THE
SWORD OF THE LORD

A ROMANCE OF THE TIME
OF MARTIN LUTHER

BY

JOSEPH HOCKING
AUTHOR OF " THE WOMAN OF BABYLON," " A FLAME OF FIRE,"
" LEST WE FORGET," ETC.

NEW YORK
E. P. DUTTON & COMPANY
31 WEST TWENTY-THIRD STREET

CONTENTS

CONTENTS

THE SWORD OF THE LORD

THE SWORD OF THE LORD

CHAPTER I

HOW THIS HISTORY CAME TO BE WRITTEN

WHEN my good friend and master the Earl of Devonshire asked me to commit to paper my impressions on the events I witnessed in Germany during my sojourn there, I accepted the task almost eagerly. And this for many reasons. It was by his request and through his influence that I undertook the mission, which I hope to explain in due course, and therefore I was, and still am, anxious to comply with his desires. Moreover, not only were the events which I witnessed of vital interest to me, they were of world-wide importance, and are even at the present moment occupying the attention of those on whom the welfare of many nations are supposed to rest. In addition to this, unimportant though I am, I was so mixed up with grave matters that I had opportunities which fall but to few men of understanding events which have set the whole world ablaze. I do not presume on the latter fact, however. As my master repeatedly says, the man who is on the scene of a battle is not as capable of judging how the battle is going as are those who watch from a distant hill. His own opinion is that men will be better able to judge of the rights and wrongs of the things which are evidently changing the life of Europe a hundred years hence than are those who are blinded by the smoke of battle and deafened by the clang of weapons. It may be that he is right; nevertheless, he agrees with me that the personal experience of one who, like myself, was enabled to witness the breaking up of the old order of things, and that at the very fountain-head must be of great value to those who may come after us.

I repeat, then, that when my good friend and master asked me to write down my experiences, I accepted his suggestion almost eagerly. On reflection, however, I almost regretted my hasty decision. For although I have had some experience in penmanship, I find it no easy task to present a true picture of what I saw. If I am asked to relate an isolated incident which came under my notice, I can perhaps do it as well as another; but isolated pictures may not convey the truth concerning things of which they are but a part. That is doubtless why I have sat hour after hour seeking so to arrange my thoughts that all those events which I saw and which befell me may be described in such a way that nothing may be out of true proportion, and yet may not, at the same time, lose the interest which belongs to them.

After much thought, and after discarding many methods of writing, I have come to the conclusion that if I am to in any degree satisfy either myself or my master, I shall have to set down, as far as my memory will serve me, a complete history of my experiences, and leave others to form their own impressions. Let it be understood, then, that I claim no authority for my opinion, my work being to set down in due order certain events, and, if necessity compels, what caused those events to take place.

If I am to do this, however, it seems a necessity that I shall have to commence by telling who I am, and how it came to pass that I came to be an eye-witness of some of those happenings which, as Master Thomas More says, has set Europe on fire.

My name is Brian Hamilton. I was christened Brian because my father was influenced so to name me by the Abbot of the Rochford Monastery, whose own name was also Brian. As is well known, this monastery belongs to the Order of St. Francis, and is one of the largest and richest in England. My family owned at one time a great deal of land around the monastery, but as one generation succeeded another, most of the land, for one reason or another, passed into the hands of the holy fathers. Indeed, as my father more than once declared, it was well I was an only child, for so poor had he become that he was unable to dower more than one son in a fashion becoming his name and station. Be that as it may, more than forty fat farms once belonging to the Hamilton family had passed to the Church, so that I, bearing one of the oldest names in England, and an only son into the bargain, possessed scarcely sufficient land to enable a paltry squire to keep up appearances. It is true, Hamilton House belonged to me, with a few hundred acres of land, but, compared with what once belonged to the family, I was little better off than a yeoman.

Gossip had it, moreover, that the Abbot had his eye upon the little that remained to me, and had declared more than once, when he had taken more than ordinary of strong liquors, that it should, before he died, belong to Holy Church. However, that is all by the way just now. He persuaded my father to call me Brian, slyly hinting at the same time that it would be a fine thing if I should be some day Abbot of Rochford.

My father, religious man as he was, shook his head at this, saying that the Hamiltons had always been either brave soldiers on the field or wise counselors of the King, and hoped that I should be true to the traditions of my race. The Abbot had great power over my father, however, as, indeed, the heads of religious houses have over landowners all over the country, which accounts for the fact that while the Church has grown fat, men have grown lean. So great, indeed, was his power, that I was trained more as a clerk than as a soldier. I was placed under the care of certain of the most learned of the monks, under whom I made good progress. I became fairly skilled as a penman, learned something of letters, and, what was more, owing to the fact that one of my teachers was a Frenchman and another a German, I became fairly proficient in the languages of these two countries.

I was also trained to be a good churchman. I learned to hate all heresy, and had a proper anger toward

Lollardism in my own land, as well as of Hussism in Bohemia.

When I was seventeen the Abbot again urged that I was called of the Lord to a holy life, and tried to persuade my father that his own salvation depended upon him being another Abraham, and sacrifice his only son at the altar. But in this he did not get his way. The Earl of Devonshire made it known that it was the King's will that I should go to Court, as my father had done, and although the Abbot urged that the call of the Lord had more authority than the call of the King, I was sent off to London, where I quickly forgot that I had well-nigh become a monk.

During the next five years I lived the life of a gay gallant. I became renowned as a swordsman, I got some repute as a brave soldier on the field of battle, and during the time we were at war with France, I gained much valuable experience in warfare. Indeed, when I came back from the wars, there were those who sung songs about young Brian Hamilton, the language of which was so extravagant that I wonder I did not lose my head altogether.

One of those songs lies before me as I write, and it was my purpose a minute ago to copy it here, but as I read it I blush at the very thought of perpetuating such high-sounding praise. After all, although I happened to do certain things which brought me some renown, I attribute my victories more to the brave fellows who followed me, and who faced fearful odds, rather than to my own prowess. Moreover, the learning which I gained from the monks was often just as valuable to me as a keen eye and strong sword arm.

After the wars, however, we fell upon a piping time of peace, and then I, like many another poor fool, began to write sonnets to my mistress's eyebrows. In fact, if the truth must be told, I lost my head and my heart to as gay a coquette as ever danced at Whitehall. There is no need to dwell on the period when I danced attendance on Lady Patty Carey, or how I fetched and carried for her, like a well-trained dog. I suppose most young fools pass through such experiences in their callow days, and I was no exception to the rule. When presently, however, I went to my father and asked him to approach old Sir Henry Carey with a view of my marrying Lady Patty, he called me a fool.

"Why a fool?" I asked.

"Because, first of all, the minx is heartless, and second, because she has only used you to attract Sir Edwin Pinner's son, who on his father's death will be one of the richest men in England."

I did not believe it, and I told him so plainly, but events proved that my father was right. She who had led me like a lap dog is led by a string, and made me believe that I had won her heart, presently plighted her troth to young Ned Pinner, for whom she had been angling, and left me in the cold.

It seems foolish enough now; but at the time I became nearly crazy with grief. I picked a quarrel with Pinner, and should have killed him in a duel but for the coming of an emissary from the great Cardinal. As it was, Pinner married Lady Patty, while I behaved like a lunatic.

I love not to think of those days, for when one has since gained a reputation as a wary counselor, and one who never loses his head under the most exciting circumstances, he has little pleasure in being reminded of a time when for a coquette's smile he would barter his birthright, and at whose frown he had become a sullen clown. Yet so it was. After my encounter with Ned Pinner (and I ought not to have challenged him, for he was no swordsman) I became as morose as a Jew who has lost his money, and even contemplated suicide.

Then, for troubles never come singly, my father died, leaving me without guide or counselor, save the monks of Rochford Abbey. And here again I was like to take a step which, had I taken it, I should never have written this history. No sooner was the breath out of my father's body than the Abbot told me that the condition of my father being prayed out of Purgatory was that I should become a monk.

He held out all sorts of flattering promises, too.

"Brian," he said, "it is the will of God. You were

named Brian after me, because I had it in my heart that you should succeed me. I have not many years to live, and if you embrace the holy life now, you will doubtless take my place. Then you will not only be the Squire over the few acres left to you, but ruler over all those rich, fat acres which once belonged to the Hamiltons, as well as other farms belonging to the Monastery of Rochford."

I saw what was in his mind. In order to obtain the benefits of the Church at death, my forefathers had given farm after farm to the Abbey, leaving each successive Hamilton poorer and poorer, and now he wanted to grab what remained. If I became a monk, I should, of course, take the vow of poverty, and make over house and lands to the Church, and then the Abbot could boast that the Abbey lands of Rochford were the fattest and richest in England.

"Your father's speedy escape from Purgatory depends on it, too," he urged, "while no man obtains salvation for himself, if having the call of God, he disobeys it."

I was in a fit frame of mind to receive his arguments kindly, nevertheless I hesitated.

"It was not my father's will that I should become a monk," I said, "else had I never gone to the King's Court."

"Your father was led away by false counselors," was his reply, "neither did he realize the benefits which would accrue to his son by living the holy life."

"Holy life," I repeated, for I had not been educated at the Abbey for naught. As all the world knows now, the monasteries of England were not noted for their piety, nor were monks called holy men save in jest.

"Ay, holy life," he repeated, "for holy life depends upon the offices which are performed. I say not that the monasteries which were founded immediately after St. Francis's death were not more strict in their discipline than is the Abbey of Rochford; but what then? When a man becomes a monk he enters the great Ark of God, in which he is safe, whatever the world may say."

"Then a man may live a holy life though he flee not from wine and women?" I asked.

"Are the value of sacraments nullified by the private life of the priests?" urged the Abbot. "Have some of the Popes been less Popes because they have broken some of the Commandments?"

I was taken aback at this method of argument, for I knew that if all sacraments were nullified because the priests who administered them were unchaste, or if their priestly powers were taken away because they obeyed not the Commandments, there was little chance of salvation, even for the best. It is true Erasmus had written books which set all tongues wagging, and which showed that monks were guilty of sins which laymen like myself would shudder at committing, but he never argued, as far as I know, that souls were left unshriven because of it. If they were, God have mercy upon us all, for the power of the Church was gone.

Moreover, the Prior's appeals to me to become a monk gained in plausibility as the days went by. I was tired of the world, or thought I was. My heart was bleeding because of the way Lady Patty Carey had treated me, and I assured myself that naught in the world had attractions for me. Then, as chance would have it, naught was stirring in England which saved me from brooding over my sorrow, and, added to all this, it turned out that my father left me so little in the way of lands and money that I, who belonged to one of the best families in England, possessed only the patrimony of a small squire.

"I tell thee, Brian," said the Prior, "that nothing need stand in the way of thy stepping in good time into my shoes, for, added to the influence which I possess, thou hast friends who will make thy election as Abbot a certainty."

But this latter argument did not appeal to me. What charmed me was not the thought of authority, or even of riches (for as Abbot of Rochford Monastery I should be rich beyond what I could ever be as a layman), but I did long to get away from the world and spend my days in study and prayer.

So I said I would give it six months' trial, and that, in the meanwhile, my father's and my good friend the Earl of Devonshire should look after my lands. To this the Prior at length agreed, although he desired to make shorter work of my novitiate.

Three months were enough to open my eyes about the life at the monastery. Most of the Brothers were low-born and low-bred fellows, who had scarcely a thought above eating and drinking and lewd talk, while ghostly offices were to most of them a weariness beyond words. Therefore, although I was as sick at heart as ever, and had little desire for the world, when my good friend the Earl asked me to become his secretary, assuring me that I should have abundance of time for the study of the books I loved, I told the Abbot that I gave up all thoughts of ever stepping into his shoes.

"Leave the holy life to become the scribe of a King's Minister," he cried. "Surely thou art tempted of the devil. The world, the flesh, and the devil hath mastered thee."

"As to that, I have seen more of the world, the flesh, and the devil in Rochford Monastery than at the King's Court," I answered, and although the Abbot called me a saucy, unregenerate varlet, I entered the service of the man who has been my friend, and in some senses my master, ever since.

The years passed quickly while I served my lord of Devonshire as his secretary. I did his work faithfully and to his satisfaction, and yet I had much time to pursue those studies, which became more and more pleasing as the time fled by. Although my master often railed upon me for living a monk's life, bade me clothe myself in gay apparel as of old, and offered to choose for me a rich and beauteous wife, I paid no heed to his wishes, declaring that I hated all women, and cared not for their society.

In truth, although young in years, I was in a fair way of becoming a hermit, when one day my master came to me with such a great purpose in his eyes that I saw something unusual was stirring.

"Brian," he said, "I have come to tell thee that for the present thy quill-driving is at an end."

I spoke not from pure amazement, for not only did his words portend much, but I saw by his face that he had something of importance in his mind.

"You speak the language of the Germans?" he said eagerly.

"Passing well," I replied. "Old Father Schneider found no fault with me."

At that he started walking excitedly around the room, sometimes muttering fiercely to himself.

"I have just come from the King," he said presently.

"From the King?" I repeated. "What doth the King know of me?"

"Much," he replied, "for I have told him much."

In spite of myself, I felt my heart grow warm. Although I had become a recluse, and reckoned little of Court life, the King is still King.

"And the King hath work for you, Brian."

"What work?" I asked.

"Work that, if it is well done, will mean great reward. Work that should appeal to thee; work that may bring back some of the fat farms that Holy Church hath robbed from thee; ay, and work that may make thy house into a barony."

I do not think it was his language, so much as the way he spoke, which stirred my blood. His voice was tremulous, his eyes gleamed with excitement.

"I am fit for no such work," I replied, "and, for that matter, I do not desire it."

"Wait until I tell you what it is," he said with a laugh. "I tell you, man, I wish I were thirty again and had such a chance. Why, the thought of it sets my own sluggish blood running fast, and makes me forget that I was born years before your father."

"Then be pleased to tell me what the King wishes me to do, my lord," I urged, "and why I am chosen to do it."

Upon this he laughed in great good humor. "I little thought," he cried, "that when I derided thee upon living a monk's life, and wasting thy spare hours upon musty folios, instead of living in the sunlight as others of thy kith were doing, that thou wert thereby qualifying thyself for this mission. Little did I think when I chided thee as a fool, that I should say to the King, ' I know the man your Majesty wants,' and all because thou hast been a bookworm and a woman-hater."

" My lord," I said, " I was always bad at riddles. Be pleased to tell me what is in your mind."

" This is in my mind. It is the King's will that you go to Germany on a difficult, and perhaps a dangerous, mission. A mission on which the King sets such store that my heart almost came into my mouth as I named thee for it."

" And what may it be? " I asked.

The Earl stalked around the room again before he spoke. Now and then he looked at me questioningly, as if he were afraid to speak, but presently he blurted out, almost stammeringly:

" In a nutshell it is this: You are to go to Germany, and bring back to England — secretly, mark you, secretly — one of the noblest of German ladies."

Had an earthquake shaken the City of London I could not have been more startled. I started to my feet, and stared at him as though both he and I were demented. Indeed, at that moment I thought we were.

" Bring to England, secretly, a lady of noble birth ! " I cried.

" There is none nobler, nay, not in the whole of Germany," he cried.

" A princess, then? " I gasped.

" Well, scarcely that, but yet just as good," he replied. " Her mother was the daughter of an English peer, her father was a German noble, who was of the same blood as the — but I have said enough. There is no lady in Germany of nobler blood ! "

" And her father and mother? "

" Both dead."

My head whirled. I scarce remembered where I stood. A few moments before, I was the secretary of the Earl of Devonshire, who had no other thought than

to look after my lord's papers, study such affairs as he
required of me, and read the books I loved; while now
I was called upon to substitute sword for pen, horse and
open air for quiet solitude and books. I, Brian Hamilton, who, because a woman had wounded my heart, had
determined never to have aught to do with the world
again, and whose greatest dream was to in some way
emulate the great Erasmus, who had dazzled the nobles
and divines of England by his learning, was called upon
to forsake solitude and go out into the world on a difficult mission.

And such a mission! To bring, secretly, a lady of
noble birth to England. A thousand questions came
rushing into my brain. I was bewildered at the thought
of it, and I made up my mind there and then, even although I might bring the King's anger upon me, to
declare that I was unable to take it.

"Are you mad, or am I, my lord?" I asked presently.

The Earl laughed with great good humor.

"Neither," he replied; "and if I know thee aright,
Brian, thy nerves will be all a-tingling in a few minutes
at the thought of what lies before thee."

"But — but —" I began.

"Ay, I understand," he laughed. "You have lived
so long doing a scribe's work that you have forgotten
you are your father's son. But shake yourself, man!
Do you think, when I took you from Rochford Monastery
and offered you the post of secretary, that I ever had
it in my heart to keep you always at it? Have I not
known all the time that your manhood is only slumber-
ing? Is such a swordsman as you have proved yourself
to be to wield no other weapon than a pen? Is Brian
Hamilton going to shut himself up within four square
walls all his days because a silly coquette bestowed her
favors elsewhere? Man, the bones of your forefathers
turn in their graves at the thought of it. The work is a
great work, man — such as any gentleman should covet.
And the command is the command of the King. Why,
man, when once you feel a sword by your side, and feel
a horse's shoulders between your knees again, you will
live anew. Don't you feel it, Brian? A horse under

you, a sword by your side, the wind whistling free around you, and dangerous, difficult work to do! Does not the thought stir your pulses?"

My heart grew warm as he spoke. I knew not why. All I could say was:

"Tell me more about it."

"Ay, that I will," he said. And I, forgetting that I had made up my mind to have nothing to do with the work he had called me to do, fell to listening eagerly.

CHAPTER II

"THIS is how matters stand, Brian," said the Earl. "Twenty-five years ago Count Rudolf Rothenburg came to England on matters of state. While here he wooed and won for his bride the second daughter of the Earl of Lancaster, who, as you know, is closely associated with the Royal house. One child was born of the marriage, a daughter. The mother did not live many years after her birth, and when the child was ten years of age the Count also died, leaving the child to the care of the present Count of Rothenburg. Now certain facts have come to his Majesty's ears. I must not tell you what they are, for he will not have them mentioned, neither do they directly affect the work you have to do. This, however, I may tell you. Owing to the death of various members of the House of Lancaster, the Lady Elfrida became the heiress of great possessions in England. Moreover, the King hath certain intentions concerning her, which necessitate her being brought to England. The Count Rothenburg having his plans concerning the disposal of her hand in marriage, and this with Elector's consent, she cannot be brought here openly. In truth, while the King wills that she shall be brought to England, neither his will nor his desire must be known. It is true you go on the King's mission, but you cannot go in the King's name, nor with the King's authority. His Majesty hath grave and important reasons why the Lady Elfrida shall come to England, reasons which affect the peace and well-being of the nation, yet so secret are they that none may know them. Suffice to say that there are certain people in the realm whom the King desires to please, that he may thereby obtain what is dear to his heart. Beyond that I must

13

not go, but this I may say: the man who brings the Lady Elfrida Rothenburg to England, in such a manner as I shall presently indicate, shall receive the King's smile, and he shall not be lacking in rewards that the highest in the realm might be proud to receive."

I had not yet got over the surprise which the Earl's first words gave me, yet I saw plainly that the mission upon which I was to be sent was full of apparently insurmountable difficulties.

"The lady must not be brought by force," I suggested.

"There is no nobler lady in Germany," he made reply; "therefore must she be treated with all respect and courtesy."

"But if she be not willing to come?"

"Then must the King's messenger persuade her."

"But if the messenger goes not in the King's name, or with the King's authority?" I urged.

"If the King's reward be in accord with the difficulties of the situation, all things should be possible," replied the Earl. "To be frank, the work is not for a fool, nor a coward. It is the work of a learned man, a man of resource, a man who can gain the ear of a proud maiden, as well as of one who hath no small gifts in persuading her, it may be, against her own judgment. It is also the work of a brave man, for many difficulties are in the way; it may be there will be much fighting, for the man to whom Count Rothenburg hath promised her is said to carry the best sword in Germany."

"You had better get another man, my lord," I replied.

Again the Earl laughed good-naturedly.

"Long have I talked with his Majesty on this important matter," he said presently. "There is no man who can appreciate the difficulties of the situation better than he. 'There are many things we must bear in mind, Devonshire,' said he only to-day. 'For one thing, the Lady Elfrida is under close espionage; for another, she is as proud as Lucifer; and for a third, Rothenburg is determined on her wedding a German clown, who hath a keen eye on her estates. Germany is in a state of turmoil just now because of the new ideas which are springing up, and God wot what will come to pass. More than all that, the man who brings her to England must not dare to cast eyes on her, and he must regard her as sacredly as though she were our Blessed Lady in the flesh. Putting all these things together, and remembering that she must come hither of her own will, the man we send must have special qualifications. He must be a man of noble birth, else will she not deign to hold converse with him. He must be one of wit and resource, else will he not be able to gain entrance to her presence, safely guarded as she is. He should be a man who knoweth something of the questions which distract Germany so that if need be he can thereby gain the confidence of Rothenburg, who, fighter though he is, is learned in matters pertaining to the Church. In addition to all this he must be a soldier, for I can see many difficulties in his way; and, above all, he must be one who is not moved by the flash of a woman's eye, for I am told that the Lady Elfrida hath driven half the gallants of Germany mad about her, so beautiful is she. Where can you find such a man, Devonshire? A man who can be unmoved by a woman's wiles, a daring fighter, a swordsman, a man with a steady head, a sound judgment, and one who can be trusted to hold his tongue whatever may happen; for I tell you again, he takes his life in his hands and can have no help nor protection from me.'"

"'You ask much, your Majesty,' I said.

"'Ay, because I need one of special qualities,' he made answer, 'but if you can find such a man, and will accomplish this work, then shall he not grumble at the reward.'"

"But I am not such a man, my lord," I said.

"I have ransacked my brains much," went on the Earl, as though I had not spoken. "I have considered the merits of at least a score of men, then suddenly it came to me that I had such a man with whom I was in daily contact. Brian Hamilton hath a good name, and though not equal in birth to the Lady Elfrida, can still enter her presence as one of noble blood. There is no better swordsman in England, nor one who hath shown himself more wary in counsel or more sane in judgment. Brian Hamilton also loves danger, and although he hath lived the life of a monk for years, is thirsting for adventure. He is also one who will faithfully do what he undertakes, and because he is a woman-hater will not make eyes at a fair lady, although she be as wise as Sibil, beautiful as Venus, and hath a voice like a siren."

"Brian Hamilton is content to be my Lord of Devonshire's secretary, and to live with the books he loves," I replied.

"Brian Hamilton is a soldier at heart, even as all his fathers were," he made answer. "Even now his heart is burning at the thought of going to Germany on such a mission; and Brian Hamilton hath another thing which the King urged: he hath a knowledge of the German tongue, and can therefore do what another may not."

"And you have mentioned my name to the King?" I asked.

"I have sounded thy praises to such a tune that if thy ears have not burned there is no truth in the old adage, and what is more, I have convinced Henry the Eighth that thou art the man. I reminded him of thy deeds of prowess in France, I have told him that thou wert on the point of becoming a monk, and that thou hast not for years looked on a woman. As thou know'st, he is much given to the study of questions of divinity, and I have told him of thy love for books, and, above all, I have sounded thy praises as one who is discreet beyond the ordinary, and who is sensitive on matters of honor even to foolishness."

"And in your praises you have done me injustice," I said. "You have made the King expect more than I can ever perform."

"I have made thy fortune, Brian, and thereby I have lifted myself high in the King's favor. And more, I have so interested him in thee that he hath commanded thee to his presence this very night."

"I to go before the King?" I cried.

"This night," he made answer.

Again, although I doubted much concerning my fitness, I felt my heart grow warm. Little by little the thing which the King would have me do was getting hold of me. In spite of myself I had to admit that my love for adventure was not dead, while the thought of doing a scribe's work day by day became more and more distasteful. In short, although I still kept up the show of refusal, I was more and more inclining to the work. But even as I did so incline the unusual nature of the mission loomed larger and larger, and difficulties arose before me thick and fast.

For, be it remembered that although a young man I had reached that age in which one is led to look before one leaps, and I was ever one who had a habit of calculating before taking an important step. Men said of me, years before, that I fought against what seemed like impossible odds, and succeeded where others failed wholly because I did not know when I was beaten. But this was not so. I know that the very essence of life is risk, nevertheless I always reckoned carefully upon my risks before I took them, but having once taken them I would never spare myself nor others in order to carry out the thing which I had attempted.

"Do others but you know what is in the King's mind?" I asked.

He shook his head, but not, as I thought, with conviction.

"There is doubt in your mind, my lord," I said.

"The King hath a hot head," he replied, "and it may be that he hath mentioned his desires; but not with my knowledge."

"Your *knowledge*, my lord?" I said, emphasizing the word.

"Of course, the King speaks freely to his other counselors," he replied.

"Who may have spoken to others," I suggested. "They have their favorites."

"If they have spoken of men who might do this work, they have not convinced the King of their fitness," he made answer, "for before I spoke of you he declared

2

he knew of no one whom he could dare to send on such a mission."

"Still, others may be in his secrets," I said.

"And if there are it will not affect you," he answered. "They are his trusted counselors, and would, therefore, speak to no one who would betray the King's mind."

"A small leak hath been known to sink a ship, my lord," I said.

"I see no leak," he replied, almost angrily.

"Know you aught of this Lady Elfrida Rothenburg?" I asked.

"But little," he replied; "indeed, naught but what the King told me when speaking of his need."

"You say she hath been much sought after by the German gallants?"

"So it is said."

"And hath she given her heart to the man whom her uncle hath chosen for her?"

"That I do not know."

"It would seem not," I suggested, "else would she not be under close espionage."

"That would seem true," said the Earl, almost carelessly, I thought.

"It is of importance," I urged. "If she be content with her uncle's choice, then will it be more difficult to persuade her to come to England. But concerning that I must ask the King."

At this the Earl laughed loudly. "Then thou hast already consented in thine heart," he said. "In truth, I am glad of this, for, as thou knowest, the King hath a hot temper, and brooks not opposition. This thing is dear to his heart, else had he not discussed it with me so seriously, neither would he have asked so many questions about thee."

"The King is King," I replied, "and therefore must he be obeyed. Still, a man must be a fool to undertake what is impossible to accomplish."

"But I tell thee it must be accomplished. The King hath promised."

"Whom, and what?" I asked.

"That I may not tell thee."

"If I go, there are many things the King must tell me," I answered, almost angrily. "The King hath a project dear to his heart. He hath made a promise — what, I know not — concerning the Lady Elfrida Rothenburg; he hath also made it to some person. Whom, I know not. And I am requested to bring this lady to England secretly that this unknown promise may be fulfilled to this unknown person. He admits it is dangerous, and yet I am to go without safeguard or authority. I am to accept the King's commission without the King's protection. I am not even to mention the King's name. Can you not see my position, my lord? I am to persuade this lady of high degree to come to England, and yet I am not provided with the means to persuade her."

"Ay, I know, I know," interrupted the Earl. "And yet if you refuse, after his Majesty hath set his heart upon you, I —" He shrugged his shoulders, but did not finish the sentence.

"I would rather bear the brunt of the King's anger by refusing to undertake this work than to come back to him telling him I had failed."

"You would never dare to show your face in England again," said the Earl.

"Then must the King tell me many things of which I am ignorant," I replied.

"That's as may be," said the Earl. "He is but young, yet hath he already thrown more than one from his high estate. He demands obedience without question, neither is he willing to tell what is in his heart. Nevertheless, he loves not a coward, and would rather that a man should speak out boldly than to obey him through fear."

As I well know, the Earl spoke truly in this; it was true that never King came on a throne in whom the people had higher expectations, yet no sooner was he firmly seated than he showed the iron hand. Empson and Dudley, favored by his father as they had been, were brought to the block, while although it was be-

lieved he would rule with justice, it was quickly seen
that he would show but little mercy to them that angered
him.

Moreover, he was ambitious beyond measure. He
desired more power in France, and for that reason he
became engaged in the war which enabled me to obtain
what little reputation I possessed as a soldier. I was
one of those who took part in the sudden rout of the
French cavalry near Guinegate, and although I may be
called a boaster in saying so, it was generally admitted
that it was through my advice that the engagement became " A Battle of the Spurs," because of its bloodless
nature, rather than a carnage which might have ended in
the loss of many of our best men.

Moreover, but for the fact that Henry's purse became
empty, the fate of France might have been different,
and instead of falling upon those piping times of peace,
which led to my losing my heart over Patty Carey, I
might have risen to high position in French wars.

Disappointed as the King was in his contest with
France, he sought an outlet for his energies in the
encouragement of the new learning. Instead of giving
honor to knights and nobles, he bestowed them upon
such men as Erasmus, Colet, and More, who made it
the fashion everywhere to know Greek, and to talk of
the new learning. Perhaps it was owing to this spirit
that I, belonging to a race of soldiers, longed more to
read the tragedies of Sophocles and the orations of
Isocrates and Demosthenes than to seek forgetfulness
of my disappointments in adventure.

Nevertheless, it was true what the Earl said. No
sooner had he proclaimed to me the King's will than
my pulse began to beat fast and my heart grew warm
at the thought of action and danger. It was true Pope
Leo had declared for universal peace, and urged that
the nations should encourage literature and the arts
rather than warfare, and yet, now that the Earl had
spoken to me of work which meant the necessity of skill
and bravery, I felt even as a hunter feels when he hears
the cry of " Tally ho! "

" You will obey the King's command? " said the Earl.

" A subject can do no less than obey the call to his Majesty's presence," I answered.

"That is all I ask," said the Earl, "and so to-night at eight o'clock I will present you to his Majesty."

There was no more reading to be done that day. The time was yet early afternoon, but no book attracted me. "Utopia" and "Praise of Folly" might never have been written for all I cared, while the writings of the Florentine scholars seemed tame and uninteresting when compared with the thought of feeling a good horse beneath me, a good sword by my side, and work to do. In this it will doubtless be seen that I was no true bookman like Erasmus or More, and was at heart more a man of the sword than of letters.

When the Earl had left me I went out into St. James's Park in order that I might ponder over what he had told me, and to make my plans accordingly. No sooner did I reach the park, however, than, hearing a familiar voice, I turned around and saw Master Thomas More by my side.

"Why, Master Hamilton," he said, "this is a strange sight. Little did I expect to see you strutting in the park like a gallant instead of learning the wisdom of the Greeks."

"Erasmus saith that folly is a wise thing, Master More," I replied.

"Ay; but what are you dreaming of?"

"Utopia, the land of Nowhere," I answered.

"And thou hast wasted thy time in reading news concerning it?" he said, somewhat pleased.

"Nay, I am rather determined to seek it," I replied, "even as Master Thomas More did when he spent his time writing concerning it, rather than getting an aching head by poring over learned law books."

A serious look came into his eyes.

"Hast heard aught from the King?" he said, after first looking around.

"I hear many things from the King, seeing I am the Earl of Devonshire's secretary," I made answer.

He eyed me, I thought, keenly. "Which is the greater folly," he said, like one musing, "for a youth who was once a soldier to live a monk's life, or for one who hath lived a monk's life to take to saddle and sword?"

I felt my color rise, but I gave no confidences; nevertheless, his words confirmed my suspicions. My master was not the only man to whom the King had spoken.

"Ask Erasmus," I said, with a laugh.

"That is not bad advice," he said. "And do you know what Erasmus would say? Methinks he would say this: 'When the man has been living a monk's life takes to sword and saddle, let him take heed to the man who knows naught of books and thinks that all matters of action should be left to fools.'"

"It is but little harm a fool can do," I said.

"A fool can set fire to a house; a fool can also make a wise man's work difficult. But how is thy study of Greek progressing?"

"But slowly," I replied, "seeing I am but watching the ducks."

"And fancying thyself sailing, eh? But the new learning is spreading, Master Brian. It hath even reached Germany. Therefore, the man who goeth thither should ever remember that men's eyes are opened."

He left me at this, while I pondered over his words. For I well-nigh loved Thomas More, even as did almost every other man who knew him. For, besides being a great lawyer and scholar who stood high in the estimation of the King, he had a heart full of the milk of human kindness, and forever sought things true and good.

"He knows the King's will," I thought, "and he warns me against secret enemies. Perchance this mission is known to many, and those who would undertake it desire to frustrate the efforts of the one who is chosen."

But this thought did rot trouble me, for now that the thought had got possession of my heart I rejoiced in difficulties rather than feared because of them. It was, therefore, with a light step that just before eight o'clock that night I made my way to the King's presence.

CHAPTER III

KING HENRY VIII

" HA ! " said the Earl, as he met me in the ante-
room, " my cavalier is in time, but not too soon for
the King's impatience. He awaits thee, man."

" It wants ten minutes to eight," I said.

" Ay, I have no fault to find; but had'st thou been
a minute past the time thou would'st have found his
Majesty in a bad temper. But thou art here, and, what
is more, thou hast doffed the somber attire of the secretary and donned that of a courtier."

I blushed as he spoke, for I had hesitated much before effecting the change in my raiment. Yet, though
I had grown accustomed to black hose and a somber
cloak, I felt I could not appear before the King in such
a fashion, so although I had no attire of the latest fashion, I selected from my wardrobe the gayest finery I
possessed, and having put them on, I scarcely knew
myself when I looked into the mirror. Nevertheless,
I was pleased with the result, for, as I thought, I looked
years younger and presented a far braver appearance. I
also sent for a wig maker, who arranged my hair in a
becoming fashion; indeed, so much was I changed that
I began to feel a different man.

" A little out of fashion," commented the Earl as he
gave me a second look, " but passably becoming, for all
that. Brian, whatever is the outcome of this venture,
I can see that I have lost my secretary. Thou wilt never
be content to drive the goose's quill again. Ay, and the
King will be pleased — he will be pleased. He always
is when he sees a man after his own heart."

I had thought little of my personal appearance for
many a long month, but now I began to have a sort of

23

pride in it. I had passed my youth, yet, as I was not thirty years of age, I was still a young man. I stood over six feet high, and men said, when I tilted in the tourneys, that there was no stronger lance in Henry's Court than mine. Like all my race, I was strong and large of bone, and even during the years I had lived like a monk I had a soldier's bearing.

This may seem somewhat boastful, but it will not be out of place in this history, as it bears upon later events. Besides, as the Earl had truly observed, the King was partial to men who knew no fear, who stood erect, and who were blessed with pleasant features and strong limbs.

"Come," said the Earl, and a minute later we stood in the presence of Henry VIII. The King was seated at a table as I entered, and was busy examining some parchments; nevertheless, he turned quickly on hearing us, and rested his bright eyes upon me.

At this time Henry was twenty-eight years of age, and although inclined to stoutness, did not present the appearance by which he became known in later years. He was bravely attired, yet not so gaily as many of his Court gallants. His face was florid, yet not unpleasantly so, while I thought I detected a kindly humor playing around his lips.

For a moment he did not speak, but looked at me searchingly. It was commonly said at this time that the King boasted of his being able to read a man's heart at a glance, and although he, doubtless, made mistakes, he had great powers of penetration. Anyhow, I felt as though he were reading me through and through, and that he took note of every detail of my person from foot to crown.

"How now, my Lord Devonshire?" he said in a not unmusical voice.

"This, your Majesty, is Master Brian Hamilton of whom I spoke to you."

"Son of the late Edward Hamilton, of Hamilton Manor, near Rochford Monastery, and faithful servant of my father?" said the King.

"The same, your Majesty."

Again he looked at me steadily, and then held out his hand.

I took a step forward, knelt, and lifted the hand to my lips.

"Your faithful servant, your Majesty," I said.

"Rise, Master Brian Hamilton, I would speak to you," he said, while he settled himself in his chair.

I retreated two or three steps from him and awaited his will, and here I must confess that my heart fluttered somewhat, for it seemed to me that momentous issues were to be discussed.

"Hast thou acquainted Master Hamilton of the purpose for which I commanded him to our presence?" asked the King, turning to Devonshire.

"Of the purpose, and the general outline of that purpose, sire," replied the Earl.

"And he?"

"He is here to receive your commands, sire."

Again the King turned his piercing eyes upon me and looked at me steadily.

"Thou hast the appearance of a strong man who can be faithful," said Henry VIII presently.

I stood silent before him, waiting for him to continue.

"I have need of a faithful man," he went on; "but, as you may know, I have no mercy upon the man who betrays my trust. Neither have I patience with a dull-witted clown; but I love a man who hath a keen wit and can act with judgment."

Still I was silent, for I saw no reason why I should speak.

"You do not make answer, Master Hamilton," he said, sharply, I thought.

"There is no need for speech on my part until your Majesty is pleased to ask for it," I made answer.

He gave a short laugh as I spoke, and then fell to examining the documents which lay on the table.

"You have for some years acted as secretary to my Lord of Devonshire," he said, and then went on: "Before that you were a soldier, and were not a stranger to the King's Court. Why did the soldier turn monk?"

"Perchance your Majesty has been informed," I made answer.

"I love not weather cocks," said the King, "and a disappointed soldier maketh but a poor monk."

"A secretary to the noble Earl of Devonshire is forever doing the King's business," I replied.

"Art thou he of whom men spoke brave things after the Battle of Spurs?" he asked.

"Many gave me much undeserved praise, your Majesty."

"Nay, I desire no mock modesty. Thou did'st act the part of a good soldier in France, and wert reputed to be wise beyond thy years. For such a soldier to drop the sword and to live the life of a monk is to play false to a soldier's heart."

"Even the King favored the new learning, when the treason of the League of the Italian States made it impossible for him to continue the war," I replied, risking everything at a hazard; "and it is said that his Majesty well-nigh complimented Dean Colet when he preached a sermon against war."

For a moment I did not know which way the scales were to turn. I saw his eyes burn with a strange light, and he half started to his feet. I also thought I heard the Earl muttering angrily, but of that I was not sure. Perhaps the King was in a good humor that night, or it may be that I had measured him rightly, for presently he gave a great laugh and said:

"The thrust was good, even although it exposed thee to the man who carrieth a more powerful sword. But we waste time. Can'st thou be faithful, Brian Hamilton?"

"Never hath one bearing my name been accused of unfaithfulness yet, your Majesty."

"But if I remember truly a Hamilton refused to obey the King's will," he retorted.

"That was because my grandfather thought your Majesty's father commanded an impossible thing," I replied.

"I love not the word impossible," he said.

"Yet would a man be unfaithful to the King and

a fool into the bargain if he undertook a work beyond the skill of man."

"Not if the King wills?"

"A man may die in attempting an impossible thing," I replied; "ay, it is doubtless his duty to do it if the King commands. Nevertheless, he is but a fool who attempts it without telling the King plainly, and that is all my grandfather did."

"And the work of which my Lord of Devonshire hath spoken to thee?" he said quickly.

"Nothing is impossible where a woman is concerned, sire," I replied.

"Then thou wilt undertake it?"

"Since it is the King's will."

"But thou wilt succeed?"

"That depends, your Majesty."

"On what, sirrah?"

"On the help your Majesty may afford me."

"I can give thee no help. Thou goest alone, in thine own name. I must have no quarrel with Germany at the present hour, therefore I can give thee no protection, no authority. Only this I promise: the man who succeeds shall not grumble at the King's reward."

"And if he fails?"

"Then had he better keep from English soil."

"Will your Majesty permit me to speak plainly?"

He nodded impatiently.

"Your Majesty hath reputation for wisdom," I said. "Never since England was a nation hath it had a King more renowned for learning, for piety, for valor, and for kingly qualities."

"Well, and what then?"

"Then the King will know that he would have me undertake work which is well-nigh impossible."

"And what of that? I told my Lord of Devonshire that I had no need of a carpet knight, a dullard, a clown, or a coward. I told him to choose a man who could overcome the impossible through sagacity, and wit, and courage, and a strong right arm. If the work were easy I should not want such a man, but since it is difficult let me have a man, and not a blockhead."

"Will your Majesty be pleased to reflect," I said. "I am asked to go to a strange country, and to bring to England a lady of high degree. She is not to be brought by force, and yet have I no means whereby I can persuade her to come of her own free will. She is closely guarded, yet am I provided with no means whereby I can obtain leave to enter her presence. I am to go in ignorance of the King's will concerning her. I am to treat her as though she were the Mother of our Lord, yet am I to bring her for many hundreds of miles of difficult country, and —"

"Hath not the Almighty given thee brains, man?" he cried angrily. "Of what use is a man to me if he cannot devise means to overcome all these things?"

"Since it is the King's command, I will do all that a man may do," I replied. "Nevertheless, I care not to have dealings with women."

"Thou dost hate women, Devonshire tells me?" he said hastily.

"The word doth not describe my feelings," I replied. "Rather I despise them, and I dread them as a burnt child dreads the fire."

"It is well, Brian Hamilton," said the King; "for let me tell thee this: the Lady Elfrida is not for thee. She is for — But that is naught to thee. My will is this: Thou must go to Germany, and by thine own devices thou must persuade her to come hither. Thou must guard her safely. Thou say'st that thou dost despise women. It is well, for if thou dost lift thine eyes to her, then — but thou understandest."

"But I know not in what part of Germany she resides," I objected.

"Instructions shall be written for thee," replied the King; "that is, the name of the castle where she resides, the town by which it is situate, the name of the man to whom her uncle would bestow her in marriage. These and other things shall be fully made known; with the rest I have naught to do. Thou will travel as thou wilt, by what route thou wilt, with as many servants as thou wilt. Thou canst go as a mendicant friar, or a preaching monk. Thou canst use what means thou wilt for entering Rothenburg Castle, or wherever she may be living. All that is thy business. Only mind, the name of Henry Tudor must not be spoken; even to save thyself from the dungeon or the scaffold, thou must not breathe my name. I have made diligent inquiries concerning thee. Thou hast learning, thou hast wit, thou hast strength of arm, thou hast courage. Let them all be used in the King's service, and if thou dost succeed the King will not be ungrateful."

I bowed, determined to see the thing through, although I saw but little chance of doing it.

"A moment more," cried the King. "Thou hast money?"

"The rents of the Hamilton estates are not great," I replied, "but since I have been the Earl of Devonshire's secretary I have not spent half of them."

"Nevertheless, thou shalt be liberally supplied," replied the King. "Thou hast promised but little, Master Brian Hamilton, yet I believe in thee."

"There is another thing I would say," I said.

"What, more difficulties? Beshrew me, but provoke me not too far."

"Nay, not difficulties, your Majesty, but questions," I said.

"Well?" he cried impatiently.

"Are there many who know what is in the King's mind?" I asked. "When I leave England will many know why I have gone?"

"Why?"

"Because if others know, I should like to know who they are!"

"What matters it to thee?"

"This, your Majesty," I replied respectfully. "If there are I have needless difficulties placed in my way even at the commencement of my work. I have already received intimations that others know of the King's will concerning me."

"Others? Who, then, sirrah?"

I felt I had made a mistake here, for if I mentioned

Master Thomas More's name I should seem like a tale-bearer, yet was not the King in a humor to be denied.

"I have perhaps said too much, your Majesty," I said, "for perhaps what I have heard hath no meaning; but ever since my Lord of Devonshire told me of your Majesty's will, my mind has been full of strange thoughts and many suspicions. Thus doubtless I misinterpreted what Master Thomas More said in idle joke."

"Master Thomas More!" said the King with a laugh. "He lives in Utopia, the land of Nowhere, Master Brian Hamilton; therefore pay no heed to what he may say. And yet methinks he might be more chary of speech."

There was a tone of petulance in his last words, which convinced me that I had hit upon the truth, even although he tried to make light of it. Neither was his explanation satisfactory. It was true that all London was agog concerning the book which More had written; and whenever he was more than ordinarily humorous, men said that More was off to the land of Nowhere again. Yet was I not convinced that he did not know what was in the King's mind concerning me.

"But what did Master More say to thee?" he went on, after a pause.

"Nothing of seeming import, your Majesty. He only told me that even in Germany the new learning was advancing, and that whoever went thither should keep his eyes open."

"Well, how doth that concern thee?"

"A few hours ago I had no thought of going to Germany," I made answer.

"And if I have spoken to others, none will dare to repeat the King's words," he said. "Besides, think you that you are the only man I have thought of for this work? A king may examine many men before he chooses one who may commend himself to his judgment. But what of that?"

"Nothing, since it is your Majesty's will," I made answer.

The King was silent for a few moments, and then I thought he was on the point of speaking, but he evidently thought better of it, and so I was left in ignorance as to what was in his mind.

"There is another thing, your Majesty," I went on. "Perchance when I reach Germany I shall find the Lady Elfrida wedded. Is it still your Majesty's will that she shall be brought to England?"

"If she is wedded before —" He stopped in the middle of his speech, as though my question had made him uneasy. "But there is no fear of that: she cannot be wedded to the man her uncle hath chosen for her for three months. Still, there is no time to waste. Get thee to horse, man, and that right quickly. By to-morrow morning thou wilt have all necessary information, and see that no unnecessary time is wasted."

"Your Majesty shall be obeyed," I said as I stepped backward toward the door; but before I reached it he lifted his hand as if bidding me to stop.

"Stay, Master Hamilton," he said. "Perchance I have spoken somewhat hastily to thee, and I would ever treat my faithful servants with due consideration. That upon which I send thee requires the bravest qualities a man may possess, and the work I have given thee to do is only for a brave man and a loyal gentleman. Therefore, if thou dost succeed thou shalt have the King's gratitude and the King's favor. Nay, more; if thou dost succeed, I shall know that I have no more faithful, or valuable servant in the realm."

My heart grew warm as he spoke, not only because of his words, but because of the kindly tone in his voice. For was he not the King, and was not I his humble subject?

"Therefore, beware lest thou dost fail in any particular," he cried, his eyes flashing again. "As for thy question concerning what others may know, thou hast the name of being one who hath a nimble wit, and it is said that a red-haired man who is past thirty hath always many schemes in his mind."

He dismissed me without another word, while I made my way into the open air. As may be imagined my mind was well awake, and especially did I give good heed to the King's last words.

When presently I had reached a lane off Fleet Street, for I had walked thither musing over what I had heard, and calling to mind every red-haired man whom I had ever met, a strange thing happened, and one to which I found myself obliged to pay heed.

CHAPTER IV

THIS was what happened: A hand was placed on my shoulder, while a voice whispered in my ear:
"Listen, as you love your life, Master Brian Hamilton."

I turned and saw a man with his face well-nigh hidden by his cloak.

The night was dark, so that I could not discern his features, but I knew that he was deadly in earnest by the tones of his voice. There was something coarse in the texture of his' speech; nevertheless, he might be a man of quality, for all that.

"You have just come from the King," he said.

"And the King loves not mysteries," I made answer.

"There you make a mistake," was the reply; "but I have not come to argue with you. I have come rather to warn you; ay, I have come as a friend to warn you."

I must confess to it. The man troubled me, for it seemed to me that the King's will concerning me was known to all the town. And more than that, from what was said in parables, I knew less of the business on which I was sent than the hooded stranger who chose to speak to me.

"We are quiet here and may speak freely," went on the stranger. "The town is abed, and even Fleet Street is well-nigh deserted. So let us return. You have just come from the King, and you are in danger."

"If you will honor me," I said, "well, be it so. It is little I know of such matters; but I did not know that Henry the Eighth gave audiences freely. Rather I have been told that those in high places go away from his doorkeeper in anger, because he is so chary of letting men enter his presence."

3   33

This I said to gain time, for the man had come upon me suddenly; and I had to fence in the dark.

"The King's will is the King's will, and the King's command is the King's command; woe is he who sets himself against them. But there are some who seek the King's commands and yet are not entrusted with them. Hence evil thoughts."

The man dropped his cloak somewhat as he spoke, and as I had slowly led the way nearer Fleet Street, where a light shone from a window, I saw his face. I tried hard to recollect if I had ever seen it before, but it was strange to me. I say this because it was a face not easily forgotten. It was hard-featured, large and bony. The eyebrows were bushy, the eyes deep set, and although he had his beard trimmed carefully the face suggested an unkempt condition. His hat hid his hair.

I knew not why, but the man angered me. He had stopped me in the street, he had, unsolicited on my part, sought speech with me, and he had suggested that he desired to be my friend. But he spoke in riddles.

"Your name, my man," I said sharply. "I am not one who gives speech freely to nameless night-walkers."

"No more a nameless night-walker than yourself, Brian Hamilton," he said quietly, "ay, and as much a gentleman to boot. I come to you as your friend, man, for, by the Mass, you walk on a sword's edge."

"If you come as a friend, cease to speak in riddles," I replied, "for my temper is not of the longest to-night."

"I speak in riddles until I know my man," he replied as sharply as I had spoken.

"Then good-night," I replied, turning on my heel and making my way toward Fleet Street.

Quick as a thought he placed his hand on my arm, and said, "I tell you, if you listen not to my words, you will rue it to your dying day."

"Then speak plainly," I retorted.

"You have stood before the King to-night," he said eagerly.

"You have already given me this news," I answered.

"But you have?"

I shrugged my shoulders French fashion, for there was a question in his voice, as though he were not sure.

"If I have stood before the King," I said presently, "I am not one who cries it aloud from the housetops. If I have not, then will I not divest myself of the honor which you have bestowed upon me unasked."

"But you have," he replied, like one who tried to convince himself. "And I can tell you why."

"It would please me much to know," I made answer.

"To receive the King's command," he said, "to receive the King's commission, which is no commission, to undertake work which cannot be accomplished."

"Is Paul also among the Prophets?" I laughed.

"Let us not be at cross purposes, Brian Hamilton," he said. "Believe me, I know what would much advantage you."

"And you are my friend?"

"Your friend," he cried eagerly.

"Then make known to me what would so advantage me."

He hesitated a moment, and then he spoke boldly. "You have friends more than one, Brian Hamilton." he said, "but you have your enemies also. Go to, man. But is the lady beautiful? Is she of high degree? Hath she great possessions? Can she bring a dowry fit for a king? Why should she be brought to England? Do your ears tingle? Why should the King send you? Now, do I know? Now, will you speak freely?"

"If all this were plain to me instead of a riddle, why should I speak freely?" I made answer.

"That you may be protected, and that you may know those of whom you may beware."

"Why should I speak freely in order to know that?" I answered.

"Doth a man give all for naught?" he cried.

I saw what was in his mind now. Either he had something to sell or he desired to know what the King had told me. How could I obtain knowledge of what was in his mind without giving aught away?

"The King is young," I said, "scarcely older than

myself, and all the Tudors speak freely. He favors the
new learning, and the monks curse it. Why? The fairest lands in England are owned by the monasteries, while
the King's coffers are far from full. But what then?
Is not the King loyal to the Church?"

It was a bow at a venture, but it went straight to its
mark.

"Ah, you know that!" he cried. "And are the King's
favorites the Church's favorites? And why should
Henry favor a man on whom the Church's wrath is resting? Answer me that."

"Methinks I am not called upon to answer your questions, Sir Stranger," I retorted. "I sought not this
meeting, neither did I desire it. Besides, who is the man
upon whom the King's wrath is resting?"

"Are you the Earl of Devonshire's secretary and know
not that?" he replied. "Are the King's coffers full?
Are the ways of his father forgotten? Is it true he hath
not a Cardinal Morton, who hath a fork to lift money
out of his nobles' coffers. But hath he not tried? Tell
me that, Brian Hamilton."

"Why should I tell you, Sir Stranger?" I retorted.
"The Earl of Devonshire's secretary knows his business
too well for that."

He seemed at a loss how to answer me, while I assumed a careless air, as though it were a matter of indif-
ference to me whether he spoke further. Yet, if the
truth must be told, I longed greatly to know what was in
his mind, for I felt sure he could tell me things I longed
to hear.

"When do you start?" he asked abruptly, after a
silence.

To this I did not answer save by humming a song
that was popular at the period.

"By the Mass, you are a fool, although you think
yourself wise," he snarled. "You know as well as I
that the King hates the fat abbots; you know, too, that
he would send all the monks about their business before
one could count ten if he dared; and you know that both
the abbots and the King seek the favor of the Earl of
Lancashire. Isn't that enough to make you speak?"

"Not quite," I answered.

"Then I'll say this," he cried, as if in desperation. "The abbots also have a man who is as powerful in his way as the Earl is in his, and that man also desires the lady of Germany. He hath treated me badly, but what of that? He is as good a swordsman as you used to be before you dropped the sword for the pen, Brian Hamilton. With me to help him, he can frustrate any plans of yours, Sir Secretary, and the abbots have offered him better terms than the King hath offered you. Now, then, will you take me with you? For if you will not, I would not give the last goose's quill which you ever used for your life."

My mind has a habit of working quickly when I am aroused, and I knew that I had need of all my wits. The words of the King came back to me. "It is said that a red-haired man over thirty always hath schemes in his mind." Up to that moment the words conveyed nothing to my mind, but now I thought I saw their meaning.

A red-headed man past thirty!

Rufus Dudley! A man past thirty, a man who was practically an outlaw, and who yet had a great following. A man shut out from the King's presence, and yet who longed to have the King's smile. And Rufus Dudley had many satellites and was mixed up with many strange enterprises. A man who feared neither God nor man, and yet was said to be in the secret councils of the Church.

"You wish to change masters," I said.

"A man bearing my name calls no man master," he cried angrily, "no man save the rightful King. But I can be a loyal comrade, Master Brian Hamilton, wise in counsel and as secret as death. I can back a horse, couch a lance and wield a sword with the best, and I never fail a comrade at a pinch."

"And you bear a good name?" I asked, like one who would take him into my confidence.

"As good as your own, Brian Hamilton," he cried eagerly. "I have no churl's blood in my veins, even although I have made a mistake in choosing my friends."

"You also seek the favor of the King?" I asked.

"A man grows tired of being forever at war with those who are mightier than he. He remembers also that he has a name which has been mentioned with pride in the presence of kings."

"Dudley is a good name," I said, like one reflecting.

The man started, while I went on, "But your name is not Dudley."

"If it were, you would be dead ere this," he cried.

"I carry a good sword," I replied.

"Dudley hath many ways of killing the man he wants to get out of the way," was his answer.

"And you know his methods?"

"I know him altogether," he cried. "I know his secrets; that is why we quarreled. He threw me off like an old cloak, and now — Now, will you give me confidence for confidence? I tell you that I alone can save your life, and your mission from defeat."

"Your name is John Mainwaring," I said.

"And is not that name good enough?" he asked.

"Old Sir Richard Mainwaring was an English gentleman of high degree," I replied. "Report hath it that his youngest son hath strange friends."

"But he hath never betrayed a comrade."

"There is a lonely spot in St. James's Park," I said quietly; "it is at the west end of the lake; perhaps you would like to walk there at ten o'clock to-morrow night."

"It might be good for my health," he answered. "Besides, I might then have the pleasure of your society?"

"And in the meanwhile," I made answer, "I could think over a proposition which hath been suggested to me. It is this. Shall I take into my confidence one who is brave, is a sage adviser, a good swordsman, and one who hath been able to obtain knowledge which will be of great value to me."

"Ah," he said, "you grasp the situation."

"That being so," I said, "I bid you good-night."

"I use the French phrase," he replied. "Au revoir, Monsieur Hamilton; but German will be more to our purpose in a week from now."

With that he turned on his heels, and in a few moments was lost to my view. I, for my part, went quickly into Fleet Street, and walked with a rapid step toward Whitehall.

I felt very happy. The battle of wits through which I felt I had come out unscathed had removed the gloom which, in spite of everything, my visit to the King had caused to surround me. I had told the man nothing, and I had learned several things. It is true he had not explained many things which were still dark to me, but he had nevertheless opened my eyes to many things.

I did not trouble about the political aspect of the business. There was time enough for that yet. What motives the King had for desiring the Lady Elfrida Rothenburg to be brought to England was not my affair. It might be made plain to me afterward, it might not. But one thing was plain: there was more than one in the secret. Rufus Dudley evidently knew, and Rufus Dudley was one of those men who stopped at nothing where his own interests were concerned. It had been reported more than once that, but for Dudley's powerful connections, short work would be made of him, but that he was so strongly supported that even the King dared not touch him. He was a handsome, red-haired, dare-devil fellow, a little over thirty, who, report had it, had broken more than one lady's heart. He was one of the best swordsmen in the kingdom, and seldom rode abroad without a number of men-at-arms at his back.

I did not doubt that he was the red-headed man whom the King had in mind; moreover, report had it that, although he was in no way renowned for piety, he was hand in glove with the Church.

All this came to me in a flash as I passed near the Globe Theater, and saw the boys holding the horses of those who were witnessing the play within.

I say I felt very happy, and yet I realized that I had put my hand to a difficult task. Evidently the King's business was more complicated than I had first imagined, and I saw that I should be lucky if I came out of it alive. I felt that I was alone amidst a network of schemes of which I had no intimate knowledge. I had heard of John Mainwaring as one of Rufus Dudley's chosen companions. What Little John had been to Robin Hood, John Mainwaring was to Rufus Dudley, who was youngest son of Lord Robert Dudley.

Now, then, what led John Mainwaring to offer me his help? Had he quarreled with Rufus Dudley, or was he trying to obtain knowledge of all the King had told me that he might acquaint his master?

Anyhow, I did not trust the man, neither was he the one I should think of choosing for a companion. Nevertheless, his offer gave me an idea. I needed a trusty lieutenant, I needed a man of quick wit and a strong arm. To go on my mission alone was to court defeat, and probably lose my life in the bargain. Besides, my brain always worked better when it was brought into contact with the wits of another man.

The thought grew in favor with me. I would seek out a companion who would be to me all that John Mainwaring had boasted. The question was, where could I find him?

I had by this time reached the Strand, and was calling to mind all the likely men I could think of when I heard the laughter of a group of young men who came toward me. They were evidently very merry, and seemed on pleasure bent. When they came up to me they stopped.

"Here is a dangerous night-walker," one exclaimed. "He must explain to us why he is away from the sound of his mother's voice. It is not good for young men to be out alone. Come, young master, tell me who you are, and where you've been?"

"And then?" I asked.

"If your answers are satisfactory we may let you go in peace."

"On condition that you accompany us to the nearest tavern and pay for drinks all round," suggested another.

"I think you've drunk enough to-night, Dick Branscombe," I said, for I knew the speaker well.

"By the Mass, it's Brian Hamilton!" cried Branscombe. "But what doth my lord's secretary in this gay attire? Come now, who is the lady?"

"Ay, you must tell me that," cried the one who had spoken first. "How dare the Earl's secretary be abroad so late, when he hath the reputation of spending his nights studying divinity. Ah, Master Hamilton, it'll be strange divinity you've been studying to-night."

I knew the man slightly. He had but lately come from Cornwall, and was called David Granville. Like many more who belonged to old families, he had come to the King's court to seek his fortune, and had been introduced to me by the Earl of Devonshire. I had liked him when I saw him first, and I liked him now as he stood there before me laughing. He was little more than a boy. Perhaps he was four-and-twenty, but he had all the beauty and grace which characterize the men of the West Country. Even there in the dim light I could see him plainly, tall and straight as a young fir sapling, and with all the dash and daring of youth in his every movement.

"Come now, Master Brian Hamilton," he went on, "by Tre, Pol, and Pen, of which I am an unworthy representative, we must know the truth, or we shall have in duty bound to tell the noble Earl that his secretary keeps late hours."

"And then," I replied, "I should be like young David Granville, a gentleman without occupation, eh? But, seriously, whither go you?"

"To the Globe Theater," cried Branscombe. "There is a play on the boards there which should interest you, Hamilton, a student and lover of the Church."

"Let me go with you?" I said, for a resolution had sprung into my mind.

"Shall we let him off easily like this?" they laughed. "He hath told us nothing, and yet he carries the secrets of State with him."

"He shall go with us on condition that he pays admission money for all," cried Granville.

"Agreed," I cried, leading the way; and a few minutes later we were watching the concluding act of a play that

had set London talking. Indeed, many wondered that it
had been allowed to appear on the boards, for although
the King was no lover of the monks, he had the name
for being deeply pious. There is no need that I should
describe it here, save to say that if it had any serious
purpose at all, it was to show the ignorant and brutal
opposition of the monks — who were set forth as a
drunken, loose-living set of men — against the new learning. In truth, those who have read "Julius II Ex-
clusus," which is supposed to have been written by
Erasmus, will know the kind of thing it was. The
monks, backed by the devil, protested all through the
play against any reform in morals or any increase of
learning, declaring that such reform would result in the
downfall of religion. The thing had no great merit, yet
it was, to an extent at all events, a picture of the times.
As all the world knows, the monks were howling all over
Europe against the diatribes of the scholars, and calling
every plea for reformation devices of the devil.

My companions laughed heartily at much of the buf-
foonery which was introduced, all save David Granville,
who took a more serious view of the question.

"Tell me, Master Hamilton, you who know the inside of monasteries and thought of becoming a monk,"
he said, "is there aught of truth in this?"

"No man doubts it," I answered.

"And the King, knows he of it?"

"Else why the anger of the monks at hints of reform? But of that later. Granville, where go you
when the play is over?"

"I know not. Branscombe and the others have suggested a tavern in Covent Garden."

"Do not go," I replied; "I want to have a talk with
you alone."

He looked at me questioningly, and my heart warmed
as I returned his glance. The large, gray, intelligent
eyes, the broad, smooth brow, the finely-chiseled features could belong only to a fine nature. It was easy to
see, moreover, that he was a youth of brains and courage.
Impulsive, and sometimes foolish, perhaps, but brave and
loyal.

"You have not made your fortune yet?" I said.

"There is nothing moving," he replied: "for the moment all the world's at peace, and my sword lies rusty. Unlike you, I have no store of learning."

"There is much doing," I answered. "What say you to a delicate mission abroad, a mission which requires a keen wit and a strong arm?"

"I should love it," he cried, his eyes sparkling; "but tell me more."

"Not here," I replied. "It is not for the world to hear. But when the play is ended come with me to the place where I live."

We had a great ado about getting away from the other men, who insisted on our making a night of it at a tavern in Covent Garden, but at length we succeeded, and by a little past midnight David Granville and I sat alone, he with an eager, questioning look in his eyes, I watchful and observant, yet convinced that here was the man I needed.

CHAPTER V

"NAUGHT has happened since I have been in London," said Granville, "and although the King, for my father's sake, promised me fair, he hath given me naught to do. A war now!"

"The King professes to love peace," I said.

"Ay, but if there is peace what is there for an English gentlemen to do save to look after his farms? As it is, I have spent much of my patrimony, and while the smiles of the fair ladies at the King's Court are well enough, I need a man's work,"

"What kind of work?"

"A soldier's work," he cried. "Work that a gentleman can rejoice in."

"A soldier's work doth not always consist of fighting," I said. "Did not the knights of old go forth into the world to right wrongs and rescue fair ladies?"

"Ah!" he cried, his eyes gleaming.

"Would that work meet your need?" I went on.

"Would it!" he cried excitedly. "But we live in a practical age, Master Hamilton. It is true I have a horse to ride and as good a sword as was ever forged, but money, my master, money!"

"That can be forthcoming."

"You mean it?"

"Else you would not be here."

"An honorable mission?"

"By the King's command."

"To do what, to go where?"

I reflected a moment, but another look into his face told me I could speak freely.

"To bring a lady of high degree to England."

"From where?"

44

".From Germany."

I had expected a shout of exultation, but in this I was disappointed.

"By the King's command. To fetch a lady of high degree from Germany," he said reflectively. " Secretly, Master Hamilton?" he added questioningly.

"Undoubtedly. As secretly as death if possible."

"Then it's a serious business," he said slowly.

I was pleased at this, and was more than ever assured that here was the man I wanted. He had all the courage and enthusiasm of his race, but I saw that he was thoughtful beyond the ordinary.

"What of that?" I asked. "We are not play-actors."

"No, no," he answered. "I like the business all the more because it is serious. But I was thinking."

"About what?"

"If it is serious and secret," he said with a question in his voice, "no one knows of it save the King and yourself?"

I shrugged my shoulders.

"Ah!" he cried, "I begin to understand now."

"What?"

"I was wondering why Mainwaring followed us to the play, and then kept out of sight as though he did not want you to see him."

The youth startled me, not only by his quick observation of that which had escaped my notice, but by his mention of Mainwaring's name.

"What do you know of Mainwaring?" I asked.

"I know he is Dudley's right-hand man," he replied. "I have heard, too, that he hath a big scheme on foot. There is gossip afloat that Dudley is to marry a foreign lady who hath great possessions in England, but I have paid but little heed to it. There are always stories on foot about Dudley."

I was silent for a second.

"What would you say if Dudley and I have the same project in mind?" I asked. "He for his own ends and I by command of the King."

"I should say you will be kept busy," he replied. "Since I have been in London I have had naught of im-

portance to do save to listen to stories of plot and in-
trigue, and Dudley is the hero of many tales. Besides,
he hath a wonderful henchman in Mainwaring. You
never know which side he is on. Some have it that he
is against Dudley, some that he is his bosom friend. It
was but yesternight that he asked me to join him in the
affair he had on hand."

"What?" I asked eagerly.

"I know not," he replied. "He would not tell me
until I gave my promise to join him. As though the
son of a Cornish Granville would promise to draw his
sword at the command of such a parti-colored beast as
John Mainwaring! But he promised well."

I looked at him again, and the more I looked the more
I liked him. He was in every respect the man I needed.

"David Granville, I will speak as plainly as I dare,"
I said. "I have received the King's command to go to
Germany to bring to England a lady of high degree
named Elfrida Rothenburg. I am afraid the affair is
known to more than one, and it is known to John
Mainwaring, who this night hath asked me to take him
as a lieutenant. I left him not an hour before I saw
you."

"And you told him —?"

"Nothing."

"And you have the King's countenance?"

"The King's command, but not his countenance. His
name must not be mentioned."

"Ah, these Tudors!" he cried, as though he had
great knowledge of that house.

"And if you succeed?"

"I shall have the King's smile."

"He promised that?"

"Yes."

Again he looked thoughtful. I could see he was
weighing everything with great care. Presently he rose
from his seat.

"There is my hand on it," he said, holding it out
to me.

I grasped it eagerly and my heart beat light. The

fever of adventure got hold of me too, and I longed to
be away.

"By daylight to-morrow I shall have all particulars in
my hands," I said.

"We must not start at daylight," said Granville.
"John Mainwaring knows I am with you now."

I told him what was said about my meeting Mainwaring on the following night.

"But he will not be there," said Granville. "Think,
man, think. He asked me to join him in an affair; he
asked you to be allowed to join you ; he saw us together to-night, and he is as cunning as the devil.
Besides, if Rufus Dudley —"

"Yes," I replied, "I see. Therefore must we not sail
from the nearest port. He will have all the boats on the
river watched as far as Gravesend."

"If what is said concerning Rufus Dudley and Mainwaring is true, he will have every road out of London
watched," said Granville. "But what of that? We
must outwit them. By the Mass, Hamilton, but I see
great times ahead!" And he laughed with boyish glee.

"I know the road to Ipswich," I said; "it is but sixty
or seventy miles from London, and there will be a moon
to-morrow night."

"And by the early morn on Thursday we should be
there," he said. "But we must not be seen riding out of
Whitehall together."

"No, the cross roads beyond Aldgate pump is the
place to meet," I replied. "You come to it from Is-
lington, and I from the river."

"It is well," he cried eagerly. "We have more than
twenty hours to make our preparations. Between now
and then we must not be seen together."

"At midnight to-morrow night, then," I said. "You
say you have a horse and accoutrements."

"I have everything," he cried gaily. "And, you
when you come, you will have — but you are reported
to have a wise head, Master Brian Hamilton. Have you
another way out than by the front door?"

I led the way to a narrow, dark alley which led

from the house to the river, a way which was difficult to find save by those who knew it well.

"I do not think John Mainwaring will see me to-night," he said, as he gripped my hand.

The next day I had another interview with my Lord Devonshire, and by eleven o'clock at night I was on my way to a hostelry near the Tower. I took a crooked route, but I need not have feared, as I quickly found I was not followed. Arrived at the hostelry, I found my horse saddled as I had arranged, and by midnight I was at the cross roads I had mentioned. But no sight of David Granville greeted me. All was silent as the grave. Neither horse nor living being of any sort was to be seen. I waited it may be ten minutes, and still all was silent. I did not doubt Granville, but I was afraid something had happened to him. Presently I heard hobbling footsteps, and an old man crept up to me.

"I am not from Germany," he said, "but you can do worse than follow me."

I thought I remembered the voice, and leading my horse followed. We were now outside the city, and I soon found myself in a narrow lane, and as the grass grew rank scarcely a sound was made. Presently my companion stopped and gave a low whistle, while I, thinking I had been betrayed, drew my sword. Before the blade had left the sheath, however, I heard David Granville's laughing voice.

"I am only whistling for my horse, Hamilton," he said, and almost immediately a great gray horse bounded to his side.

In an instant he had thrown off the old ragged cloak which had enshrouded him and had leapt on the horse's back. A few minutes later we were galloping eastward.

Presently we dropped into a walk, and there being open country all around us, we were able to talk freely.

"The thing grows interesting," he laughed. "I have been watched all the day. I think Master Mainwaring depended on me to know which way we were going. So I had to send Nimrod by the only man who could take him to our meeting-place, while I must needs follow the best way I could. You see," he went on, " Nimrod was broken to the saddle by myself, and with the exception of Tom Juliff, my lackey, who I brought from Cornwall with me, he will allow no man to go near him. Seeing I was watched, I had to disguise myself; but I think we have escaped. No man followed me, and Tom Juliff hath an old head on his shoulders. Nevertheless, I did not let Tom see you. I thought it best he should not. As for Nimrod, he knows my whistle as though he were a Christian."

" You think you were watched through the day ? " I said.

" I am sure I was; that was why I walked to the cross roads, and was late. You see, I knew I could trust Tom. For some things I wish we could have taken him with us. Naturally, I told him nothing of the affair we have on hand. I have given him instructions to come to Ipswich with all speed, as Nimrod must be taken back to London."

" But I hope we shall be gone before he arrives," I urged, " and how will he be able to claim the horse ? "

" As to that, I found out that there is an inn called the King's Head, where the landlord is an honest man. He will come there, and I will make all things easy with mine host. That is, if we are gone before he comes. But I am not so sure about that. For one thing, vessels do not leave every day, and, for another, Tom hath a great gift in obtaining horseflesh."

He laughed as he spoke, as though he were in great spirits, as indeed he was, for the spirit of adventure had got hold of him, even as it filled my own heart with joy.

" We have got away with seeming ease," I said; " nevertheless, I hope your sword lies loose in its scabbard and that your dags are easy to hand."

Before the words were out of my mouth he covered me with his pistol. " How is that for quickness ? " he laughed as he replaced it. " But, seriously, Brian Hamilton, my trouble is that we have got away with

4

too much ease. I have been expecting to see Master Mainwaring ever since we started."

"That hath been haunting me too," I said, "and yet why should it? Therè are many roads out of London, and we have taken every care."

"You carry your instructions with you?" he asked.

"Ay, but not in writing."

"That is well. You are sure you have committed everything to memory?"

"I have it all here," I said, tapping my forehead. "Names of places and names of people. But not a scrap of writing do I carry; it would not be safe."

"Where go we?" he asked. "North or south of the country?"

"Rather to the northward," I replied. "But I gather from my Lord of Devonshire that no one but myself knows of this. Thus it is that Mainwaring cannot judge from which port we should be likely to sail. We might have gone to Folkestone and crossed to France; from Dover, and gone to Belgium; or from Gravesend, and sailed down the river."

Granville shook his head gravely. "Master Mainwaring, if report be true, could place men on every road," he said.

We galloped steadily on, I noticing in the moonlight how easily David Granville sat on his horse, and as I saw him I rejoiced the more that I had him with me. I reflected that it would have been lonely riding alone, and I should not have felt half so confident if I were without his aid. For the young Cornishman convinced me that he was no ordinary man. He had all the dash and daring of a youth of twenty-five, with the caution and judgment of one twenty years older.

Presently, on reaching the summit of a hill, we stopped as if by one consent. Half a mile or so in front of us there was a fork in the road, and I knew that we might take either the right or the left turning and still get to Ipswich. Between us and the fork, however, we saw several dark forms, apparently in a life and death struggle.

"Footpads," said Granville.

"Maybe it is Mainwaring," I suggested doubtfully.

But here, as though in contradiction of my words, we heard the scream of a woman. "Help! help! Murder! murder!" she cried.

"Let us on, man," said Granville. "There is some devilry on foot, and we cannot let a woman suffer."

As we drew nearer we heard the clash of swords and angry curses, while the woman's voice was still plainly to be heard, although I judged someone was seeking to stifle her cries.

"Faster! faster!" cried Granville, and we urged our horses forward at a full gallop; then suddenly, as if by magic, even while we were well-nigh a furlong away from the fighters, our horses came to a sudden stop, as if they met with an invisible obstacle. Almost before I realized what was happening I lost my stirrup, and I felt myself pitched forward, while my horse rolled heavily on the road. I felt myself flying in the air, then I reached the ground with a terrible thud. I thought first that I was done for, as all life seemed to be shaken out of me, but by a wonderful stroke of Providence I had well-nigh turned a somersault in my fall, and while I had not fallen on my feet, I had nearly done so. Thus, beyond bruised knees, bleeding hands, and a terrible shaking, I was unharmed. All the same, I lay huddled up on the road in a dazed condition, incapable of rightly comprehending our happening. What had become of Granville I did not know; neither for that matter, did I think. We were riding downhill when I fell, and the shock of my fall had nearly scattered my senses.

As I said, then, I lay huddled up in the road, wondering in a dazed way what had happened, when I heard running footsteps. What this portended I could not tell, yet was I incapable of moving.

"This is the one," I heard a voice say, and although my senses had not fully come back, I knew it was Mainwaring who spoke. "My lord's secretary hath had a sudden fall, it seems, and there will be little trouble in dealing with him."

At this I heard the scramble of horses, but I did not heed. In a dumb sort of way I realized that Mainwaring and I had an account to settle.

He stood close to me, not more than six feet away, and I heard him laugh.

"This is neither the time nor the place we arranged to meet, Master Brian Hamilton," he went on, "but what of that? We meet, and I have a shrewd suspicion I shall get the knowledge you refused me last night. My friend Rufus Dudley needs it."

"I believe the other is unharmed," said another voice. "He moves."

"Then attend to him. I will deal with Master Brian Hamilton."

At this all my senses came back to me, and all became clear. I knew what had happened. A rope had been tied to a tree each side of the road and pulled taut; thus, as our horses had come full tilt down the road, we had suffered our mishaps. The cry of the woman had been uttered to bring us forward at greater speed. It was an old trick, and I ought to have been prepared for it. Indeed, I believe it was my anger at being befooled so easily that roused me to my senses quickly. I was surely old enough to know better. How many of them there were I knew not. I had heard the voices of two, but doubtless there were more. I realized that I must act with caution.

A pistol-shot rang out clearly, which was followed by angry voices, and in a moment I leaped to my feet, feeling a great pain in my left leg as I moved. I sprang away from Mainwaring, as if it were my intention to take flight. He rushed after me, as I knew he would, but before he could reach me I turned and faced him with my sword drawn. At the same time I kept my left hand upon the new kind of fire-arm, the pistol or dag, which had lately come into use in England. I concluded that Granville had used his, and was still able to fight, for there was a clash of steel close beside me.

Before I had time to attack Mainwaring, however, he had also stepped back and drawn his weapon.

" I meant not to have hurt you further, Master Brian Hamilton," he said, " but since you will have it so, on your own head be the blame."

I knew I was fighting not only for my life, but what seemed of more import at that moment, the success of my undertaking. For although I had not been over eager to obey the King's bidding, yet now that I had embarked upon my mission I had sworn in my heart that I would carry it through. Still he had me at advantage. I was scarcely my own man, owing to my fall, and though I tried to fight warily, I did it in a dazed kind of way, for there was a ringing noise in my ears and strange sparks of light flashed before my eyes. Moreover, I did not know the kind of swordsman he was, nor what tricks he knew; so I fenced warily, determined not to take any risks. This, however, did not keep me from holding my dag in readiness and feeling that the thing was fit for use. Had the affair taken place before my fall I should have had but little difficulty, for I had not obtained my name as a good swordsman for nothing, but, as I said, I was far from being my own man, and I also felt anxious as to how David Granville was faring.

Still I held my own, watching his every movement, when I knew by Mainwaring's guard that something new was afoot, but whether it was to his or my advantage I could not tell.

CHAPTER VI

DESCRIBES OUR JOURNEY TO BURG

THINKING that Mainwaring's guard seemed uncertain, I redoubled my caution, for, although still far from clear in my mind, I felt that he might be devising a new trick whereby he might have me in his power, but ere long I saw that he fought uncertainly. And this I believe was because he heard, even as I had heard, a new voice on the scene; and I felt sure that David Granville was receiving help from an unknown quarter. The new voice was altogether strange to me. It was deep and sonorous, and spoke, as it seemed to me, a peculiar and incomprehensible dialect. Now and then I caught a word, but again words were spoken altogether unknown to me.

Suddenly there was a cry for help. It did not come from Granville, nor was it spoken in the voice of the newcomer. This was followed by someone falling with a groan. After that I heard Granville's voice quite plainly.

"I can manage now, Tom," he said. "Go and help my friend if he stands in need. Be careful that you befriend the right man. You know Mainwaring."

The light was good, for the moon had peeped out from between a thin place in the clouds, and I believe that each of us looked out of the corner of the eye to catch a glimpse of the newcomer. I was not fool enough to be thrown off my guard, but I saw, as it seemed to me, a giant coming toward us. Mainwaring made a great lunge, and I barely succeeded in parrying his thrust, but he paid no heed to the slight advantage he had gained, for in another moment he was running down the hill as though the Furies were behind him.

"Aisy, aisy," shouted the giant after Mainwaring's

54

retreating figure; "fight like a vitty man, do 'ee now."

But no reply was forthcoming, whereupon the giant laughed as though he were well pleased.

"Doan't zeem ta like my comp'ny, do a thun?" he said cheerfully. "But be 'ee braave, maaster? No brok boans nor nothin' that way?"

"I'm all right," I panted, "but what of Granville?"

"'Ee's enjyin' 'isself, maaster, that's wot 'ee's bin doin' ever since I shawed one of they chaps how to do the flyin' mare."

"All right, Hamilton?" cried Granville, coming up to me.

"A bit bruised, nothing more. And you?"

"Right angry, my master. We deserved not this. Tom, thou great hulking lout, what didst thou mean by throwing the fellow on the road and breaking his neck?"

"Man 'gin man, maaster. Vair play. Tha's wot we allays zay in a rastlin' ring. Bezides, his neck ed'n brok. He'll come too after a bit."

"But Mainwaring?" cried Granville to me.

"Listen," I cried.

As if in answer to his question, we heard the sound of a horse galloping eastward.

"'Ee ded'n zeem to like me," said the giant. "Dreckly 'ee zeed me 'ee turned tail like a rabbut."

"Then there were only three," cried Granville. "Master Hamilton, I'm glad it's not daylight. I should have been ashamed to look you in the face. Fooled by the first trick, and I thought myself clever."

"And I ought to be made to wear cap and bells," I cried. "But tell me what happened? Art hurt badly, Master Granville?"

"Ay, I'm covered with scratches, and my finery is torn so that I'll not be fit to be seen. Directly we came to a dead stop I saw what had been done, so I minded me of a trick which Tom taught me years ago, and threw myself into a prickly thorn bush. I had but barely got out when two men attacked me. I was not doing so badly, when Tom here came rushing up and practised a Cornish wrestling trick on one of them,

And, well — it's not that which troubled me, Hamilton. We've got out all right; all the same, we fell into the first trap they set for us."

" Did you kill your man? "

" No, but he needeth his mother right badly," and he laughed with boyish glee.

" Master David," said the giant solemnly, " if so be that you do think of goin' furder, it do zeem to me it may be so well fur us to pack up our traps like. Ted'n aisy braithin' 'ere."

" Right," I cried, and I looked around for the horses.

As fortune would have it, neither seemed much hurt. Mine was trembling mightily, but Granville's was picking grass from the roadside as though naught had happened. But what surprised me was to see another horse standing close by Granville's.

" Tom, thou hast been horse-stealing again," cried Granville.

" No, Maaster David, I only borried one for the night, so to speak."

" Come, now, tell me what this means."

" Well, arter you'd gone from up by Aldgate Pump, I bethink me of what to do. Ses I tes a goodish way to the place naamed, and I never boasted of bein' a walker. I be wot you may call a 'eavy man, I be. Twelve score pound, maaster, and no vlesh to spaik of, tha's wot I be. Zo not long after you wos gone a chap camed up in a 'urry. 'Seen three horsemen go along this road, my good yokel?' ses 'ee. 'Ah,' ses I, puttin' on a knowin' air. 'Tell me quick,' ses 'ee, 'or I'll lay my whip across your back.' 'What would his worship Maaster Mainwarin' zay to that, I wonder?' ses I, all quiet like. 'Mainwaring,' he cries, 'then I must catch him. This is the Ipswich road, isn't it?' and I, think no 'arm would come of tellin' 'im, zaid it was."

" Well, what then, you rascal?" cried Granville. " Tell me quickly."

" Well, I thought what a keenly 'oss he had, and 'ow 'twas a long way to Ipswich, and 'ow sorry I was not to 'ave the 'oss I rode from 'ome, and zo — I borried this waun."

"Stole it, you mean? Now, Tom, this is a serious matter. You know what your father suffered because he was a horse-stealer."

"Iss, pore dear vather ded 'ave a leanin' to 'osses," said Tom sadly, and then he became silent.

"Well, what do you propose doing with this animal? You'll be hanged, you know."

"Doan't think zo, Maaster David. But this was wot was in my mind. I zaid to myself, I knaw Maaster David would 'ave liked to have tooked me with un, but 'er cudden't cause he 'adn't got no second 'oss, nor money to buy noan. Zo I throwed the genleman over the adge and comed along. Maaster, the air ed'n good 'ere, and ef so be that you'll 'arken to me you'll ride on to where you was goin', and then, when we do come back to England again, I could return the 'oss, wot es a mare, that I've borried."

I could see that Granville was pleased, although he pretended to look vexed, and as I looked at the gigantic proportions of the man I did not wonder. I judged him to be about thirty-five years of age, and looked in point of strength to be a match for any two men. There was a homely wit about him, too, which would doubtless serve him well in emergency.

"Do you speak French or German, Granville?" I asked.

"French, but not German," he replied.

"Is this fellow faithful?" I asked in French.

"He would die for me. He cared for me as a baby, taught me to ride, followed me to London, although I told him he would have to live like a dog. He's as strong as a horse and wary as a fox. He stole that horse for love of me, and is never happy unless he's near me."

"Mount," I cried, "and as for you, varlet," turning to Tom Juliff, "do you come also. We must decide what to do with you another time."

A minute later we were going eastward again, but when I reached the cross roads of which I have spoken I bore to the right.

Granville looked at me questioningly.

"We dare not go to Ipswich," I said. "Remember that Mainwaring is still on the road. There are vessels to be had at Shoeburyness, let us go thither."

"As you will," replied Granville.

When we had got a few miles farther I waited till Juliff came up.

"I have a few words to speak to you, you rascal," I said.

"'Ard words braik no boans," was his reply.

"Do you know what you have done?" I cried. "You have stolen a gentleman's horse, and you deserve to be hanged for it. Probably you will."

"Iss, I've bin a miserable sinner, there's no doubt," he replied sadly.

"Still, I'm loath to send you back to London to such an awful death, because I hear your mother would grieve about you. So for the time we've decided to take you with us. When our work is done you will have to return the horse or send twenty crowns to the gentleman from whom you stole it."

"Oal a man can do I'll do," he said solemnly, although I felt sure there was laughter in his heart.

"The thing that troubles me is what to do with our own horses now," said Granville. "If Tom goes with us, how's he to take my Nimrod back to London Town?"

"We shall never git three 'osses like this in no furrin country," remarked Tom. "Ef the boat es a big wawn, we can take 'em with we."

Granville looked to me for confirmation. I could see that he longed to take Nimrod with him.

"It would be easy to get a boat to take three men, but horses are a different matter," I replied.

"The King's command must be obeyed in a kingly way," laughed the young Cornishman. "We must charter a big vessel."

I said not a word but galloped on. Certainly our horses were good and we were going to a strange land. It might be, therefore, that Tom Juliff's advice was good. The only difficulty lay in carrying it out.

Morning was beginning to break. A purple haze

showed itself in the east, and the birds began to chirp. A few miles farther, and Tom came up to my side.

"I smell salt water," he said.

"Then we are near the sea," said Granville. "A man is not born and reared in Cornwall for nothing. He knows the smell of the sea just as a farmer knows the smell of new mown hay."

"Lead the way, Juliff," I said, for by this time I had lost my bearings.

The giant stopped a minute, threw back his head and sniffed. Then without a word he led the way. A little later we heard the splash of waves upon the shore.

"Harken!" cried Tom. "There's something afoot." He said this in his curious dialect, which I will not try and write down.

It was still nearly dark. Black clouds had obscured the sky, and the day promised to be stormy. The country-side seemed utterly desolate, and I racked my brains sorely for the means by which we could get a vessel to take us across the seas.

We entered a narrow, grass-grown lane. Juliff was no longer the cumbersome, sleepy-looking man for which I had at first taken him. Since he had taken the lead in the road he seemed a new man. A moment later we heard a strange sound, which was half a moan and half a whistle, whereupon Tom leaped from his horse and spoke in a low tone to his master. Then he threw the reins to Granville and turned to me.

"Maaster," he said, somewhat sheepishly. "Maaster David 'ere have said as 'ow my father was a horse stealer. He might have said he was other things as well. We Cornishmen be rough, maaster, our life hath made us so. But we know the sea as well as the land. And I've just heard sounds which have told me things. I may be wrong, I may be right, but I believe we're in luck's way. Would you mind if I went on here a little, way by myself?"

He still spoke in his strange Cornish dialect, but I understood him.

"Never doubt Tom, Hamilton," cried Granville. "He hath more than five senses, I believe."

A minute later Tom leaped a hedge and was lost to our sight. Ten minutes later he was back again.

"The greatest luck man ever had," he cried as he came up. "Five miles from here a vessel lies anchored, and she only waits for the tide to go to that foreign land where you wish to go."

"How did you find out?" I asked.

"Wouldn't it be better, maaster, to make the hay while the sun is shinin' and to explain afterwards?" he said, lapsing into his old manner of speech.

I felt angry with the fellow for answering me in this way, for a man should never bear insolence on the part of a servant, but his news was so important that I followed him without a word. In this I did right, for in less than an hour we had entered a creek, where in very truth a vessel lay at anchor.

"Surely our patron saints are working on our behalf," cried Granville. "When I go home again I will give public thanks to St. David for his great goodness, and will give as liberally as my purse will enable me for Masses to be said for souls in purgatory. Who is thy patron saint, Hamilton?"

"St. Martin," I replied.

"I know him not," was the answer; "nevertheless, he hath served thee well. First, we have escaped from Mainwaring's crew, and that with unbroken limbs, and now we find a vessel waiting for the sea, as though the Blessed Virgin herself were seeking to show us favor."

"If Tom Juliff hath informed us rightly."

"I never found Tom at fault yet," replied Granville.

He had scarcely spoken when a tall, black-bearded man approached, and immediately he and Tom were talking eagerly in a language which, try as I might, I could not understand.[1] I saw, however, that Tom seemed to have great influence with him, and before long had apparently won the man to his way of thinking.

"He will take us all over, men and horses," said Tom to us presently, "on one condition."

"And what may that be?" I asked.

[1] It will be remembered that the Cornish had a language of their own until the end of the eighteenth century.

"That we ask no questions," replied Tom.

I did not altogether like this, but I was anxious to be gone. Besides, Granville had told me that I might trust his servant.

"And where will he take us?" I asked.

"On any part of the coast five miles from the town of Amsterdam," he replied.

"I tell you the saints are with us," cried Granville gaily. "I will surely build an altar to St. David and pay for many Masses; that is," he added with a sly look in his eyes, "when my purse is filled."

In less time than it takes me to tell, a rough gang-way had been made from the bank to the vessel, over which we led our horses, and before two hours were over we were at sea, with all sails set.

The day, which had promised to be rough, turned out to be fair enough. Contrary to custom, the wind went down as the sun rose, and as there was no sea to speak of, our voyage was both pleasant and speedy.

Neither the black-bearded man, who was the captain of the vessel, nor the sailors spoke to us, and as I was desirous of keeping my part of the bargain, I asked no questions. I was all the more ready to keep silent, how-ever, as, owing to the fact that we had a following wind, we made good headway, neither were we troubled by any passing vessels. The day passed and the night fell, and we saw no sight of land, and when the next morning appeared we were still in the open sea. Toward evening of the next day, however, we spied as grim and desolate a shore as a man is ever likely to see in this world.

At this I made my way to the silent captain.

"We shall land in the daylight, captain?" I said.

He shook his head in reply, and I saw that he de-sired no speech of whatever sort.

Night had fallen before we found our way into a lonely creek, and then, without a word of any sort, the captain made preparations for our departure.

Before I left, however, I asked him what I should pay him for his great goodness.

"What you will," was his reply.

"You are a good, honest fellow," I said as I put a number of rose nobles in his hand.

The fellow looked at the money and laughed. "I thank your worship for your good opinion," he said. "As to the truth of it, ask Tom Juliff."

"You know Tom?" I said.

He laughed again, but gave no answer, but I knew by the way that they bade each other God speed that it was owing to Tom's acquaintance with the fellow that we had such great good fortune. By what means Tom knew of the fellow's vessel, however, he would not tell me, neither do I know to this day, although I have many shrewd suspicions. Enough, however, that I have told of the means by which we got out of England and landed upon what was surely the strangest country God's sun ever shone upon.

For this we found as soon as ever we had mounted our horses and begun to travel. We were in a land with but few roads, and, for that matter, with but few people. The country was as flat as a table, and consisted for the most part of great tracts of sand. Of course I knew where we were. We were in Nederland, which the people had reclaimed foot by foot from the sea. We kept our faces eastward, and traveled with what speed we could, until presently we came to a town called Leyden, which seemed a flourishing enough place, where we thought best to rest.

We stayed not long here, however, because now that I was well on my way, I desired to reach my destination quickly, which was a castle no great distance from the city of Magdeberg, where I was told my work would lie. Moreover, I knew nothing of the language which these people of Holland spoke, and although I thought it seemed much like the German tongue, I found that a man might know the latter language and still not be able to understand the former.

These Dutch people struck me as being a brave, strong, and sturdy people, however, betraying a respectful independence pleasant to see. They were cleanly too; even the peasants had learned the art of cleanliness, which was far from being so common among the poor in our country.

We traveled several days without ceasing, but without meeting any adventure worthy of notice. No robbers molested us. That may be because we were three men, young, strong, and well mounted and armed, or it may be because, as a rule, robbers do not form themselves into bands in flat countries so readily as in hilly regions. And this country is as flat as the table from which one eats one's food. Even when we had left Holland and had entered the countries which make up Germany, we still found the same thing. All the way from Leyden to Hanover we went without seeing scarce a hill worthy the name, until we were tired to death of the eternal levelness and longed for the sight of a hill.

Mostly, we stayed at such inns and taverns as we passed, but on two occasions we passed the nights at monasteries which lay in our line of march. We were received with great kindness at these, and fared right royally, for we found that good tables were kept, and as much Rhenish wine and beer was placed before us as any lover of good drink could desire. In both cases, however, we found the Brothers were very angry at some heretic fellow, who had seriously disturbed them. I found, too, that they had nothing but hard words for Erasmus, who had been so kindly received by our own good King, urging that he, by praising learning and telling lies about the monks, was doing great harm to religion.

"Even the common people are asking questions," said the good Abbot to me at the last monastery we visited, "and this heresy of learning, if it is not checked will spread like a pest. This accursed Erasmus hath been speaking about the wealth of this house, and hath urged less drinking and more study of the Scriptures, when all the world knoweth that study leadeth to doubt, and doubt to heresy."

But they seemed most concerned about some monk who lived at a town called Wittenberg, whose name I did not catch at the time, but who seemed to be setting the whole country-side agog.

"He must be taken, sent to Rome, and treated as Huss was treated at Constance," cried the sub-prior of the monastery; but as I knew nothing about it, and having but little acquaintance with the writings of John Huss, I thought it better to be silent. I little dreamed at the time how soon I should be dragged right into the very midst of the trouble that was brewing, and how it would affect the whole tenor of my life.

I noticed, however that David Granville asked many questions, and weighed their answers very carefully, so much so that he was led to being questioned himself, but his answers were evidently of a satisfactory nature.

As we drew near Magdeberg we saw the peasants in groups, talking excitedly together, some evidently holding one opinion and some another. Presently we saw that we were a part of a great procession of people, who were all evidently bound for the same place as we were.

"There must be a fair," said David. "It seemeth that the whole world and his wife are going to Burg."

And indeed, as I saw these peasants gathering from every side I asked a man if there was a fair at Burg.

"Ay," he replied, "a great fair, a kind of fair which has only been known in these later days."

"What kind of fair?" I asked.

"Mayhap your worships are going to Burg?" he said.

"Yes."

"Then you will be able to see for yourself," he replied, looking suspiciously at a monk who had just come up.

Upon this we rode on, and soon after entered the town of Burg, where we saw the strangest sight it had ever been my lot to see.

CHAPTER VII

HOW DAVID GRANVILLE BOUGHT A PARDON FOR HIS SINS

WHEN we had entered within the walls of the town we saw a great concourse of people, mainly of the lower orders, although many men of the yeoman and merchant class were present. Everyone seemed excited, and each talked to his neighbor with great earnestness. So great was the throng that we found a difficulty in threading our way to the market-place, which was close to the eastern gate of that town. At length, however, we found a hostelry, and having left our horses to the care of Tom Juliff, we found our way into the square again.

"Ask what may be the meaning of this tumult," said Granville; "there seems naught to sell, and yet it might be a fair."

"It may be the feast of some saint," I urged.

"But there is no procession," replied Granville, "and priests and monks are mingling with the people as though they, too, waited for something to come to them."

So I went up to a man of grave countenance, and asked him what was afoot.

"Is it possible you do not know?" he made answer.

"I am but a stranger here," I replied, "but I thought mayhap it might be a fair."

"Ay, it is a fair."

"But there is naught for sale," I protested.

"There will be presently," and he laughed, half angrily, I thought.

"What?" I asked.

"Pardons," he replied.

"Pardons?" I repeated, for the word conveyed no meaning to me.

"Ay, pardons," he replied, "pardons for your sins, master, pardons for the living, pardons for the dead."

" For sale, at the fair? "

" Ay, for sale at the fair, master. Ah, here he comes!"

At this there was a great rush to the gate, but a road was presently made, and we saw enter a gaudy carriage drawn by fine horses. In front of and on either side of the carriage rode a horseman, gaily liveried, while in the carriage was a stout, elderly-looking man, who showed his large yellow teeth as he looked around among the people.

A man of evident importance approached the carriage, whereupon another who accompanied the carriage came forward, and said:

" The grace of God and of the Holy Father is at your gates."

And then, as if by magic, there came from a monastery near by a number of priests and nuns, bearing lighted tapers in their hands, and approached the carriage and bowed many times, with great reverence, before the man who sat therein.

Upon that bells began to ring and music to peal. One might have thought that the Pope himself had come to the place, so great was the commotion and so profound was the reverence paid to the man in the carriage, who by his dress I took to be a monk.

Presently the carriage moved slowly into the town, followed by a long procession, some of whom sang while others swung censers and offered prayers.

Ere long we reached a church in the center of the town, and, being anxious to see what was afoot, I found my way with the rest, David Granville being close behind me. The church was large and most gorgeously decorated, while a huge organ, which stood in a gallery at the western end of the building, pealed forth triumphant music.

Then I saw that the man who sat in the carriage lifted a huge cross and placed it at the front of the altar, and on the cross I noticed the arms of the Pope, and to this cross the people paid great homage.

" This is a strange business," whispered Granville,

" while the man who carries the cross might be a mounte-
bank at a fair."

" Or a cheapjack," I could not help saying. And this
was no wonder, for the man, whatever his office, was
a coarse-looking fellow, who looked fitter to clean dog-
kennels than to deal in holy matters.

" Look," said Granville, " he goes into the pulpit."

The which was true, and I could not help noticing
the assurance with which he climbed the pulpit stairs
and looked around upon the great concourse of people
which had gathered together. Every available inch of
room was occupied. Galleries, aisles, and crowding up
even to the altar rails, the excited, eager people waited,
and watched the man in the pulpit. Near to him, and
guarded by the three men who had accompanied him
outside on horseback, I saw a big box, which was evidently of great strength.

No sooner had the man entered the pulpit than the
organ ceased, while the priests stopped chanting, and
the censers ceased to swing. In truth a great silence
fell upon the multitude, so great that each man seemed
afraid to breathe. When the monk began to preach all
listened eagerly, as though not to miss a word.

He had an easy flow of speech and a rough humor
which held the attention of all. Indeed, he began by
complimenting the people on the pleasant weather, the
women on their comely attire, and the authorities on the
evident prosperity of their town. After this he went
on to show that earthly prosperity, while very good,
was as nothing compared with the joys of heaven, while
many a man who wore rich attire and fared sumptuously
every day would for his sins suffer terrible tortures in
hell fire.

" But I have come to show you how to escape those
tortures, I am come to offer you pardons for your sins,
which, if you refuse to take advantage of what I offer
you, will drag you down to the pit of Tophet, to the
fires of hell, where you will be tormented everlastingly
by grinning devils.

" In truth I have great good news for you. I come

to sell you indulgences. These indulgences are the stored up merits of our Lord Jesus Christ, they are in the keeping of our Holy Father the Pope, who in the infinite goodness of his heart hath commissioned me John Tetzel, to sell to his people indulgences, pardons for sins past and future, and a free passport to eternal bliss. All of you have sinned, all of you deserve to suffer eternal perdition, and here is your chance, and now is your time to escape eternal doom. Reflect, O, people. For every mortal sin you must, after confession and contrition, do penance for seven years, either in this life or in purgatory. Now how many mortal sins are there not committed in a day, a week, a month, a year, a lifetime. Alas! these sins are almost infinite, and they entail an infinite penalty in the fires of purgatory. And now, by means of these letters of indulgence, you can once in your life, in every case except four, which are reserved for the apostolic see, and afterward in the article of death, obtain a plenary remission of all your penalties and all your sins."

On this he took a letter from under his monk's garb and held it on high.

"Look!" he cried, "here is one of the letters, all properly sealed, by which all sins can be pardoned.

"I would not exchange my privileges for those of St. Peter in Heaven, for I have saved more souls by my indulgences than the Apostle by his sermons.

"There is no sin so great that an indulgence cannot remit. Only pay for my indulgences, and you can be forgiven."

At this moment there was silence, and I took a hasty glance around me. I saw some priests who I thought looked distressed and almost angry, but they were silent like the rest, but in the eyes of others I saw different looks. One great sensual-looking man I saw drank in every word eagerly, as though he delighted in all that was uttered.

"What is the fellow saying?" asked Granville. "I cannot understand a word."

"He is offering pardons of sins for sale," I said. "I will tell you all presently."

"Most of you," went on the man who called himself John Tetzel, "although doubtless well-to-do, are not rich, and so I will sell you these indulgences cheaply. Kings, queens, princes, archbishops must pay twenty-five ducats for an ordinary indulgence, abbots and counts and barons pay ten, while other nobles, some of which I think I see here"— and I saw that his eyes rested upon Granville and myself —"must pay six; but to you who are poor I will only charge half a ducat.

"For particular sins," he went on, "more must be paid. For polygamy six ducats, for sacrilege and perjury nine, for murder eight, and for witchcraft two.

"Now, I appeal to you, was ever such an opportunity known before? Was ever the grace of forgiveness so abundantly shown?

"Will you not buy? Ay, even if you had but one garment on your back you should sell it that you may buy these precious letters bearing the seal of the Holy Father.

"But these indulgences avail not only for the living but the dead, and for this even repentance is not necessary. Priest! noble! merchant! wife! youth! maiden! do you not hear your parents and those belonging to you who are dead cry to you from the abyss of purgatory? 'A trifling alms would deliver us,' they cry, 'and you will not give it.'

"At the very instant your money rattles at the bottom of the chest the soul escapes from purgatory and flies liberated to heaven.

"What must you do, then? Bring! Bring! Bring your money and buy these precious indulgences!

"And now one word more. To what will this money go? It will go to the Holy Father, who will expend it for the building of a great Basilica in Rome. The House of the Lord lieth waste, and it is for you to re-build it." [1]

All this I heard, and much more, delivered in the most vehement manner, while the people, many of whom,

[1] The above is a correct description of one of the sermons actually delivered by John Tetzel the Indulgence Merchant.

with blanched faces and eager eyes, stretched forward to listen.

No sooner had he finished his harangue than he hurried down the pulpit steps and put a piece of money in the box, which rattled loudly as it fell.

"This is a strange affair," cried Granville. "Will you explain to me what the fellow hath said?"

Whereupon I told him the purport of the sermon to which I had just been listening and of the fellow's authority.

"If he has his authority from the Holy Father there seems naught more to be said," cried Granville. "God knows, all of us have sins enough, and I think I will buy one of these pardons."

It was the first time I had heard Granville say, so much about religion, even though he had not neglected to confess at the two monasteries and go to Mass at various villages where we had stayed. For that matter, I had never broached the subject to him myself, for while I had no doubts concerning the claims of Holy Church, I had as little as possible to do with either priests or monks, and this, I expect, was because of my early experiences. Not that I had ever thought of saying aught against them. Indeed, but for the Dutch wit, few men dared to criticise their doings, seeing that the Church was all-powerful everywhere. Every man confessed and went to Mass because he dared not do otherwise. Kings obeyed the Church because the Church could make and unmake them; and the example of the Lollards was enough to make men everywhere fearful of the Church's power. Moreover, as all the world knows, the abbots and monks had laid their hands upon so much of the lands of the nations that their wealth was well-nigh incalculable, and this wealth, as may be imagined, made them almost all-powerful. So much was this so that few men dared to oppose the religious houses or cry loud concerning their sins. Not that there was no need for this. There was. There was scarcely a monastery or nunnery in England but was looked upon with suspicion, while many were notorious because of the loose living of the friars and the monks.

In truth, it became a question with many as to whether
the Masses sung by monks who had just come from
their cups or their orgies could be of avail. But no
man dared to say aught aloud; besides, if the life of the
monks meant that their offices availed not, what was
to become of religion?   After all, the priests, whatever
their lives, were the channels through which divine grace
flowed, and if their evil lives destroyed their powers, how
could man be saved, seeing they were the divinely appointed means of salvation?

But these public sales of pardons for sins I had never
seen in England.   There were certain images which
were supposed to work miracles, and which, on receipt
of gifts, granted many graces, notably the one at Box-
ley, in Kent, but a public sale like this I had never
seen.

"If a man hath one of these pardons he can do what
he will, and all is well," said Granville.   "Truly, the
Holy Father is making salvation easy."

I had it on my lips to answer him, for there was
something about this sale that was displeasing to me;
but I could say naught.   If the Holy Father had granted
this boon to the people, and if he had declared that for
a few groats sins could be forgiven, what could be
said?

Meanwhile, money was chinking in the box at a
great rate, while acolytes went among the people, shouting "Buy! Buy! Buy!" as though we were at a fair
in an English market-place.   As for the man Tetzel, he
stood by the box cracking rough jokes, as if he enjoyed
his business.

I saw David Granville find his way to one of the
many confessional boxes, but I did not follow him, for
though I was as anxious to get rid of my sins as any
man there, one thing stuck in my throat.

A minute or two later he was at my side again.

"You have got through your confession quickly," I
said.

"Ay," he replied, "the man was in a hurry and many
were waiting, but it is all right."

There was a laugh in his voice, as though he made

light of the whole matter, and then he made his way to
the man Tetzel.

Tetzel eyed him keenly. " You come to buy an indulgence, young master," he said.

" I do not know the German tongue," replied Granville.

" But you know Latin," cried Tetzel.

" I am no scholar," replied Granville, " but I know
Latin indifferently well."

" Ah, then," cried Tetzel in the Latin tongue, " you
are not a German?."

" No, I come from England."

" Why, young man, why? "

" For private reasons and my pleasure," replied Granville not altogether graciously, for he was proud and
came of an old Cornish family, while Tetzel, in spite
of his attire, looked like a clown. " Still, as I was traveling through this town and such a boon came in my
way, I bethought me that I would buy my pardon."

" It is well, young sir. Hitherto men have had to
make pilgrimages to obtain indulgences, while they have
only been obtainable at given times, but now is the grace
of God come to the doors of the people, such is the
goodness of the Holy Father. You want pardons for
both yourself and your friends who are dead."

" For both," said Granville.

" Truly a worthy young man. The saints will smile
on you and you will find favor at the day of judgment.
With this pardon you will be able to walk boldly up to
the gates of heaven."

Granville placed his money in the box, whereupon
Tetzel gave him a sealed letter, which the young man
looked at curiously.

" And you, my master," said the monk to me, " have
you bought your pardon? "

" Not yet," I replied.

" Then is your guilt on your own head, but my
hands are free of your blood. If you had not known of
this, then might you be forgiven. But when a free pardon is to be had for the paying, and when the souls of
your friends who howl in purgatory can be liberated

by paying, and yet you refuse, I tell you it shall be better for Sodom and Gomorrah in the day of judgment than for you."

I felt angry with the fellow in spite of all his pretensions, for although I had no answer for him, yet did all he said seem as so many idle words.

"Let us away," I said to Granville.

"Ay, away," yelled Tetzel, so loud that many people could hear. "But remember this, although your friend will go straight into heaven through the pardon I have sold him, you will go away among grinning devils. For the grace of God hath come to you and you have refused it."

"Let us see the thing he hath sold you," I said to Granville, when we had got away from the fellow.

He took the letter from his pocket and showed it to me. It lies before me as I write, and I set it down here in my own tongue that all who care to do so may read.

"May our Lord Jesus Christ have pity on thee and absolve thee by the merits of His most holy passion! And I, in virtue of the apostolical power that has been confided to me, absolve thee from all ecclesiastical censures, judgments, and penalties which thou mayst have incurred; moreover, from all excesses, sins, and crimes that thou mayst have committed, however great and enormous they may be, and from whatsoever cause, were they even reserved for our most Holy Father the Pope and for the Apostolic See. I blot out all the stains of inability and all marks of infamy that thou mayst have drawn upon thyself on this occasion. I remit the penalty that thou shouldst have endured in purgatory. I restore thee anew to the participation in the Sacraments of the Church, I incorporate thee afresh in the communion of saints, and re-establish thee in the innocence and purity which thou hadst at thy baptism. So that in the hour of death the gate by which sinners enter the place of torment shall be closed to thee, and on the contrary the gate leading to the paradise of joy shall be open. And if thou shouldst not die for long years this grace will remain unalterable until thy last hour shall arrive.

"In the Name of the Father, Son, and Holy Ghost.

"Friar John Tetzel, Commissary, has signed this with his own hand."[1]

"It is full and complete," said David Granville. At this I was silent, for I knew not what to say.

"It seems I can do what I will and all will be well," went on Granville with a laugh. "What can a man want more?"

"If it is any use," I said, almost without thinking.

"It were heresy to deny it," cried Granville. "Hath not the Holy Father authorized it? Nay, Hamilton, thou art a fool not to buy one of them. In any case, it is but a few ducats, and it can do thee no harm. Besides, remember what the fellow said to thee."

"I'll take my chance," I said grimly. "Meanwhile, I'll think about it. It seems we shall have many more opportunities, for these things are sold all over Germany."

"Never did I think heaven was so easy of access before," laughed Granville. "Hamilton, I thank thee for bringing me here."

"I have things of more importance to attend to than this," I answered angrily.

"What can be more important to a man than saving his soul?" cried Granville. "However, whatever happens, I am safe."

"We are but a day's journey from the castle where my Lady Elfrida lives," I said, half to myself. "I must e'en obey the King's command."

On this we made our way to the market-place, for by this time the people were congregating there again; we saw, too, that stalls had been set up for the sale of beer and wine, and the people were drinking and carousing gaily. We noticed, moreover, that those who had bought indulgences were loudest in their revelry.

[1] The above is an exact copy of one of Tetzel's letters of pardon.

It was not long before Friar Tetzel came out of the church, whereupon a great cheer went up for him, as though he were some conquering hero.

When he had entered his carriage he looked around among the people.

"I rejoice with you who have bought my letters," he said. "It hath been a great day for you. But I pity those who have refused to buy. Ay, I pity them; so great, indeed, is my pity that I may return once again, but this I cannot promise. Still, if I can come again I will, and bring my priceless letters."

"Are they any good?" shouted someone in the crowd.

"Who asked that?" cried Tetzel angrily. "Who dares question the value of the pardons of the Church?"

"Dr. Martin Luther," cried a voice.

"Martin Luther!" cried Tetzel, and his eyes burned red. "What is he but a vermin-covered mongrel! A blaspheming heretic! An enemy to the Church! I tell you hell is yawning for him!"

"He is a man of God," cried someone.

"A man of God! Nay, a child of the devil. Hath he not denied God's word, seeing that he hath denied the power of the Pope? I tell thee, the Holy Father will deal with Dr. Martin Luther. What did the Council of Constance do with John Huss? Ah, cursed be those who gave him the name of John, seeing it was the name of the holy evangelist, as it is also the name given in baptism to me, who have saved even more souls than the holy evangelist! But what was done to that arch heretic Huss? He was burned! And he was a holy angel compared with Luther. I tell you, Luther shall be treated a thousand times worse than Huss; and both of them shall, like Dives, lift their eyes in hell, being in torments, and shall cry for a drop of water to cool their tongues.

"And what is more," went on Tetzel, warming with his theme, "if there be anyone here who takes sides with this accursed Martin Luther, then my curse be upon him. My curse be upon him!"

"What can your curse do, seeing we have letters of

pardon?" cried a voice, and someone waved a piece of parchment above his head.

"My curse, my deadly curse, be upon those who take the part of that child of Belial," cried Tetzel as the carriage drove away.

We stayed in that town one night, and never in my life had I seen a place so given over to wickedness. It seemed as though the people took the letters of pardon as a license to sin, for there seemed no manner of evil which was not committed that night.

The next day we rode hard, and toward evening we saw the walls of a great castle rising above the plain, on which it was built.

"Is that the place?" asked Granville.

"If I am rightfully informed it is there I must find entrance this night," I said as boldly as I could. Nevertheless, as I saw the men-at-arms who kept guard, and the grim walls of the castle, I wondered much how we should fare.

CHAPTER VIII

I HAVE said that the castle was built upon a plain, and this is true. And yet I must correct this statement somewhat, for while the country all around was as level as a table, and stretched for many miles in every direction without the sight of a hill, yet the castle itself stood upon an eminence. In truth, it seemed as though a hill had arisen right in the heart of the vast plain by some strange freak of nature. It was not a large hill: rather it looked like a huge mound, the base of which might measure nearly two miles around. It rose from one to two hundred feet from the country around, while a sluggish river almost entirely surrounded it. Huge trees grew on the banks of the river, and a great part of the hill was also woodland. There was a drawbridge on the side by which we approached, and a winding road led up to the summit where the castle stood. At some little distance from the drawbridge was a village containing, as I imagined, people who would in the main be retainers at the castle.

" That," said I to a man in the village, and pointing to the castle, " is Rothenburg Castle, is it not? "

" Yes," he answered, and then he eyed me closely, as if he desired to understand my station.

" The Rothenburg family is at home? " I queried.

For answer he pointed to the men-at-arms who stood by the drawbridge, but no word did he speak.

I thought he desired to hold communication with me, and yet I was not sure. I judged him to be of superior intelligence, and was desirous of learning what things I might from him.

" The Count of Rothenburg is a great man in these parts? " I suggested to him as pleasantly as I could.

"You are a stranger?" he asked curiously.

"I come from another country."

Again he looked at me as though I were a curiosity. Then his eye traveled to Granville, and I could see that he noted the young Cornishman's rich attire. After this he turned to Tom Juliff, whose mighty proportions evidently impressed him greatly.

"Another country?" he repeated. "But not from France, or the Nederlands?"

"From neither," I replied. "I come from England."

"The land with water all around it?" he asked curiously, whereupon I nodded.

"The Lady Elfrida's mother —" Here he stopped, as though he had said too much.

"She is dead," I replied, "but yes, she was an Englishwoman. A lady of high degree."

"Your worship knew the Lady Elfrida's mother?" he questioned.

"Scarcely," I replied, "since she left England when I was but a boy. But I know members of her family."

"And you know the Count?" he asked.

"I have affairs at the castle," I replied.

He looked toward the men-at-arms who stood by the drawbridge, then beyond them toward the castle, after which he turned his eyes to me again. Upon this he moved a step nearer me, and placed his finger on his lips.

"You need not be afraid to speak," I said; "neither my friend nor his serving man understand the German tongue."

Still he hesitated, and then, looking toward the village, and noting that no one was near, he came close to my side.

"Your worship desires to enter Rothenburg Castle?" he said.

I nodded, for I did not see the harm in acknowledging so much.

"Are you a friend of the Count of Rothenburg?" he asked. "Go you there at his bidding?"

"Why?" I asked.

"Because if you do not, you go at your own peril,"

he replied, and I could not help thinking the man was earnest and sincere.

I shrugged my shoulders French fashion, as though I thought but little of his warning.

"You are young," he went on, "and, although a foreigner, are still a Christian. If you were an Italian I would not speak thus to you: they are all liars, liars every one, and would deserve what they would get. But you are English, and Father Brandt hath read to me something of the writings of Erasmus, who hath been to England, and who speaks great things of your people. Besides, was not the Lady Elfrida's mother English? Young master, you are young, and you love life and liberty. Therefore go not to Rothenburg Castle if the Count doth not call you friend, or if you are not protected by a safe conduct."

I laughed as though I recked not of danger, but in reality I wanted him to say more.

"Perhaps you speak mere gossip," I replied. "If he be such a man as you say, then as Germany is a Christian country he would be punished by your law."

He laughed scornfully.

"What doth the Count of Rothenburg care for law?" he cried. "Is not the Elector his cousin? and is not the Elector afraid of him? Hath he not friends among the other nobles? What of Duke George of Leipsic? What of the King of Bavaria? What of him who reigns over Hesse? Doth not the Elector Frederick fear the King of Bavaria?"

I looked at the fellow more keenly, because I realized that he knew more of the affairs of the land than was generally known among people of the class to which I had taken him to belong. I saw now that while his clothes were plain they did not appertain to the peasant class, and I noted, too, that his eyes gleamed with intelligence.

"You seem to know much concerning the reigning dukes," I suggested.

"I speak to warn you," he cried. "I tell you this. A man had better put his head into a lion's mouth than to anger Count Karl of Rothenburg. And he is easily angered. He hath many friends, not because any love him, but because all fear him. Duke George dare not thwart him, while the Elector Frederick, honest as he is, dare not say ' no ' to him. The States quarrel, my master, and Count Karl can command many swords at twenty-four hours' notice. What would you? Because many fear him he is at enmity with all. Therefore doth he regard every man with suspicion."

" From whom do you know all this? " I asked. " If the Count of Rothenburg be the man you say, he is not one who speaks of his affairs so that the villagers on his lands know his mind."

" I speak what I know, young master. More than that I need not say. Know you Count Hans von Hartz? "

" No," I made answer.

" Then do not go thither, unless you must."

" I must," I said quietly.

" You said you did not know the Lady Elfrida? "

I shook my head.

" But you know her mother's family? "

" Yes."

He placed his hand on my horse's neck, and I saw that it was not the hand of a serf, but of one who had done no servile work.

" You are a man of honor? " he said. " You are a lord in your own land? "

" Well? "

" If you must enter Rothenburg Castle, then God's will be done. But beware of treachery."

" Why should I beware of treachery? "

" Because the Court of Rothenburg —" He did not finish the sentence, but looked around him, as though he were afraid.

" It is the custom in your land, as in ours, to help the distressed; to care for the honor of women? " he said questioningly.

The man had lost the rough German brogue in which he first spoke to me, and betrayed by his speech that he was of some learning and quality.

"Always," I replied, quietly, although I wondered why he spoke after such a fashion.

"If you must enter, you must," he went on. " Perchance it is God's will. Who knows but —"

He hesitated again, and then went on:

"'The man who can help the Lady Elfrida will do God's work," he said, and then he walked away hurriedly, as though he were afraid he might be led to say more.

Now this set me wondering greatly. For the man whom I at first took to be a clown proved to be, according to my thinking, a man of quality. Moreover, he had hinted at many things which were beyond my comprehension. He had made me feel that the castle on the hill was full of secrets, and that he who reigned there was a man to be feared.

During my journey I had formed many plans as to the reason I should give for seeking to gain lodgment at the castle, but the more I reasoned out the matter the greater did the difficulties of my task appear to me. I reflected upon the night when I had received the King's command to bring the Lady Elfrida of Rothenburg to England, and the more I reflected the more did I realize that when I entered Rothenburg Castle I must do so by stratagem, and that I had no sufficient reason to give to the Count for my appearance.

Not that this daunted me. I was not yet thirty, and now that I had thrown aside my pen and my books, and had come upon a dangerous mission, my blood tingled at the thought of adventure. Moreover, I had as my companion one who was keen-witted beyond the ordinary, and a brave, loyal gentleman to boot.

I therefore made my way to the drawbridge, which was guarded by men-at-arms, David Granville riding by my side, while Tom Juliff kept a few paces in the rear.

A soldier blocked the way as we came to the bridge, and asked me my business.

"The sun hath set, and we have ridden far," I replied. " I claim the usual hospitality."

"There is a monastery a few leagues hence," he replied.

6

" The Castle of Rothenburg is but a mile away," I answered.

He eyed me closely, and then spoke to his companion, as if in doubt what to do. The companion gave a hoarse laugh, and pointed toward our horses.

" Bear you letters for my lord? "

" I have that to say to the Count of Rothenburg which he would be sorry to miss," I answered. " Meanwhile, stand out of the way, for I am not accustomed to being stopped in my way after this fashion."

" From whither come you? " he asked.

" If your master is anxious to know, I will tell him when we meet," was my reply.

Again he murmured something to his companion, which I did not catch, while the other laughed as before.

Presently he stood aside. " Blame me not for the welcome you get," he said surlily.

I threw him a silver coin instead. " I never blame lackeys for doing as they are bidden," I replied, and then we rode across the bridge, and made our way under the dark trees up the hill toward the castle.

" It hath become dark in a moment," said Granville, pointing to the dark trees which hid the light of the dying day. " As for the man at the bridge, I did not like the look on his face."

I heard a rustling among the undergrowth near by, but it was too dark to see what made the sound.

" The Count hath a strange reputation, Granville," I said. " We must play a wary game. We must keep our trump cards ready."

" What are they? " laughed the Cornishman.

" England is at peace with all the German States, as well as with the Empire," I replied. " We are two men of quality traveling in a foreign land."

" By the King's command, but not with the King's warrant," he replied. " We have the King's signature for nothing."

" Not so bad as that," I replied. " For I have the Earl of Devonshire's writing that Master Brian Hamilton is a man of quality who travels in Germany with my lord's approval, and the Earl of Devonshire is

known to every European Court as the King's right
hand."

" You did not tell me that."

" Because it is a trump card that I do not intend to
play except in direst need," I replied.   " And let me tell
you something else.   The Lady Elfrida is behind those
walls."

" The man with whom you spoke so earnestly told
you?"

" He told me that which makes me sure of it."

" I will learn this outlandish tongue," said Granville
as if to himself.   Then to me, " Told he you aught of
the Count himself?"

" The Count hath a strange reputation, but what to
make out of it I know not.   We must be wary, and
expect surprises."

At this moment we emerged from under the dark
trees, and the castle came suddenly into view.   I saw
in a moment that it had not the appearance of most of
our English castles; neither was it so compact or imposing.   Rather it was large and rambling, being evidently
built at various times, and without adhering to any
given design.   As all the world knows, many of our
English castles are round, while all of them are built according to a carefully wrought out plan.   This, on the
other hand, was straggling.   There was a block of buildings here, and another there, while two great towers
had been erected evidently without regard to the castle
as a whole.   Still, it was of great size and immense
strength.   One part of it impressed me especially.   At
first I took it to be a chapel, but presently I found it to
be a great hall, more than a hundred feet in length,
with gallery all around.   In this hall many of the noble
families had met in past years on festive occasions, the
feasts being kept for many days.

I noticed a great tilt-yard, too, while it was told me
in after days that the armor-room, which I presently
saw, contained the finest suits of armor to be found in
Germany.

On reaching the castle I saw that some soldiers were
on the point of closing a door of immense weight and

size, and that in order to reach this door we had to cross yet another drawbridge, for a deep fosse had been dug around the very base of the castle.

"Halt!" I cried as I saw the soldiers closing the door. They were all of them large-limbed, strong fellows, but seemingly rough and uncouth beyond measure.

"What would you?" asked one curiously.

"Lodgment," I replied, "for this worshipful gentleman and myself. Stables and food for my horses, and supper and a sleeping place for our serving man."

"Two gentlemen of quality with one serving man," sneered one soldier to another.

"But he's as big as two," said the other, with a laugh.

"Did Hans pass you on the river drawbridge?" said the first who had spoken to me.

I looked at him as though his question occasioned surprise.

"You are a friend of my lord's?" he said in a more courteous manner.

"It is for you to lead the way to your master's presence," was my answer.

"It's Hans's affair," I heard him mutter, but he made no further ado, and led the way under the great doorway, through which five horsemen could ride abreast.

It was not until I entered the doorway that I realized the magnitude of the castle buildings, and the great thickness of the walls. Doubtless the house of Rothenburg was of great importance, for there seemed no end to the many buildings.

The horses' hoofs made a great noise as we clattered over the cobbled roadway, and then giving a hasty glance around, I saw what made my heart for a moment stand still.

Standing by a window and watching us I saw a maiden, whose face was clearly revealed to me by the light, which was evidently close by her. I had in my day seen the proud beauties of the English Court, but I thought then, even as I think now, that I never saw one which I could compare with hers. It was not that the face was more beautiful than many others known

to me, but it was different from them all. A prouder
face it had never been my fortune to behold, but with
the pride something else was visible, and that was an
expression of unutterable longing. Perhaps the sadness, the longing, was more noticeable than the pride,
and yet I was not sure. But I knew it was a face that
I should never forget to my dying day.

It may be that in writing this I seem to be using
extravagant language, for what could there be in a face
which one saw at the window of a castle which should
so enthrall a man who was not unacquainted with the
beauties at the Court of Bluff King Hal? I repeat
what I said, however. I knew I should never forget the
face, even though I might never see it again. For, although she might not, feature for feature, be more
lovely than many of the fairest women of which England can boast, yet, as every man who has lived thirty
years knows, there comes to his vision at some time one
who possesses what none other has possessed: a something which cannot be written down but which is nevertheless real; a quality of the soul which, shining through
the eyes and overspreading the features, gives a quality
which is not in the power of man to put into words.

Only for a moment did our eyes meet, but that moment changed my first impression. I had thought that
the two things which the face betrayed were at once an
insurmountable pride and an unutterable longing. When
our eyes met, however, I knew there was something else
which was as great, if not greater than these. I knew
then by instinct, as I know now by many strange experiences, that the young girl whose face I saw at the
window for a space of time in which one could barely
count thirty, was one who might be broken, but could
never be bent, against her will. Who she was I did
not know. For a moment I associated her with the
Lady Elfrida, although I had no sufficient reason for
doing so. But I knew that here was one, though young
in years, and, perchance, unused to the ways of the
world, who would never be led to do aught that she
willed not to do. That dungeons might imprison her,
that racks might torture her, that men might seek to

persuade her, but she would remain firm by the purpose in her mind.

I came to this conclusion by no process of reasoning, but I became conscious of it in a moment, and I knew then, as I know now, that I was right.

I am aware in all this that I have given no description of her as I saw her there for the space of thirty seconds. For that matter, I did not at that moment realize whether she was tall or diminutive, whether she was fair or dark. Neither would I have it believed that because I saw in her face a great pride and an unconquerable will that she was in any way masculine or unwomanly. Rather, whether it was the look of sadness and longing which I had noticed or whether it was because of that other indescribable quality which I have mentioned, but I felt that here was a woman who could stir the heart of a coward to do brave things; one for whom a brave man would venture a hundred lives, if he had them, that he might win her smile.

No sooner did our eyes meet than she stepped into the shadow, and I saw her no more, and it seemed to me then that for the space of half a minute I had been in a trance. I looked at Granville, who was glancing around him with a gay laugh in his eyes.

We came to another great door, where we waited, it may be two minutes, and then a serving man came to show us into the presence of Count Karl of Rothenburg.

CHAPTER IX

HOW I OBTAINED SPEECH WITH LADY ELFRIDA ROTHENBURG

" THE Count is at supper," said the man behind whom we followed; " but he will see you."

I heard loud voices as he spoke, and I knew that the Count of Rothenburg did not sup alone; I judged, too, by the excited tones that he and his companions were supping well.

I knew naught of German customs, but I did not expect to be shown into his presence while he supped. Had I dared I would have liked to have asked permission to attire myself in a befitting manner.

The serving man threw open a door, and I stood in a large hall in the middle of which stood a great table. Beyond this I was unable to take note of the furniture of the room, as my attention was attracted toward the men who sat at the table. Eight of them there were, all gaily attired as if for some revel or dance, but no woman sat at the table, which struck me as strange. From their appearance I judged they had finished eating, for although the remains of great joints of meat and huge pies and pasties lay on the table, their trenchers were empty, while before each man stood great goblets of beer and wine.

For a moment our entrance was unnoticed, and I saw that one man was telling a story of evident interest, for the listeners broke in every now and then with excited remarks.

" And thus he carried her on his crupper for seven leagues," cried the story-teller, " while behind him was her father and seven knights, besides men-at-arms, together with the disappointed lover. No man helped him. Alone he entered the castle, alone he took her away, and that very night, while the Baron and his men stormed his castle, Count Albert Dorndorf wedded her. The priest who lived in the house was unwilling to celebrate the marriage sacrament, but Count Albert would have no man say him nay, since he had sworn a solemn oath that the lady Rotha should be his. The arrows and bullets rattled against the windows while the priest muttered his prayers. Then, when they were man and wife, Count Albert went out and asked the Baron, the disappointed lover, and all the men of quality to come and partake of the marriage supper. Ay, and what is more, they came, after which there was a feast which lasted for three days."

A great shout went up as the man finished his story, while more than one laughed heartily. Amongst those who laughed was he who sat at the head of the table; but it was not the laugh of merriment but rather of scorn.

"Let us drink to Count Albert Dorndorf," cried a voice.

"Ay, let us drink to him," cried he at the head of the table. "He will need good luck. Every man who saddles himself with a woman hath need of it."

At this they all rose and drank deeply, and no man drank more deeply than he whose laugh had no merriment.

As he set down his huge goblet he turned his head and saw me.

"Ah!" he said, "I had forgotten; we have other guests."

He made a step toward me as he spoke, and then stood still, as though something had struck him. I could not help being impressed by the man. He was of immense height and girth, but this was not what any man of judgment would be most impressed by. It was rather his dark, sad face, the deep-set, piercing eyes, the suggestion of authority which marked his every movement.

I had no doubt that this was Count Karl of Rothenburg.

"You come as strangers to seek the hospitality of

Rothenburg?" he said, after he had gazed on us for some seconds.

"We are strangers," I said. "We have traveled far, and the road is long to any place where one can rest in comfort."

"And you, my masters, I doubt not fare royally in your own land, for though you speak our tongue yet you are not Germans."

"The Earl of Hamilton was bosom friend of Henry VI. of England," I said, "and I bear his name. As for my friend, there is no better name in England than Granville, since it boasts of royal blood."

"Then welcome. We have supped, but the board is not bare. Meanwhile, you will doubtless want to tell us why Englishmen should come to Germany."

"The private ear of Count Karl of Rothenburg should hear of everything which appertains to his house," I said.

I saw that he caught my meaning, and then, without more ado he bade us be seated. "Ho there, George, Phillip, Martin, bring platters, food and drink for the worshipful strangers."

We fell to right heartily, and the fare being of better quality than we had known for many days, we showed that we were good trenchermen, as every true Englishman should be. Meanwhile, both Granville and I became objects of great interest to the assembled guests, who asked us many questions concerning the land from which we came.

"Erasmus, the wit and scholar, says that the ladies of England are of rare beauty," said one.

"Erasmus hath a keen eye," I replied.

"Monk though he is, he says that when he went to great houses the maidens kissed him at coming and at going. Is that the custom of the land?"

"It may be for the favored few," I replied, "but not for all. But Erasmus was a monk, and therefore fared royally."

"Ay, the monks have the best of everything," said Count Karl of Rothenburg; "the best lands, the best wine, the best food; money they have in abundance, even though they beg from house to house. As for the women —" He looked around darkly, and then set his teeth savagely.

"And are the Englishwomen as beautiful as those in Germany?" cried the man who had told his story of which I had just heard the end.

"I have seen but few ladies of quality since I have been in your land," I replied warily.

"But even our farmers' dames are fairer than your women of quality. How can it be otherwise, when your King hath wedded an ugly Spaniard?"

"Perchance if you visited England you would tell another tale," I answered.

"Nay," cried another, and I could see that strong wine had gone to his head; "although I have seen no women but our own, I challenge any man to prove to me at the point of the sword that any woman from another country can vie with ours. Will Master Hamilton meet my challenge?"

There was general laughter at this, while more than one declared that I was in honor bound to meet Hans of Hartz.

No sooner had I heard his name than I called to mind that I had heard it before. This led me to pay him special attention, moreover a plan was at that moment born in my mind which I hoped would bear great results.

Count Hans of Hartz was a giant of a man, of perhaps twenty-six years of age. He was not of prepossessing appearance, his face being pitted by small pox; moreover, his cheeks were heavy and fleshy. His forehead was low and his eyes small. And yet, I saw that he was no fool. True, he had been drinking heavily, and he was much excited by it, nevertheless, there was a suggestion of wariness and caution about him which showed me that he was not to be despised.

"Fight you to the death?" I asked.

"For some causes, such as a man's or a woman's honor, most certainly," was the reply; "but in such a cause, he is conqueror who draws first blood or disarms his opponent."

"Why," asked the Count of Rothenburg — and there was a sneer in his voice —"do men from your land fear to fight to the death?"

"The history of my land is not a history of cowards," I replied, "yet do we not throw away our lives without cause. I would fain draw my sword to defend English beauty, yet would I not do so without cause. Show me a German beauty. It may be you have such in your castle; if, after I have seen her, she appears to me more beauteous than English women I will e'en say so, and admit that we have none to compare with her; but if not, then I will even trust to my sword to uphold the beauty of my countrywomen."

At this there was a silence for a moment, and had I made this challenge before supper I do not believe it would have been taken up, for I found that the German nobles and knights held their ladies in high esteem, and did not willingly allow their names to be bandied from lip to lip. As it was, I saw that the Count of Rothenburg shook his head and looked at me angrily. Not so Count Hans von Hartz — as I found out afterward he was commonly called. He had been either drinking more heavily than the others or he carried not his wine so well.

"Spoken like a man of honor," he cried, "and I will meet any man sword to sword who declares there is in the whole wide world a beauty so perfect as that of the Count of Rothenburg's own blood relation, the lady Elfrida."

At this the Count started like a man stung; but I had my game to play, and I determined to play it. Before he could protest, therefore, I rose to my feet.

"Doubtless this lady is fair," I said, "but how can I fight with certainty unless I have seen her? It is said that the fairest lady at the Court of Henry the Eighth is the Countess of Buckingham. She hath dazzled the eyes of many, but how can I maintain that her beauty is peerless unless I have seen the lady whom Count von Hartz hath named?"

The Count looked at me angrily; then he said, "It is not our custom for our ladies to present themselves to passing strangers, even though they claim to be nobles. Yet it shall be as you say. The stranger shall see her who hath been more than once proclaimed the greatest beauty in Germany. The dance we had well-nigh forgotten shall begin forthwith. We will have the fiddlers in, and we will adjourn to the great hall for a dance. After that mayhap there will be fighting."

His eyes gleamed savagely as he uttered the last words, while a young man who sat next to me said, with a laugh, "You might have known the Count's weakness, Master Englishman. He will do aught for a fight."

"If the ladies are to appear I would crave permission that my friend and I make some change in our apparel," I cried.

"Thy friend is gay enough even now," replied the Count grimly; "but e'en so. Your baggage hath been taken to your sleeping chamber."

A few minutes later Granville and I found our way to an apartment which was evidently used for visitors without aught to distinguish them. But I was not likely to complain of this. I had not expected to enter Rothenburg Castle so easily.

I told Granville all that had taken place, whereupon he laughed with great good humor. He had gathered but little of what had been said, but enough to tell him that something stirring was on foot.

"You play a bold game, Master Brian Hamilton," he said, "but I love you for it. I would, however, that I knew the tongue of these people. Still, I will learn many words every day."

"We will speak in Latin," I said; "doubtless many among them will speak it. It is the language of the Church, therefore doubtless some of the nobles will know it."

It was little finery I had been able to bring with me, but as we were travelers naught much could be expected of us. I was pleased, however, with Granville's appearance when he presently appeared. In truth, I have seldom seen any man who presented a braver presence than the young Cornishman. Straight limbed, perfectly proportioned, and on a generous scale, and a noble, fearless countenance, no man could take him to be other than what he was, an English gentleman of the first order.

When presently we were led into the great hall I saw that it blazed with light, while the sound of music told me that the Count had made good his promise.

I must confess that my heart beat quickly as I saw a group of ladies at the farther end of the hall, for I wondered much whether she whom I had seen at the window would appear.

As I have said, it struck me as strange that those who sat at the supper table, and who had been attired as if for a banquet, had been unaccompanied by the ladies, but I afterward discovered that not only Count Karl of Rothenburg but many other nobles supped apart from the ladies of the house. Whether it was that they felt they could drink more freely when they were not present I cannot say, but certainly it was as I have described.

Granville and I stood together, apart from the others, but although the Count saw us he took no steps to present us to the Countess and others whom I took to be members of his family. Those with whom I had been supping, however, spoke to them freely, but either he was not sure about our rank or it was not the custom to present chance strangers, even although they claimed to be of noble birth, to the ladies of his household.

As we stood apart watching them I wondered that they did not commence dancing, for the music sounded merrily, and all seemed to be in readiness. Still they kept on talking, casting from time to time inquiring glances toward David Granville and myself as if they could not understand our presence. This, moreover, I noticed, Count Hans von Hartz was not with the rest, but stood moodily apart, as though something had happened to vex him. Presently, however, his heavy face brightened, and I was not long in knowing the reason, for coming in at the door I saw another lady for whom I imagined he had been waiting.

" Holy Mother, what a beautiful creature! "

It was David Granville who spoke, and yet it seemed as though the words passed my own lips, so truly did they express my feelings. But this was not all. I knew as soon as I beheld her that she was the one whose face I had seen at the window. She stood well-nigh a head higher than any one of the other women, but so perfectly was she proportioned that no one would have spoken of her as too tall.

No sooner did she enter than Count Karl went to her side, and the dance commenced.

" We are but strangers and aliens," said Granville, as the dancers swept by us.

" Wait," I answered. " We must indeed be slow witted if we gain not the smile of these German dames before the night is over."

" Noted you the one with whom the Count led the dance? " said Granville. " She might be a model for Michael Angelo himself."

I replied not, for I noticed that Count Hans von Hartz was still standing moodily by himself. What did his behavior portend? But an hour before he had challenged me to deny that there was no woman in England equal in beauty to the Lady Elfrida of Rothenburg, and it was she, I could swear, who led the dance with her uncle.

I made my way to his side.

" You are not among the dancers? "

He shook his head, with a scowl. All the ardor which he had betrayed an hour before was gone.

" Those ladies — would you be pleased to tell me who they are? " I asked.

" They are the Countess and the ladies of the household," he replied sullenly, but nothing more could I get from him.

A moment later the dance ceased, and I saw that the young girl who had so attracted me stood for a moment apart. Instantly Count Hans von Hartz hastened to her side. His face lit up; he had changed from the heavy-jawed, beer-drinking, slow-witted German, to an ardent lover. But she met him coldly. I could see him pleading with her, but there was an icy look in her eyes which even he could not help but see. Presently he came away crestfallen, looking more gloomy than ever.

Another, and still another dance passed, and still David Granville and I stood apart. None spoke to us. We were allowed in the hall on sufferance; but we were not treated as guests. Presently I saw that the girl to whom Hans von Hartz had spoken was not dancing, but that she stood for the moment behind a pillar under a kind of gallery which was placed around the hall.

Daring all consequences, I made my way to her side. I was not sure, but I believed she was weeping. She did not notice my approach, but kept her eyes on the ground.

"May an Englishman claim the privilege of speaking to one whose mother was an Englishwoman, even although, according to the laws of this household, he is not presented to her?"

This I said in English, and in a low tone.

She started, and looked at me eagerly.

"Who are you, sir?" she said. "And why come you to my side when, seeing you have not been presented to me, you cannot claim to do so by the laws of courtesy?"

"If I were a courtier I would reply that the moth is ever drawn to the flame, and that the bee ever flies to the sweetest flowers," I answered. "But I am not. It is years since I foreswore Court life and became a man of the pen and of books. I am Brian Hamilton, an English gentleman who hath more than once spoken to those who claimed kinship with the late Countess of Rothenburg."

Her eyes flashed eagerly.

"And why do you speak to me?"

"Because I would befriend you."

"I need no friends."

I was silent, but I did not leave her side.

"How could you befriend me, supposing I needed one?" she asked presently.

"I could match my wits against those of Count von Hartz," I said at a venture. "But that would be a small matter. He is a dull-witted German boor. The real battle would be between me and Count Karl."

"You guess. You know nothing," she said quickly.

At this my heart gave a joyful leap, for I saw that I was gaining her confidence.

"I keep both my eyes and my ears open," I said, "and I do not make either dull by sitting too long over my cups."

"Leave me now," she said, "and when the music strikes up again come and ask me to join you in the dance."

Again I found my way to David Granville's side.

"Hans von Hartz has been at the wine cup again," he said.

"You have seen him?"

"I have seen you too. Brian Hamilton, you play a bold hand. I did not think you had it in you."

The dance ceased, and again Hans von Hartz came to the Lady Elfrida's side; but ere he could speak five words she had moved away, and was speaking with an elderly lady, whom I took to be the Countess of Rothenburg. The man followed her with his eyes, eyes filled half with mad love, half with black, murderous hate. I could see his giant form rocking to and fro with rage.

"My duel with him will be to the death," I said to Granville as I left his side. "Keep both ears and eyes open, and report to me."

Again the music clashed, and again the couples were formed. I went up to the Lady Elfrida as though I knew her well, and led her into the hall. I knew that many eyes were upon us, but it was for me to keep my nerves steady. As for the Lady Elfrida, she passed by the other dancers with that look of pride on her face which I had seen at the window, that expression of unutterable will in her eyes which bade defiance to all.

"If you would be my friend," she said, laughing gaily as she spoke, although I heard the tremor in her voice, "go to Dr. Martin Luther at Wittenberg, and tell him what you have seen."

I laughed as though we were exchanging pleasantries, but my reply was grave enough.

"You mean the man who is called a heretic?"

"Yes. He hath influence with the Elector. He knows Hans von Hartz for what he is."

"I will do what you ask," I said, still keeping a smiling face, for I knew I was being watched. But I may not be able to leave the castle easily. Nevertheless, you may trust me."

"You are the first Englishman I have ever seen," she replied, "and I have heard my mother mention the name of Hamilton often. I trust you because you are of my mother's country and bear a noble name. Besides, you look honest."

"Then is my face an index to my heart," I answered.

The music ceased suddenly, and seemingly without reason. But I knew that Count Karl had spoken to the musicians. Therefore I led the Lady Elfrida back to her seat, and left her with a bow, but only to see Count Karl coming toward me with a face as black as night.

7

CHAPTER X

THE FIGHT — AND AFTER

" SINCE when, Master Hamilton — since you choose to call yourself by that name — hath it been the custom for strangers to take a lady to the dance without being presented ? "

" In England," I replied, " when a man hath been received as a guest in a house, he may, if his host hath forgotten the usual courtesies, seek means whereby he can claim to speak to any lady who sits alone."

" But we are not in England."

" English and Germans spring from the same blood, most noble Count," I replied. " Therefore a German will understand an Englishman when he is drawn to speak to a lady of peerless beauty."

" Know you who the lady is ? "

" She told me naught concerning herself."

" But you must have possessed some famous talisman, for she is not free in granting favors."

" I spoke to her in the English tongue ; perchance that was the talisman," I replied, drawing a bow at a venture.

" Told she not her name ? "

" She told me nothing."

The Count scowled, and I saw he was thinking deeply. I heard him muttering something about flouting von Hartz, and then I realized that only men were in the hall.

" Truly, the Count governs his household strangely," I thought within myself. " The women come like shadows and depart as noiselessly."

But I quickly saw that the play was not yet played out, for coming toward me were men who had sat

with me at supper, and in the midst of them was Count
von Hartz.

"The wager! The wager!" they cried. "Will the
stranger fight for the peerlessness of English beauty?"

"Ay, willingly," I replied, and I laughed as I spoke,
as though it were a jest.

"And thou, von Hartz?"

"Ay, I fight," he said sullenly and hoarsely.

"Then let us understand," I said gaily. "I declared
that the Countess of Buckingham hath dazzled the eyes
of many, and although the German ladies are fair beyond words, yet will I defend English beauty as best
I may."

"The Lady Elfrida against the world," cried one of
them. "She hath not smiled on thee to-night, von
Hartz, but wilt thou fight for this?"

"Ay, to the death," cried Hans von Hartz.

"Nay, I will not fight for that," I cried. "If I did
I should be placing one English beauty against another."

"What mean you, sirrah?" cried Count Karl.

"I mean that I claim the Lady Elfrida, since such, you
say, is her name, as an Englishwoman."

"Then I will fight thee for another cause," cried von
Hartz, as though he were anxious I should not escape
him. I saw, too, that his eyes were inflamed with anger,
and that he could scarce control himself. "I say," he
went on, "that thou art a spy and a coward. I say
that thou hast broken the laws of hospitality."

I kept my head, although I saw, not only by the look
on the face of von Hartz, that he meant my death, but
also by the grunt that Count Karl gave, that von Hartz
had expressed his own feelings.

"If I have broken the laws of hospitality I crave
pardon," I said. "In that matter, doubtless, the English have much to learn from the Germans. In England, when a stranger comes to us, bearing a good
name, we receive him with honor. We protect him
from insult, and if he transgress our custom, we attribute it to lack of knowledge. Still, Count Hartz hath
called me a coward and a spy. That is an insult which
must be wiped out. My friend and I are but strangers;

therefore I appeal to Count Karl of Rothenburg to see to it that neither of us has undue advantage in our quarrel."

I watched the Count's face as I spoke.

" Be it as you say," he cried. " Never shall it be said that Karl Rothenburg played foul in a fight. Ay, you shall fight; but, by Himmel, the best man shall win ! "

" He longed for this," I heard one say to another. " Karl of Rothenburg is never happy unless swords are clanging."

" A fight, a fight ! " went on the Count. " But follow me, where the sound of steel may not reach my lady's ears."

A change had come over his face, and he laughed with boyish glee.

" Welcome, Master Stranger," he cried; " and I trust that thou art as ready with thy sword as with thy tongue."

He led the way as he spoke, while I told David Granville all that had taken place. Ere long we found our way to a large vaulted room, which I judged was underground, seeing we had descended many stone steps to reach it; and when the great door slammed I knew that aught could be done here, and no man might know. There was no window to be seen, and the stone walls which surrounded us were damp and covered with fungous growth. This I saw by the light of the torches which had been brought, which was also sufficient for the fight.

It was easy to be seen that no man counted on my victory. I heard one saying to another that Hans von Hartz was in a savage mood, and that he would show me no mercy, while another declared that the Count should keep him from killing me.

And, in truth, the look of a devil shone from the eyes of the man who had called me a coward, for the which I knew the reason. He loved the Lady Elfrida, and she had flouted him. But that was not all, for she had smiled on me directly afterward, and had allowed me to lead her to the dance. Thus he, maddened by jealousy, and excited by strong liquors, longed for my death.

"Things look black, Brian," whispered Granville.

"I have a plan," I replied.

"Can you carry it out?"

"If my hand hath not lost its cunning through the years I have neglected sword play," I replied.

"If he kills thee, Brian, I will e'en take up thy quarrel," he said, and it was then I knew that David Granville loved me.

"If he kills me, David, you must take up my work. The Lady Elfrida is unhappy. Count Karl wills that she shall wed this boor, von Hartz, and she loathes him — that is plain. If I fall, seek out Dr. Martin Luther at Wittenberg."

"What, the heretic?"

"Ay. But methinks he must be a good man."

"To swords, my masters!" cried Count Karl. "Ay, but the clash of steel is sweet to the ears."

Hans von Hartz rushed at me like a whirlwind. So terrible was his attack that I was well-nigh carried off my feet at the first pass. Had I been a man of little stature, and small of bone, he would have had me at his mercy. But, as fortune would have it, I was tall, and of as large a bone as he, although he carried at least twenty pounds more flesh. Moreover, I had not gained my reputation as a swordsman for nothing. I maintained my footing, therefore, and received no scratch. Ere long I knew that a change was coming over the spectators; they were no longer so sure about Count von Hartz's victory. For, being swordsmen themselves, they could see that while not being a stronger man, I was more skilled with my weapon. He fought madly, but with no great adroitness. He sought to break down my guard by brute strength, and this, as all the world knows, goes against a man if he faces one skilled in swordcraft. Besides, I think heavy drinking had made his eye uncertain, while passion made him less dangerous to a man whose strength was at least equal to his own. Therefore Count Karl no longer uttered excited

cries of joy; and, indeed, but for the sound of the clashing and slithering of steel, the great stone vault was
silent.

As for Count Hans von Hartz, his frenzy increased
the cooler I became. Seemingly he was unaccustomed
to meet a man whom he could not bear down at will.
Ere long I saw that he struck out wildly, and then I,
who had kept on the defensive, began to attack. He
was a strong man, that I admit — ay, and under ordinary
circumstances would be a dangerous opponent; but he
was mad with jealousy and much drinking, and therefore I had him at mercy. The sweat stood out like
great beads on his forehead, and his breath came heavily,
as, inch by inch, I pressed him back. He gave a wild
thrust which led to his undoing, for when I had parried
it I seized the opportunity for which I had been
watching. His sword flew from his hand and clattered
on the floor, while he fell with a gasp, his doublet
crimsoned with blood.

The silence was like death as he fell. It seemed as
though the onlookers could not believe what they saw.

As if by instinct, David Granville came and stood by
my side, while I, without a word, wiped my sword.
Count Karl was the first to recover himself. He went
and knelt by his side.

"The fellow hath killed him; he will die," I heard
him say.

"No, I have not killed him; he will not die," I said.

"How do you know?"

"Because I took care not to kill him. But if you
have a leech in the castle, it will be well for you to get
his aid."

"Father Sylvester is in the castle. He hath some
knowledge of surgery and medicine," said someone.

"If he hath not been too deep in his cups," added
another.

"Fetch him with all quickness," cried the Count;
then he looked at me darkly, and turned to the man
who had been telling a story when I had first come upon
them, and whose name, I learned, was Herr Henricus
Amsdorf. What he said to him I did not hear, but

Amsdorf replied, "You cannot; the man is a swordsman, and fought honorably. The very stones would cry
out if he be not treated with all chivalry. Besides, the
laws of hospitality are sacred. By Himmel, he is a
man worth securing!"

"You are right, Amsdorf," cried the Count. "But
here comes Father Sylvester, and, by Gott! he looks
sober."

A priest entered as he spoke, and knelt beside von
Hartz.

"Peace be with you, noble lords," he said. "He that
killeth by the sword shall fall by the sword; nevertheless, no vital part hath been touched; he will recover.
But he must be taken to bed at once." This he said in
Latin.

"Master Brian Hamilton, you have borne yourself
worthy a brave gentleman," said the Count Karl, coming
to my side. "But methinks I would learn more concerning you ere we sleep."

"Willingly," I replied. "I did not expect, most
noble Count, when I entered this castle, that aught of
this nature would happen. As you know, I sought no
quarrel with any man."

"Ay, and you could have killed him, and no man
have right to complain."

Then, turning to the others, he cried, "Enough, my
masters, no harm hath been done — a little blood-letting,
that is all. But what say you to a tourney in the tilt-
yard to-morrow?"

At this there was a general shout of approval, and
we left the dungeon in high good spirits, even as though
death had not been brooding over us five minutes before.

"Thou art a man, Brian," cried Granville as we ascended the stairs. "The whole matter seemeth like a
dream; but thou art a man. I feel ashamed that I
have done naught."

"We live from moment to moment, David," I replied,
"and I wot not what will happen next; but we must
be wary. We are now to have speech alone with Count
Karl."

Not long after we sat together in the supper-room,

the Count with a great goblet of wine before him. At
first he talked of matters having no import; then,
turning suddenly upon me, he cried:

"Why came you to Germany, my masters?"

"To have speech with the Elector Frederick of
Saxony," I replied boldly.

I saw that my answer staggered him.

"You know the Elector Frederick?" he asked
presently.

"Only by name, most noble Count."

"You have matters important with him?"

"They are for his ear only," I made answer.

After this he asked me many questions, but I fenced
warily, and I saw that David Granville, seeing we spoke
the Latin tongue, listened like a dog.

"It will pleasure me much if you stay many days,"
he said at length. "I would e'en know whether thy
friend is master of the sword even as thou art, and
whether thou canst couch a lance as well as wield a
sword, whether thou canst fight on horseback as well
as on foot."

"I would not abuse your hospitality, most noble
Count, and I would now plead forgiveness if I have in
any way angered you by taking the Lady Elfrida to
the dance."

He looked dark, and for some time spoke no word.
Nevertheless, he drank deeply from his goblet of wine.

"I was angered for von Hartz's sake," he said presently. "Know you, Master Hamilton, it is my wish
that she shall be given to him in marriage, but she refuses me — she defies me."

"She refuses to wed him?" I asked with seeming
carelessness.

"She refuses to speak to him with civility. And this
after my commands. But I will be obeyed. Since
when have women had wills of their own?"

"Since the time of Adam," I replied. "When doth
not a woman gain her way in the long run?"

"With others they may, but not with Karl of Rothenburg," he replied. "But this proud minx is self-

willed in everything. In truth, I believe she is a believer in the heretic of Wittenberg."

"What, Dr. Martin Luther?"

"Ay; she hath read his theses. For that matter, she hath read the writings of Dr. Erasmus, who is nearly as great a heretic as Luther. But that is not all. She refuses to go to confession. Not that I wonder much," he added presently. "The priests and monks have a .bad name, and with reason. They are sworn to a holy life and to celibacy, yet they are — But enough of that. It is dangerous to offend a friar. Is this also the condition of things in England?"

"There is no revolt against the Church in England," I replied, "although the morals of the clergy are a by-word. But what of that? Bad as they are — drunken, loose-living, and all the rest — yet only they have the power to shrive us. Therefore must we obey the Church."

"Ay, ay," he cried; "and yet all Germany is ablaze because of Luther. And, by Gott! I admire him, even though he makes no allowance for a man of the world. When my Lady Elfrida declares that she will not confess because the priests are unchaste, unholy, and drunken, I can say but little, although I fear for her soul."

"Sins seem to be forgiven easily in Germany," I said. "But yesterday, for a few ducats, my friend purchased a pardon which absolves him from all the consequences of sin."

"Ay; and while the monks uphold it the people, backed up by Dr. Luther, cry out against it."

He took another deep draught of wine, and then continued, "I make but little of her refusal to go to confession," he said, "for these monk fellows are a filthy, drunken lot as a whole, even although they do profess to open the gates of Paradise. But for this other matter — she shall wed Hans von Hartz; it is my will. I tell you, Master Hamilton," and his voice was husky with passion and much wine, "if you had killed him it would have gone hard with you."

I saw that he spoke words which would not have escaped his lips but for much wine.

"Still, it was a good fight," he went on; "but never did I see Hans von Hartz fall back from any man as he fell before you. I know more than one noble who would rejoice in such a swordsman as you. Are you rich as well as noble, Master Hamilton? or would you follow the fortunes of a German noble who never forsakes a friend?"

"I have all I need in England, most noble Count," I answered, "and after I have fulfilled my mission I must return to my own land."

He looked at me questioningly and darkly, but spoke no other word on the matter, even although he did not look as though he had given up the project he had in mind.

"But you must be weary, Master Englishman," he went on. "To-morrow we will meet again. I trust you will stay with us many days, long enough to see the Lady Elfrida wedded to Count Hans von Hartz."

"Then must he be wedded speedily," I answered.

"Unless the sword-thrust you gave him is worse than I think, she shall be wedded to him within a month," he cried angrily. "It must be so; else I — But it shall be so. It is my will."

When I arrived at my sleeping chamber I found myself much wrought upon. The events of the night had followed in such quick succession that though I prided myself upon my steady nerves, I found myself starting at every sound, and saw to it that my pistols and sword were ready to hand. As for David Granville, he slept soundly, for he was much wearied; but the events of the night had not come so near to him as to me.

I held the candle close to his face, and noted how free he looked from care. There was not a line on his smooth cheeks, not a fear upon his sunny face. He smiled as he slept, and presently I saw that he dreamed.

"Brian," he murmured, "such a peerless maiden should not wed such a clown. Ay, man, but we must take her to England. But for the King's command I would pay court to her myself."

He laughed as he dreamed. It was easy to see that the scenes through which we had passed and our strange surroundings ruffled him not at all.

But his words set me thinking. It was for me to gain the Lady Elfrida's confidence. It was for me to take her to England.

I noted that the room in which we were housed looked out on the stone causeway by which we had first entered the castle, and soon it came to me that on the other side of the causeway, not more than twenty feet away, was the window at which the Lady Elfrida had stood when I had first seen her.

Instantly a plan entered my mind, and I at once set to work to find means of carrying it out. I looked to the right and to the left, but no sentinel was to be seen. I knew that there was a guard-room where soldiers would be close to the great door, but that was at least thirty paces away. Beneath me was the causeway, perhaps twenty feet down. I knew that even if I desired, escape from the castle would be impossible. But I did not desire to escape. I looked steadily at the Lady Elfrida's window, but nothing could I see, and although I listened carefully no sound could I hear. The great castle was silent save that in the distance I heard the stamp of horses on the stable floor.

After searching carefully I managed to get several pebbles and bits of hard mortar, which had by some means fallen on the ledge of the window. Clouds hung in the sky, but as there was a moon, the Lady Elfrida's window was plainly to be seen.

Taking careful aim, I flipped one of my pebbles toward her window. It struck the stone wall just below, and made but little sound. I tried again, and again failed to accomplish my purpose. A third time I tried, and struck the center of the window with a clatter.

Nothing came of this; but I kept on. Again and again did I strike the window with a pebble, and then I heard someone moving. There was no wind, so that every sound reached my ears with distinctness.

Presently I saw a face, but whose it was I could not tell. I stayed where I was and watched. I was in no great danger, for even although an alarm was made, or a sentinel were to appear, there was but little chance of my being detected.

I shot another pebble, and again it struck the window. At this the face appeared plainly. My plan had succeeded. It was the Lady Elfrida whom I saw.

"Hush!" I whispered. "It is a friend. You remember me? I am the Englishman whom you saw tonight. I want to tell you something."

I spoke slowly but distinctly, in a whisper. The night, all windless as it was, allowed my voice to reach her. She stood there rigid and silent, listening for what I had to say.

CHAPTER XI

" I want to speak words of cheer to you," I said. " To-night, after the dance, the man who owns this castle was angry with me, and tried to fasten a quarrel on me."

I heard her answer plainly, even although her voice was low. So silent was the night that the sound of her voice easily spanned the gulf between us.

" I crave your pardon. I knew when I allowed you to lead me to the dance that I should place you, a stranger, in danger; but if you only knew —"

Even on that cloudy night I thought I saw her shaken by sobs. A great pity came into my heart.

" Listen," I said, " and do not fear. I know the Count wills that you shall wed the Count Hans von Hartz. But you may be at ease. I have frustrated his purposes. I evaded the quarrel which your uncle tried to fasten on me, but I could not evade that which the man whom you repulsed sought. He insulted me. He was mad with jealousy and drink, and he called me a coward, and a spy. We fought."

She gave an exclamation of astonishment.

" You fought with Hans von Hartz," she said, and her voice rose above a whisper.

" Listen and be quiet," I said. Again I looked to the right, and to the left, and harkened for any sound which might be heard.

" But are you wounded?" she asked. " But no; if you were, he would have killed you. There is no more terrible fighter anywhere, unless it be the Count him-self. And he has no mercy on a fallen enemy."

" I am not wounded," I answered, " but, by good fortune, he is. He will be in bed for many days to come. Therefore you have a respite for a month."

I heard her give a cry of thankfulness.

" In the meanwhile, if you will trust me I can help you," I went on. " The Count hath asked me to stay many days at the castle."

" Then hath he some plan, some scheme against you. Believe me you are in danger here. He is as merciless as death to all who do not fall in with his wishes. Besides, why should you desire to help me?"

" Because no Englishman can see a lady in distress and not seek to aid her," I cried. " By the Holy Mother of our Lord I will aid you if you will trust me."

" But you do not know all, neither can I tell you. And more, I do not need your help, Sir Englishman, for it is my purpose to go into a nunnery forthwith."

For a moment my heart was chilled by her words, I know not why; but I made no show of it.

" I fear, fair lady, that that may not be," I said. " For, first of all, you cannot leave this castle, and even if it were in your power to do so, if nunneries have the same name in Germany that they have in England, it might not be a safe asylum."

At this she was silent, whereupon I went on:

" But be comforted, lady. Think over what I have said, and if you can trust me, we will find means to confer together again, and then I promise you that if the wit of man can encompass your escape you shall be taken to a place of safety."

" Whither?" she asked.

" To England," I replied.

" But I do not know that I am welcome in England. My kinsfolk send me no messages. Whither should I go in England?"

" I could provide you a safe asylum," I answered, even although I felt uncomfortable at her words. For was it not my business to take her to England by strategy.

" But why should you? You know naught of me. Until to-night you did not know of my existence. What motive have you for running yourself into danger to befriend me?"

"Since when was chivalry dead?" I made answer; "since when could an Englishman see a lady in distress, and not go to her rescue? As for danger, doth not a man love danger? Is it not the salt of life?"

She was silent at this, and in the dim light I thought she looked as though she were thinking deeply.

"Would you really help me?" she asked presently. "Is it your desire to come to my aid, and are your motives such as you would have another man have, if your own sister needed help?"

"I have naught but honorable feelings toward you, lady. Tell me how I may befriend you, and both my friend and I will be willing to lay down our lives for your service."

Now this may seem extravagant language for a man who was an avowed enemy of women. But this I have found: while a man hath a man's heart, he can never see a woman in need of help, and not desire to rush to her side. Nay, I knew at that moment, that had even Lady Patty Carey been in such distress I would have struck a blow for her liberty. Such is the power of woman. Besides this, the spirit of adventure was upon me, and I rejoiced in, rather than feared, the thought of danger.

"I will accept your offer of help," she said, "if, indeed, I do not presume too far upon a stranger's kindness."

"Command me, lady," I replied, "and your slightest wish shall be obeyed."

"Then will you go to the only friend I have whom I can trust," she said. "Will you go to Dr. Martin Luther, at the Augustine Monastery, in Wittenberg, and tell him that Count Karl hath willed that I shall wed Count Hans von Hartz, and that I will die before I obey his commands."

"Yes, I will go," I replied.

"But you must e'en be very cautious," she made answer, "for if the Count hath bidden you to stay here many days, he will take every means to prevent you from leaving the castle."

"My wits against his," I said. "Sleep in peace, fair lady, for all that man may accomplish shall be accomplished."

I drew back quickly at this, for I thought I heard the sound of approaching footsteps. I think the Lady Elfrida must have heard them also for I saw her no more that night.

Truly I had much food for thought, and I felt no, sleepiness as I lay down on my couch, yet no sooner did my head touch the pillow than I became unconscious, neither did I awake until I heard David Granville's voice telling me it was time to wake.

"Wake, man!" he cried. "Methinks there are gay doings. I hear the stamping and neighing of horses; and if my ears do not deceive me I hear sounds which tell me that knights are fastening on their armor."

I listened, and judged that he had opined truly, and then I called to mind the Count's words about a tourney in the tilt-yard. I therefore hastened to attire myself, and a serving man having told us where we might obtain food, we were quickly in the Count's presence.

"Good morrow, my masters!" he cried. "And a great day is before us. Eight guests slept beneath my roof last night, and because I desired great doings today, more are coming. I sent out messengers through the night. Seeing there are no wars afoot, we will even enjoy ourselves as gentlemen should. Master Hamilton, both thou and thy friend shall take part in the tourney in the castle tilt-yard this day. In an hour from now many ladies, besides those of my own household, shall watch brave deeds of arms."

The Count's eyes shone with joy, and I called to mind what a man had told me the night before. He loved a fight beyond all things, and was never happy save when he heard the clang of steel.

"I have no armor, most noble Count," I said; "neither for that matter hath my friend."

"Then shall you go into my armor chamber," he cried. "Thou hast good horses, I am told. Let us see, then, whether thou canst use the lance as well as the sword."

"I do not know the laws of your tourneys here in this land," I said, "and it is years since I couched a lance."

"Then must you make amends," he cried. "As for the laws, they are simple on such days as this. There will be sixteen in the tourney who will fight two and two, horse against horse, lance against lance. That number will be quickly reduced to eight, for each man who shall be unhorsed, or who shall be bested in the shock, shall be declared *hors de combat*. The eight will thus be reduced to four, the four to two, and the two to one, and then that one after he hath dined, and rested, shall meet me."

He laughed with great glee as he spoke. He had evidently forgotten all care and trouble.

"It is the only way we can keep our arms from rusting," he went on. "And more, he who is conqueror hath a right to claim a gift from the lady whom he deems fairest, and she shall proclaim him her knight before all who are assembled."

On this he led the way to the armor chamber, where suits of armor belonging to many generations had been preserved.

The thing had been arranged suddenly, for such was Count Karl's way. In this way he spent vast sums of money, although I heard it whispered that he had impoverished his estates, and that no one knew where he obtained means whereby he feasted his neighbors so royally.

In truth, after I had chosen a suit of armor, and had come into the tilt-yard, the place was full of knights and ladies, making one feel as though the time of Richard of the Lion Heart had come back again.

In quicker time than I can write it down the tourney was arranged, and the rules were proclaimed aloud by a herald. I found myself pitted against a young German noble who I thought regarded me sullenly; while David Granville was matched by a short, middle-aged man, who looked for an eager victory over my friend. David, however, was in great good humor. The joy of youth sparkled in his eyes, while I knew that he determined

8

in his heart to bear himself bravely in the day's tilt.

On one side of the yard the ladies were seated on a raised gallery, and I noted with a sharp feeling at heart that the Lady Elfrida was there, and that she watched all that took place with an eager eye.

"I would that von Hartz were here," cried the Count; "alas! he is sick. But what of that? On the day following his wedding, the greatest tourney in the history of the castle shall be held. Seven days shall it last, with seven nights feasting afterward."

He made his great horse prance as he spoke, and he gave a laugh which showed how dear to his heart was the clash of steel.

Both David and I had good fortune in the first tilt. Both our lances struck sure, and our opponents were unhorsed. In the second encounter, moreover, we were both declared to have obtained advantage over our opponents; but in the third Granville slipped one foot from his stirrup, and was declared vanquished.

Presently it came to pass that I, who had never expected to come out of the jousting with so much honor, found myself face to face with a redoubtable warrior, the Baron von Freunberg, who had fought in many battles, and who had unhorsed each man he had met. Truly I had not expected so much good fortune, for years had passed away since I had gained such honor, and since I had dropped the lance to be my Lord of Devonshire's trusted secretary. Still, I had found during my previous encounters that I had lost neither strength nor skill. My first adversary had been of no great strength, and my victory over him had given me confidence.

"Ho, Master Englishman!" shouted Count Karl, "if thou dost not unhorse the Baron, then the tourney is over, for the Baron and I have taken an oath never to meet in tilt-yard or in battlefield."

It was at this moment that I felt in doubt about the issue, for the Baron was a mighty man, and bore himself as though he were a conqueror already. I think, too, that the Count must have guessed the thoughts which passed through my mind.

" Keep a brave heart," he cried. " It will be no disgrace to be unhorsed by the Baron, for mightier men
than thou art have fallen before his lance."

I could see that he reckoned on the Baron's victory,
and thought of me as the weaker man, and this stirred
all the pride of my heart. Besides, at this moment I
turned and saw the Lady Elfrida's face through the
bars of my vizor, and then I vowed that, come what
would, I would not yield before the doughty warrior.

It all comes back to me now as I write. The great
castle loomed in the near distance overlooking the wide
plains which surrounded it. Mile upon mile in every
direction stretched the lands, all was unbroken save by
a few villages, the sluggish river, and here and there
belts of trees. The castle itself was *en fête*. On the
one side sat the ladies of the Count's household and
many guests; on the other were the serving men and
maidens, while scattered around the tilt-yard were those
who had been engaged in the tourney, but who had
in turn been conquered. Only the Baron von Freunberg and myself remained, and each of us sat motion-
less on his horse, waiting for the signal to tilt.

I say I had determined not to yield to the great
Baron, for although he was a heavier man than I, he
was full fifteen years older, and even though such
jousts as these were an everyday occurrence with the
German nobles, all the old love for fighting came back
to me as I sat there. And more, were not the eyes of
the Lady Elfrida upon me? If I were victor, would
she not trust me more fully, and had I not the King's
command to bring her to England.

At length the signal was given, and the Baron and
I rode against each other full tilt. I gathered all my
strength together for the meeting. Every muscle was
in tension. I held my breath while every power I
possessed was concentrated to meet the mighty shock.

Great sparks of fire flashed before my eyes, and then
came a darkness; I felt my horse sinking under me.
It seemed as though I had bolted against the castle
wall, and I felt my lance shiver in my hands. Still with
set teeth and strained muscles I held on, and a minute

later I found myself still on my horse's back. The noble creature had recovered the effects of the shock of meeting, and now with flesh quivering and eyes dilated was ready for the next charge.

I heard a great cheering from the assembled nobles and ladies, and then I saw that the Baron also retained his seat, while his spear had, like mine, splintered in his hands.

"*Hoch! hoch! hoch!*" I heard the deep-voiced men cry, but the silver-toned voices of the ladies were just as jubilant.

"New lances!" cried Count Karl, to a serving man. "Noble knights choose wisely, for this is a great day!"

I chose a new lance, and right careful was I that the wood should be straight in grain and of fine quality. It came to me then that I was not the weaker man; as for the Baron, I heard him talking excitedly to the Count, but what he said I know not.

Again I looked around, and this time I caught the Lady Elfrida's eye, and then it seemed to me that much depended on the next encounter. Her face was pale as death, but the pallor robbed her not one whit of her beauty. Perhaps this was because I thought she gave me a smile to encourage me. For this I noticed: many there were who shouted for the Baron, but not one gave the stranger Englishman a cheer.

Perhaps that was the reason that I seemed to regard myself as a kind of grim fate, rather than as an Englishman who tilted for pleasure in a German noble's tiltyard.

Again the herald blew his trumpet, and our horses which knew the signal even as we did, rushed forward, and we rode furiously against each other. This time I saw that the Baron pointed his lance not at my breastplate, but at my visor. I knew, too, that if he struck me full and fair, he would have me at advantage, for while the aim was more difficult, it was more dangerous if true. I knew it was dangerous to swerve my head a hairbreath, yet this I did, and thus the Baron's lance well-nigh missed me altogether, but by good fortune I caught him fully in a joint of his armor, and a moment

later I found myself breathless, but unhurt, and not
unhorsed.

An almost deadly silence pervaded the tilt-yard. No
man save David Granville gave me a cheer. The faces
of both nobles and ladies were set and stern, but whether
it was with surprise or anger, I knew not. Still, I
sat there the victor in the day's tourney.

Now it may seem like boastfulness to tell of my
good fortune in this way, but I trust I may be pardoned,
for although doubtless I owed as much to good fortune
as to strength and skill that day, yet I am not ashamed
to own that my victory gave me great joy. Indeed, it
comforted me somewhat in the days which followed,
when not victory, but defeat, dogged my footsteps.

"Beshrew me, a brave lance," said Count Karl at
length; and then as if to himself, he added, "but I did
not think that a man lived who could have done it."

As I have said, no man save David Granville gave
me a cheer, and this seemed strange to me, for by the
laws of our English hospitality, we ever applauded a
knight from foreign lands who came to break a lance
at our tourneys. Moreover, I wondered much at such a
jousting as this being held without due notice having
been given to the nobles and knights around the country; but, as I afterward learned, feats at arms were
meat and drink to Count Karl of Rothenburg, who,
whenever possible, held tournaments, and that without
great proclamation.

"And now to feasting," cried the Count, and to-
morrow, Sir Englishman, we will commence the day
with a meeting between us two, for always at our tourneys the victor hath to meet Karl of Rothenburg."

I cannot say I was displeased at this, for I was
weary, and much spent. Never before had I met such
a man as Baron von Freunberg, and even as I sat on
my horse my ears were singing in a distracted way, and
it seemed to me that all my strength had gone. Each
of us therefore took off his armor, after which we repaired to the great feasting hall, where we fed right
royally. Again the men sat at the great table alone,
while the ladies went away together, although it was

promised us that they should presently join our revels.

Presently it was announced that strangers sought admission, and upon the Count asking whether they were visitors of quality he was told that they were cunning as astrologers and soothsayers, having much learning in secret things, and by the aid of wisdom, known only to them, could read the hearts of strangers, and foretell coming events. By this time the men had drank deeply, and though never in my life have I known those who could drink so deeply, and yet carry a steady head, they had quaffed enough to have merry hearts, and to speak at random.

"What would you, my masters?" cried the Count. "It is true that Holy Church loves not soothsayers, yet doth not the King of France keep them at his Court? We need diversion till to-morrow's fray begins, and who would not know the future? Ay, there are many things I would love to know. As for the secrets in the hearts of strangers — what would you, lords and knights?"

I saw the Count glance toward me as he spoke, and I knew that he had not yet made up his mind concerning me, although I had made it plain to him by many infallible proofs that both David Granville and myself could claim a line of descent equal to his own.

A great shout went up as he spoke.

"I would know whether Duke George, and he of Bavaria, will settle their quarrel, or whether we shall have war," cried one.

"Marry, and so would I?" cried Count Karl, "for as Captain of the free-lances I sadly need work."

"And I would know whether Dr. Martin Luther will defy the Pope," cried another.

"Be chary of speech as to that," cried another, "for the Pope hath many arms and long. And he who speaks a kind word of this disobedient monk may have to repent of it."

"Besides, he would destroy the joy of life," cried another. "He will have it that there is no means of entering Paradise save by a holy life. He would stop

all buying of pardons, and declares that all pilgrimages
to holy shrines are but a waste of time."

"To purgatory with the refractory monk," cried another.   "Let us drink, and let the soothsayers come.
They may tell us if the stranger Englishman will unhorse our host to-morrow."

At this Count Karl swore a great oath.   "Let them
come in," he cried; "I have many questions to ask them.
Fill your goblets, lords, knights, and gentlemen, and
drink to the confusion of all cowards and all traitors
to the house of Rothenburg."

Each man of us filled our goblets, and as we drank
two men entered, who called themselves by some outlandish name, and declared that their minds were filled
with the wisdom of the East, and that their eyes were
keen to pierce the hearts of men.

"Convey my desires to the noble ladies that they repair hither," cried Count Karl.   "As for you, Master
Mystery-mongers, do you go to the end of the room and
prepare for our entertainment."

The two soothsayers went to a raised daïs at the end
of the room, and there, after having made a deep
obeisance, they squatted on the ground, and without a
word let their eyes travel from face to face.

Both of them bore signs of having lived many years.
Their forms were bent, and their hair and beards were
long and white.   Each wore a long gown, not unlike a
monk's frock, and each wore a leathern girt around his
waist, to which were attached many mystic symbols.

There was great laughter, and much eager questioning as the ladies entered the great chamber, and I saw
the glittering eyes of the soothsayers turn from the faces
of the men to those of the women, as though they eagerly
sought some one.

CHAPTER XII

PRESENTLY all was quiet, for each one watched with great care the two soothsayers, who took from under their garments the implements of their trade. Worn parchments they brought forth, also a huge piece of glass that was smooth and round as a ball, in which strange figures appeared. They likewise had a large piece of polished steel shaped somewhat like a horse-shoe. I noticed, too, that one of their scrolls was marked like a mariner's chart, while another contained a map of the heavens on which the names of the planets were written. They also carried many curious instruments strangely marked, the like of which I had never seen before, neither can I think of anything to which I can compare them.

After they had taken these things from under their scarlet robes, and having placed them near their persons, they again scanned those of us who surrounded them, and spoke to each other in a lingo that was incomprehensible to me.

"Stay," said Count Karl, "what tongue speak you, Master Mystery-mongers, or know you only one tongue?"

"We speak all tongues," said one, in good German. "But as good Christians we would speak the language of the Church. It is most befitting our sacred calling."

"Good Christians," cried the Count, "but hath not Holy Church proscribed you?"

"We have had audience with His Holiness," he replied, "and have revealed many things to him by the sacred heavens. Here is a letter from the great de Vio, the Cardinal Cajetan who is the mouthpiece of His Holiness, recommending us to the Mighty Prince, the

Archbishop of Mayence. If Churchmen be present we will speak in Latin. We will speak in German for those to whom it is their mother tongue. I perceive also that there are two strangers from a land beyond the seas, to them also we will speak in words which they can understand."

I felt that every eye was upon David Granville and myself, and I knew by the look on every face that these men had well nigh convinced them that they were indeed seers of mysteries. Moreover, the silence of the great hall had become profound. The men had forgotten to drink, while the ladies were eager to know what would take place.

"Come, begin your necromancy," cried Count Karl, "if ye be holy men, and have the blessing of Holy Church so much the better; but by the Mass, all is not holy that hath the Church's blessing."

"Most noble Count, where would you that we begin?" said the spokesman.

"Begin!" cried the Count, "begin with me, and if you deceive me, Pope or no Pope, Cardinal Cajetan or no Cardinal Cajetan, I will have you hanged on the highest tree that grows around Rothenburg Castle."

"Life and death are naught to us," said the astrologers, "seeing what is called death doth not exist. But, enough, if you will place your right hand upon this crystal, then shall your past and future be made known."

The Count placed his hand upon the piece of crystal as he was commanded, and then took it away. The man who had not yet spoken lit a small lamp, and the crystal was held close to it. Then the astrologer who had been the spokesman, after having examined the glass with great care, began to speak.

Every ear was strained to catch his every word, and I noted that the Lady Elfrida looked eagerly toward the men even as did the others.

"Your name and your destiny are not confined to the land of your birth, most noble Count," said the man. "Not many weeks ago your name was uttered by a mighty monarch, in a tongue unknown to you. Many plans are made concerning you. You have under your protection one who is also linked to lands beyond the seas. She is very fair, and her star looms large in the heavens. She is sought in marriage by —"

He ceased to speak, and gazed intently at the crystal.

" It is not clear by whom, I must gain the secret of this alone. Besides, I see many conflicting currents of life. Most noble Count, you have enemies; you must be as wise as a serpent."

" Speak more plainly, Master Mystery-monger," cried Count Karl. I could see that he was much wrought upon, and there was no caution in his words.

" More I may tell you in privacy," said the sooth-sayer, " for I see that which is only for your private ear."

" Ay, and you expect to fool me as though I were a half-witted woman," cried Count Karl. " Speak on, man, or I will have thee hanged."

" Methinks Count Karl of Rothenburg recks not that he speaks to one whose blood is as noble as his own," replied the other; " neither hath it come to him that if I were to tell him all I see, he would be angry and with cause. But this will I say, he hath promised the hand of the noble lady of whom I have spoken to — no, he is not here. I see a wounded knight — but the sword that wounded him is —"

" Ay, who is he?" cried the Count, for the man had ceased speaking.

" It was held by the hand of a stranger, who hath strange devices at heart."

Again every eye was turned toward me, and then the Count cried out, angrily:

" Speak on, man. Tell me who the stranger is? Tell me what he hath in his heart?"

" It is not clear," said the soothsayer. " He is of noble blood, and speaketh fair. But methinks I see treachery everywhere, yet am I not sure, for mists sweep over my eyes, as though lies obscured the truth. Never-theless will I find the truth of this, if the Count so desires; in silence, and with no light save those of the stars, and the light of the sacred lamp of truth, I will pierce the falsehood, and reveal what may be revealed."

"Tell me more, caitiff," cried the Count. "Thou hast spoken too much or too little. Tell all that is in thy mind."

"I may not, for the thing is not clear. Save this. All here are of one race save two, nay, three. Yet am I not sure concerning the third. Yet, most noble Count, I tell thee this, there are strangers here, ay, one beyond all others, but I cannot read his heart unless he will place his hand as thou hast done, upon this sacred crystal."

"What ho! Sir Englishman," cried Count Karl, in a strange voice. "Come thither, man. Let the light shine. Thou hast come hither claiming hospitality. Let us know what the wise man hath to say concerning thee."

"That willingly," I cried, for though the fellow seemed to know many things, yet did I feel that he was but a charlatan.

I laid my right hand upon the ball of crystal, and as I did so a great silence fell again upon all present. It seemed as though they suspected some secret, and wondered much if the soothsayer would be able to penetrate it.

"It is the hand of a man who hath noble blood in his veins," said the fellow; "it is a hand also which hath won renown in feats of arms. In truth, it is not long since that this hand hath born a victorious lance."

"It needeth but little wisdom to know that," cried Count Karl; "there is not a serving man or man-at-arms in the castle but speaks of it."

There was a general laugh at this, for the Count had pricked the bubble of professed knowledge without difficulty.

"It is not the only fight in which he hath been victorious," went on the soothsayer, quietly. "It is scarce a month ago since he put to flight another warrior. Who or what he was I know not, but it is e'en so."

"Speak he truly, Sir Englishman?" cried the Count.

"My friend and I put some footpads to flight some weeks ago," I made answer, "but one doth not boast of such things."

"But his days of victory are over," said the sooth-sayer, looking into the piece of crystal.

"Mean you that he will fall before my lance?" cried Count Karl.

"I see no meeting between this stranger and the noble Count of Rothenburg," said the soothsayer. "If there is to be such a meeting it is hidden from me. But wait awhile! The shadows disappear. There is a deadly feud between this stranger and the noble Count, but their battle will be of wits, and not of lances, swords, or battleaxes."

"Speak plainly, Master Mystery-monger," cried the Count, "for I am not good at guessing riddles."

"There are secrets in the stranger's heart which are hidden from me," said the soothsayer. "When they begin to appear, shadows come and hide them. Yet is this man's destiny bound up with that of the noble Count. More I must not say to the ears of many."

I cast a glance at the Count as the soothsayer spoke, and well I knew that before the morning's sun arose he meant to have private speech with the soothsayer. Moreover, he did not ask him any more questions, but listened quietly, which was a manner strange to him.

"I also would ask a question of the soothsayer," I said, for at that moment a strange suspicion came into my mind.

"Speak on," he said.

"You are very old," I said, "and your hair is white. But it is a strange kind of white. Was your hair red in your youth?"

"It is an idle question," was the reply, "and I deal with mysteries, for I ever answer foolish questions according to their folly."

"That is shrewdly said," I made answer. "But me-thinks the hands of soothsayers should be smooth and white. Do soothsayers in this land wield a sword as well as a pen?"

At this I saw him hide his right hand under his robe as though I had pricked him to the quick, but his voice altered not as he answered:

"This is but playing at questions, and methinks there

may be others who would know what the planets in their courses tell concerning them."

"But thou hast told me naught," I cried. "What do they say of me? Is my future to be dark or bright?"

"He in whose heart dark secrets are held; he who dares not proclaim his purposes; he whose footsteps are stealthy ever finds doom in his pathway," he replied; whereupon he turned from me as though he would speak to others.

"Methinks I have your secret, Master Soothsayer," I said in English, "and I can with ease obtain a private hearing with the Lord of Rothenburg. Methinks if your wig were pulled off, we should see a merry sight."

At this I stepped back, and fell to thinking deeply, for truly matters were serious.

"Hamilton," whispered David Granville to me, "if I am not a blind fool, thou hast been speaking to Rufus Dudley. The other is Mainwaring who hath not spoken because we know his voice."

"We must escape to-night," I said.

"And leave the Lady Elfrida to his tender mercies?" he asked.

I spoke no more to him for I saw we were being watched, even although the soothsayers were telling the fortunes of others.

Presently the Count seemed to grow tired of the "wise men," and commanded some of his serving men to come in and show us feats of strength. Great strapping fellows they were, who lifted heavy weights, broke ropes, and performed clumsy tricks.

"As you see, we have strong men in our land," cried the Count. "Have you as strong in your land?"

"As to that," I replied, "we have brought as serving man one to whom your strong men would be as children?"

"Let him come hither," cried the Count, and ere long Tom Juliff appeared in the room.

"Tom," I said, "I have had thee brought hither that thou mayest show these fellows what a strong man is; but more, I have to tell thee that we must escape this night. The warder on the castle walls must be silenced, and our horses must be waiting for us beyond the draw-bridge. Canst thou manage this?"

"Yes, master," he said, "it shall be done."

"Can I trust thee?" I urged, eagerly. "The horses must be beyond the river. As for the rest, thy master and I will see to it."

He gave a great laugh, and I knew that he had spoken with confidence.

"What is this," cried the Count; "naught calls for secret councils?"

I could see that he regarded me with suspicion, and that if my suspicions concerning the soothsayers were true, both David Granville and I would hang on one of the castle trees on the following morning, even though he had hitherto treated me as a guest of honor.

"He knoweth not your tongue, most noble Count," I said, "and I must needs instruct him concerning what he must do."

"Come hither, Fritz," cried the Count, calling to a heavy-limbed fellow, who had proved himself to be the strongest man in the castle. "Thou hast to wrestle with the stranger. If thou dost not throw him I will surely have thy ears cropped to-morrow morn."

I saw the German look at Tom Juliff solemnly, and even as he did so a look of doubt came into his eyes. But he gave no sign of fear. Rather he hardened his mighty muscles, and seemed to be gathering his strength for the struggle.

As for me I did not trouble now. I had given my instructions to Tom, and it was for that reason I had schemed to get him into the hall.

The German made a poor show at wrestling, for first of all he did not know the tricks of the sport as Tom did. For as all the world knows, there are no better wrestlers in the world than the Cornish, and Tom had been for years the champion of his county. But besides this the German's strength was not equal to that of the Cornish giant, who presently caught him up, and lifted him at arms' length above his head.

"I trust, most noble Count," I said, "that you will

not be angry with Fritz, for my serving man hath no
equal in such matters."

The Count looked at me keenly. "Thou and I must
talk together to-morrow," he said. "I tell thee, man,
if thou wilt place thy fortunes in the hands of Count
Karl of Rothenburg, both thou and thy friend shall have
money and lands in abundance."

"But if I have to meet you in the tilt-yard to-
morrow, methinks I need rest," I replied.

"Thou hast borne thyself well to-day," he cried.
"Thou art the first man beside myself who hath borne
down von Freunberg for many a year. But thou hast
secrets, young man. Perchance England is too warm
to hold thee? If so, thou hast done wisely in coming
to Karl von Rothenburg. He is hard on his enemies,
but he never deserts a loyal friend, mind that. But to-
morrow we will speak freely."

With that he went and spoke to one of his men-at-
arms who had been commanded to appear before him,
and the two left together. Without a moment's hesitation I made my way to the Lady Elfrida's side.

"Listen," I said in the English tongue. "I must
escape from this castle to-night. I go to Wittenberg
to speak to the man of whom you spoke. You must beware of those soothsayers. If I am not deceived they
come from England to do you harm. They are not soothsayers, but are noblemen who have turned robbers. And
they rob by the aid of the Church, with which they are
hand in glove. See here is half a chain. Accept no
help from any who do not bring you the other half.
Meanwhile, know that I am planning your escape from
the castle."

She spoke no word, but I knew by the look in her
eyes that she was well nigh distraught. Perchance she
doubted me as she doubted others, for what reason had
she to know that I had vowed that I would suffer death
rather than harm should befall her?

She held the chain which I had privily placed in her
hand, but she thought not of it. I knew that many
other thoughts filled her mind.

Presently she spoke. "You cannot escape," she said.

"The Count hath willed that you shall not. That I know."

"My wits against the Count's," I said.

"What would you that I shall do?" she asked, for — as it seemed to me — my words had given her confidence.

"Count von Hartz is lying wounded in the castle," I said. "The Count wills that you shall wed him in a month."

"I will never wed him," she said. "I would sooner die. Neither is there need. To-day I have received a message from the convent at Juterbock. The Mother Superior was a friend of my mother. But for the letter I have received from Dr. Martin Luther I would go thither."

"Who brought you the message?" I asked.

"A monk from the monastery close by."

"And you trust the monk?"

"I trust no one." And then, as if to belie her words, she went on. "Leave me. The Count is returning. Half an hour before midnight I will be in the tilt-yard. There is a great tree growing close by the tower."

Why it was I knew not, but my heart seemed too big for my bosom when I heard her speak after this fashion; but I moved away before the Count entered, noting as I did so that the hand into which I had put half the golden chain of which I have spoken was clasped tightly.

The Count looked around sourly as he entered, but he spoke not unkindly to me, and when, soon after the revels ceased and the ladies departed, he did not demur when I said that I desired rest.

"Granville," I said, "we must away to-night."

"That is plain, although I see not how," he replied.

"I have spoken to Tom Juliff. He says he will take our horses beyond the river."

"Did he promise this?" he asked eagerly.

"Fervently."

"Then will it be done. How, I know not; but the horses will be there. Tom hath never failed me yet."

"As for our own escape, I have a plan," I said; "but not before midnight. Half an hour before midnight I meet the Lady Elfrida under the great tree in the tilt-yard."

He laughed gaily. "The noble earl did wisely when he saved you from being a monk," he cried.

At this I grew angry, although I held my tongue concerning his words; but I gave him instructions about things which I thought it wise that he should do.

I had kept my eyes open through the day, and so I found the means to find my way to the tilt-yard. The Count, I felt sure, was holding secret conclave with the soothsayers, who, I was certain, were no other than Rufus Dudley and Mainwaring, while the other guests at the castle were still drinking.

It may seem strange, but I could not keep my heart from jumping wildly as I made my way to the great tree. I felt no fear, and my sword was ready to my hand, and yet I had a difficulty in breathing, so much was I wrought upon. In truth, so little was I my own man that no sooner did I see the Lady Elfrida than I rushed to her side and said foolishly:

"You trust me, then?"

"Why do you say so?" she asked.

"Else you would not have met me here alone."

"And yet," she replied, "if I were to cry aloud you would be seized and thrown into one of the many dungeons which are underneath the castle."

"But you would not."

"Why?"

"Because I would die to serve you."

"How do I know that?"

"Have you not seen my face? Have you not heard my voice?" I made answer. "Do they not proclaim aloud that I will obey your lightest word?"

"Master Englishman," she said, and there was that in her voice which made falsehood impossible, "tell me why you are here, what came you from England to do?"

"To take you to England." The words had escaped from me before I knew I had spoken.

"You knew of me in England? You have heard my name spoken?"

"Yes."

9

Her words seemed to drag my answer from me, whether I would or not. Enough that I answered her truly.

" By whom were you sent? "

There was a tone of command in her voice, and as she spoke she moved two or three steps, which brought her to an angle in the great tower, where her form was completely hidden.

" Lady Elfrida," I said, " need I answer that? I swear by the Holy Mother that I have naught in my heart but that is honorable. I hold you as sacredly as ever a pilgrim holds the saint at whose shrine he kneels."

" And you would take me to England? "

" I will give my life to guard you until you reach there."

" And when I am there? "

" You will be in a land where men die to defend woman's honor," I said.

" But for what purpose were you commanded to bring me to England? "

" That I know not," I answered, but my heart grew heavy as I spoke.

She did not speak for several moments. She might have been listening whether footsteps were approaching.

" Then you are the paid servant of another? "

There was scorn in her voice, and it seemed to me that from that moment she regarded me much as I might regard a friend's lackey.

" And yet you should be a man of honor." She murmured as though she were speaking to herself.

" Else should I not have been entrusted with such a mission," I said.

Although she spoke no word for some time I knew that a battle was going on in her own heart. As for me, I was angry with myself that I had obeyed her bidding to speak as though I were her bond slave. For truly she had dragged words from me that I had no thought of speaking.

" And if I refuse to go with you? " she said presently.

I was silent, for what could I reply?

Presently her mood seemed to change.

"I will not go with you," she said.

"I think you will," I made answer, for I was becoming angry.

"Why?" she cried.

"Because," I answered, "any fate is preferable to that of wedding von Hartz, and that is what the Count Karl hath willed."

"If I put myself under the protection of the Church neither Count Karl nor von Hartz can touch me."

"Why is the Church so anxious to befriend you?" I asked. "Is not the Church in Germany, even as it is in England, eager to grasp your property? And if you become a nun, do you not enter a place of living death? Besides, you doubt the Church."

I knew I had spoken her feelings, for her head drooped as I spoke, but she uttered no word.

"Besides," I went on, "even now the Count is with the soothsayers. Both my friend and I are sure we have penetrated their designs. There are no two more dangerous men reared within the four seas of England than they. They have also their purpose in coming hither."

"What purpose?"

"To get you into their power."

For some time she was silent. Then she said: "I am safe until the Count von Hartz hath recovered from his wounds; but if you would aid me, bring to me a letter from Dr. Martin Luther and the other half of the chain you gave me."

She fumbled among her garments and took therefrom the image of a saint.

"If you will give that to Hans, the keeper of the drawbridge, he will obey your bidding." On this she placed the image in my hands.

"Now tell me how you would escape," she said.

I told her the plan I had and what Tom Juliff had promised.

"Bring your friend hither," she said, "and if you are men of courage, I will show you a better way."

CHAPTER XIII

HOW I FIRST SAW DR. MARTIN LUTHER

I BROUGHT Granville to her, whereupon she led the way up some steps to the ramparts of the castle.

"Listen," she said. "I am putting much trust in you, for I am showing you the way by which I have planned to escape rather than obey the Count's will. I have secreted this strong rope here, because it is a part of the castle seldom visited; moreover, I have found this iron ring, which is securely fastened to the wall. You can lower yourself to the base of the castle by means of this rope. That done, I will pull it back again. I have also written a letter for Dr. Martin Luther, which you will take to him. When you have brought back his answer, I shall know what to do. God preserve you, Sir Englishman."

With her own hands she took the coil of rope and flung it over the battlements. I heard it fall among the leaves fifty feet below.

"I cannot serve you better by staying here, can I?" I asked eagerly, for truly it went to my heart to leave her thus.

"Go quickly," she cried, like one afraid.

"Do you go first, David," I said.

The young Cornishman caught the rope, and tested the knot by which it was fastened to the chain.

"The saints preserve you, fair lady," he said. "I bid you fear nothing, for my friend is both wise and loyal. What he promises he fulfils."

He lowered himself as he spoke, while I stood by her side speechless. Presently the rope slackened. He had reached the bottom.

"I go to this Dr. Luther, only to come back to you,"

I said eagerly. "Believe me, fair lady, I live only to serve you."

"May God send you good speed!" she cried. "And I—I—believe I am well-nigh friendless."

There was a sob in her voice, which, although I had vowed never to trust a woman again, drew my heart more and more toward her.

"Lady Elfrida," I cried, "I swear by all I hold sacred, by the bones of my ancestors, by the sword my father bequeathed to me, by the faith I hold, that —"

"I hear footsteps," she cried. "Descend quickly. Nay, fear not for me. I will trust you."

I seized her hand and lifted it to my lips. She did not resist me, and then, although I but barely touched her long, tapering fingers, there was kindled a fire in my heart which I knew would never die out.

"I will never betray your trust," I said; "never, never. I will pray for you continually. I will ever hold myself ready to fly to your side."

In less time than it takes me to tell, I lowered myself to Granville's side, and then, even while I stood there, dazed at the happenings of the night, the rope disappeared from my sight, and all was silent.

"Who said it was hard to escape from Rothenburg Castle?" laughed David Granville; but his voice was low, for he knew as well as I that we were still in danger.

"But 'tis not everyone who is aided by the lady of the castle," he added presently.

As for me, I spoke not. It was for me to take the Lady Elfrida's letter to Dr. Martin Luther, the man who, if reports were true, was setting all Germany in a blaze. I saw what was in her mind. Evidently she trusted this man completely, and if he bade her place herself under our protection she would do it. Moreover, he had great influence with the Elector of Saxony. This much I realized, but little more, for I was much wrought upon. In truth, I desired only one thing, and that was to get back to the Lady Elfrida's side again, recking naught of the danger which surrounded me.

It was with some difficulty that we found our way

through the wood, although we made not bad progress, for, in spite of the thick undergrowth, our road to the river was downhill, and ere long we found our way to the bank of the sluggish stream.

"Our difficulty will be at the drawbridge," I said. "It will surely be drawn, for it is now midnight. It is true we can swim across, but I do not relish the thought of spending the night in my cold clothes."

"I have faith in Tom," said Granville.

"But he knows no German," I urged.

"Tom hath a way with him," was Granville's answer. "He hath been at the castle more than twenty-four hours, and, seeing he hath promised to have our horses on the other side, we may depend on him."

In this I found that Granville was correct, for when presently we came to the drawbridge we found it crossing the river, and, what was more, not a soul was to be seen. No light was in the guardhouse, neither were there signs that anyone was near. Nevertheless, we crossed the bridge very gingerly, making little or no noise, although we both saw to it that our weapons were ready to hand.

Having gone some distance down the river, Granville made a sound, not unlike that of a night bird, and ere long we heard the stamping of horses.

"Mount quickly, sir," said the giant, and in but little time we had left Rothenburg Castle behind us.

"How didst thou manage, Tom?" asked Granville, whereupon the Cornishman answered him in a tongue which was strange to me, but which set Granville laughing in great good humor. But I did not ask my friend to explain to me the means he had used, for, first of all, we were riding hard, and, besides, my mind was so full of the work that I had in hand that I troubled but little about the means by which he had got his way.

It was early morning when we reached the town of Wittenberg, and after some little difficulty we gained entrance at the western gate, not far from the great Schloss Church.

"Whom come you to see?" asked the watchman at the gate.

" Dr. Martin Luther," I made answer.

" Art thou friends of his, my masters? " he asked.

" And if we are? " I queried.

" Then, even though the devil himself should bid me keep thee out, yet would I open the gate."

" And wouldst thou not be afraid of the devil? " I asked.

" Nay, for I should know that Dr. Martin would best the devil."

" But is he not a heretic? "

" Nay, for he hath made known to me the word of the Lord," he replied.

" I go to him for counsel, for help," I said.

" Then enter, in God's name," he answered. " It is yet early, but methinks he will be at his books and his prayers.   Tell him as you have opportunity that Nicholas Bucer hath let thee in, and that he rejoices in the word of the Lord."

" Is the Augustine Monastery far from here? " I asked.

" It is the other end of the town, close by the Elster Gate," he replied. " As you pass, note the great door of the Schloss Kirche. It was there that Dr. Martin nailed his theses. Ay, that was a great day, and Wittenberg hath been a new town since. But you cannot miss the monastery, for the road is straight. You pass the market-place and the Rathaus, you leave the town Kirche on your left, and then, having gone along the street for five minutes, you will see the monastery on your right. Be sure and tell him that Nicholas Bucer neglects not the Word of God, and that he rejoices in his book on the Babylonian Captivity, and that he prays night and day that God will give him strength."

" Evidently Dr. Martin Luther hath one friend in Wittenberg," I said to Granville after telling him what the man had said.

" But if he defies the Holy Father," said Granville, " methinks no blessing will fall upon us. As for this man, he may be led away by lies."

To this I found no answer, and I wondered much that Lady Elfrida should put so much confidence in the

words of a man who was an enemy to the Church. I
learned afterwards that the whole town of Wittenberg
had gone after him, and that after he had nailed his
theses against the church door, concerning which the
watchman had spoken, a new spirit was stirring, not
only in Wittenberg, but all over Germany.

Wittenberg consisted mainly of one long street, the
houses being of a comfortable nature as far as I could
judge; but as the morning was yet early, we saw nothing of the people.

Ere long we came to the Augustine Monastery, where
the monk lived, and without ado we rang a bell which
quickly brought a porter to the gates. We saw at a
glance that the building was large, for not only was it
a monastery, but a university to boot, and we were afterwards told that many hundreds of students came hither
that they might have the privilege of listening to Dr.
Luther's lectures. Some, indeed, had it that Duke
George was angry with Dr. Luther because the Wittenberg University was gaining greater fame than even
that at Leipsic, which he had under his own special care.

"No man can see the doctor at this hour," said the
lay brother who spoke to us, " seeing he will for another
hour be at his orisons; but there is an inn across the
road where you can rest until he can speak with thee."

We therefore repaired to the inn, where, early as
it was, we were received without question, Tom Juliff
seeing to it that the horses were well foddered and
attended to. A stout German woman gave us each a
bowl of steaming bread and milk, on which we break-
fasted, after which, leaving Granville at the inn, I again
sought admission to the monastery.

I had no sooner entered the outer door than I saw
a great courtyard, where many young men were conversing. These I judged to be students, for I heard
one saying that, according to the Word of God, there
could be but three sacraments: baptism, repentance, and
the Lord's Supper; but as I was at this moment led up
a stairway I caught not the opinion of the others.

On reaching the top of the stairs I was met by a
brown-frocked monk, with soft eyes and a kindly face,

who I afterwards found was the Prior of the monastery, and who spoke to me in Latin and gave me a blessing.

" Thou would'st see Brother Martin? " he said kindly.

" If it so please you, reverend Father," I made answer.

" I doubt much if he can see you this morning," he replied.   Then looking at me, he said, as I thought, tenderly: " From whom came you, Sir Stranger? "

" That I can only tell to Dr. Luther," I made answer.

" As to that, Brother Martin hath no secrets from me," he said, and yet he spoke not as his superior, but as of one whose will he obeyed. " But come you on matters of the Church or of doctrine? "

" On neither," I answered; " nevertheless, I come on behalf of one who seeks his counsel and trusts him without question."

Again he looked at me questioningly, as though he would read my mind, and then, without a word, he beckoned me to follow him.   We entered an outer door, which admitted us into a room of good dimensions, and then, having crossed this apartment, he placed his hand timidly on another door and entered.

" Pax vobiscum, Brother Martin," I heard him say, and in reply I heard a deep though musical voice give answer, but the words that were uttered I did not catch. Presently, however, the monk I had followed beckoned me to enter, and I came upon a room somewhat larger than the rest.   In the corner of this room was a large stove which, although not in use, caught my attention because it seemed of a quality superior to any I had ever seen in any German house of any sort whatever. In the middle of the room was a table covered with books and parchments.   I paid but little attention to these things, however, for my attention was drawn to the window, for here, seated on a curiously shaped chair, which looked like a chair and desk in one,[1] was evidently the man I had come to see.

He rose to his feet as I moved toward him, and as

[1] Luther's chair, table and stove may be seen in Wittenberg to-day, preserved in the monastery where he was professor.

the light from the window shone straight upon him I
was able to see plainly the kind of man he appeared to
be. That which struck me first of all were his eyes,
so large and piercing were they. He turned them full
upon me, and seemed to be reading my very secret mind.
Not that they were ferocious, although there was a
strange light in them; rather they suggested a kindly
humor and a tenderness somewhat strange in eyes so
piercing. Nevertheless, they gave his face an appearance of power, of command, of unutterable will. The
face itself was large, and although not fleshy, did not
suggest the ascetic. But even of that I was not sure,
because although ruddy, there was a look on his countenance which told me of lengthy vigils. He was
dressed in a monk's garb. His frock was old and well-
nigh threadbare, and fastened around his waist by a
leathern girdle. He was strongly built, being deep of
chest and broad across the shoulders. His neck, which
was bare, suggested, as I thought, great strength and
power of endurance, and yet it was not physical strength
which impressed me, but qualities of the mind and soul,
which one became conscious of by entering into his
presence rather than arriving at the conclusion by any
process of reasoning. In a word, I felt I was in the
presence of a strong man, a great man — great not only
because of intellectual powers, but great because of an
integrity of purpose which nothing could shake.

"You would speak to me, my son," he said.

"I crave an hour's speech with you, if you are Dr.
Martin Luther," I said.

He laughed as he made answer, a laugh which
showed that he loved a jest and had a keen sense of
humor.

"Ay, of a truth I am Dr. Martin Luther," he said,
"but an hour's speech — an hour's — ah, but, my master,
if every day had forty-eight hours instead of twenty-
four, and my strength were doubled, then, perchance,
I could give thee what thou asketh. But come, tell me
the thing of which thou wouldest speak."

His voice was so musical and gladsome that I could
scarce believe it was he. For I had thought of him as

a peevish fellow who sought to draw people away from
the true fold of the Church, one who was churlish by
nature and sour of temper. Therefore, the cheer in his
voice made me look at him again. I had been told he
was a miner's son, and therefore I expected him to be
a clown; but although no one would think of him as
a gay courtier — for he suggested the plebeian — I felt
myself to be in the presence of a master of men.

"I bring a letter from the Lady Elfrida Rothenburg,"
I made answer.

He started as he heard the name, and then looked
at me shrewdly.

"You speak the German tongue, but it smacks of
something foreign," he said.

"I am an Englishman," I replied.

He was silent for a few moments, and I knew that
his mind was working quickly.

"The Lady Elfrida is partly English," he said.
"Perchance you know her family?"

I shook my head.

"How came it, then, that thou, a stranger, art chosen
as a messenger?"

"Perchance her letter will explain," I made answer;
whereupon I took the missive from under my doublet
and gave it to him.

Again he looked at me, then going to the window, he
sat down in the curiously formed chair to which a kind
of desk was attached, and broke the seal.

Once only he stopped during its perusal, and then it
was to lift his head and look steadily at me. I felt then,
as I know now, that here was a man who would only
be content with truth; that his eyes pierced all trappings
of lies and saw the kernel of truth that lay beyond.
I knew, too, that it would go ill with the man who tried
to deceive Dr. Martin Luther, for he probed both men
and things to the very bottom; that his was a mind
which sifted wheat from chaff and threw the chaff from
him.

"Your name?" he said abruptly.

"Brian Hamilton."

Upon this he spoke no other word, but turned to the

letter and read to the end. I saw that he regarded the
purport of the letter as grave, for his face clouded somewhat. He again gave me a searching glance, and then
turned his face toward the window, where something
evidently caught his attention. There was a rumbling
noise outside, and I heard the angry voice of a man
belonging to the peasant class.

His face lit up with anger.

"Henrick Klein," he called, "cease pricking the oxen.
Thou art a cruel varlet, Henrick, and I forbid thee to
persecute the poor dumb beasts. God gave them life even
as He gave it to thee."

"They be stubborn, Father Martin," shouted the man.

"Then be patient with them. I tell thee, God's blessing can never rest on those who treat His creatures
thus. I forbid thee either to strike or prick them, Henrick; meanwhile, pray that God will have mercy on
thy soul."

He kept his eyes on the sheet for some moments, then
he turned to me again.

"This letter is grave, Sir Englishman," he said, "and
I must think of it carefully. But I have not time to
devote to it now. There are lectures I must give, letters
I must write, and people in darkness who are waiting
to be led to the light. Therefore must this wait until
I have done what clamors to be done. But God forbid
that I should be neglectful of such a plea. Therefore
must I think carefully and, if God gives me grace,
wisely, for there is more than appears on the surface."

He started to his feet as he said this and walked
across the room, after which he stopped suddenly before me.

"Ay, and I must satisfy myself concerning the
thoughts which fill Master Brian Hamilton's mind," he
went on. "I must assure myself whether he is a lover
of truth or is one who is willing to live on lies. Nay,
man, let not thine anger rise," he added, for I doubt
not I looked not pleasant as he spoke, "there be better
men than thou or I who find it hard to leave Egypt and
go to Canaan. For there are lies which, because they

are sanctioned in high places, look like truth, and truth which has been spoken of as lies. Besides —"

Again he walked across the room; then he said:

"I must see thee further, Master Brian Hamilton. We must have converse together. Ay, thou shalt have the hour thou didst ask for, e'en though I have but few to spare. But not now, for every minute between now and the hour of six this night is carefully planned. But at six to-night come again. Meanwhile, be assured of this: my lady's welfare is as dear to me as my eyes. If thou art an honest man, a brave man, and if thou art not a fool, methinks there is — But of that, to-night. If, on the other hand, there is a foul desire in thine heart, or a lie on thy lips, doubt not but I will speedily discover it. Ay, I will discover it, and then thou wilt rue the day that thou didst come to see Dr. Martin Luther. What! Thou dost scorn the threat of a monk, and dost trust to the sword by thy side! That shall avail thee not, man. But enough; thou dost look an honest man, and my Lady Elfrida hath ever been able to winnow the chaff from the wheat. Go, then, in God's name, if thou be an honest man, and come again at the hour of six to-night, and I shall have something more to say to thee."

This was how I met and spoke with Martin Luther the first time, I little thinking then of what would happen to us both in the days to come.

CHAPTER XIV

THE STUBBORNNESS OF MARTIN LUTHER

THROUGHOUT the day I learned many things about the man who had impressed me so strongly. Indeed, I had no difficulty in doing this, for his name was on the tongue of every man. There was scarcely a man or woman or child in the town of Wittenberg but who loved him, while the doctrines he had preached had changed the life of the whole neighborhood. I found that he was born in the little town of Eisleben, which lay some seventy miles away on the borders of the Hartz Mountains, and that his father, who had been a miner, had by thrift and industry risen to be a man of importance in the town of Mansfield. I learned, too, that Martin had gone to a town called Eisenach to school, where he had received much kindness from some motherly dame. At Eisenach, moreover, he had shown much aptitude for study — so much, indeed, that his father had, after his school-days, sent him to the University of Erfurt to study law, in order that he might become a Doctor of Laws. While at Erfurt he had been led to give up all thoughts of the law, in order that he might gain holiness through becoming a monk. I was told that he had been a great worker while he was a student, being content with nothing but a thorough mastery of whatever subject which presented itself to him. Moreover, when he became a monk, he became as thorough in relation to his religious duties as he had been in his study of law.

It was while he was at Erfurt that he had come to the conclusion that salvation was not to be obtained by Church offices, by Masses, or by pilgrimages, but only through repentance for sin and faith in Jesus Christ, the Savior of the world. While at Erfurt he fasted, prayed, and underwent all kinds of penance without realizing that he was God's child, and then he came one day across a Latin Bible, in which he learned that man was not saved by those things which the Church declared essential, but by God's grace, which was given to all who repented and believed; and that no sooner did he thus give himself to God than light came. Afterwards he went to Rome expecting to find holiness and truth, but found instead filth and lies. He found also that the priests of Rome believed not in the religion they taught, but held to the semblance of it, just as the pagan priests had held to the rites of paganism at the time when St. Paul first brought the gospel to Rome. One day Dr. Martin was at a feast amongst the prelates and great men of the Church in Rome, and he was much shocked to hear them jest about what he held most sacred. He found, too, that so little faith had they in the Mass that, instead of the words of consecration, they sometimes used the words,

" Panis es, et panis manebis,"

and then amused themselves by watching the people adore what was, after all, no consecrated Host, but a mere piece of bread.

He found that Rome was a cesspool of iniquity, and that the people had a couplet which ran like this:

"Vivere qui sancte vultis, discedito Romæ;
Omni hic esse licent, non licet esse probum." [1]

So much was this the case that the foulest deeds were done, while justice was often impossible, because families high in the Church participated in the dark deeds done.

I was told, too, that Brother Martin, while in Rome, was induced to climb the Holy Staircase near the great Church of St. John, Lateran, or, as the Italians call it, the Santa Scala. It was believed that a thousand years' indulgence was granted to all who climbed this staircase on their knees, and the monk anxious to obtain

[1] Ye who would live holy lives, depart from Rome; All things are allowed here except to be righteous.

this great favor determined to perform the ceremony. As he went up, and had reached the thirteenth stair, he seemed to hear a voice saying to him, *"The just shall live by faith,"* and that then the ceremony seemed not only senseless, but sinful, and he got up from his knees and walked down.

Soon after Luther returned from Rome he was made professor of the New University of Wittenberg, he having been made a Doctor of the Holy Scriptures.

Then I heard something else which interested me greatly, for I found that the man Tetzel, of whom I have spoken, had some time before come near Wittenberg, selling his indulgences, and had declared that if men bought his pardons there was no need for repentance. It seems, too, that a woman who had bought one of these letters had come to Dr. Martin Luther for confession, and when the Doctor had told her that she must repent of her sins and amend her life, she had showed him Tetzel's letter, which granted her full forgiveness.

"This is an emparchmented lie," said Dr. Luther. "It hath no merit. No sins are forgiven without repentance and faith."

I learned, too, that this had led to Luther preaching in the town church, which I had seen, and that Tetzel had answered him. Whereupon Luther, who ever since he had found peace through faith, had been much given to reading the Scriptures, wrote to the Archbishop of Magdeberg, who had laughed at the monk's protest, and threw his letter to the rubbish heap, and that thereupon the monk had, after a re-examination of the Scriptures, written ninety-five theses, containing an utter denial of the value of indulgences, and then invited the people of the town to follow him to the great Schloss Kirche.

"Here is my answer to Tetzel," he cried, "and here, too, is my answer to the Archbishop of Magdeberg," and then he nailed his theses against the church door, while the assembled crowd gave a great shout of rejoicing. I was told, too, that ever since that time Dr. Luther had written much about the abuses of the Church, and that thousands all over the land were professing faith in the doctrines he taught.

"And what is your opinion of this man Dr. Martin Luther?" I asked of one of the men who had told me these things.

"There is but one opinion here in Wittenberg," he made answer. "That is among those who love the truth and live sober, God-fearing lives. Of course, he hath many enemies, who say he hath a proud stomach, and will not suffer Church discipline, while others have it that, as an Augustine monk, he was jealous of the greatness of the Dominican order, to which Dr. Tetzel belongs; but all who know him truly know that he hath naught to gain and everything to lose. For my own part, I should not wonder, if Dr. Luther is not taken away secretly and burned."

"But why secretly?" I asked.

"Because even the Church dare not take him openly. He hath gained too many followers. Nevertheless, many of us remember the fate of John Huss of Bohemia, and are afraid for him. Ay, I see trouble ahead, and I dread aught happening to Dr. Martin, for surely the Lord hath raised him up to set His people free."

"You seem to love him."

"Love him!" he cried. "Sir Stranger, I am a teacher of a school in Wittenberg, even as my brother, Master Trebonius, was a teacher of a school in Eisenach, He was a greater man than I, although he always declared that I, his brother Paulus Trebonius, was a sounder scholar than he. When he was alive he ever lifted his hat to his scholars, because, he said, the great ones of the future were among them. Thus every day, as he entered his school — and I have gone by his side many times — he always saluted his boys, and when I saw the boy Martin Luther's eyes kindle, I wondered much concerning him. Now I know how wise and great my brother was." [1]

"And what think you the future will be?" I asked.

[1] The schoolroom where Trebonius taught Martin Luther may still be seen in Eisenach.

10

"As to that who shall say? Dr. Luther will have naught but truth. At present he maintains that the Church is the Church of God, and he still remains a monk in the Church. But he is marching forward. Already he hath traveled far since he wrote his theses and nailed them against the church door; already he hath begun to ask whether the Pope is the Vicar of Christ, or Antichrist. I tell you, Sir Stranger, that, even although the matter of indulgences be settled, there are graver matters which remain unsettled."

Now all this set me thinking gravely, as may be well imagined. As I have already said, I knew something of the life of monasteries in England, and while I had never doubted the truth of the Church, or its sacredness and authority, it seemed to me as though what I had heard came as a kind of expression of the thoughts and feelings which had been lying dormant within me. All the same, my heart revolted against this same Martin Luther, because it seemed to me that he was attacking the Church of God, and thus must be accursed.

Nevertheless, I determined to go and see him again. For not only had the Lady Elfrida Rothenburg spoken of him as a friend, and bidden me take a message from him, there was something in his presence which fascinated me. His strong, masterful personality, his great good humor, and his evident desire for truth, made me feel that he was a man to be trusted. All the same, I determined that David Granville should go with me, for I had great faith in the young Cornishman's judgment; moreover, he knew so much of my plans that there was nothing Dr. Luther could say to me that he might not hear.

Accordingly, when six o'clock came both David Granville and I made our way to the Augustinian Monastery, and with but little ado was again shown into the monk's presence.

I watched David Granville as his eyes met those of Dr. Martin Luther, for I was anxious to see how the two would strike each other; all the more so as David had spoken very strongly through the day concerning the man who had dared to lift up his hands against the Church. Neither spoke, for Granville knew not yet the German tongue, while Martin Luther examined the young Cornishman's face closely, even as he had examined mine that same morning. Yet I knew that each man impressed the other, for a pleasant light flashed from the monk's eyes and a smile played around his rugged features, while there came a look on Granville's face which ever came when he was interested beyond the ordinary. As he told me afterwards, he felt he had come into the presence of a man who laughed at danger and looked into the very heart of things.

"How now, Master Englishman?" said Martin Luther presently. "For what purpose hast thou brought a witness to our meeting?"

"He is my friend and companion," I replied. "I have no secrets concerning the matter of our interview which I desire to keep secret from him."

"Even if you had such a desire it would be vain," replied the monk.

"Why?" I asked.

"Because he hath a keener eye and a nimbler brain than thou," he replied. "Otherwise I might refuse his presence. But enough; he is here as thou art. I have read the letter thou didst bring me, and although I have had much to do I have weighed it well."

"And you have an answer that I may take back?" I made answer.

"Nay, I know not," was his reply. "It is easy to see what is in your mind, Herr Hamilton. You would take the Lady Elfrida to England. She asks my advice concerning this."

He had touched the core of my desire in a single sentence, even although I doubted if the Lady Elfrida had said so much in her letter, seeing that at the time she wrote it my mind concerning this matter had not been mentioned. But, as I afterwards found, a small window was large enough to enable Dr. Luther to examine a large room.

I made no answer to his remark, however, for I was anxious to say nothing of which I should afterwards be sorry.

"The question which comes to me is why you desire to take her to England?" he said, and I felt his piercing eyes upon me.

"Is not the lady in distress?" I said.

"And how did Master Brian Hamilton know she was in distress?" he asked. "One question, Sir Englishman — what did you know of her before you left your country?"

His questions angered me. I had fancied that I should easily deal with this miner's son who had spent his days in a cloister, yet at the very outset he had assumed the position of one who would make his own terms with me.

"Any man can ask questions," I replied, "but they do not always get answers."

The monk laughed as though he had a merry heart.

"Is it not well that the ground should be cleared?" he said. "Believe, Master Englishman, I am no fool, though I have spent most of my days in a cloister. This is how I understand matters are. Two strange Englishmen, one of whom knows not the German tongue, come to this land. They enter a certain castle and discover a beauteous lady there, who is promised in marriage to a German noble. They discover that such a marriage is not pleasant to the lady, and one of them obtains speech with her. The lady, who is in sore distress, listens to the offers of this Englishman, but is chary of accepting help from a stranger of whom she knows nothing. Moreover, she is so situated that she finds it difficult to obtain information concerning him. She therefore sends him with a letter to a poor German monk whom she trusts and loves — ay, and one who would shield her as a shepherd shields a pet lamb from a wolf. The stranger brings the letter, but the German monk is no fool. Before he advises her what to do he would know something of the strange Englishman.

"I tell you," and his eyes flashed, "had she been the humblest peasant maiden instead of one of the highest born dames in this nation, so great is my love for her that I would not trust her to any man's care unless I

knew his most secret thoughts. Yes, yes; I know the
lady loathes the thought of wedding Count von Hartz,
and is willing to catch at any straw whereby she can
save herself, especially as she is under the control of
and fears her uncle's power. Otherwise she would never
have dreamed of paying heed to a stranger that came
within the castle gates. But she trusts the poor monk
and seeks his advice. If the monk says, 'Trust yourself to these unknown strangers,' she will trust herself.
But why, Sir Stranger? For the Lady Elfrida Rothenburg is no giddy-pated child. She hath not only brains
but learning. She hath a mind to plan and a will to
carry out her plans. Why, then, will she trust herself
even to strangers if the monk advises herself to do so?
Because she knows that before Dr. Martin Luther will
give advice he will know the truth. Before he will tell
her to trust any man he will look into his heart, read
his motives, know his history. Is a man a fool in matters of men and things because he is a Doctor of the
Holy Scriptures? Nay, not so, Sir Englishman."

He spoke not angrily, for I could now and then see
humor gleaming from his eyes, but he spoke as one
who knew his mind and who was determined to have
his way.

"What would you have me tell you?" I said, half
sullenly, for I liked not the trend of things.

"Many things, Master Hamilton. For what purpose
did you come to Germany? Was it by chance or by
purpose that you entered Rothenburg Castle? Is it only
because of desire that you would free the Lady Elfrida from a hateful situation, or is it because of some
motive at the back of your mind and which you are
afraid to make known?"

"Are you not asking a foolish thing?" I said. "It
would be easy for me to tell you a pretty fairy story,
easy to frame a reason for entering Rothenburg Castle."

"Not for you, Master Hamilton."

"Why?"

"Because, first of all, thou art passably honest — in
some things, at all events — and would stumble mightily

in telling the fairy story; and secondly, because even if thou wert gifted in that way, lies do not deceive me."

" If you believe me to be honest, why not trust me? " I said, fastening upon his own words.

" In some matters I might, Master Englishman, but not in this. If God had willed that I should have stayed in the world, and married and had children, I could not have loved them more than I love Lady Elfrida Rothenburg. Thus would I protect her as my own eyesight. Besides, it is not altogether a matter of honesty; it is a matter of judgment. If thou art not a knave thou mayst be a fool."

" Neither, Dr. Luther."

" What then? "

" As honest a man as thou art," I answered.

Again he laughed heartily.

" And what if I told thee I thought thou wert both? " he said.

" I should know that thou didst not speak the true feeling of thy heart," I made answer.

" And why? "

" Because men speak of thee as one whose eyes peer into the heart of men and things," I made answer.

I felt we were on better terms. Unconsciously we had changed our manner of speech. The feeling of antagonism had been swept aside.

" Think, Dr. Martin," I went on. " If I have a secret in coming to Germany it may not be my secret. Perchance I may not tell why I sought entrance into Rothenburg Castle. Yet may I be an honest man, and yet may my motives toward the Lady Elfrida be honorable. Remember this, too: Is what I offer easy to perform? Is the anger of Count Rothenburg nothing? Is the Count von Hartz a coward? When a man offers to undertake a dangerous mission —"

" He must have a serious reason for undertaking it," he broke in.

" Ay, and a worthy one," I retorted.

" That must be proved," he replied.

" May not a man be taken on trust? "

"Trust must have foundation. A man doth not trust without reason."

"Hath the Lady Elfrida written any suspicions concerning me?"

"What the Lady Elfrida hath written is between me and her," he replied.

"Then you will allow her to be sacrificed to a brutal clown rather than trust her to one whom you feel convinced is an honest man?" I retorted.

"Nay," he replied; "I will not allow her to be sacrificed. Believe me, Sir Englishman, thou art not the only man who breathes German air, neither is Dr. Luther altogether without resources. If thou dost not convince me that I may safely trust her to thee, then go thy way, and I will take other steps to protect her."

"What steps?" I asked, for I was becoming angry.

"That concerns me," he answered.

"You cannot protect her!" I cried.

"And why?"

"Because your only powerful friend favors her marriage with Count von Hartz," I replied, "therefore will he not aid you against him. As for the other thing in your mind, even you, monk as you are, will not admit of it."

"What is it?" he asked.

"A convent," I replied.

"And why may she not go to a convent?"

"Because, if they have the same name in Germany as they have in England, then is not a lady's honor safe in them," I replied. "More than that, she loathes the thought of being a nun, while you —"

"Yes, I, Master Hamilton?"

"Think that even if convents are good for women she is not fit for such a place."

I felt that my back was against the wall, and that I must fight for my ground, for truly the desire to take the Lady Elfrida to England grew stronger and stronger, yet I dare not betray the trust placed in me.

"What do you know of convents?" he asked.

"What every English gentleman knows," I replied.

" As for monasteries, I received what education I have within the walls of one."

He hesitated for a few seconds, while all the while his eyes rested on me.

" So far we have been skirmishing," he said presently; " now we will come to close quarters. Already I have made up my mind concerning thee. Perchance, too, we may come to an understanding. There are certain questions I would ask, which thou canst answer without betraying any trust. If thou dost answer them to my satisfaction, then will I write a letter which thou shalt take to Lady Elfrida, and then will the fulfillment of thy desires depend on thine own courage and brains."

I made no answer, but waited for him to proceed.

CHAPTER XV

"MASTER BRIAN HAMILTON," said the monk presently, "I would place before thee two propositions. First, I would that thou shalt tell me something of thy past life and career; and second, I would have thy solemn vow that thou hast naught in thine heart toward the Lady Elfrida Rothenburg but that is honorable. Upon thine answer to these two propositions depends everything."

"Willingly, to both these," I made answer; whereupon I told him much that I wrote down at the commencement of this history, to the which Dr. Martin Luther listened carefully, never speaking a word.

"And that is the story of thy life?" he said, when I had finished. "Praise God, man, that thou didst not become a monk."

"And yet thou art a monk," I made answer.

He did not reply to this, but went on, "Tell me, Master Brian Hamilton, doth the sale of pardons go on in England as here in Germany?"

"In a way," I replied, "yet not as I have seen them in Germany. There are pilgrimages, and penances, and miraculous images —"

"And money," he interrupted. "Is money ever at the end of these things?"

"The Church must be upheld," I answered.

"Ay, but God's grace is a free gift," he cried. "It cannot be obtained by money. Hast thou read the Holy Scriptures, Master Hamilton?"

"As to that, the Holy Scriptures are but little known either by churchmen or the laity. But what of that? The Church is the channel of grace. Besides, have we not the lives of the saints?"

153

The monk laughed. "Lives of the saints!" he cried. "Fairy stories for ignorant children. And tell me, then, where is thy proof that the Church is the only channel of grace? Where in Holy Writ is it set down? As for salvation by penances, and pilgrimages, and masses, and miraculous images, what saith Holy Writ? 'There is no other Name given under heaven whereby a man may be saved, save the Name of Christ our Lord.'"

"But the Church is the treasury of grace," I cried.

"What is the Church?" he made answer. "John Huss was excommunicated and burned at Constance because he held to the Word of God, but was not Huss in the Church? Jerome of Prague suffered death at the hands of the Church, and his soul was condemned to everlasting flames; but is he not safe with God? What are we to believe, Master Hamilton, the Word of God, which is the sword of the Lord, or the words of those who send out men like Tetzel, who hawk pardons for the sins of the soul, even as a hawker sells sausages in the streets?"

"But was not Tetzel sent out by the Holy Father Leo X?" I cried, "and is he not the Vicar of Christ?"

"Was Alexander VI, the greatest libertine who ever betrayed women, the Vicar of Christ; or was Julius II, who delighted in bloodshed, the representative of the Prince of Peace? What saith the Word of God? Whose word are we to believe? The Word of God or priests who mock the holy faith?"

"Are they not in the ark of God?" I cried.

"Between Wittenberg and Magdeberg are many beer-houses kept by priests," he cried. "What are those places? Haunts of drunkenness, gambling, and lewd women. What are these priests? Forbidden to marry, and yet— But, by God's grace, the Church shall be purified!"

Now, to this I could make no answer, for had not Erasmus, the friend of Henry VIII, written the same things? Had not Master Thomas More cried aloud against them?

"Can these men be channels of divine grace?" went on Martin Luther. "Moreover, how can monks save a man? Salvation is of the spirit; it is by the grace of God, which comes into the hearts of all who repent and believe. That was why I made answer to that roaring bull Tetzel; that was why I made a hole in his drum. As though the things he sold had aught of efficacy, Pope or no Pope."

"My friend and I did listen to one of Tetzel's sermons less than a week ago," I made answer.

"And bought his pardons?"

"My friend did."

"Hath he the thing?"

I spoke to Granville, who took it from under his doublet and gave it to Martin Luther.

The monk read it, and as he read his eyes burned like fire.

"A lie — a great, black, damning lie," he said as he handed it back. "And thou, Master Hamilton, didst thou buy one?"

"Nay," I answered; "the thing seemed to me but a mockery."

He placed his right hand on my shoulder and looked straight into my eyes, and it seemed to me as though he read my very soul.

"Tell me, Master Brian Hamilton," he said, "on thine honor as an English gentleman, and on thy faith as a Christian, that if I do write a letter to the Lady Elfrida, advising her to trust herself in thine hands, that thou wilt allow no harm to befall her, that thou wilt guard her even as thou wouldst guard thine own mother if she were alive; that whether in Germany or in England thou wilt give thy life to save her from aught that is wrong or harmful, or from which her soul revolts?"

"I will swear to it on the cross of Christ," I said.

"And there is naught in thy purpose to take her to England but what is honorable?"

"Naught," I replied, for had not the King commanded me to bring her thither?

"Then surely it is the will of God," he replied, and without more ado he went to the table in the room and wrote a letter.

"God deal with thee as thou dost deal with her,"
he said; "and if thou dost in aught fail, be sure that
God will bring thee into judgment."

He placed the letter in my hand as he spoke, which
I held doubtfully, for it was not sealed.

"Nay, read it, man," he went on, "for I do not trust
men by halves. Moreover, it may be that thou wilt
not subscribe to what I have written."

The letter is before me as I write, and I set it down
here because it is not only of import to a right understanding of what will follow, but it gives something of
an insight concerning the kind of man Martin Luther is.

"Augustinian Monastery,
"Wittenberg.

"MY DEAR CHILD—

"My prayers are ever at your service, and I trust
you rejoice daily in the great love of Jesus Christ our
Lord. Know, my daughter, that there is no salvation
but in Him, even as it is revealed in the Word of the
Lord. Much have I thought and prayed concerning you
for many days, neither have I been unmindful of the
perils that surround you. It has grieved me much that
the Elector Frederick consents to your marriage with
the man we wot of, for he is one of evil passions, and
hath no love for the Lord. Moreover, I fully believe
that the Count would not have consented to this marriage but that he hath entered into an agreement with
him concerning your possessions. Have a care, my
child, concerning this, and if ever you find it possible,
go to Duke George and ask him concerning the estate
of Rothenburg, the which the Count Karl seized after
your father's death. Methinks there is much there which
requires the services of an honest man of the law. To
this end, be wise, and sign no papers whatever of which
you do not understand the full import.

"And now concerning another matter. The Englishman, Brian Hamilton by name, who is the bearer of this
letter, even as he was the bearer of your letter to me,
is, I believe, honest and trustworthy. I have looked
deeply into his mind and heart, and I not only believe

him to be a man of honor, but one who is not far from the Kingdom of God, having in his heart already, even although he may not know it, sifted the wheat from the chaff, and laid hold upon truth. He hath some knowledge of matters of faith owing to early training, and because he loves truth, hath already cast off the works of darkness. It is because I believe this that I commend him to you, for even although he only sees as yet, even as the man to whom our blessed Lord gave his sight, 'men, as trees walking,' yet am I sure that he sees plainly that the Word of God must be supreme.

"Therefore, seeing the plight you are in is a sad one, I can think of naught better than that you should trust in him, even although he is a stranger to us both. But God hath not given me the power to read men's hearts for naught. Wherefore, look forward with a bold, brave heart, knowing that the Lord is everywhere, and that they who trust in Him shall not be forsaken.

"As for me, I am full of affairs, and although the Word of God is becoming known, yet am I beset on the right hand and on the left. Many in high places are set on my destruction, and, in truth, unless God gives me special protection for His own purpose, I shall soon suffer the fate of those who a hundred years ago upheld the Word of God. Yet am I not afraid, for God lives. What matters the lives of twenty Martin Luthers? If I am cut down, He can raise up others. And yet I have it in my mind that He hath a great work for me to do in cleansing the Church of Christ, which is truly full of filth and false doctrine.

"May God graciously preserve you at all times, my child, and may His word become dearer to you day by day.

"Always your faithful adviser and friend,

"MARTIN LUTHER,
"Augustinian Monk."

I read the letter through with great care, much wondering at the words he had written concerning me, yet much rejoiced because of his trust.

"Would you that I shall alter aught?" he asked.

I had it in my mind to tell him that what he had written concerning me as touching my faith in the Church was not true, and yet I could find no words to utter my thoughts. Moreover, so rejoiced was I that he had bidden the Lady Elfrida to trust me that I would not have it altered, and told him so, whereupon he laughed merrily.

"And now go, for I have many things to do," he said; and, indeed, at that moment there was a knocking at the door.

"Ah, Philip!" cried Martin Luther, as he turned his eyes toward the door, "I grieve to have kept you waiting so long, and, in truth, I would talk carefully with you concerning the authority of the Pope before I write down what is in my heart."

The newcomer was a young man, pale of face, and of thoughtful eyes. Altogether different was he from Dr. Luther, for he looked as though a strong gust of wind would blow him away.

"These be Englishmen, Philip," cried Luther; "and this, Master Hamilton, is Philip Melanchthon, the best scholar in Germany, and the youngest. Ay, look at him well, for even Erasmus knows not Latin and Greek better, neither is he his master in Aristotelian philosophy, the which I hate. I wonder if God wills whether we shall all meet again?"

"God go with you," said Philip Melanchthon as we left the room, and truly his voice was almost as sweet as Luther's, although not so strong and joyful.

"Trust in God, keep a brave heart, and have naught to do with lies of any sort save to defy them, even although they may fall from the lips of an archbishop or cardinal," he said as we left him, and his words rung in my ears as we went down the steps from his room and into the street.

No sooner did we get back to the inn than a great storm came on, with thunder and lightning and much rain, so that had we willed to travel that night we should have found it impossible, for no man could have found his way to Rothenburg Castle, so dark and terrible did it become.

The following morning we started to return to Rothenburg, but by strange mishaps not only my horse, but
David's, fell lame, and although both of us were passa-
ble farriers, as every man trained to arms should be,
we could do nothing for them, neither could we discover
the cause of their lameness. Thus it came to pass that,
in spite of my utmost endeavors to push forward, we
could make but little headway; indeed, from morn till
evening we did not cover more than twenty or twenty-
five miles.

I discovered, moreover, as we drew near a town where
I proposed to spend the night, that Martin Luther
was as much hated there as he was loved in Wittenberg.
More than one spoke evil of him, and expressed the
hope that the Archbishop of Magdeberg, who seemed
all-powerful in those parts, would throw him into prison
till he learned better manners.

When we came to the town, which was called Kessell,
we made our way to an inn, which was a wretched
place, and under ordinary circumstances I should never
think of entering. For the sake of our horses, however,
we determined to make the best of it, and ere long were
partaking of such rough fare as the place provided.
As we ate our food the place became filled with a number of people, not only men, but women. I noticed,
moreover, that among the company there were two
priests and three monks, each of whom drank freely of
the strong German beer which was provided. I was not
long in seeing that the place was the resort of an evil
crowd, for the jests which were bandied were such that
had stable-boys bandied them in England I would have
thrashed them without mercy. In truth, as it seemed
to me at the time, it was my anger at the behavior of
those who gathered there which led to the trouble that
followed, although I know now that the cause of this
same trouble lay deeper.

"Are you a man of God or a stable scullion, Master
Monk?" I said to one of the churchmen who had been
drinking deeply, and who was talking loudly to one of
the women in the company.

"What is that to you, Sir Stranger?" he asked, "and what is your business here?"

"As to my business here, it doth not matter," I said; "but if you do not cease this vile talk, I tell you that your monk's frock shall not save you from my horse-whip."

"I talk as I will," said the monk, for he was a big, powerful fellow, evidently of peasant origin. "Things are come to a strange pass, I ween, if a layman begins to talk to churchmen about their behavior."

I did not want to be engaged in a tavern brawl, yet was my anger so aroused, not only by the man's speech, but by that of others, that I recked not of consequences.

"Either you cease this talk or you taste my riding-whip," I said, rising to my feet, for the thing had gone on some time before I opened my mouth.

"Not before you feel the weight of my fist," he cried. "You think because I am a churchman that I must needs allow thee to crow like a bantam cock, and ne'er say a word; but I say what I will, and kiss whom I will — mind that."

At this the whole company, including the other church-men, shouted greatly, and I saw that if we came to a skirmish, David Granville and I would have to fight the whole crowd. Even those who had been gambling left their cards and their dice to take sides with the monk. It was with pleasure, therefore, that I saw Tom Juliff come into the room, although at home I would not have had any servant of mine come into a room where I was sitting. But, as I said, it was a small inn, and this was the only place of entertainment in the house.

"I wonder any honest innkeeper allows his house to be given over to such things," I said. "What ho! mine host, do you give a lesson to these churchmen for giving your house a bad name."

At this there was great laughter, especially when one of the priests told me that the house was his, and that he knew his own business without the interference of meddling strangers.

"What!" I cried. "Dost thou, a churchman, keep a place like this?"

"I am an honest innkeeper," he cried, "and I do mine offices at the church none the worse for it."

"With the consent of the bishop?" I cried, for the fellow had been worse than any farm laborer there.

"As though the bishop cares what I do," he cried. "Is a man, because he is a priest and sworn to celibacy, never to kiss a pretty woman? Is he, because he hears confession and says Masses, never to drink his ale? Doth not Holy Writ say that wine gladdeneth the heart of man?"

"The Archbishop of Magdeberg shall know what goes on here forthwith," I cried.

At this all laughed again, as though I had uttered a good joke.

"It is no wonder that the people of Wittenberg have gone over to the teachings of Dr. Martin Luther," I went on, "when such a vile house as this is kept by a priest."

"A heretic! A heretic!" was the general cry. "Here is a follower of that son of Belial, Martin Luther, the disobedient monk."

At this moment there was a great stir outside, and immediately afterwards two men, evidently of some authority, entered.

"Have two strangers been seen traveling by here, with a servant?" one of them asked.

"Why?" asked the priest-innkeeper.

"Because complaint hath been lodged against such," he said. "They are followers of Luther, and go around from place to place stirring up strife."

"Ay, their wickedness hath overtaken them right quick," said the innkeeper, who I found was commonly called Father Peter, "for this pestilent fellow hath been abusing the Church, and hath been disturbing the quiet peacefulness of the evening. Even at this moment I was about to give orders that he should be thrown into the street."

"Who are you?" I said to the man who had just entered, and who had uttered the charge.

"I am the magistrate for this district," he cried. "Lucas Breimer is known to all respectable, peace-

loving, and law-abiding people. The names of the men
against whom I have signed a warrant are Brian Hamilton, a fellow who hath had to fly from England because
of his evil ways, and his boon companion, named David
Granville. They, with their servant, found lodgment
at a nobleman's castle, where they did much mischief,
and then, after having maltreated two warders, escaped
as thieves in the night. They are in league with Martin
Luther, the heretic, and are suspected of having some
of the monk's writings with them. My charge, however, is chiefly against Brian Hamilton, who, though
calling himself a gentleman, is in truth a low-bred fellow,
besides being a vile heretic. The other, Granville, I am
willing to allow to go free, also his servant. Know you
aught of this Brian Hamilton?"

"I am Brian Hamilton," I said. "But have a care
Master Breimer, before you dare to lay hands on me."

"I am but the servant of the law, and must do my
duty," he cried. "The Rector of Brigberg hath sworn
a deposition against you, and it is for you to prove yourself innocent at the Town Hall to-morrow."

Granville, although he could understand but little of
what was said, saw that something serious was afoot,
and quietly drew his sword. As for Tom Juliff, he had
noted the action of his master, and prepared to do battle. Seeing the state of things, therefore, I drew my
sword, and before one could count ten the place was
in an uproar. Women were shrieking, the priests and
monks were uttering maledictions, while the rest stood
staring at us, not knowing what to do, but evidently full
of anger against us.

For a moment we seemed to be masters of the situation, for, quick as a thought, we had cleared a space
around us, Granville and I with our swords, and Tom
Juliff with his great arms.

"I command you to yield to me as prisoners," cried
Master Breimer excitedly. Evidently he had not expected such resistance on our part, and was now well-
nigh frightened out of his wits. As for the churchmen,
they continued to pour malediction upon us, calling us
all the vile names they could invent.

"This comes of heresy," yelled Father Peter. "This comes of Martin Luther's lies. His foreign minions stir up strife, and breed lies. Down with them! Drag them to prison!"

"Master Breimer," I said as soon as I could make myself heard, "if you dare to lay hands on us you will have to answer for it to the Elector Frederick, who in turn will have to answer to his most gracious Majesty of England, for we are his subjects, traveling quietly. We have stirred up no strife, and should not have said a word had not we found these churchmen talking to these women in such a manner that any man who hath mother, or sister, or sweetheart, must blush for shame at hearing them."

"A lie! A lie! A foul lie!" shouted Father Peter. "They are heretics, and spies, all of them."

"If you are innocent you shall be set free to-morrow," said Master Breimer.

"I will run my sword through the man who dares lay hand on me," I cried.

At this every man crept back as far as they could from us, for, in truth, we did not look like men who could be played with. As for Father Peter, he fled from the room like a man frightened out of his wits.

"Put down your sword," said the magistrate.

"We shall not put down our swords," I made answer. "As for you, Master Breimer, it would surely befit your office to keep a churchman from keeping such a vile house as this, which is plainly a harbor for loose women, drunken men, and gamblers. As surely as I speak to the Elector I will advise him on the matter."

"As though the Elector would care!" he cried. "Besides, what can I do? I am but the servant of the law, and the law says nothing against priests keeping inns."

"Then is your law in a bad way," I cried.

"Listen to his foul heresy," cried one of the monks. "Is not the law of the State also the law of the Church? And is not he who speaks against it guilty of heresy? At him, men!—at him! He is but a boasting bully."

At this, three or four fellows, watching their chances, fell upon me, whereupon there was a regular mêlée, during the which two or three were wounded.   How the matter would have ended I know not, but Father Peter, who had gone out, presently returned with several armed men, who fell upon us, and so, borne down by numbers, we were presently bound and dragged off to jail.   But, worse than all this, our belongings were stripped from us, and with them the letter which Dr. Martin Luther had written to the Lady Elfrida Rothenburg.

CHAPTER XVI

MY TRIAL AND IMPRISONMENT

PRESENTLY I found myself lying in a room at the base
of the Rathaus, much bruised, and feeling very sore, yet
with no broken bones. Granville and Tom Juliff were
lying with me, so that I was not wanting in company.
Moreover, the place was clean, and there was a quantity
of straw to lie on, so that, but for the fact that we were
prisoners, I doubt much whether we were not more com-
fortably situated than we should have been in Father
Peter's inn, which, as I have said, was an evil-smelling
hole. My greatest trouble was the fact that Dr. Martin
Luther's letter to the Lady Elfrida was taken from me,
while I was also sore distressed that I was not able to
return to Rothenburg Castle, from which I had planned
to take back to England the woman the thought of whom
was never out of my mind. Even while lying there I
called to mind that which we had said to each other,
while her proud face was ever before my eyes — a face
that was to me more wonderful than any I had ever seen.
Forgetting the King's command, I found myself weaving
all sorts of fancies about her, and picturing myself daily
gaining her confidence as I accompanied her to my native
land.

While these fancies filled my mind, I wondered much
that I had ever thought of casting my eyes upon Lady
Patty Carey, who was but a wayward, flippant minx,
and who, as it seemed to me then, had naught but a
pretty face to catch any man's attention. I made a great
vow, too, that, in spite of my present straits, I would
quickly return to Lady Elfrida's side and be her servant.

But with this vow the difficulties which surrounded
me rose up thick and fast. What would happen the
next day? Would Dr. Luther's letter be returned to

me? Would I be able to clear myself from the accusa-
tion which would be brought against me, and by what
means should I be able to return to Rothenburg Castle
to render my lady the help she needed? For I realized
now that everything centered in that, and I found my
heart all aflame at the thought of it. I, who, when
Lady Patty Carey had jilted me, had declared I would
never think of a woman again, knew that my whole
life was bound up in this German maid. And more,
the thought gave me joy which I had never felt before,
but at the same time it brought me much sorrow, for
I called to mind the conditions on which I had come on
my mission. I had promised I would never lift my eyes
to her for a reason that caused a pain in my heart as
though I had been stabbed with a knife. For although
the King had not told me so in so many words, I knew
she was destined for some noble whom the King had
in his mind. And, besides all that, even although this
were not so, who was I that I should lift my eyes to
such a maid? For was I not poor? Had not the Hamiltons lost well-nigh all their lands? And, even though
my family was perchance well-nigh as noble as hers, a
landless man had no right to wed a maid, even though
he could win her love, whose dowry was so great that
the King regarded it as worthy to give to some noble,
perchance of his own line.

And yet I hugged the thought to my heart, even although I lay a prisoner in that German Rathaus, and
the more impossible it appeared the more did I cherish
it, in spite of the commands of the King.

"Hamilton."

It was David Granville who spoke. He had doubtless been thinking even as I had, while Tom Juliff snored
loudly.

"What would you?" I asked impatiently, for my fancies were so pleasant that I was angered at having them
broken.

"I see a light."

"It is midnight," I replied, "and we might be in the
bowels of the earth for all the light that can come."

"The lame horses, the coming of Master Breimer — it is all a part of a plan."

"Nay," I made answer. "It was but an unlucky mishap that led us to enter that vile inn."

"It was Rufus Dudley and John Mainwaring," he said quietly.

I gave a start, and, sitting up, rubbed my eyes, as though such an act would enable me to see more plainly. The scenes which had passed flashed through my mind, and I felt sure he was right. While I had been thinking of other things, his mind had been piecing together the reasons which had brought us thither.

"You were a fool to meddle with those monk fellows," said Granville. "It is always well to let sleeping dogs lie. What, man! Are things so free from wrong in England that we must needs fall afoul of German ways? If monks keep low taverns, what is that to us? We cannot, like Erasmus, write books which set the world talking. Even if we could, I do not see that it could do aught of good. These things have not improved in spite of all his fine writings. All the same, that was not the cause of the happening. Master Breimer came with his warrant not knowing of what had taken place at the inn. How came he to get it? Who informed him concerning us? Who knew that we had gone to visit Martin Luther? Who suspected that you might have some of his writings on you? I tell you, it was Dudley and Mainwaring."

"How could they know?" I asked.

"What doth not Dudley know? Did he not find his way into the castle? Is he not as cunning as a fox? He hath more learning than half the monks; he is hand-in-glove with the Church. He, so gossip had it in England before we came away, had sworn he would marry a German lady. Is it not all plain? Think of the necromancy business at the castle; think of the things he said. It is all of a piece, man. Mainwaring and he have been ferreting out secrets ever since they came. Besides, who knoweth what spies he may have? What happened, think you, when Count Karl found out that we had gone through the night? Was it not for you to meet him in the tilt-yard? Think, man, think!"

Doubtless he was right. His mind had been weighing and analyzing events; he had been piecing things together while I had been dreaming, and he had seen what had never occurred to me.

"I do not see how the knowledge of this can be of help to us, even if it is true," I said, somewhat pettishly, for I felt a passing pang of jealousy that he should be quicker of brain than I.

"The knowledge of truth is always of advantage," said the young Cornishman. "We know now where our danger lies; we know with whom we have to fight."

Instinctively I felt underneath my doublet, where I found the half of the chain, the other half of which I had given to the Lady Elfrida, and I felt comforted.

"It is we two against they two," I said musingly.

"And the deciding factor is the woman," he made answer.

"What mean you?" I asked.

"A woman always is the deciding factor," said the young Cornishman sagely. "But besides this, the Lady Elfrida is no ordinary woman. Did you not notice the flash of her eyes, the quiver of her nostrils? She will govern her own life in spite of all you or they can do."

"If naught is done for her by us, she will either be kidnapped by Dudley, or she will be wedded to von Hartz in a month," I said.

"Taken away by Dudley, perhaps," replied Granville, "but married to von Hartz, no."

"Why do you say so?"

"Because I saw the flash of her eyes as she looked at him," he replied. "If I am not blind and a fool, she will wed no man against her will. She will defy Count Karl and the Church."

"But you do not reflect," I made answer. "The position of woman in England is bad enough, but here in Germany it is worse. Ladies of high degree are wedded without their being questioned in the matter. Their parents or guardians decide, and they have no word to say. It is interwoven into the very life of the people. A woman no more dare question the command of the Holy Father himself on a matter of faith than she dare question the will of her parent or guardian as to whom she shall marry."

" The Lady Elfrida dares question both — ay, and defy both — or you may put me down to be as blind as a mole and as witless as my father's fool. And, what is more, I have no fear concerning her, even although we shall not be able to help her."

" But we must help her," I cried.

" If we can," he made answer.

" You do not believe we shall be able? "

" We have Dudley and Mainwaring to deal with. Think you they have not arranged their plans? And Dudley is as cunning as the devil. If one thing fails them they will have another in readiness. Of a truth, I look forward to many days' imprisonment. Long enough to enable them to believe they stand in no danger from us."

" Then you think —"

" That our hope lies in the Lady Elfrida's wit and will," he answered. And this was all the satisfaction I got from him, although I asked him many further questions.

In truth, as I reflected afterwards, our case seemed well-nigh hopeless, although I framed many plans which at the first blush promised well. I reflected presently, however, that everything depended on what might happen at the trial on the following morning, and so I composed myself to sleep, having as I thought, prepared myself for anything that might happen.

When we were brought before our judges there was a great stir in the building, for, attracted by the stories which had got abroad concerning us, a great crowd had gathered together.

The first charge brought against us, namely, of brawling in the tavern, was got through with commendable quickness. The magistrate said that, although our conduct was very grave, and deserving of severe punishment, he would, bearing in mind the fact that we were strangers and did not know German ways, deal with us very leniently. He would not even send us to the whipping-post, but would put us for one day in the stocks, and afterwards keep us in prison for a week.

Now this, as may be imagined, was hard to bear. What would the Lady Elfrida think, and what would happen to her during the time of our imprisonment? But this, as I discovered, was not all, as will quickly be seen. The magistrate began to ask us questions concerning our faith, seeing we were accused of being followers of Martin Luther, the heretic monk.

At this I protested strongly, making it clear that I had always been faithful to Holy Church, and knew naught whatever concerning the teachings of the man of whom all Germany was talking.

"You say you know naught of Martin Luther," said the magistrate; "then be pleased to explain to me why you paid him a visit but two days ago."

As will be seen, I dared not answer this question for it would bring the name of the Lady Elfrida to light, and would cause her to be the subject of gossip among a lot of German clowns. I therefore declared that my own visit to the Augustinian monk was of a truly private nature, having nothing whatever to do with matters of doctrine.

"If that is true," said the magistrate, "what have you to say to the letter which Martin Luther hath written concerning you, and which you carried on your person?"

"The letter was a private letter," I replied.

"It bore no name or superscription," answered the magistrate, "yet from its contents I judge it to be written to a lady of high degree, and one, moreover, whose mind hath evidently been poisoned by the lying teachings of this rebellious monk. It speaks of you as one who is well-nigh a follower of this fellow, and one who is evidently concerned in some matter which is not lawful."

After this there was much asking and answering of questions, which, as far as I could see, ended in nothing, for I took great care to say nothing that should in any way implicate the Lady Elfrida. And this angered the magistrate much, for I could see that he was eager to know to whom the letter was written as well as the causes which led to its writing.

One thing, however, comforted me, slight as the matter seemed to be. It was evident from the eager way in which the magistrate asked questions concerning this matter that neither Dudley nor Mainwaring, if, indeed, they were the cause of our imprisonment, had told anything of the matter we had at heart.

As may be imagined, I now repented much that I had not requested Dr. Martin Luther to omit the words he had written concerning me, for they now came to be the chief charge against me. The matter of the brawl in the tavern seemed to be as nothing compared with the question of doctrine. So serious did this become, indeed, that the clerk of the court presently announced that it was an affair on which that court could not judge, but must be specially remitted to the Church courts, whose province it was to deal with traveling strangers who were suspected of heresy and who went around the country stirring up strife.

It being dinner-time, therefore, and the members of the court having become very hungry, they decided to pack us all off to jail again — Granville and Tom Juliff to be punished only for brawling in a well-conducted tavern, and to be set at liberty in due time; but I, being the leader of the whole business, being kept in prison until such time as the bishop or some person of note in the Church had time to deal with me.

All this, taken alone, did not surprise nor, indeed, trouble me much, for I had conceived a plan whereby I believed we could escape from jail before the days of our punishment for our so-called brawling had expired. What troubled me, however, was the fact that we were no longer to be imprisoned together, I having been put in a category different from them. In truth, it was only a moment's speech I had with them before I was huddled into a dark cell by myself, and this, as I said, grieved me sorely, for it was partly on Granville's quick wit and partly on Tom Juliff's great strength of arm that the success of my plan for escape depended.

" Granville," I whispered, " you must take my purse.

You will need it. As soon as you are at liberty find
some means of telling the Lady Elfrida what hath happened to me. Tell her, too, that I still have the other
half of the chain, and that I will present it to her in
due time; and bid her beware of Dudley and Mainwaring."

"Be not downcast," cried Granville; "we will soon
set you free."

"Do as I bid you," I cried. "Tell the Lady Elfrida
that whether bound or free, I still seek to be her friend,
and that I shall be thinking night and day of her welfare."

"I would do your work, and take her to England myself," said Granville, "but perchance she would not go
with me. Neither will I leave you here in prison."

In spite of myself, his words made me glad, for much
as I desired that she should be taken away from her
uncle, who would wed her to Count von Hartz, I loved
not the thought of any man but myself being her companion to England.

"Keep a good heart, and fear not for the Lady Elfrida," he said. "Had she a man's strength of body
she would need no aid from you or me. As it is —"

But he could not finish what he had on his lips to
say, for at that moment we were separated, and many
and many a long day was to pass before I should see
my friend again.

I gave up all thoughts of escape as soon as I was
placed in my new prison cell, for it was underneath the
Rathaus, and dug out of the earth. No light came to
me except from a small aperture at the top of the cell,
which was grated by strong iron bars, and was not half
big enough for a man to squeeze his body through, even
although the iron bars were not there. The only other
way out of the place was through long corridors, where
guards were constantly watching, and these corridors
were guarded by the door of my prison house, which
was securely locked and bolted from the outside.

As may be seen, therefore, my plight was a dismal
one, and gave no promise whatever. Still, I determined
to keep a brave heart, especially as I felt sure that my

experiences in Rochford Monastery would enable me to clear myself directly I was brought before the Church courts. I imagined, too, that not many days could elapse before my second trial would take place, and I set myself with a good heart to prepare my defense.

How many days I lay there I knew not. At first I counted them eagerly, but as the time passed on I forgot to count. Indeed, for some time I was well-nigh swallowed up in despair. And this, I think, was no wonder. It seemed to me that I was beaten at the first bout. I had imagined that everything was well, and then suddenly I had been outwitted, tricked, and cast into as evil a smelling jail as I thought could be found in the whole of Germany. Moreover, I had no means of redress. I had come hither at the King's command, but not with the King's authority. I dared not mention his name, neither had I friend in Germany whose help I could claim. For that matter, I was not yet assured of what lay at the root of my misfortunes. Sometimes I reflected that it was not Dudley and Mainwaring who had encompassed my ruin at all, but Count Karl of Rothenburg, who had divined something of my plans, and regarded this as the best way of being rid of me.

Of my disgust with myself I need not write, for those who read these pages will be able to judge of it. That I, who had been recommended to the King because I had a quick brain and a ready arm, should be thus outwitted and thrown into a common jail like any German boor goaded me to anger more than any bodily discomfort which I suffered.

At length the time came, however, when the fellow who brought me my food, and who from time to time changed the straw on which I had to lie, told me that some great churchmen had come to a town near by to deal with Church matters, and that I was to be packed thither at once. As may be imagined, I was greatly rejoiced at this, and when at length I was led to this place I felt that the hour of my deliverance was nigh.

The town at which I was tried was no great distance from Magdeberg, which was a city of great size and the seat of an archbishopric. Indeed, I hoped that the archbishop might preside over the courts, seeing he was reputed to be a rich young nobleman and of great good nature. But in this I was disappointed; as I afterwards learned, the archbishop, being a prince and a man of pleasure to boot, had little care about the spiritual matters of the diocese. Indeed, it was to this same archbishop that Martin Luther appealed about the affair of Tetzel selling indulgences, and who treated the monk's letter with scorn. This action of the archbishop caused the monk to nail his theses against the door of the Schloss Kirche at Wittenberg.

Still the Church court was imposing enough, for many bishops and abbots walked in procession to the hall of justice, which was close to the Town Kirche. Masses were sung, and the Sacred Host was carried on high through the streets, which many people followed with heads bared and many signs of reverence.

At length my turn came to be judged, and I could not help rubbing my eyes at all the fuss that was made about me. Lengthy screeds had been written about me by the Church lawyers, charges were read against me both in Latin and in German, and many maledictions were uttered against Martin Luther. Moreover, it was urged that, as it was necessary to the well-being of both the Church and the realm that all heresy should be destroyed and obedience to the Church in all forms be exacted, anyone favoring either of false doctrine or of the teachers thereof must be put down with a strong hand.

And all this because I had foolishly allowed certain words which Martin Luther had written about me to remain in his letter to the Lady Elfrida!

I found myself subjected to many questions of which I should never have known the meaning but for the years I had spent in Rochford Monastery, but as far as I could see, they had naught to do with the reasons for the treatment which had been meted out to me. Presently, however, we got to the matter at hand, and I was questioned closely about my visit to Martin Luther, concerning which I was enabled to affirm boldly that it had naught to do with matters of faith. This led to the words the monk had written about me, and here I quickly found myself in a quagmire.

"Did you know of the words which the rebellious monk had written?" asked a fat bishop.

"I did," I replied.

"Then why did you not declaim against them?"

"I did not think them of any great import," was my answer.

At this there was a great outcry. Such an attitude of mind told of great carelessness about the faith.

Presently one of my judges said he would bring the matter to a head by asking me one direct question. Did I or did I not believe in the teaching of the Rebellious Monk?

I replied that I had never read his writings or heard him preach.

"Hath thou read the blasphemous theses which he nailed up at the Schloss Kirche?" he asked.

I replied, "No," whereupon someone quickly handed the bishop a copy, for, as I have said, these theses were scattered all over Germany with the speed of light almost directly after he had written them, the printing presses of Wittenberg being glutted in the printing.

The bishop read many of these theses aloud, some of which I will set down here, for they contain the marrow of the matter of the first disputation between Luther and the monks.

"The Pope cannot remit any condemnation, but only declare and confirm the remission of God. If he does otherwise the condemnation remains entirely the same."

"They preach mere human follies who maintain that as soon as the money rattles in the strong-box the soul flies out of purgatory."

"Those who fancy themselves sure of salvation by indulgences will go to perdition along with those who teach them so."

"Every Christian who truly repents of his sins enjoys an entire remission, both of the penalty and the guilt, without any need of indulgences."

" Doth thou believe that these propositions are lies? "
thundered the bishop after he had read them, and it was
easy to see that the reading had made him angry.

Now the question staggered me, for although I believed myself a good churchman, there seemed naught
but truth in these propositions. In truth, they came
to me like a breath of pure wind in foul air, and, in
spite of myself, I felt my heart grow warm. And yet
I knew that, did I not condemn them, the anger of the
court would be more than ever aroused against me, and
then where would be my chances of helping my Lady
Elfrida?

" They are bold words," I said, wishing to gain time,
" and as I have never heard them before I may not have
grasped their true import."

" Ay, but thou hast," cried the bishop. " Thou hast
proved thyself to be a man of some learning, and thou
understandest well. Dost thou believe the monk Martin
Luther a heretic in writing these things? "

" It is not for me, a layman, to pass judgment on
matters ecclesiastical," I said, " surely your lordship
must see that."

" Thou art accused of being a heretic, and of stirring
up men to heresy," cried the bishop. " Yet, to show
my patience with thee, I will e'en ask thee another
question. Dost thou believe that these letters of pardon
are efficacious, seeing they are authorized and sanctioned
by our Holy Father the Pope? "

" Whether the man who buys the letters repents or
not? " I asked.

" Yes," he thundered, for I had made him more angry
than ever by my question.

My answer escaped my lips before I realized that I
had spoken.

" No," I said; " it doth not stand to reason that any
man can be pardoned unless he repenteth."

At this the outcry was greater than ever, and I knew
now that, instead of being set at liberty, another form
of punishment awaited me. But concerning this I could
see that the court was undecided.

One was for having me sent back to England, and I

was asked who was the bishop of the diocese in which
I lived; but I refused to answer this, as I preferred
being imprisoned in Germany rather than to return to
England without having done my work. Presently, however, it was decided that as I had refused to give any
account of the part of England where I lived, they must
e'en deal with me in Germany, and the court further
decided to send me to a place of confinement until I had
repented of my naughty ways and confessed a full belief
in Church teachings.

It was after dark when I was taken to my new prison
house, which was some distance from the town where
I was tried; but I judged from the fact that some monks
took me thither that the place belonged to a religious
house of some sort.

12

CHAPTER XVII

THE NEWS OF FATHER NICHOLAS

I OUGHT to state here that on leaving my prison I made
diligent enquiries concerning my friend Granville and
his servant, Tom Juliff; but, although no clear information was forthcoming, I learned that they had been
set at liberty some days before. I gathered, too, that
while they had been set free, they were ordered to leave
the town without delay, and on no account to return
thither. If they did they would be immediately seized
and dealt with in a summary fashion. I thus found myself doubly cut off from my friends, and all chance of
communicating with the Lady Elfrida seemed impossible. Otherwise, my circumstances were much improved.
The room into which I was ushered was clean and airy,
neither was it infested by rats as the other place had
been. Indeed, as I afterwards learned, I had been taken
to a monastery and confined in a disused monk's cell.
From time to time, moreover, I could hear distant chant-
ings, which led me to judge that my cell was situated
not far from the monastery chapel.

As may be imagined, my mind was busy during my
imprisonment, and I speculated much concerning my
chances of escape, for, as it seemed to me, the longer
the matter was delayed, the harder my work would become. All the same, no opportunities came. The window of my cell was strongly guarded by iron bars, while
the two Brothers who brought me my food day by day
seemed to look upon me as a dangerous prisoner. After
the first three days two monks came to instruct me in
religious matters, but beyond declaring that the greatest
sinner out of the bottomless pit was Martin Luther, they
told me but little. In truth, these Brothers were not
likely either to convince anyone of the heresy of deny-

ing the efficacy of indulgences, or to teach him concerning
the true path in which to walk. They smelt of beer, and
were not always sober when they came to me. Nevertheless, I made pretense to listen to them attentively,
partly because they were supposed to be holy men, and
partly because I hoped to gather from their conversation
that which might be of value to me.

Several days passed without aught of importance happening. My food was plain and wholesome, and although I had no liberty my health continued good. One
or two books were given me to read, but I got but little
comfort from them, my mind being full of other matters.

Presently, however, I heard that which set me thinking. The two Brothers who came to instruct me had
evidently dined well, for they talked freely, and, among
other things, spoke of a postulant who had been refractory.

" Why not send her away? " asked one, without heed-
ing my presence.

Upon this the other put his forefinger on his lips and
winked knowingly.

" We desire that she shall enter the Kingdom of
Heaven, Brother Judge," he said. " And is it not easier
for a camel to go through a needle's eye than for those
having great riches to enter the Kingdom of God? "

" And hath she great riches? "

" Ay, and is a great lady into the bargain. That is
why the Mother Superior thinks she hath a vocation."

" She told you this? "

" Ay, but two hours since. It seems she fled hither
because she was destined to wed a man she did not
love, and who is eager for her possession."

As may be imagined, this aroused my interest to a
very high degree. It is true, their talk might have
naught to do with the Lady Elfrida; but, on the other
hand it might, and although I showed no signs of excitement, I listened eagerly.

" She fled hither of her own accord? "

" Ay, and yet not without some persuasion. Father
Lucas, who goes thither to say Mass, proved to her that
it was her only means of safety and salvation."

" Then why hath she been refractory? "

" Ah, we may not know. I enquired diligently of the Mother Superior, but, as you know, the reverend Mother is not free in imparting knowledge."

" Especially to such as you," laughed the other.

At this much banter followed; indeed, so much were these men under the influence of wine and gossip, that they forgot all about giving me instruction, and left without speaking a word on religious matters.

Nevertheless, they gave me much food for thought. First of all, I gathered that there was a nunnery close to the monastery where I was imprisoned, and that the monks had opportunity to speak to the Mother Superior. Next, it was perfectly plain that a young lady of high degree had entered as a postulant entirely under such circumstances as the Lady Elfrida herself might have entered. But what was of still greater interest to me, this postulant had, for some reason or other, become refractory, and would as a consequence have to undergo the discipline of the convent.

All this was full of interest to me, and I found myself making many plans in order to verify my suspicions. The more I thought of the matter the more I was convinced that the Lady Elfrida was the refractory postulant, and that by a strange combination of circumstances, we were dwelling practically under the same roof. Naturally, I was much rejoiced at all this; nevertheless, the more I thought about it the more difficult did the task I had set myself appear. Had this information come to me while I was free and had friends at my side, I would quickly have framed devices whereby I could have discovered the truth; but I reflected that I was closely imprisoned, and that both my horse and my weapons were in the hands of the holy Fathers of the monastery. Still, I did not abandon forming plans of escape, one of which, as I thought, promised well, but which I will not describe here, as I never tried to carry it into effect, good as I thought it was.

And for this reason. Not many hours after the conversation of the two Brothers had set me thinking so vigorously, an old monk whom I had never seen before sought an audience with me. I have called him old, and yet perchance the description was not true, for he was barely sixty years of age, and although somewhat wan in appearance was hale and strong. He entered my cell timidly, and looked around like one afraid. Then he carefully locked the door, and having put the key in his pocket drew near to me.

" My son," he said, " I have come to have speech with you, if I may."

" To what end, Father?" I asked. " The two Brothers who have visited me have spoken much, yet do I find myself as much in the dark as ever concerning the reasons I am brought hither."

" But surely, my son, the reason is plain," he replied.

" Plain or not, I have not been able to understand it," was my answer.

" Thou hast become tainted with Luther's doctrines," he made answer, " and thou hast been brought hither that thou mayst be led to repentance."

" I know little or naught of Luther's doctrines," I said. " I have never read his books."

" And yet thou didst convince the bishop that — but tell me, my son, if thou canst, the story of thy coming hither."

The old man's kind face and soft voice destroyed the suspicions which arose in my mind, and without telling him of the purpose for which I came to Germany, I told him much of what I have written down here.

" And you saw Luther?" he said eagerly at length.

" I saw him twice and had lengthy speech with him," I replied.

" Tell me what you thought of him," he said tremulously. " Repeat to me what he said to you."

" To what purpose?" I asked, for the look in his eyes and the tones of his voice made me pause.

" Nay, doubt me not," he replied. " I will not use a word against you. I —," and here he stopped, like one afraid to go on.

" Master Englishman," he said presently, " I have been an inmate of this monastery for more than forty years. I know little of the ways of the world, but something

tells me you are an honest man. Since you have been
here there has been much talk concerning you, so
much so that I have been led to come and see you. I
swear that I have no thought in coming to see you that
I would use to your harm. Perchance if I were to
tell you all that is in my heart, I might give you power
to harm me. Nevertheless, I would give much to know
what a stranger such as you thought of Martin Luther
and of the doctrines he holds."

"But surely you regard him as a heretic," I made answer. "You look upon his doctrines as dangerous lies."

He looked eagerly around the cell, and then out of the
window.

"Tell me," he said tremulously, "do you look upon
him as a tool of the devil? Is he an evil man? You
saw him, you heard him, you looked into his heart. Tell
me what you think, and I will swear upon this crucifix
that not a word you tell me shall escape my lips."

"Why do you so much wish to know?" I asked.

"Because, because — look, young master, as I have
promised to be faithful to you, will you be faithful with
me."

I think it was the tone of his voice which made me
promise, for there was that in it which touched my
heart.

"I have lived here, as I told you, for many years," he
went on when I had spoken the words he desired, "and
although I have gone but little into the world, I have
seen strange things. Oh, it is no use denying it, no use
trying to keep it back; have I not seen the life of many
of the Brothers, have I not wept in secret? Young sir,
our Church is full of corruption, full of false doctrine,
full of filthy lies. It is said that Luther's eyes were
opened through reading the word of God. I, too, have
read the word of God, I have read the blessed Gospels
again and again, not only to learn the words of our Lord,
but that I might see if our Church is according to His
will. And this I have found: there is but little sim-
ilarity between the Church as I have seen it and the
life and teaching of our Lord. May God forgive me for
saying it if I am wrong, but I feel I must speak. For

many days it hath burned in my heart until I feel I can keep silence no longer."

"But could you not tell your difficulties to your confessor?" I asked.

"My confessor!" he cried. "How can one confess one's deepest thoughts to such as he? His life is foul, man, foul. How doth he spend his days, his nights? If half the filthy abominations of the monasteries were made known the people would raze them to the ground."

"But they are made known," I said.

"Who hath made them known?"

"Erasmus," I replied.

"Ah, yes, Erasmus; that is true, but the people do not know it. The truth hath not been made known in the German tongue. Besides, hath Erasmus the root of the matter in him? Why, think, man. Here is our archbishop, a prince, a spendthrift, a worldling. Cares he for the souls of the people? As for the bishops, with but a rare exception, it is money and pleasure and earthly pomp that they rejoice in. The Church is not the home of the meek and lowly Jesus, it is a great corrupt institution. Real sins are made light of, while all sorts of innocent things are spoken of as sins. Commit adultery or fornication, and you can be forgiven; be guilty of thinking, ask some innocent question about this or that doctrine, and the vials of wrath are opened upon you. If Martin Luther had lived a loose life, if he had been a drunkard, or kept an evil tavern full of vile men and lewd women, naught would have been said, providing no public scandal were made; but because he proclaimed against the vile trade of indulgences everyone pounces upon him. Monks bleat until they are hoarse, bishops pronounce curses on him, abbots revile him. Here are you in prison. Why? Because you are accused of heresy. What have you done? It is said you have shown favor to Luther, condemnation of Tetzel, and stirred up strife. That is why I, who have been so sorely troubled, have come to see you. I want to hear what Martin Luther said to you, I want to know whether you think him a man of God."

"As to that," I replied, "no man can doubt it. With

regard to his doctrines, I will not argue, but that he is an honest man none who have met him can deny. Rough of speech he is, but kindly. He hath a merry heart, too, and although he hath much to cause him pain, he laughs like a boy, and can tell a pleasant story."

"Ay, but tell me concerning his doctrine," he cried. "There is many a monk who can tell a story to laugh at, too many, for that matter. Speak to me concerning his doctrine."

Thereupon I told him what I have set down concerning my conversation with Martin Luther, also many other things which I have not set down here.

As I spoke a bright light came into the old monk's eyes, and more than once he gave exclamations of joy.

"That is it," he cried again and again. "A man is saved by repenting of his sins and believing in the infinite love of God as revealed in our Lord. The Lord requireth not the devices of men, they are but as thistledown. Christ is our Savior, it is for us to believe in Him, to accept Him, to allow Him to fill our lives with His spirit. That is salvation. But what said he concerning indulgences, young sir?"

"He seems more pronounced against them than when he nailed his theses against the door of the Schloss Kirche at Wittenberg," I made answer. "He is of opinion that not only have they no efficacy, but that they hinder salvation, seeing that they cause men to rest upon a rotten reed. He claimeth that salvation is the free gift of God to those who repent of their sins, and who trust in Christ as their Savior. That the Pope's indulgences are but emparchmented lies."

"It is according to the word of the Lord," he cried, "and it comes as spring water to my poor thirsty heart. And thou, young sir, dost thou believe this?"

"As to that," I replied, forgetting all caution, "the more I have thought about these things the more it hath come to me he is right. It was my fortune to be at one of the fairs where Dr. Tetzel sold indulgences at Burg, and it seemed to me a vile traffic."

"Surely God hath raised up another Joshua," he cried; "but tell me what the people say at Wittenberg?"

"They have nearly all accepted his doctrines," I replied, "and the people have become more sober, more God-fearing. There is but little else spoken of in the streets of Wittenberg than the doctrines of Luther, who is regarded as one who hath been raised up to cleanse the temple of God."

"Ah, but he will never do it," cried the old monk.

"Why?" I asked.

"Because all the archbishops, the abbots, and the superior clergy are against him. They will put him to death. Duke George of Leipsic is his enemy. I doubt much if he will return in safety from his disputation with Dr. Eck."

"What disputation?" I asked.

"Did you not know? Did he not tell you? He is even now at Leipsic disputing these matters with the great doctor. If he is not equal to Eck, as most men think he is not, all his doctrines will be laughed at, but if he holds his own and confutes the great champion of Rome, then will he be killed even as Huss was killed. Many bishops and priests have sworn his death, and he is being encompassed about by many devices. Yet who knows; if the Lord hath raised him up for His own work, will not the Lord protect him? Moreover, hath he not the mightiest of all weapons?"

"What weapon?" I asked.

"Doth he not for ever appeal to the Word of God, which is the Sword of the Lord?" he cried. "Will not the Lord take care of His own? But thou, Sir Stranger, is it true that thou hast proclaimed Luther's doctrine aloud, as it hath been alleged against thee?"

"I have proclaimed nothing, except that it seemed to me a vile thing for priests of God to keep vile taverns, where lewd women and evil men resort together," I said. "For that reason was I thrown into prison."

"But did you not carry a letter of Martin Luther, which declared that you were a believer in his doctrines?" he asked.

It was at this time that I decided to trust the old monk, for I felt sure that he was a good and honest man, and I hoped that he could help me. I therefore told him something of my purpose in coming to Germany, and my suspicions that the lady I desired to help was at that time in the convent which was close to the monastery. I saw, too, that he was strangely affected by my words, and I felt sure that he knew much of what I told him, even before the words passed my lips.

"You swear this to be true?" he cried at length.

"I swear it," I replied.

"Then may I tell you what otherwise would not have passed my lips," he made answer. "I did not come to you wholly because of my desire to hear from your lips concerning the doctrines of Luther, although I greatly longed to hear them. What you have told me confirms much that I knew before. Herr Hamilton, she whom you seek is in the convent close by."

My heart gave a great leap at his words, even although I felt sure of what he said.

"Father Nicholas," I cried, for such he told me was his name, "you must help me to see her; I must have speech with her."

He was silent at this, although it came to me then that this thought had been in his mind all the time.

"Truly, I am sore distraught," he said. "According to my vow of obedience I should scorn your suggestion, and instantly acquaint the abbot of your desire. Yet is the convent a house of God? Do poor persecuted souls find peace there? Are they not urging her to take vows, not because she hath a vocation, but because she hath vast possessions? Ay, and is it not a place of sin?"

"Doth she know I am here?" I asked eagerly.

"No, but I was appointed as her confessor, and presently she told me what was in her heart and what had happened to her. Thus when I heard our Brothers speak of you, and hearing of what had passed, I put two and two together and —"

"Yes, I see," I cried. "Father Nicholas, I must have speech with her. God hath sent you to me for this."

"To arrange this is but too easy," he said at length. "In three days there is to be a fast in honor of the founder of this monastery, and so there are special indulgences allowed to all the Brothers until then. Consequently there will be much wine-drinking in revelry. I could help you to find your way to her. But I must first of all tell her that you are here, and acquaint her of your purposes."

"Do this, Father Nicholas," I cried. "Waste not an hour."

"God knows I would take the lamb away from the wolves," he said as if reflecting. "Moreover, she hath appealed to my heart, for she is in sore trouble, and it seems like God's will to deliver her from this place. I wonder whether its secrets will ever be made known to the world."

"She must be delivered," I cried, snatching at his words.

"Tell me," he said like one still in doubt, "will you, when you are again brought before the Church tribunals, deny Luther's doctrines?"

"No," I said, for although I was not fully grounded in them, I could not deny that much of what he told me appealed to me as true.

"Then unless you escape I fear for your future," he said. "Young sir, could you, if I gave you a monk's frock, act as became one?"

"I did not spend much time in Rochford Monastery for naught," I made answer.

"Wait," he said. "If I can help you I will be back in less than an hour, and if I do not come back, then may God help you, for I cannot."

With that he left me alone, and surely no man was ever tossed to and fro between hope and fear as I was after he had gone. It will seem but a little time to those who may read this, yet to me it seemed like an eternity. Would he come back, or would he not? If he came, then I hoped soon to stand face to face with my Lady Elfrida, and if he did not I felt I must go mad.

And so minute by minute I waited, listening for every sound. Now lifted up into heaven by hope, and again cast into the depths by fear.

CHAPTER XVIII

MORE than an hour passed away, and yet no one came. The time was night, so that all was silent. Naught broke the stillness of the night save the sound of laughter and song which at times penetrated my cell. Evidently the monks were carousing in good earnest, and knew nothing of Father Nicholas's visit. At least such was my hope. If they believed there was a chance of my escaping from the monastery there would be excitement of a different nature. At least, I was fain to believe so. But still Father Nicholas did not come. Was he an enemy who had come in the guise of a friend, was he tool of Dudley and Mainwaring who had led me to utter words of which would make my position more hopeless than ever? The thought haunted me, and yet I could not believe it. Then why did he not come? Had the Mother Superior of the convent obtained an inkling of Father Nicholas's desires, and frustrated them? Or had the Lady Elfrida refused to take heed to my desires?

My brain seemed likely to burst at the thoughts which haunted me. Had I been at liberty I could have borne it better, for a man can bear much if he is able to act; but I was closely immured in the cell, so closely immured that it would pass the wit of a man to escape.

At length I heard a stealthy footstep in the passage outside. This was followed by a fumbling at the lock, and then Father Nicholas entered. His face was pale as death, but I paid little heed to this, as I saw that he carried a bundle of some sort under his arm.

"Perchance I am sending my soul to hell by this action," he whispered affrightedly. "Have I not taken my vows? What right have I to doubt? How dare I act unworthily of my calling?"

" Tell me what to do. Have you seen her? " I cried,
for at that moment I cared but little about the monk's
religious fears.

He did not answer, but, holding a candle in his hand,
looked straight into my eyes.

" Swear to me on this crucifix which hangs on my
breast that you believe you are doing the will of God by
seeking to lead this woman to forsake the life which is
called holy! " he cried.

" I swear it."

" Even though the Bishop and the Holy Father were
to forbid you? " he cried.

At that moment the behests of the Pope himself
seemed but as naught.

" I swear it! " I cried again.

Still he seemed to argue with himself. " I have read
the Holy Gospels diligently," he said, " and there is
naught in the words of our Lord upholding such things.
And you will swear that you have no thought toward
her but what is honorable? "

" Yes, yes," I cried; " I would rather die than see her
dishonored."

" But would you not take her out of the fold? "

" What fold? " I asked. " Is the convent safe for such
as she? Is it God's will that she should spend her life
there? " and at that moment the sound of laughter and
song reached our ears.

" No, no," he cried as if convinced; " be quick. Place
this monk's frock over your own clothes. No one will
ask questions then. And look, I have brought your
sword. That is why I am late. I had difficulty in obtaining it; but I thought you might need it. And I will
show you the way to the stables. Your horse is there."

, I had thrown the monk's frock over my clothes before he had ceased speaking. " Come quickly," he
whispered, " and make no noise."

He blew out the light before we entered the corri-
dor, but he evidently knew every inch of the way, for,
holding my hand, he led me through the darkness without hesitating in a single step. A few seconds later I

could scarcely repress a cry of joy, for I breathed pure air and saw the twinkling of the stars above me.

For a second he stopped and listened, but nothing save the singing of songs and the shouts of laughter came to us. And these came to us indistinctly, for evidently the revelers were in a room on the other side of the building.

"They call themselves priests of God!" he whispered hoarsely. "They say they have taken the vows of the holy life. They are sworn to celibacy, and yet — oh, Holy Mother, it makes me sick when I think of it. They are going to make pretense of fasting, and so they feast and revel. And yet they bark like mad dogs when Martin Luther speaks of the Word of God and demands a holy life!"

"Whither now?" I asked; "we must needs haste."

"Ah, yes! I had forgotten. Come!" He pointed as he spoke to a twinkling light. "That is the door of the stables. My Lord Abbot's horses are there," he said, "and yours is among them. He already calls it his own."

He laughed bitterly as he spoke, and I reflected then, as I learned afterwards, that Father Nicholas had not always been the patient, studious monk who had gained a reputation for holy living, but a gay young gallant who had entered the monastery because he believed a woman had been unfaithful to him.

He led the way along a garden path until we came to a high wall, where was a closed door. This he unlocked and opened for me to enter.

"Turn to the left directly you get inside," he whispered. "Walk twenty steps, and you will be under a tree. That is all I can do. God forgive me if I have done wrong!"

"You will not go farther?" I asked.

"I must go back to my cell," he cried. "I must find out God's truth. It hath come to me that if I have been in the wrong I must do the right. If Martin Luther fights for God, then he needs help. Oh, that I were worthy! We may never meet again. God forgive me if I have done wrong! May He also guide my footsteps."

He closed the door as he spoke, but did not lock it, while I turned to the left as he had bidden me and walked eagerly forward. When I had taken twenty steps I halted and looked eagerly around. Close to me were the overhanging boughs of a great tree, so I judged I had rightly followed Father Nicholas's directions, although I could see no one.

The night was not very dark. The pale crescent of the moon hung in the sky, and the stars shone brightly. It was a cold night, so cold that I felt grateful for the warmth of the monk's garb that had been placed over my own clothes. Now and then a breath of wind sighed through the tree branches, but not often, indeed, the night was almost windless.

"Surely I have made no mistake," I thought, as I continued to examine every spot where my lady might be, and at the thought of it my heart grew cold. I knew then, as I had never known before, how much the Lady Elfrida was to me. I felt that my whole life had gone out to her, and that, compared with her safety, and honor, and happiness, the smiles of princes and the rewards of kings were as nothing. But my love, while it filled me with a strange joy, also filled me with many fears. Had her plans been discovered? Was she unable, after all, to keep the tryst the old monk had arranged?

I reflected that Father Nicholas had not told me that she would be waiting for me, otherwise I should have done some rash deed, and thereby jeopardized all my hopes. Even as it was, I, after waiting some minutes, was on the point of making my way to the convent, when I heard a slight rustling of garments. A minute later I looked into my lady's eyes.

"I have come to take you whithersoever you will," were the only words that came to me. I thought not of explaining why I had not returned to Rothenburg Castle as I had promised; there seemed no need. Moreover, although my words may seem like boasting, seeing I had been outwitted almost at every turn since I had left her, there was no thought of boasting in my heart. And this was because no sooner did our eyes meet than

it seemed to me as though my brain was clearer and
that my strength had increased tenfold. I had no more
thought of fear than if I had a hundred stout lancers at
my back, I had no more doubt that I could fulfill my
promise than if there were no difficulties in the way.

For a moment she did not speak, and I saw that although she had put great restraint upon herself, she was
strangely wrought upon. And in truth this was no wonder. She had, as I learned afterwards, escaped from
Rothenburg Castle because the Count had commanded
her immediate marriage with Count von Hartz. The
wound I had inflicted on him had healed more quickly
than they had dared to hope, and the Count Karl of Rothenburg had told her that he was making all preparations
for the wedding to take place as soon as the man whom
he had sworn she should wed was able to stand by her
side in the castle chapel. These preparations had been
pushed forward with all the more eagerness the day following my escape from the castle. It was said also that
the Count Karl had had much converse with the astrologers who had come on the night I had escaped, and who
had told him that he must look upon me as an enemy.

Upon this the Lady Elfrida, who waited some days in
the hope of my coming, at length heard that I was in
prison, and then, on the advice of a priest who had come
to the castle to perform his offices, had adopted a disguise and had fled to the convent, where I had found her;
and with so much circumspection had she gone, that the
Count had no inkling of her whereabouts. Moreover, although he had scoured the whole countryside, he had
found no traces of her.

There was, I thought, a look of pity in her eyes as I
spoke.

"You have suffered much since we saw each other
last, Master Hamilton," she said.

"There hath been no suffering worthy a thought save
the knowledge that I have been unable to help you and
the fear lest you should think I had failed you," I replied.

She was silent at this for a few seconds, then she said,
"And your friend and his servant, where are they?"

"I know not," I replied. "Only of this I am sure, they are even now planning for my liberty."

"Tell me what hath happened to you since the night on which you left Rothenburg Castle," she said; and I wondered at her calmness, for I reflected that if the inmates of the convent knew of her absence there would be a hue and cry without delay.

I told her right quickly what had happened to me, for I was eager to make our escape, seeing, as it seemed to me, Providence had made escape easy.

"You say Dr. Martin Luther gave you a letter. Do you know where it is?"

"It was taken from me when I was imprisoned," I made answer.

"But you know its contents?"

"Dr. Luther showed it to me before he sealed it," I replied. "It was also read as a proof of my belief in his doctrines."

"Will you tell me what it contained?"

I repeated it to her as well as I could remember, while she listened with great quietness.

"It was brought to me but three nights ago," she said. "It was conveyed to me in secrecy."

"How? By whom?" I asked eagerly.

She did not speak, but seemed to be thinking deeply.

"The Sister who brought it said it came from you," she said at length.

"Dudley and Mainwaring," I could not help saying. "The astrologers who came to the castle."

She uttered no word of surprise at my words. Evidently she had thought of everything.

"I seem to be beset with enemies," she said, but there was nothing plaintive in her voice. "The Count, for reasons I have not yet fathomed, hath determined that I shall wed the man whom to look on makes me shudder. The Church hath her reasons for urging me to enter religion, while the men who sent me the letter which Dr. Martin Luther gave to you have also their reasons for getting me in their power. What are your reasons for wishing to take me to England, Master Hamilton?"

13

" I have told you," I replied.

" In part, but you have not told me all the truth."

" I have told you there is naught but what is honorable in my heart."

" You told me you came to Germany to take me to England," she said quietly. " I learned that someone sent you. It was the King, was it not? "

I could have bitten my tongue out in anger a minute later, yet it seemed to me at the time that the word was dragged from me.

" Yes."

She showed no surprise. It might seem that she was not ignorant of the fact before I had spoken.

" And what is his will concerning me? "

At this my heart became like lead, for was I not sure, even although I had been told nothing of a definite nature, that Henry VIII. had willed that she should be the wife of some noble whom he desired to please? This was why I was chosen for the mission. I was regarded as one who had forsworn women, and I was told that if I dared to lift my eyes to her in love it were better I had never been born. And yet I knew that I lived only for her. That, asleep or awake, my thoughts would be of her, that never, until my heart grew cold, would I cease to love her.

All this came to me as I stood there, and for a moment my brain whirled, and I was ready to cast everything to the winds that I might win her smile. What were the King's commands, what his smiles? What was all the world compared with the woman the love for whom had come to me in spite of myself?

I opened my mouth to tell her of my love, and the dark sky seemed to grow bright at the thought of it, and then I remembered. I came of a race which prided itself upon loyalty. " Death, but never disgrace," had been the motto which had been emblazoned upon our shields. And I had promised the King — I, Brian Hamilton, who had boasted that my promise was as sacred as an oath taken upon a crucifix.

Then it was that my heart was torn with conflicting

thoughts. Honor on the one side and love on the other. The King's command and the promises I had made pleaded against the desires of my heart.

It was over at length — at least, I thought it was. A man must be true to his promise, he must be true to his honor. I had admitted to her the fact that King Henry had sent me, but I knew that this was safe in her keeping. Besides, I had betrayed the fact, not to save myself from danger, but in an unguarded moment. Foolish I had been, but in my heart of hearts I had not betrayed the King.

"What is his will concerning me?" she repeated, for I had not spoken during the time the battle had waged in my heart.

"I do not know," I replied.

"Why doth he desire that I shall go with you to England?"

"He hath not told me."

"But you have your suspicions."

I was silent at this, for what could I say?

"The King of England must have but a poor opinion of Elfrida of Rothenburg," she said proudly. "He must have thought that I would be willing to obey the behest of the first passing stranger and follow to England one who dares not tell me of his Majesty's wishes. He sends me no token of his royal will, and I am kept in ignorance of his desires. Yet, doth his envoy think I will leave the land of my father and allow myself to be blindfolded while I fulfill his purpose."

In spite of my love her words made me angry, for had not my action made me seem even as a clumsy clown? So angry, in truth, did she make me, that there came to me a great desire to bend her will to mine, and to conquer her even in spite of herself. All the same, I knew that I must not attempt to deceive her. She was quick of understanding beyond the ordinary, and she scorned subterfuges.

"The Lady Elfrida comes of a race renowned for its honor," I said. "Not only on her father's side, but on her mother's. Suppose the Lady Elfrida had been a man and not a woman, and suppose the King had said to her, ' Do this, do that '— the work might be beset with difficulties, it might seem impossible, but would she not seek to do it? What hath the subject to say when the King's word is spoken? Must he not go forward and do the best he may?"

"Must not a man's God be before his King?" she asked.

"Wherein doth that question touch the matter?" I said, for I did not see the trend of her thoughts.

"Even to obey a King a man must not be unfaithful to honor," she replied, " for honor is of God and truth is of God. When a man takes a woman from home and country, is he not responsible for the woman's happiness? Must an English gentleman, even to obey his King, deliver a woman to a fate which her soul loathes?"

"I would rather my hand rotted from my arm than I would lead you to such a fate," I replied.

" And yet you would take me to England not knowing what is in store for me?"

"Except that I trust the honor of Henry the Eighth," I replied, "except that I cannot believe he would have you brought to England save for a purpose that is worthy of a king. Because of this I promised that I would treat you as sacredly as I would treat the image of the Holy Mother herself."

"Tell me what you believe is in the King's mind concerning me," she said.

"I have been wrong in admitting that I am here at the behest of the King," I replied, " and I trust in your honor to save me from the disgrace which my weakness deserves. For remember this — a woman hath her duties as well as a man. If a woman is not powerful to wield a sword or couch a lance like a man, yet hath she the power, because she is a woman, to make a man forget his resolutions. You ask me to tell you what I believe to be the King's mind concerning you. In doing that I at least break no promise, though I may be unfaithful to the King's will. I believe then that the

King would have you wedded to one of England's greatest nobles."

" For what reason? "

" The knowledge of that is beyond me, and my suspicions are of no value. You at least can guess what is in the minds of monarchs when they will the marriage of a lady to some noble whose career they desire to advance."

" You believe I have possessions in England," she said quietly. " You believe that as my mother's child I have become the inheritor of estates which your King would have pass into the hands of one of his favorites. I am to be taken to England not because the King cares aught for my mother's child, but that he may enrich someone who may be as dull of mind and of as vile a nature as the man to whom Count Karl of Rothenburg would give me."

" I do not believe the King of England would have you wed any man whom your soul abhors," I replied; and I thought I believed what I said, although I did not speak with any conviction.

" And suppose there is in England some noble who is young, and fair, and brave, yet not brave enough to come and fetch me himself "— and there was bitterness in her voice as she spoke —" and suppose I go with you and consent to be his wife, would it content you, Master Hamilton? "

" Content me! Great God in heaven, no! How could it, when —"

I stopped, and only just in time, for the confession of my mad passion was on my lips. I knew that my voice trembled and that every fiber of my being quivered at the anguish of the thought. It was many moments before I mastered myself, and even when I did I was scarce able to speak in my natural voice.

" Content me! " I went on. " Who am I to content? I am only the hand that carries the King's sword, the envoy to do the King's bidding. If I succeed, I shall be rewarded by the King's smile, and if I fail I shall not dare to put foot in my native land again during the King's lifetime. And as the King and I are of an age, and as he will in all likelihood live as long as I, then —"

I did not finish the sentence, but shrugged my shoulders angrily, for in truth I had uttered words which made me feel but a sorry clown.

Both of us were silent for a few seconds after this; I because I felt I had already said too much, she perhaps because she was angry with me. Whether she had forgotten that both of us were in danger at that moment I do not know. Certain it is that I thought nothing of the fact that I had escaped from my prison cell in the monastery but an hour since, and that, even in spite of the fact that the monks were feasting near by, I might at any moment be called upon to fight for my liberty.

"You told me but a few minutes ago that you would take me whither I desired to go," she said presently.

"You know I will," I replied. "What one man can do for you I will gladly do."

"Even although I will not accompany you to England?"

"Even although you will not accompany me to England," I repeated.

"And I will not," she made answer. "I am not disposed to be a pawn on the King of England's chessboard, to be moved at his will."

I could not help rejoicing at this, even although it made my own future not a whit the less hopeless, but rather more so.

"What is your will?" I asked. "All I have and am are at your command."

She hesitated before answering, and then it came to me that she only desired this conversation to know what was in my mind, and that she purposed to go back to the convent again. If she had gone thither to be free from Count Karl's commands, would she not be safer there than elsewhere? A convent was sacred ground into which, it was said, no man might enter with impunity, and if Count Karl was ignorant of her whereabouts, she was free from his power. I did not know then all that I learned afterward, and hence I feared that she had determined to return thither. For, as it will be seen, if she had willed to remain there, then I should never see her again.

Thus I waited even like criminal waits for the pronouncement of a judge, not knowing what the sentence would be.

CHAPTER XIX

THE ESCAPE

" HAVE you ever heard of Count Ulrich von Hutten? "
she said presently.

" He that is spoken of by many as a vile heretic? " I
queried. " He who favors the teaching of Dr. Martin
Luther? "

She looked around anxiously, as though she feared
someone was listening.

" And if so? " she said. " Did Dr. Luther speak the
truth concerning you in his letter? "

" What he wrote hath been given as the cause of
much of my troubles," I replied; " but, of a truth, I
have read none of his writings."

" But you have seen Dr. Martin Luther. Do you
believe that a follower of the teachings of such a man
may be trusted? "

" No sane man can doubt that."

" Then you do not fear to be called heretic? "

" I fear nothing if I can be of service to you," I replied.

" He hath a castle on the road between Halle and
Weimar," she said. " If I am once within his castle
gates I am safe."

" When can you be ready to depart? " I asked.

" I am ready at this moment."

" You have a horse? " I asked.

She pointed in the direction of the stable of which
Father Nicholas had spoken.

" My horse is there," I said, " and I go to get it.
Perchance you will deign to ride on mine until I obtain
one for you."

" The Abbot hath received enough from the Rothenburg estates to obtain many horses," she replied.

"Come, then," I said boldly enough, although I had many doubts at the back of my mind. For although I feared nothing, I knew that the taking of horses from my Lord Abbot's stables would be surrounded with difficulty, even although Father Nicholas had seemed to make light of it.

She followed me without a word, and I rejoiced in the thought that, although she had refused to accompany me to England, yet she trusted me to take her to the Count von Hutten's castle, with nothing but my word as a guarantee of my faithfulness.

The convent, which was but a little distance from the monastery, was in darkness, but we could hear the shouts of laughter coming from the house where I had been imprisoned, and I judged that by this time the monks must be deep in their cups.

The light still burned dimly in the Abbot's stables, and thither we made our way with as much speed as we were able. To my delight I found the door open, and on entering I saw two horses saddled, my own and another. There were other horses there, but they were unsaddled, and were standing idly in their stalls. How many there were I did not note, but I could not help noticing that my Lord Abbot's stables were princely in their appointments compared with the hovels in which the peasants of his domain lived.

I thought at first that, but for the horses, the stable was empty, and I wondered much that so little guard should be given, but I made a clattering sound as I entered, and thus awoke a man who was clothed in coarse attire, but whether it was clerical or whether it was lay I could not tell. It appeared to me, however, as a strange uniform for one of my Lord Abbot's stablemen to appear in. I gripped my sword, determined to make short work of the fellow if he opposed me, but as he half rose I saw that he was well-nigh drunk.

"All right, Father," he said with a drunken giggle. "All's ready, and no one knows. Some are feasting indoors, and some go larking outside, so let's be merry. I don't know anything, except that I've got two golden crowns."

The fellow wandered on in a sleepy way as I led the horses from the stalls, seeming only to be half conscious of what was taking place.

"Quick!" I whispered to my Lady Elfrida; "I like not the ease with which we get away. I am afraid there are enemies near."

"Oh, a lady," giggled the fellow, who had watched me in a stupid sort of way. "By the Mass, I'll not rest until I am a holy monk, for of a truth all the good things come their way.\ Feasting indoors, plenty of wine and beer, and an open door to Paradise. Ay, and that's not all, for here is a holy Father taking off a lady for a midnight ride. Oh, yes, I'll never rest until I'm a holy monk, especially seeing it's so easy and so pleasant to be holy."

"Silence, you fool," I cried, "or I'll lay this whip across your back!"

"Ay, as silent as death. For what would you? Would I betray a holy Father who is eloping with a fair lady? The saints forbid! Besides, have I not been well paid? Two golden crowns, two pints of good strong wine, and full absolution for all my sins. You are earlier than I thought, but what of that? The saints speed you, holy Father."

And so the fellow meandered on while I got the Lady Elfrida into the saddle and prepared to depart.

"Good luck to your wooing, holy Father," giggled the fellow. "The porter is asleep, and the gate is unlocked. Ah, I would I were a holy monk."

I led the horses along the road until we came to the monastery gates, and there, even as the fellow had said, the way was clear, and no one appeared to ask us who we were or whither we were going. Indeed, so sudden had everything been that I felt as though I were in a dream. But two hours before I was immured in a monk's cell, not knowing what had become of the Lady Elfrida, and now I was outside the monastery gates, well mounted and unharmed, and that, too, without striking a blow.

Still I was far from satisfied. The escape was too

easy, and I could not help feeling that something was afoot which I could not understand.

"Father Nicholas hath planned everything well," I said presently.

At this she did not speak, and I imagined that she too had been wondering at the smoothness with which the escape had been made.

"Hath Father Nicholas much authority in the monastery?" I asked.

"Why?"

"Because he did not strike me as a man who could plan things so well."

"You have your sword?" she said as if in answer to what I had said.

"Ay, I have it," I replied, "but a monk's garb is no help to the using of it."

"I cannot understand," she said presently, "but I think things are getting clearer to me."

I had scarcely asked her what she meant by this when a couple of men leaped out from the wood we were just entering.

"Early, my masters," said one.

"Ay, but it was necessary," I replied at a hazard, for my suspicions began to take tangible form.

"There should be three," said the other man. "Where is the other?"

"I had to alter my plans," I said, still at a hazard, for I knew not what was in the fellow's mind.

"It is all well," replied the first. "Two foreigners who spoke German indifferently well, and dressed like monks, but it is not yet midnight, and an hour past midnight was the time. But the password, Master Monk?"

Now this put me in an awkward fix, and I was in doubt whether I should not strike them down with my sword, when I bethought me of the old monk's formula, so, still trusting to good luck, I cried out:

"*Pax vobiscum.*"

"Ay, that was not it," cried one.

"But it was," said the other. "At any rate, it was 'Pax' something."

"Nay, it was 'lux,' not 'pax,' but hang me on the highest gallows if I have not forgotten. I know no Latin and I knew I should forget."

"*Pax vobiscum,*" I said again, then, judging the kind of men they were, I went on:

> "In hâc urbe, lux solemnis
> Ver æternum, pax perennis."

"Go on, in God's name, seeing you are a holy monk," cried the man, "but say no more Latin to me or I shall swoon. Latin always makes me think of the devil. But what a holy monk who can spout Latin is doing with a wench passes my wit to tell."

At this the other laughed, but they let us pass, for the which I was thankful, for with a monk's garb on my back I was ill prepared for fighting the sturdy rogues they appeared to be.

"I tell you it must be right. He said both 'pax' and 'lux,'" I heard one say to the other as we rode away.

"Can you understand this, Lady Elfrida?" I said, "for it passes my wit."

She did not reply, but I thought she appeared anxious, so, making sure that we were riding in the right direction, we clapped spurs to our horses' sides and rode faster.

We had ridden perchance an hour or more, when, stopping to tighten the girth of Lady Elfrida's saddle, I heard the sound of galloping horses.

"Methinks I begin to understand," I said. "You say you received the letter which Dr. Martin Luther gave me, and you were told it came from me?"

"Take off your monk's gown and throw it away," she said, for by this time the sound of the horses was plainer.

I was glad enough to do this, for the thing sadly encumbered me, but I felt I had been mistaken in thinking she had trusted me. Still, I threw the brown frock from me, and leaped on my horse's back, feeling my own man again as I did so.

"Perhaps you understand more than I," I said rather angrily.

"The Sister who brought me Dr. Martin Luther's letter brought also another," she said. "The other letter told me that you would be at my Lord Abbot's stable door to-night an hour after midnight, and all things would be made ready for my escape. I should not have gone, for it did not contain the other half of the chain. After that Father Nicholas came to me."

"Dudley and Mainwaring," I said.

She said nothing at this, nevertheless I felt sure she understood.

"But the two men who demanded a password?" I said, half to myself.

"That must be a part of their plan," she said. "Are these men good swordsmen, Master Hamilton?"

"I have only met one of them in that way," I replied, "but Rupert Dudley is reputed to be one of the strongest blades in England."

"And the other?"

"I can scarcely tell," I replied; "we fought on unequal terms, and he ran away when he thought it wise."

"Who will be most dangerous of the two?" she asked.

"Dudley," I replied. "Without Dudley, Mainwaring would be like a hilt without a blade."

We were riding on side by side, and now that the road led through a broad, open plain, I could see her face plainly, for she did not wear her mask. I thought it was very pale, but of that I was not sure, for every woman looks pale in the silver light of the moon.

Meanwhile, the sound of galloping horses behind us became plainer and plainer. Although we were riding as fast as we dared, those following us rode faster. Either they were better mounted or they were heedless of the pitfalls in the road.

"I think my horse could go faster if I urged him," I said.

"Mine could not," she replied quietly.

"Then, if my suspicions are correct, it will be a matter of fighting," I said, feeling that my sword was loose in its sheath.

She made no sound, while I began to plan how I could do battle with my pursuers.

"I would I had a lance as well as a sword," I said aloud, "then the odds had not been so great."

Still she did not reply, while I went on: "I think we had better ride more slowly. If they are not enemies, they will wonder at the speed we are making."

We slackened our speed therefore, and before one could well count a hundred our pursuers were upon us.

"You ride late," said a voice in English. "Therefore, we will ride together. It is not right that those of the same land should travel alone so late at night. Even as in England, the roads in Germany are full of footpads, and three swords are better than one."

"That is well thought of," I said, "but even as in England, travelers sometimes desire to go alone, and such is our case to-night. So, good-night, my masters, and good speed to you."

"Nay, not so, Master Brian Hamilton," was the reply. "What, shall not one Englishman help another? Your charge is too great for you single-handed. Therefore, we will relieve you. By the Mass, it will be a great joy to me to do so."

The man laughed as he spoke, and I had little doubt but that it was Rupert Dudley. I could see in the moonlight, moreover, how easily he sat his horse, and I heard Mainwaring laugh quietly.

"Things have not happened exactly as I schemed them," he went on, "but what of that? He is put a poor soldier who doth not advantage by his enemies' plans. Besides, I doubt not the fair lady will willingly change companions. Fair lady, deign to smile upon your slave, and then shall the moon shine as brightly even as the sun."

I saw the Lady Elfrida swerve in her saddle, but what it portended I did not know. Then, before I could guess what was in her mind, she had dismounted, giving a cry as she did so. I leaped from my horse instantly and rushed to her side, only to be met by the swords of my two antagonists. A second later we fell to fighting furiously. I had but little hope of success, for, as I have said, Rupert Dudley was reputed to be one of the best swordsmen in England, while Mainwaring was no child at the game. Still, I was desperate. I knew that I was fighting for more than liberty or even life, for did not the life — ay, and more than the life — of the Lady Elfrida depend upon me?

For a few seconds I was borne back by the blades of the two men, and, what was more, I felt that one of their swords had reached me, how seriously I did not know, but I knew that I was yielding before them. Then suddenly I heard a cry, and only one man stood before me. What had become of the other I could not tell, neither could I tell which of the two I was fighting, for a cloud had passed over the moon, and my eyes seemed to grow dim. Still I fought on, parrying and thrusting almost without plan or purpose, save to kill the man who met me sword to sword.

My head began to swim, but with a kind of desperate feeling I fought on. I knew that I was losing blood, I felt it trickling down my body. I knew, too, that a kind of film was coming over my eyes; nevertheless, I had a kind of feeling that I was getting the better of my antagonist. Once I was sure my sword reached him. He had given that little " ugh! " which generally follows a severe sword-thrust; but although he scarcely yielded a foot, I thought his guard grew weaker. Despite the fact that my brain was scarcely capable of thinking, I found myself planning a ruse which had never failed me in sword play, but I had no sooner taken the first steps toward carrying it out when another cry reached me, and this time I knew that the Lady Elfrida, who up to now had been silent, and concerning whose fate I knew nothing, was in need of help. Regardless of consequences, therefore, I gathered my fast-waning strength into one supreme effort, and I saw my antagonist's sword fly from his hand. Before I could take advantage of this, however, I felt a terrible blow on my head, a thousand sparks flashed before my eyes, and everything began to recede from me.

In vain did I struggle and try to cry out. I knew that my senses were leaving me. I thought I heard the sound of many voices, but nothing was distinct to me. Everything became dimmer and dimmer, and after that I felt as though I were enveloped in a great darkness.

. . . .

When I awoke to consciousness, I found myself lying on a soft couch. All was silent and all was dark save for a candle that threw a strange, ghostly light around the room. The room itself was large, and I noticed, beside the bed on which I lay, a settle and two straight-backed chairs. A kind of languor possessed me, and although I tried hard, I could remember nothing that had happened to me. I was as ignorant as a child but last night born of where I was. I felt there was something which I ought to know, but what was hidden from me.

In spite of myself, I felt I was falling asleep, and then I knew no more for many hours. When I awoke again it was to know that my brain was clearer, but it was also to feel sharp pains when I moved. Indeed, I think it was the pain more than anything else which aroused me to a true sense of my surroundings. It was now daylight, and into my room came the light of day. I also saw, for my bed was not far from the window, that I was no longer in a flat country, for in the near distance a giant hill rose in front of me. Beneath me I heard the clank of men-at-arms and the sound of gruff voices, which uttered a kind of guttural speech well-nigh unintelligible to me.

It was the clank of arms, I think, which aroused my memory. It made me think of the fight with Dudley and Mainwaring. The cry of my lady rung in my ears again, and then the memory of the blow which turned everything into darkness.

"Where is she?" I cried. "I must get up, I must find her wherever she is." But on moving my body I felt as though hot irons were placed on my naked flesh.

Still, I was alive, and I could think clearly. I looked at my hands, and they were as white as those of a woman. My wrists were as thin as those of a girl of eighteen. What had wrought the change in me?

I cried aloud, but no voice answered mine, whereon
I conceived the thought that I was in prison, but this
was quickly dispelled by the opening of the door and
the entrance of a kindly-looking Frau.

For some time we looked at each other without speaking, I because I knew not what to say, and she, as it
seemed to me, because she desired to learn something by
looking at my face.

"I'm fain believe that the good Lord hath given him
back his reason," she ejaculated at length.

"Ay, my reason, good Frau," I said. "Nevertheless,
I am deep in mystery."

"Ay, but that hath been the lot of many in these latter days," she cried; "nevertheless, the entrance of God's
word giveth light."

From this I judged that the woman was in some sort
a believer in the new doctrine which had been preached
by Martin Luther, for the which I felt glad.

"Where am I?" I asked, still bewildered.

"As to that, you are in the castle of the illustrious
Count Ulrich von Hutten," she answered; "and well
was it for you that you had such a refuge in the storm,
such a shadow of a great rock in a weary land."

"Ulrich von Hutten!" I cried. "And how long
have I been here, good Frau?"

"Ay, so long that I have ceased to count the time,"
was her reply. "Render thanks to the Lord, for you
have been near the gates of death — ay, more than once
have I held a feather to your lips that I might know if
you breathed. For many days you raved with fever,
and for many more did you lie as though, in truth, you
had given up the ghost."

"And who brought me here?" I asked.

"Of that I know but little," was her reply, "neither
is it wise that I should answer any more questions. I
must even speak with the leech and tell him that you
are now clothed and in your right mind."

She turned to go, whereupon I cried aloud.

"Good Frau," I said, "but tell me another thing.
Know you aught of where the Lady Elfrida of Rothenburg is?"

14

She looked at me steadily for a minute, and then she said, "She is safe from all danger, Sir Stranger, and guarded by faithful friends."

I had to be contented with this, for the good Frau turned and left the room as she spoke, while I was left to think over what she had said. As may be imagined, my thoughts gave me comfort. Before we had started on our fateful journey my Lady Elfrida had asked me if I knew aught of Count Ulrich von Hutten, and she had told me that he had a castle between Halle and Weimar. Therefore, as I was within his castle walls, all was well. Moreover, the Frau had assured me that the Lady Elfrida was safe from danger and guarded by faithful friends. What other conclusion could I draw, therefore, than that the hands that had brought me thither had also rescued her? But who had done this? We had been attacked by Rupert Dudley and Mainwaring, and I had only wounded Dudley. How, then, had my lady escaped Mainwaring's hands, even although I had made Dudley incapable of action?

These and other thoughts filled my mind, and I had framed many more questions to ask the Frau on her return, when I heard men's voices near me, and from the sound of heavy footsteps I judged that they were coming toward me.

My heart fairly sung with joy, not because I recognized the voices, although they did not seem altogether strange to me, but because I heard the clank of armor, which is ever dear to the heart of a soldier, but more because I felt sure that I was going to hear good news.

A minute later three men entered the room. The one was dressed like a leech, and carried himself with great pride, as though he thought of himself with much complacency and pride, as I quickly discovered that he did. The other was a tall man, fully armed. But it was upon neither of these that I feasted my eyes, for the third was no other than my friend David Granville.

CHAPTER XX

COUNT ULRICH VON HUTTEN

" MAY God be thanked, Brian!" he cried as he saw me, and he was hastening to my side when the man of medicine stopped him.

" Stay, good sir," he said with dignity. " It is not well that aught should be said to a patient until the physician hath first paid good heed to his condition. For what saith the learned Pythagoras, the first duty of a patient is in all things to obey his doctor. Therefore let all stand aside until I have examined and passed judgment."

Whereupon he set to work to examine my condition, mentioning the names of Democritus, Praxagoras, and Dioctes, and quoting sayings from their writings as he did so. How long he was at my side I know not, but it seemed to me ages, especially as he treated a wound in my head and another in my side, the which caused me such pain that, weak as I was, I had difficulty to keep from crying out in my agony.

" It is well," he said at length. " The patient hath yielded to skillful treatment. Art and science hath triumphed. *Cuilibet in suâ arte credendum est* — a knowledge of scutomancy pathology and flebotomy hath overmatched disease. Yet methinks in a day or so it will be well to again practice a little more flebotomy, which the ignorant call blood-letting, and then with further application of my skill the good youth will perfectly recover."

At this he stepped aside like a man who had conquered all difficulties, and waved his hand as a sign that the others could step forward.

" It hath been a weary time, Brian," went on David Granville, " but what matters since all is well?"

"Is all well?" I asked wearily, for I was very weak, and the severe handling I had received at the physician's hands had not strengthened me.

"Ay, all is well," cried David eagerly.

"Then tell me all that took place," I cried. "How did —"

But before I could finish the sentence the man in armor came forward and claimed my attention.

"All in good time, Sir Englishman," he said, "but not now. Most learned Dr. Steinmetz, we are most grateful to you for your skill, and now we must not keep you from other sufferers who demand your attention."

"My knowledge is at the service of all," said the doctor, "for in this the doctor is alone in his profession. Not even the priest is so true to the saying *pro bono publico* as the physician. Yet am I somewhat weary, and, seeing I have ministered to the patient, I would e'en now sit awhile and learn from his own lips in what bloody fray he received that wound in his head and the sword-thrust in his side. For not only am I a physician, I am also a man of the world and love to hear of the deeds of young blood."

"Ay, but you must first go and refresh yourself," said the knight. "The journey hither hath been long, and after such attention as you have bestowed on your patient, you need a goblet of good wine and food. Besides, far be it from me to judge of a patient's condition, but he doth not seem to me in a fit state to tell of the things you desire to know."

He gave me a knowing look as he spoke, and I saw that the physician was in a strait betwixt two desires, first to know how I came by my wounds and second to taste of the knight's wine.

"I have no distinct memory of anything," I said; "perchance when the learned and skilful physician comes again I shall be better able to tell him what he desires to know."

"Ah, then I will go on my mission of mercy elsewhere," he said, going to the door, "and I will also take advantage of the most noble Count's invitation to a stoup of wine on my way."

"He is a most notorious gossip," said the knight when he was out of hearing, "and having one grain of knowledge he acquaints the neighborhood of a whole sackful of tales. But to your question, young sir. Are you strong enough for speech?"

"Indeed I am," I replied, "and even if I were not I feel as though I shall never be able to rest until I know something of what hath taken place."

"Then will I tell you my part of the tale with all quickness. I am the Count Ulrich von Hutten, of whom perchance you may have heard, and it is in my house that I rejoice to be able to give you hospitality. You were brought here many weeks ago at cockcrowing by Master David Granville, and I will leave it to him to take up the tale."

I looked into his face as he spoke, and found him to be a young man but little older than myself. He had dark, bold eyes, and carried himself as a soldier should. Yet did he impress me as something more than a soldier. He had, like Cæsar, the air of a student and warrior combined. One who loved both a Latin text and a trusty sword. Moreover, although he spoke simply, it was in the tones of a scholar, although his bright, flashing eyes and martial air seemed to contradict what I have said.

"Ulrich von Hutten, scholar and soldier, satirist and poet?" I queried.

"Ay, if you will have it so," he said, evidently well pleased that his fame had traveled so far. "But more of that later, for Master Granville hath told me that you who were a soldier gave up the sword for the pen and the battlefield for the student's quiet. But not now. Your strength is not equal to it. Yet you are longing to know what your friend hath to tell you."

I turned to David, who stood by my bed, waiting to speak. "Do not trouble to ask questions, Hamilton," he said; "I know what is in your mind. I, with Tom Juliff, had discovered your whereabouts, and was planning to set you free, when by good fortune I discovered that Dudley and Mainwaring had something on foot. Much as I hated allowing you to remain a day longer in captivity than was necessary, I thought I should be serving you best by following them. This was difficult to do, for Mainwaring hath the cunning of a fox, while Dudley is a sleuthhound. When they came to the monastery gates that we wot of, I rejoiced to learn what for a time dismayed them. But I quickly found that your danger was not over, for they started to ride after you as though the fiends were at their heels. As you may imagine, Tom and I rode after them with what speed we might, but not fast enough to reach you before they did. You follow me, don't you?"

"Ay," I replied, "go on; tell me all quickly. What happened after — after — I ceased to know what was taking place?"

"I found both of them desperately wounded, but still able to hold her fast. Whether they could have taken her away I know not, for they had no fight in them when we came."

"But both were not wounded," I said. "I remember wounding one, but only one."

"They were both wounded," replied David, "and, as I think, desperately wounded."

Weak as I was, the whole scene came back to me with vividness. I remembered my lady leaping from her horse, while both men turned upon me. Then one of them gave a hoarse cry, and I had only one to fight.

I was silent, but I am sure Granville saw what was in my mind. I knew now, as I had been sure when I had first seen her face, that the Lady Elfrida was no helpless maid, but one who could think and act as boldly and as bravely as a man. She had helped me in a way I had not dreamed of.

"The Lady Elfrida was unhurt?" I asked.

"Ay, she was unhurt," replied Granville, "and seemed far less concerned as to how she could get rid of Dudley and Mainwaring than how she could take care of you."

This he told me, and much more, especially concerning what happened to him after I was thrown into prison,

and of the steps he took to find out my whereabouts.
I discovered, too, that he had made great advance in the
knowledge of the German tongue, and that he could now
converse, although with difficulty, in that language.

"And now we will go, for you need to be quiet," he
said. "When you have rested I will come again."

"One thing more," I said, and I came to the question
which all the time had been burning on my tongue.
"You say that the Lady Elfrida is safe. Where is she
now?"

"I thought I had told you," he replied. "She is
even now in this castle."

I longed for him to say more, but I had to be content with this. For, first of all, I did not know in what
relation she stood to Count von Ulrich, but more because my strength had well-nigh departed. Besides, the
good Frau I have mentioned came in just then with
food and cordial which Dr. Steinmetz had caused to be
sent to me.

After I had eaten I lay for a long time in a kind of
stupor. I was not asleep, and yet my thoughts were
not clear to me. All the same I felt a great thankfulness in my heart. After all I had helped to take her
to a place of safety, and even then she was under the
same roof.

Presently I fell asleep, and when I awoke again I
felt much stronger. My wounds were not so painful,
and I could think more clearly. The day was gone,
and by the light of the candle I saw the good German
dame holding a dish of gruel, which I ate with great
relish, and then I went to sleep.

When again consciousness came to me it was broad
daylight. The sun was streaming in at the window,
and the air was keen and frosty. Moreover, I felt myself stronger. My brain seemed quite clear, and I was
able to think without difficulty. No one was with me,
for the which I was glad. My loneliness enabled me to
ponder over the situation, and to understand how matters stood.

And this was how it came to me: I had much to rejoice in and be thankful for. The Lady Elfrida was

in a place of safety. She no longer stood in danger of Count Hans von Hartz, nor of her uncle. It was probable, indeed, that they did not know where she was, and, even if they did, the clank of the armor of the men-at-arms in the courtyard told me that the castle was well guarded. Moreover, Count von Hutten was doubtless a man of courage, and would be a safe protector. On the other hand, however, I was no nearer the fulfillment of my mission than when I had first started on my journey. The King's wishes were not fulfilled. If I went back to England without her he would scorn me as a helpless dotard. Perchance I had done something to help her, but I had done nothing to forward my own plans. She had refused to accompany me to England, even although she knew it was the King's desire. She refused, as she put it, to be a pawn on the King's chess-board. This being so, I dared not go back to England. I had failed to fulfill the King's mission. All I had done was to play at the work given me to do, and I knew what kind of a man Henry VIII was.

And yet, I was not altogether cast down. If the Lady Elfrida had consented to go to England then would she be given to one of the King's favorites in marriage, while I, who had learned to love her with a great love, would feel that I had sold my love for the King's smile and the King's reward. The times in Germany were stirring. I would therefore remain in that country. At least I could offer my sword to one of the many free captains, such as Count Karl von Rothenburg, and as wars were plentiful it would be quickly accepted.

When the German dame brought me my food she informed me that the Count von Hutten had gone with my friend Granville hunting. She told me, moreover, that David had entered my room at sunrise, and, finding that I was asleep, deemed it wise not to disturb me.

I had the whole day before me, therefore, in which to rest; and this was to my good, for instead of being tired when night came, I found myself stronger than in the morning.

Three days passed, and I continued to gain strength,

yet never once did I see the face of my Lady Elfrida
or hear her voice. This was in no way wonderful, for
I was not allowed to leave my bedchamber, and it was
not seemly that she should come to me. Yet did I
hunger sorely for a sight of her face, for the thought
of her grew dearer to me even as my strength increased.
On the fourth day I was strong enough to leave my
room, and was able to learn something more of the kind
of man Count von Hutten was, as well as to learn something of what was going on well-nigh all over Germany.

"Another week and you will be your own man
again," he cried, after rejoicing with me over my partial
recovery.

"I trust so," was my answer.

"Ay, it is good to live," he said, and his bright
eyes sparkled. "And all the better for those who, like
you and me, Master Hamilton, are bookmen as well as
swordsmen."

"And you are renowned for both," I said.

"Yes," he cried with a laugh. "I took my Doctor's
degree in Laws in Italy, was crowned with the poet's
laurel at Augsberg, and was made knight by the Emperor Maximilian. But things have changed, Master
Hamilton. The old Emperor is dead, and because he of
Saxony refused to reign in his stead we have as emperor a Spanish glutton who thinks more of dining
than of Divinity, more of riotous living than of
righteous government. He ascended the throne through
bribery, and the Church hath taken the bribes. Meanwhile God's truth is dragged in the dust, and wisdom
crieth in the streets, while no man hearkeneth."

"Is Dr. Luther dead, then?" I asked.

He gave me a keen, searching glance.

"You know the little monk of Wittenberg?" he
asked.

"I have even seen him and spoken with him," I said.

"And you believe in his doctrines?" he cried.

"As to that," I replied, "during the long days and
nights of my imprisonment I have been led to think
much of what I have seen and heard. Surely the Church
needs reforming."

"Reforming!" he cried. "The Church is rotten to
the core. Rotten, I say. Yes, I know I may be condemned for what I have done in the past. When
Luther proclaimed against Tetzel and his indulgences,
I despised him. 'He is an ignorant monk,' I said, 'and
the son of a clown. What is he to deal with such matters?' Yet, mark you, I could not help admiring the
little monk's courage. His life hath hung upon a straw,
and yet, regardless of danger and death, he hath dared
the task of cleansing the Church of its filth.

"When Luther was called to Augsberg to stand before Cardinal Cajetan, who was sent from Rome 'to
crush the little worm,' as he said to me, I promised myself rare sport. 'I will e'en see how this miner's son
will bear himself against an Italian scholar and a prince
of the Church,' I said. And yet I knew that the Church
needed cleansing. I knew that the clergy were in the
main arrogant and filthy. I knew that the monasteries
were filled with monks who lived like swine, while
priests kept brothels. Oh, yes, I knew it; and yet I
despised Luther, who alone had the courage to speak
out for God and truth. So, as I said, I determined to
be present when the little monk had to face Cajetan.

"'What will you do with him, your Eminence?' I
said on the morning on which he was to be brought
before him.

"The Cardinal laughed. 'I will bring him to his
knees in five minutes,' he said; 'in five minutes more
he shall leave my presence like a whipped cur, promising
to be good in the future. I will show these Germans
what kind of a man this little Martin Luther is, and
what will happen if any man dare to lift up his voice
against the Church. I will show them that the Church
is a law unto herself, doing what she will and as she
will. I will show them that if the Pope makes it lawful
for a man to kill his own mother, it is naught to them,
and that they must believe and obey. I will show them
that if the clergy break every law both of God and man,
it is for them to hold their peace and do the clergy's
bidding.'"

"Well," I said, "what happened at Augsberg?"

Von Hutten laughed a great laugh. " It was the finest sight I ever saw," he cried. " The little monk stood up before Cajetan and would not allow himself to be judged. ' Revoca! Revoca!' screamed the Cardinal. ' What? The Word of God?' asked the little monk.

" ' Who are you?' cried Cajetan. ' An ignorant little monk, just an ignorant little monk.'

" ' Prove me ignorant,' cried Luther.

" ' I say you are, and that is enough,' screamed Cajetan. ' And look you, master monk, the Pope's finger is stronger than all Germany. He can crush you like the worm you are. Do you think your German nobles will protect you? I tell you no, and where will you be when the Pope's anger is aroused against you?'

" ' Then, as now,' said Luther, ' in the hands of the Almighty God.'"

" And then?" I asked.

" Then!" cried von Hutten. " Why, his Eminence grew purple with rage. He felt that the monk was his master, that he knew more divinity, more Church law. The whole matter ended in Luther escaping from Augsberg back to Wittenberg, where he hath since been digging at the very foundation of the papacy."

" And you," I cried, " do you still despise Luther?"

" I am a German," said Count von Hutten, " and a German never despises a brave man, whether he be duke or peasant. Besides, I, too, have been led to look deeper into the whole question, and I can do no other than to take Luther's side. And why? Because he fights with the Sword of the Lord, which is the Word of God."

" And are you doing aught?" I asked.

Again Ulrich von Hutten laughed. " Luther hath been denounced at Rome," he cried, " and I, too, am to be denounced at Rome for what I have done. I have set up printing presses, and I am sending out pamphlets proclaiming the arrogance and the wickedness of the clergy. I, too, am seeking to wield the Sword of the Lord."

This was one of the many conversations I had with Ulrich von Hutten, one of the most intrepid fighters in the great movement which is even yet convulsing the life of Europe.

As may be imagined, during the four days since my strength had been coming back to me, I had more than once inquired concerning the Lady Elfrida, but beyond being told that she spent her days in companionship with a sister of Count von Hutten, I learned nothing of her. This disturbed me greatly, and if the truth must be told, I felt somewhat sore at heart concerning her silence; but on the fifth day, when I was able to walk around with ease, I rejoiced greatly at receiving a message from the Lady Elfrida herself, telling me of her desire to see me.

As may be imagined, I found my way to her presence with all speed, and as David Granville had been able to secure some finery for me at the nearest town, I was able to present myself before her in some manner befitting my rank.

I found her sitting with a lady well-nigh forty years of age, who was the eldest sister of Ulrich von Hutten, and who had been widowed some two years before. Since the death of her husband she had lived with her brother, whom she regarded with great love. I discovered, however, that although she held him in great affection, she was much displeased at his avowing adherence to the work of Dr. Luther, whom she despised as low-born, and as such unfit to deal with the teachings of the princes of the Church. But naught concerning the sister of Ulrich von Hutten troubled me, for seated near the window of the room was the woman who had brought me to Germany.

She arose at my entrance and gave me her hand, and looked, as I thought, kindly toward me, but I knew not what to say, for the sight of her took away all thought of speech. For the moment I desired nothing better than to gaze on her and wonder in what way I could make my life of value to her.

It might seem as though the stars in their courses were fighting for me, for at that moment von Hutten's sister was called away, and so, before scarce a word was spoken, I found myself alone with her.

CHAPTER XXI

THE STRANGE CONDUCT OF THE LADY ELFRIDA

" I REJOICE greatly that you have escaped all harm, and that you are here in safety," I said. " But you look somewhat pale. Is all well with you? "

" All is well, Master Hamilton," she replied, " but I pray you to be seated. You are not yet strong."

" My strength is well-nigh restored," I replied, " but I can walk without pain, and my wounds are nearly healed. I want to thank you, Lady Elfrida, for all you have done for me. But for you I should have been killed."

Her face flushed as I spoke, and then became paler than before.

" What I did was nothing," she replied. " Besides " — and then she tried to laugh, but there was no merriment in her voice — " I have discovered how weak women are. Their strength and their courage are only for a minute. I think I fainted when — when one of your enemies fell."

" But not before you had made him incapable of harming me," I said.

" Not before he had wounded you," she made answer; " neither was I strong enough to keep him from giving you that blow on the head afterward."

" That is nothing," I answered, " since I am well and strong again. I shall never forgive myself that I was not able to bring you here myself. But for my friend David Granville and his servant, God only knows what would have happened."

" But your friend arrived in good time, Master Hamilton," she said quietly.

After this a silence fell between us for, I should think a minute. Much as I tried, I could find nothing to say, while she seemed strangely wrought upon.

"I am well-nigh ashamed of myself," she said presently. "I am afraid you must think me wanting in gratefulness to you. But, believe me, I am not unthankful, and I have prayed daily for your recovery."

"It seems to me that you have nothing for which you can be grateful to me," I said. "Every endeavor I have made to help you hath come to naught. Yet have I tried fervently."

"And what do you propose doing now, Master Hamilton?" she asked, and her eyes rested on the floor as she spoke.

"Since I may not take you back to England, I must even seek work befitting a soldier," I said, for the thought of my failure to persuade her to do this still haunted me.

"Do you still wish to take me to England, Master Hamilton?" she asked, still keeping her eyes on the floor. "Bearing in mind the purpose for which I should go to my mother's native land, is it still your desire that I should go?"

"Is it not ill to ask me such a question?" I responded. "Is not my honor at stake? Have I not given my word?"

"I do not ask an idle question, believe me," she made answer. "During the days you have been lying ill I have thought much, and many of the things which had weight with me in my decision have ceased to influence me. Believe me, I have a purpose in my question. Knowing, as you believe you know, the purpose for which you were to take me to England, is it your desire, your will, that I should go?"

I looked at her as she spoke, and I saw that she still looked on the floor. Her face had become flushed again, and although I was not sure, I thought I saw her lips tremble. I was about to answer as I should have answered, I tried to formulate the words which would have shown that I was faithful to the King's command, when she lifted her eyes to mine, and then all my resolves were scattered to the wind.

As I have said, the Lady Elfrida was fair to look upon, although I thought her somewhat cold and proud;

moreover, I had always regarded her as one whose will would never yield to that of another. She had defied von Hartz, she had refused to yield to her uncle, Count Karl of Rothenburg, and she had taken her own course against my pleadings. But there was that in her nature which I had not seen until that moment. As her eyes met mine I saw a new Lady Elfrida. Her words up to that moment had hardened me, and made me almost angry, but in her eyes I saw pity, I saw a great kindness.

"Would you?" she repeated, and I heard a tremor in her voice, a voice that was as sweet to me as the music of falling waters.

How could I answer her? Supposing I had said "Yes," and she had consented that I should take her to England, should I not have been signing my own death warrant? The moment I had brought her to the King I should see her no more. She would be taken to one of the favorites of Henry VIII and wedded, while I who loved her like my own life would have the King's smile, and maybe rewarded with a knighthood. I should hate myself forever after, even though I should feel I had been faithful to the King's command. For I should have sold my love for preferment, I should have sacrificed my love for honor's sake. And yet I know I ought to have urged her to come with me to England. I know that as a man who bore an honorable name I should have trampled my desire beneath my feet, and taken her to the King even as I had been bidden. But I could not. The look in her eyes mastered me, and made me the plaything of my heart's passion. If I had loved her before, that love was increased many times.

"I came hither for that," was all I could say.

"Yes, but would you now? Although it may not have been told you in so many words, you know the King's will concerning me, and you know what my fate would be. Knowing that, do you still bid me go?"

"And if I did bid you?" I asked, my voice trembling as I spoke, for I was much wrought upon, "would you go?"

She was silent for a moment; then she said quietly, "Yes, I would go."

"Then if I give the word, you will come with me to England?" I cried. "Knowing what I have told you, will place yourself under the guidance of the King of England?"

"Is not that your will?" she said. "Is not that the purpose for which you have come?"

"But would you?" I cried. "Is that your decision?"

"Yes," she said after a pause "I will come if you wish me. I can trust myself to your guidance and honor, and I will come with you."

Her voice was strangely low, and I thought I heard a sob in it.

"And what of your refusal on the night when I took you from the nunnery?" I cried.

"I have thought deeply since then."

"But why have you changed your mind?" I asked, and my heart was very bitter as I spoke, for although her words meant the smiles of a king, ay, and great reward, they destroyed the mad hope that I had once encouraged. That night, beneath the tree near the convent, as I planned her escape, I had thought that the reason of her refusal to go to England with me might be that — well, let me not speak of it here. It was a mad thought, for how could such as she think kindly of such as I, who had come as a paid servant to take her away from her home? Besides, my madness was revealed to me now. She was willing to go to England, she was willing to be the bride of the favorite for whom the King destined her. Perchance she had reflected upon her hopeless condition in Germany, and decided that it would be better for her to place herself under the control of Henry Tudor. In any case I was but the King's messenger, the King's paid servant, whose business it was to do his will and receive his reward.

And yet I could not understand it. I reflected that she had only a few weeks before refused scornfully to go with me. That she had declared that she would not be a pawn on the King's chess-board, to be moved as he

willed. I had caught the pride, the anger both in the
tones of her voice and the look in her eyes. What had
wrought the change?

I looked into her eyes, and then I thought I knew
the reason. She had consented out of pity for me. I
had told her that if I did not take her to England I
should be disgraced, and should never dare to set my
foot in my native land again, and so she, because I had
tried to befriend her and had been wounded in her
behalf, had consented to do that in which her heart
could not rejoice.

"And why would you go?" I asked. "Tell me, Lady
Elfrida, does your heart go with your words?"

"It is not a matter of heart," she said, somewhat
bitterly. "What can my heart have to do with it? You
have been sent hither that you might take me to England. At first I refused, and now I consent. As soon
as your wounds are properly healed I am ready to go
with you."

"Ay, and your reason for this?" I asked. "Is it
not out of pity for me? Is it not because I, like the
clown I am, told you I should be disgraced if you would
not go with me, and that I should never dare to place
foot upon my native land again? Is not that the reason,
Lady Elfrida?"

"And if it is?" she asked; "what then?"

"That I refuse to profit by it," I replied. "If your
heart doth not go with your words, I refuse to take
you."

"But did you not say you would be an outcast from
your own land?"

"Better that a hundred times than that you should
go out of pity for me. Nay, nay, I would a thousand
times rather be an outcast than that you should go
there for such a reason."

I saw her eyes gleam with a strange light, but what
it meant I knew not. For some seconds she did not
speak, then she said, "You refuse to take me to England, Master Hamilton?"

"Unless your heart, your desires, go with your words.
Tell me, but for pity for me and but for a mistaken
15

sense of gratitude toward me, would you obey the King's behest?"

At this she did not speak for some time, then she said quietly:

"And what will you do, Master Hamilton?"

"I have had many plans," I replied. "At first I thought I would offer my sword to one of the many free captains of Germany, but during these last days I have been reading the writings of Dr. Martin Luther. I have heard also that he is in great danger. It is my purpose to go to him, and to offer him what help I may."

"Do you believe in his doctrines?" she asked eagerly, I thought.

"I cannot help believing in them," I made answer. "It seems to me he hath gone to the root of the matter. Religion hath been but a name, and he hath made it a reality. He is endeavoring to cleanse the Church of her corruption, and his words seem to be the words of a man of God. Count von Hutten tells me that since his debate with Dr. Eck at Leipsic and his appearance before Cardinal Cajetan at Augsberg, he hath been in great danger. He tells me also that he hath been digging at the roots of the whole question of the Papacy. Because of this the vials of the wrath of the Church is being poured upon him. His writings have led me into the light, therefore I have made up my mind to go to him, to learn of him, and to offer him what help I may."

Her eyes gleamed brightly as I spoke.

"Then you will not take me to England?" she asked, and I could not understand the look in her eyes.

"Not unless you tell me that it would be according to your desires to obey the will of Henry of England," I made answer. "I will not take you if you go out of pity for me, or that you desire to secure for me the King's smile and the King's reward."

"But what of the command of your King?" she said, and I thought I saw a smile playing around her lips.

"Even the command of a king cannot make wrong right," I said, "and I would rather be disgraced a hundred times than that you should be condemned to a fate against which your breast revolted."

At this she laughed right merrily, although I saw no reason for mirth. At length she became serious again.

"When go you to Wittenberg, Master Hamilton?" she asked.

"Seeing that Count von Hutten saith you are safe here, and seeing also that he is desirous of examining those questions concerning which Dr. Luther wrote in his letter to you, I shall go in three days," I said. "By that time my wounds will be healed, and I shall be strong again."

On that she rose to her feet and held out her hand. "May God go with you," she said.

"You think I am doing right?" I said, for I could not read the thoughts of her mind.

"I believe Dr. Luther hath found the truth," she made answer. "I believe, too, he is fighting the battles of the Lord. I pray God he may be kept from harm."

Again our eyes met, and again my heart fluttered, even as I had felt imprisoned birds flutter when as a boy I had held them in my hand. I longed to throw myself at her feet and tell her of my love, longed to declare that the reason I would not take her to England and why I proved unfaithful to my King was because I could not live and see her given to be the wife of another. But this I could not do. I was even now a homeless wanderer, who had failed to carry out what the King had commanded me.

A few days later I left the castle of Count Ulrich von Hutten for Wittenberg, David Granville and Tom Juliff accompanying me. The Count had approved highly of my plan, for, as he said, he had grave fears for Martin Luther's safety. He would have accompanied us, he said, but for the time he, too, was busy doing work to purify the Church. Moreover, the ban of the Pope was also upon him, and his life was in danger. Therefore he could not be a help to the monk at Wittenberg by going to his side, but would rather increase his danger.

I did not, after the interview I have described,

speak to the Lady Elfrida again; nevertheless, I received a message from her with a letter for Dr. Martin Luther, which she desired that I should place in his hands. Moreover, I am sure that on the morning I left the castle I saw her looking at me from one of the open windows. But beyond this I knew nothing of her, and so, in spite of what I had in mind, I left with a sad heart, feeling that naught lay before me but loneliness and sadness.

This feeling, however, I endeavored to drive away, for a man hath work to do in life, and even although the hope of a woman's love doth not abide in his heart, he must do that which seemeth to him his duty.

In looking back over what I have written, it seems to me that those who may read must think of me as one who had cut but a sorry figure. I had attempted a great deal, and performed but little. I had set out to obey the commands of a great king, yet had I, instead of obeying his commands, been led hither and thither by desires and fancies of my own. But, then, I do not profess to be a hero, and I am writing down what actually took place rather than what the lover of a story of happy ending desires.

As may be imagined, David Granville and I kept a sharp look-out on our way. We knew naught of what had become of Dudley and Mainwaring, and we knew that they were men of many inventions. We saw nothing of them, however, and we traveled mile after mile without seeing aught of them. This, however, we did see; the whole countryside was in a ferment because of the doctrines of Dr. Martin Luther and Philip Melanchthon. Not a village did we pass through but we saw that the people were all agog with excitement. That which obtained when we first came to Germany was nothing to what now prevailed. Everywhere Martin Luther's doctrines were read and discussed. Again and again did we see groups of villagers gathered together, sometimes in the village smithy, sometimes in the ale-houses, and sometimes in the public squares, listening while some man read the monk's writings. Moreover, we could not help being assured that the people were with him. It is true, many of the monks and priests poured forth threatenings against those who read and received his doctrines, but this they did not seem to mind. So many were there who believed in the monk's teachings that his enemies were powerless. Moreover, we found in many places that some of the priests and monks favored his doctrines and seemed ready to follow him.

What the result of it all was to be none seemed to have a clear idea. For although Luther had written strong condemnation not only of the corruption in the Church, but concerning the Papacy itself, he was still in the Church. After his appearance before the Diet at Augsberg and Cardinal Cajetan many threatenings had been made, but nothing had come of them, and this was, perhaps, owing to the fact that Luther's followers had become so numerous that the bishops and archbishops feared that Germany would be lost to Rome altogether. But the future was altogether dark, for although Luther had many followers, scarcely a noble except the Elector Frederick of Saxony and Count Ulrich von Hutten supported him. Indeed, the Elector Frederick was faithful to the Church, and only insisted that Luther should not be condemned without giving him a fair opportunity of defending himself.

' On the third day of our journey to Wittenberg the excitement became more intense. And this was no wonder, for it was given out that the Pope had ex-communicated Martin Luther, and that commands had been given that the monk was to be condemned from every pulpit in the land. At first I could hardly believe this, but when toward the evening of the third day of our journey we came to the little town of Rochburg, I discovered that the report was true.

I will set down here what we actually saw and heard, for it seemed to me then, even as it seems to me now, a matter of much interest, and provides food for thought, no matter what shade of opinion one may hold.

Just as we entered the town we saw that much excitement prevailed. No one noticed us as we entered, but each man conversed with his neighbor with great eagerness. We saw, too, that the people were making their way toward the church which was situated in the heart of the town, and which was a great building capable of holding the entire inhabitants.

As soon, therefore, as we were able to find an inn at which we could obtain accommodations for the night, and stable our horses, I, with David Granville, made our way to the church that we might see what was taking place.

"I am afraid it is the end of the poor doctor," I heard one man say. "It is said that the Pope wrote the Bull as far back as June, and now it is October. It took a long time to be brought from Rome here, but it hath come. Dr. Eck brought it to Leipsic."

"Ay, and Dr. Eck rejoiced to do it," said another. "He did come off but badly in the disputation with Luther at the Rathaus there."

"Ay," cried the first, "he could not beat him in argument, and so he brings a Bull of Excommunication. Well, well, Dr. Luther hath fought a good fight, and he hath clipped the claws of some of the bishops."

"Ay, but it is a sorry ending to such a good fight."

"Who said it was the ending? Men said the end had come when the little monk went to Augsberg to meet Cardinal Cajetan; but was it? The Cardinal did not silence him. Hath he not been threatened again and again? Did not Tetzel burn his theses? Hath not the Archbishop of Magdeberg promised to shut his mouth? But still the little monk stands firm."

"Ay he is an intrepid fighter, whatever else he may be."

"Nay," said another, "he is but a windbag, and now that the Pope's Bull hath come the bag will be pricked, and he will collapse."

"I have faith in him," said another. "He hath never turned his back once during three years. Is he likely to turn coward now?"

"Ay, but what can a man do when the Pope curses? He hath been safe all these years because he hath been in the Church; but now he is excommunicated. He will no longer have any rights, neither will the Elector Frederick dare to protect him. Ay, and for that matter, all are cursed who give him food or a bed or a kind word."

"Men think of the curses of the Pope differently from what they thought four years ago," urged another. "Then men called the Pope Vicar of Christ, and now they call him Antichrist. I believe in Luther's courage."

"Ay, but no man will be able to speak in favor of him in Rochburg after to-night, for so Father Schmidt told me at dinner to-day."

Thus their tongues wagged as we found our way into the church which by this time was filled from end to end. By good fortune, however, we had entered at a side door, and so found ourselves not far from the pulpit.

Even here the people conversed one with another in excited whispers, some declaring that Luther's day had come to an end, while others would have it that the little monk would not be frightened by a letter from Rome, a letter which was only written by an Italian priest, even though he called himself the Pope.

Presently, however, a great hush came over the assembly, for we all saw a man climb the pulpit stairs, carrying in his hand a roll of parchment, and with a look of triumph on his face.

CHAPTER XXII

HOW MARTIN LUTHER WAS PUBLICLY CURSED

"THIS is even a greater crowd than the one we saw at Burg, when Tetzel sold indulgences," remarked David Granville.

"Ay, and things have changed in Germany since then," I replied.

"If what men say is true, this will be the end of Luther and his reformed doctrines," said David.

"Doth it seem like the end?" I asked. "Tell me, do you think Germany can ever be again as it was before Luther wrote and spoke against the evils of the Church. A new spirit hath come over the nation."

"Ay, but if the Holy Father hath sent this Bull of Excommunication?"

"Truth is not killed by Popes' Bulls," I replied.

"Hamilton, you are a heretic yourself."

"And you, David?" I retorted. "You also have during these last few months read something, not only of the writings of Erasmus, but those of Luther. Is your faith where it was?"

David Granville shrugged his shoulders. "I love a brave man," he said, "and whatever else the little monk is, he is that. But listen."

This he said because at that moment the priest who had climbed the pulpit steps began to preach.

"This is a day of sadness and a day of gladness," he began. "I am here in obedience to the command of the Holy Father to proclaim what will be proclaimed within the next few weeks in every church in Germany. It rejoices me, too, that Rochburg is the town that will be remembered as among the first in which the proclamation is made.

"Fathers and brothers and children, the Church

hath suffered long because of the foul poison of a viper which she hath nourished at her bosom. The viper is Martin Luther, the poison is the doctrines he vomits forth.

"I need not tell you the story of his naughtiness. At first he, in the pride of his heart, protested against the great love of our Holy Father the Pope, who made it possible that pardons for sins could be bought at our doors. In this way he harmed the Church. He preached against those blessed indulgences and pardons, and thus hindered the salvation of the people. He also wrote his lying theses, which he nailed to the door of the Schloss Church at Wittenberg, which theses were afterward read by the people of Germany. Many because of this have died in their sins, and are now in hell. Concerning this the Church was kind and indulgent. He was promised pardon if he would recant. He was summoned to Augsberg to appear before his Eminence Cardinal Cajetan, who reasoned kindly with him, but in vain. After his cowardly escape from Augsberg, he had the honor to meet in disputation the great Dr. Eck, who completely vanquished him. Yet did he continue his naughty ways, and pour forth his lies. Nay, he became more arrogant and more cruel. He not only attacked indulgences, but he even attacked the Holy Father himself, which hath led to our land being filled with vile heresy. He hath written innumerable books, each of which is fuller of lies than the other. He hath sown doubts in the minds of the most faithful of believers; he hath driven thousands away from their one true Mother, the Church. In truth, to such a pass hath his heresy come, and so much hath it spread in the land, that the Holy Father hath determined to put an end to this arch heretic and father of liars.

"It is but two days ago since Dr. Eck brought to Leipsic the Pope's Bull for the excommunication of this said Martin Luther, with the command that a copy of the said Bull shall be read in the churches, so that all may hear the voice of the Church, and that all may know what to do, not only with the writings of this child of the devil, but with Luther himself.

" To begin with, Martin Luther is no longer in the Church. He is excommunicate. He is no longer a Christian; he is a heathen. He ceased to be a Christian when the Pope set his seal to the Bull. And this is the Holy Father's will concerning Luther.

" First, that he be cast out of the Church, and not only he, but all who believe in his doctrines. Listen to the Holy Father's words: ' We authorize you to proscribe the said Martin Luther in every part of Germany, to banish, curse, and excommunicate all those who are attached to him, and to order all Christians to flee from his presence.'

" Second, all his writings are to be collected, wherever they are to be found. Moreover, all people are commanded to deliver up to the parish priest any writings of the said Martin Luther which they may possess, and if they fail to do this, they are excommunicate, and will be doomed to the everlasting fires which will burn unbelievers. These writings will be burned by the public hangman."

Here the preacher paused. " I have already collected many of these writings," he said, after a few seconds of silence, " and we shall presently go into the market-place, where they will be burned by the hangman.

" Third, the said Martin Luther is to be taken, bound, and sent to Rome, where the Holy Father — let us hope, brethren — will deal with him as we shall presently deal with his writings.

" Fourthly, it is the will of the Pope that these orders be carried out without delay, and if any disobey — nay, I will read to you the Holy Father's words: ' As for laymen, if they do not immediately obey these orders without delay or opposition, we declare them infamous, incapable of performing any lawful act, deprived of Christian burial, and stripped of all the fiefs they may hold, either from the Apostolic See or from any lord whatsoever.'

" And now, before going with you to the market-place, I have but one other duty to perform, and that is to pronounce the curse of the Church upon Martin

Luther. By the powers vested in me, I curse Martin
Luther in life and in death, in eating and in drinking,
in walking and in talking, in getting up and in lying
down. May he find no rest night nor day; may pains
make his life a continual agony; and because he hath
crucified our Lord afresh, and driven thousands to perdition, may his soul at death go away into everlasting
perdition. In the Name of the Father, the Son, and the
Holy Ghost. Amen."

Never have I seen such an effect upon any congrega-
tion as this discourse made upon the people assembled
there. I looked around and saw blanched faces and
wild, staring eyes. I heard ejaculations of horror and
angry mutterings on every hand. Some, indeed, seemed
to rejoice in the priest's words, but more evidently regarded him with horror — so much so that I doubt
whether if Luther were there in person he would have
made as many converts to his doctrines as did the
preacher who poured forth his curses.

As for Granville, he gripped his sword, and I saw
that his teeth were set.

"Brian Hamilton," he said, "it is little I have troubled about questions of theology, but I declare that after
this I stand by Martin Luther's side. I was going to
Wittenberg out of love for you, but now I go to stand
by the little monk who hath dared to proclaim the word
of God against the Pope and all the priests, of whatsoever sort."

Now as, from what I have said, it will be seen that
I had for some time been drawn to Luther's doctrines,
I rejoiced in his words; nevertheless, I said nothing,
but held Granville's arm as together we went with the
great surging multitude toward the market-place. Here
a kind of scaffold had been built, underneath which
some faggots of wood had been placed, and here presently
came a number of priests and monks. As they came we
heart them singing, and then the multitude, which had
been muttering fiercely, became silent.

"Veni sancte spiritus."

The words rang out on the still night air, solemn and

grand. But to many there they seemed but as blas-
phemy. How could the Holy Spirit of God come and
bless what they were going to do?

Still, no man spoke, and the silence of the multitude
became almost painful.

The priests and monks came up to the faggots, and
behind them came two men, one bearing a lighted torch,
and another a number of printed papers.

"Light the faggots," cried the man who had preached
in the church.

The man bearing the torch came forward and placed
the lighted torch to some dry straw that had been placed
in the midst of the faggots. The flames shot up, the
wood began to crackle, and in a few minutes there was
a great fire burning. Silently both priests and people
waited, and then presently the preacher's voice was
heard again.

"These," he said pointing to the pile of printed
books, "are all the writings of the heretic Martin Luther
that I have been able to maintain. Both the writings
and the writer have been pronounced accursed; therefore I command that they be thrown into the fire."

The man who carried them came forth and threw
them into the fire, and then the silence was broken by a
roar from the people, like the roar of an angry sea.

"Silence!" shouted the preacher, and his voice rang
above the roar of the crowd, and for a moment stillness
prevailed again.

He was about to speak further, when a great shout
went up, for David Granville sprang forth and seized
some of the books which had not yet begun to burn.

"Let us save the writings of a brave man," he cried,
and in a minute later each book was snatched from the
flames.

"Seize these men!" cried the priest, but none obeyed
him; rather they were ready to embrace David and myself, who were the first to step forward.

"*Hoch! Hoch! Hoch!*" shouted the crowd. "A
brave deed! *Hoch! Hoch!*"

This was followed by great excitement and much
more cheering. Then someone shouted, "Let us give

the preacher a taste of the fire with which he would burn Dr. Luther."

There was a great laugh at this; nevertheless, many of us turned to the place where they had been standing; but we saw that they had departed. Evidently they realized that they had roused an anger of which they had not dreamed, and hurried with all speed to a place of safety. Indeed, so much were the people wrought upon that I do not like to think what would have happened that night had they not taken themselves away.

As for David, men treated him as a hero; in truth, so much were we both sought after that it was with difficulty that we got to the inn and to our beds, for these quiet German people were aroused as I never saw men aroused before.

"Methinks the Pope's Bull is not the end of Martin Luther," cried Granville when presently we were alone. "It might rather be the beginning of his real victory."

At this I shook my head sadly, for I knew that what had taken place at Rochburg might not be repeated elsewhere. Besides, it was only the common people and not the nobles, who shouted "Luther for ever!"

"The Pope is not dead," I replied.

"Neither is the little monk," answered Granville with a laugh.

"But the Pope hath the armories of the world at his back," I urged.

"Ay, and if Count von Hutten is right, and truly he seemeth to be, Martin Luther hath a weapon greater than all the armories of the world," he answered.

"Ay, I know," was my answer. "Ulrich von Hutten saith that Luther will prevail, because he fights with the Sword of the Lord."

"This I know," cried Granville, his eyes sparkling. "This hath been a great day, and if ever I go back to England I will take with me the books I snatched from the flames, and if ever I marry and have children, the story of these books shall be told to them. Brian Hamilton, I believe we have seen to-day what future generations will love to have related to them. We are in the midst of a great fight, man. A fight for liberty."

A great change had come over Granville. Hitherto he had seemed to pay but little heed to the new doctrines which were being preached, but now he would talk of naught else. And this I suspect was because he realized that Martin Luther was a brave man: and if there was anything that David loved, it was courage.

The next day we left Rochburg, and continued our journey to Wittenberg; but not without difficulty. Before daybreak a crowd gathered around the inn, and it was easy to see that great excitement still prevailed. They vied with each other to do honor to us, and especially to David. But for him the books of Martin Luther would have been burned, and now they were able to boast that they had defied both priests and Church.

"Whither go you?" they asked, as presently we mounted our horses.

"To Wittenberg," I answered.

"And you will see Martin Luther?"

"Ay; we go for that purpose."

"Tell him not to fail us," cried some.

"Ay, and tell him that we will not fail him," cried others.

"Tell him, too, that he need not fear the Pope. But for him we should fear the Pope, but he hath set us free."

"Ay, and tell him that God will protect him," cried an old woman. "Tell him that all the women of Rochburg are praying for him. God hath raised him up to purify the Church and bring back the true religion of Christ, and He will never forsake him."

At this there was a great shout of approval, and when at length we were able to get away, and David Granville waved above his head the charred volume of Luther's writings which he had snatched from the flames, I thought there was not one but gave us his blessing and wished us God speed, although Tom Juliff told us afterward that some looked sourly upon us.

As we drew near Wittenberg the excitement seemed to increase rather than diminish. Naught was spoken of but the Pope's Bull, and Luther's doctrines. We

found that some believed that the monk would submit
to the Pope and cry out for forgiveness, but more believed that he would defy the great Leo, even although
he had been excommunicated. I found, too, that the
eyes of all men were turned toward Wittenberg; especially was this true of the clergy. In Wittenberg
Luther had become a wondrous power. It was he who
dictated the policy of the great university there, and it
was believed by the clergy that if his influence could be
destroyed at Wittenberg, then the stream would be destroyed at the fount.

Nevertheless, the town looked quiet and sleepy enough
as we entered it. It is true that the one subject of conversation here, as elsewhere, was the Pope's Bull. Here,
too, many opinions were expressed as to what Luther
would do. I found, however, strange as it may seem,
that although news of Dr. Eck's coming to Leipsic bearing the Pope's decrees were fully discussed, the document itself had not yet reached Wittenberg. Indeed,
some had it that Eck, although armed with the Pope's
authority, was afraid to show himself within the vicinity
of the town where the monk lived.

We entered Wittenberg by the gate at the end of the
town directly opposite to that by which we had entered
on our first visit, and it seemed to me very strange even
then that this little place should be the center of a movement which had set all Europe talking. For, as I have
said, Wittenberg is a town of no great size.

It consists of one street, which is nearly a mile in
length, and another street which is about half as long.
The chief buildings of the town are the Augustinian
Monastery and the University where Luther did his
work, and where, in the main, all interest centered; the
Town Church, where he often preached, and where he
poured forth his condemnation against Tetzel's sales of
pardons; the Town Hall, outside of which is a market
square, and where the people often congregated when
matters of interest were discussed; and the Schloss
Church, on the door of which Luther nailed his theses.
The rest of the town is made up of small dwellings
which cannot boast of any great beauty. In truth, there

is nothing in Wittenberg which marks it off from scores
of other German towns of which the world has never
heard.

Nevertheless, the eyes of all Germany — and, indeed,
of all Europe — were turned thitherward, and especially
toward the monastery, where, directly I had seen our
horses stabled, I made my way.

As I entered the gate of the monastery, which was
close to the inn where I had arranged to stay, I saw
groups of students eagerly talking, but I did not stay
to listen to them; I was eager to again enter the presence
of the man of whom all Germany was talking. As
fortune would have it, I was met by the same patient-
faced monk who had greeted me many months before,
and who again shook his head when I asked to be admitted into the presence of Martin Luther.

"Ay, ay, I remember you," he said. "I call to mind
that Brother Luther had speech with you, although I
thought he would not. But I do not think he hath time
to speak with you now. No man knoweth how he is
besieged by letters and by callers from all over the land.
Men talk of entering a monastery for quiet, but there
is no quiet here. All is excitement, all is turmoil. The
smell of battle is in the air. We were in a state of
unrest then, but it was nothing to what it is now. Ah!
a great change hath come over the land this last year."

"And Dr. Luther is well, I trust?"

"He seemeth to be the only one in the monastery
who is free from cares. When he gives lectures to the
students they meet him with anxious faces, but Brother
Martin greets them with a laugh. Yet hath he his
hours of sore travail."

"It is important that I see him," I said.

"I hardly dare go and ask him. Day and night he
toileth. In truth, it grieved me to disturb him but yesterday, when a messenger from the Elector Frederick
came; ay, and Brother Martin was none too pleased.
How, then, can I go to him? Besides, doubtless
you have heard the news. Oh, it is terrible — terrible!
I am distraught beyond words. I ought not to call him
Brother Martin at all, for hath not the Holy Father

cursed him? How, then, can I call him Brother Martin?
And yet I do. Nay, for that matter, we all love him
the more for what he hath gone through. Besides, he
hath made life and faith glorious to us. He hath
preached doctrines which we can believe. And yet the
Pope hath cursed him, and declared that all Christians
must shun him as they would shun a pestilence.

So the old man meandered on, his weak eyes blink-
ing, and his indecision marked by every word he spoke.
The new-found liberty which Dr. Luther had proclaimed
was fighting against the traditions of ages.

At length I persuaded him to go, although with difficulty, to Martin Luther and tell him that I desired to
see him.

"I will tell him, but I don't think he will see you —
mind that! Why, Brother Martin hath all Germany
to see him. The monastery might be a king's palace,
so many people are coming and going."

This he mumbled as he climbed the stairs to Luther's
rooms, and presently I heard the sound of voices over-
head. Ere long he appeared at the top of the stairs and
beckoned me to come up.

"Do not keep him long," he whispered. "Oh, my
poor head! I should go mad if I had a tithe of his
affairs to think about — to say nothing of the curse of
excommunication. Oh, Holy Mother, help us all, although he saith it is no use praying to the Holy Mother."

As I entered the room I saw him sitting at the desk
which I have described earlier in this history. He was
writing rapidly, and, as I thought, did not notice my
entrance. In this, however, I was mistaken, for without
lifting his head he said, "I will attend to your affairs
presently, Master Hamilton."

I waited for some minutes while he wrote, noting the
energy with which he swept the pen over the parchment.
It was then that I realized, as I had never realized before, that I stood before a man who was greater than
the Kings of Europe. It is true that they could pass laws
for the government of the people; but this man had
done, and was doing, more. He had changed the
thoughts of men. He had broken the chains which had

16

been, binding the people for ages.   He had aroused nations to freedom!

Presently he threw down his pen and rose from his seat.   It is true that many a long month had passed since I had last seen him, but I was unprepared for the change in his appearance.   It is true that he looked vigorous and strong, but he had become thin almost to emaciation.   His cheek bones showed plainly; his sturdy form no longer gave evidence of robust health.

"Ha! Master Englishman," he said with a laugh; "so you dare to come and see the heretic monk, eh?"

His voice was sweet and clear as of old, and his laugh made my heart light in spite of myself.

"You have brought a letter for me, Master Hamilton," he said.   "I think I may as well read that first."

It did not strike me as strange that he should know this, even although I could not imagine how he came by his knowledge.   I answered him by giving him the Lady Elfrida's letter, which he read with great care.

CHAPTER XXIII

WHEN he had read the letter a second time he turned to me suddenly.

"Tell me what hath happened to you since I saw you last," he said.

In as few words as I could I related what had taken place, although, as may be imagined, it took some time.

"The Lady Elfrida hath won your heart," he said. "You care more for her than for the will of King Henry of England."

"I care so much for her," I answered, "that I will not take her to England, when her offer to accompany me thither is to save me from disgrace, and not because she would go of her own free will."

Martin Luther laughed heartily. One might have thought that he had no cares whatsoever, so merry did he seem.

"Why think you she would go to England?" he asked presently.

"Her heart is full of gratitude," I replied. "She hath a fancy that she owes me much, although in truth she owes me nothing. Therefore, although I know full well that her heart is not set on going there, yet because she would save me from the King's anger she is willing to sacrifice her own happiness. If it was of her own free will and for her own sake that she would go to England, then would I take her thither."

"And break thine own heart in the doing it," said Martin Luther, with a laugh.

"That should not weigh with me," I made answer. "But, King or no King, I will not take her to England because she believes she owes me a debt of gratitude and because she would save me from the King's wrath.

243

Her happiness is so much to me that I will not take her there that she may fulfill the purposes of the King, even although I may thereby obtain the King's smile and the King's favor."

The monk laughed again with great heartiness.

"I have heard something of what hath happened to thee from other sources," he said presently. "Had I been able to offer help I would have offered it. But, alas! I could not. I have been beset by snarling dogs and howling wolves on every hand. Indeed, many think it is nothing short of miraculous that I am alive to this day. Surely the hand of the Lord is in it all. But tell me, Master Hamilton, for what purpose have you come hither?"

"For two purposes, Dr. Luther," I replied. "The first is that ever since I entered Germany my mind has been much disturbed. When I came to Burg, many long months ago, I came across Tetzel selling indulgences there. This led me to make inquiries and to think deeply concerning things in relation to religion. I had read some of the writings of Erasmus while in England —"

"Erasmus!" cried Luther. "He wrote to me a fair letter from Louvain. 'I cannot describe,' he said 'the emotion, the truly tragic sensations which your writings have occasioned.' Erasmus agrees with me. He knows that every word I wrote about indulgences, about the morals of the clergy, about their ignorance of doctrines, and about the corruption of the Church are true. Yet he doth nothing definite. He sits on a fence. Well, he hath found, and he will find, the seat uncomfortable. But go on, Master Hamilton."

"I had read his writings," I repeated, "but it seemed to me that naught could be done. Who could cleanse the Church, much less attack it. Hath not the Pope all power? But when presently I came to Wittenberg and heard what all men said, then did it seem to me that what men declared impossible God was making possible. Yet was I not convinced. After I had left you, and saw what I have related to you, and discovered that such evil things were being done all over Europe in the name of

the Church, and when I had been examined by the Church
courts, then did I think more deeply.   Presently, as I
have told you, I was led to the house of Count Ulrich
von Hutten, and while there I read certain of your
books.   They seemed to shake my thoughts to their very
foundations."

"Ah!" cried the monk; "and then?"

"I longed to know more, and when I found that
the Lady Elfrida would not go to England with a glad
heart, I made up my mind to come to you, that I might
learn from your own lips the doctrines you believed.   I
came that I might sit at your feet and learn."

Upon this he placed his hands on my shoulders and
looked into my eyes.   It seemed to me that he read my
very soul, so eager and earnest was his gaze.   His eyes
burned with a bright light, and I thought I saw his lips
tremble.

"I said many months ago that thou wert not far
from the Kingdom of God," he said, "but to-day thou
art nearer still.   But thou did'st mention two reasons,
Master Hamilton; what is the other?"

"The other is harder to tell," I said, "especially as it
may seem vain and presumptuous on my part.   But I
have the name of being a good swordsman and of being
a strong fighter.   Moreover, I cannot help seeing that
you are face to face with great danger.   Before I left
the castle of Count von Hutten I heard of it.   Since I
have left it I know of a certainty.   I came, Dr. Luther,
to offer you, if I may, my friendship, my sword.   My
friend is a brave man and a man of resource, and it may
be I can be of service to you.   Through you, as it seems
to me, I have come into the light concerning many things
that were dark.   Through you, religion, which had
seemed but a fable, hath become reasonable; it hath become the living voice of the living God.   I would help
you, if I could, to fight your battles.   I am not altogether a novice at letters.   If you will have me, I will
work for you.   And if danger comes, I will fight for
you."

I saw the tears gather in his eyes, and it was evident
he was much moved, but he did not speak.

"Why doth one man learn to love another?" I said. "I know not. It is among the mysteries of God. Yet ever since I saw you last hath mine heart grown warmer and warmer toward you. My heart hath burned as I have heard what you have done, and now, as I again see you face to face, I desire nothing greater than to be allowed to stand by your side and be your friend."

I spoke with a full heart, and I told him only the truth. And especially was what I said true as I stood before him that gray October day. I saw him even as I had never seen him before. One man against the world. When all had been against him he stood firm. When his voice had been as a voice crying in the wilderness he had spoken boldly and in God's name. He, the miner's son; he, when all others trembled at what he did, dared to proclaim against lies and corruption, and his voice rang throughout a nation, even as I had heard a herald's voice ring through a tilt-yard. I knew then, as I know now, that the pride of birth and riches was as nothing compared with the heart that loves truth and hates lies.

For answer to my words he did a thing which I shall never forget to my dying day. He rested his head on my shoulder and sobbed like a child. It seems so strange to me even yet that I can scarce believe what I saw and felt. This man, who had been so defiant; this man, who had been denounced as a hard-voiced, hard-hearted, unfeeling man, without sympathy and without loving kindness, and who cared only for his own vain pride, became even as a little child. He seemed as helpless as a weak woman; he might have been a timid and purposeless recluse who longed to get away from the strife of the world. But there was another Martin Luther which I had not yet seen.

"Who am I — I, who am as weak as a child — that you should come to me for light?" he said. "Hath not my name been held up to scorn as naughty and disobedient? Have I not in my dark hours been sorely tempted to deny my Lord? Ay, but my Lord hath upheld me! Without Him I am naught. He is my Lord and my God."

He turned and walked around the room, and then he stopped before me again.

"Since you come to me for guidance, Master Hamilton," he said, "all the help I can give you I will. As I have found life by going to the fount of life, even so will I try and lead you thither. May God make you wise that you may understand the deep things of His Word! I am but a fool, yet surely hath God led me in His own way. Ay, thou shalt come hither and work with me. Many helps have I, yet hath the Lord drawn my heart to you. But, Master Hamilton, I am poor. All that I earn by my writings I give away. Have you wealth? For I can offer you nothing as wages."

"On the day I left England I did give instructions that if I returned not in six months money should be placed with a certain bank in Magdeberg. By this time it will be there; enough to suffice me for many a day," I made answer.

"Then so be it, since methinks the Lord wills it," he said. "As for defending me, thou art a man of the sword as well as a man with the pen, but I pray God I may not need the sword of man. I fight only with the Sword of the Lord, which is the Word of God. Yet who knows? God may have need of thee. But hast thou heard aught which leads thee to think I stand in special danger?"

I then related to him what had taken place at Rochburg, and how I had heard him cursed in the church and his books thrown into the fire.

I saw a change come over him as I spoke, and he was no longer the man he had been a few minutes before.

"Ah! it is so, so soon, is it?" he cried. "Already they have begun, have they? The Pope's Bull — the Pope's Bull! And does Leo think, do the cardinals and bishops think, that this will stop me? Then, by the God who preserved Shadrach, Meshach and Abed-nego, I swear that they shall be mistaken. They have cajoled me, or tried to, they have threatened me, they have made fair promises! And now they will burn my writings and send me to Rome bound for the same purpose, will they? Cajetan threatened, Dr. Eck raved, and Miltitz wept crocodile's tears over me. Why? All for the same reason. 'Be quiet,' they said; ay, that hath been the devil's plea all through the ages. 'Let us alone,' said the unclean spirit to our Lord in the synagogue, and that is what the unclean spirits of all the ages have said. 'Let us alone'; but I will not let them alone. In the name of, and in the strength of, my Master, I will say to the unclean spirits, even as He did, 'Hold thy peace, and come out of him!'"

"The people are with you, even although the nobles and the dignitaries of the Church are against you," I said.

"Ay, and God is with me," he cried. "Hath He not been with me for three years, since first I commenced this warfare? What said the Pope when I first attacked Tetzel and his indulgences? ''Tis only a German boor of a monk who hath drunk too much beer,' he said; 'he'll know better when he hath slept it off.' Ay, but Leo tells a different tale now. 'I doubt whether I could take you to Rome if I would,' said Miltitz to me, 'seeing all the people have gone after thee.' In this I heard the voice of God. It was the enemy of truth confessing that the people had gone after the truth. Shall I hold my hand, then? Nay, as God is my God, no!"

He lost all signs of weariness or fatigue as he spoke. His face flushed, his foot was firm as he walked around the room.

"I have heard of this Bull which Eck hath brought from Rome," he cried. "Eck tried to crush me with arguments before Duke George at Leipsic. But God was with me, and God's truth prevailed. The work went on. And now he comes armed with the Pope's thunders. He hath now arrived at Leipsic with a long beard, a long Bull, and a long purse, but I laugh at his Bull."

"What will you do?" I said, for the spirit of the man had got hold of me, and my heart burned as he spoke.

"We shall see, Master Hamilton. But you can tell

the people who tremble, that Martin Luther will not
fail them, even as he puts his confidence in the Lord
of Hosts.   Still, although I have heard that Eck hath
taken this precious Bull, first to Erfurt and then to Leipsic, I have not yet seen it.   Eck is a liar, so perchance
it is a forgery.   On the other hand, it may be genuine.
But I must see it first.   I must see with my own eyes
the lead, the seals, the strings, the clause, the signature
— in fact, the whole of it — before I value all these
clamors even as a straw."

"But if it is genuine?" I said.

"Then I will deal with it as it deserves to be dealt
with," he cried.   "Look you, Master Hamilton, I have
even been but playing with the Pope as yet, but the battle, the real battle, is nearing.   At first, when I commenced this work I dealt only with indulgences; now I
see that it is not enough.   I must be thorough in my
work.   God delighted in truth in the inward parts.   Reform! Reform!   Ay, but we must reform thoroughly,
we must get to the roots of the business.   Erasmus
deals with surfaces.   He spoke, and he spoke right, concerning the evil living, the lying, the worldliness of monks
and priests and bishops.   I have done this also, but it is
not enough.   I will get to the root of this thing called
Papacy.   I will show what it really is.   I will sift the
wheat from the chaff, and I will tear to pieces these
rags in which the Church hath clothed itself.   Ay, they
have seen only the beginning yet.   Burn my works, will
they?   Burn Martin Luther, will they?   Yes, they will
make a bigger fire than they think.   God requires thor-
oughness; He will have it that the ploughshare go deep,
and it shall go deep, too!"

I left him not long after this, but not before he again
promised me that I should visit him often, that he would
accept what scholarship I possessed, and that if God
willed that he should need my sword, he would avail himself of it.

I took up my abode with David Granville at the inn
which stood near the monastery, and as from the window
of my bedroom I could see the huge pile of buildings
in which Martin Luther lived and worked, I felt, except

for one thing, that God had placed me where I most longed to be.

The next day all Wittenberg was in a state of commotion, for the Pope's Bull was brought there. But Dr. Eck did not bring it himself. Instead he sent certain monks from Leipsic, who brought it to the monastery, and then went away with all speed.

It happened that I was in the room with Martin Luther when it was brought. Philip Melanchthon was also there, as well as the sub-prior and two others. I call to mind, too, that Luther was in great spirits before it was brought. It was the hour of recreation, and Luther was laughing with the loudest, and telling humorous stories, as though he had not a single care.

When the messenger entered with the thing the sub-prior took it in his hand, and after he had examined it he turned pale.

"It hath come, Brother Martin," he said.

"What hath come?" asked Luther.

"The Pope's Bull. Thou art cursed with a great curse. All thy writings are to be burned by the hangmen throughout Germany, and thou art to be sent to Rome bound."

"Let me see the thing," said Luther quietly.

He took it in his hands somewhat gingerly, examining the paper and seals carefully, as though he were looking at a curiosity. Then he read it through, and as he read I saw his face harden and his eyes gleam with a ruddy light.

"*For every battle of the warrior is with confused noise and garments rolled in blood, but this shall be with burning and fuel of fire,*" I heard him say.

Then he turned the parchment over again and read it line by line a second time.

"What will you do, Brother Martin?" said the sub-prior. "You cannot defy the Holy Father."

"Cannot defy him! In God's name, why?" he asked, and there was a ring of defiance in his voice.

He seemed to grow in height as he spoke, while his eyes shone with that light which I had often seen burn in the eyes of warriors when they buckled on their armor to go into a bloody fray.   There was no longer laughter in his voice, and his features were stern and set.

"Why shall I not defy him, Father?" he repeated quietly. "Doth Leo stand on God's truth, or do I? Here is the Word of God; on this have I taken my stand from the beginning of this fight.   On what doth Leo stand?   Ay, what right hath he to exercise authority over us?   For two years have I given special study to this question, and I declare that he stands on a myth, a phantom.   There is no authority in the sacred Scriptures nor in the early history of the Church for the Papacy.   It is only an invention, a sinful invention which hath been supported by credulity and by lies.   The time for fighting hath come.   On the one side is Leo, calling himself the vicar of Christ, and all his minions.   On his side, too, are all the powers of the world.   While I, Martin Luther, stand alone — but on God's truth.   And I am not afraid.   I am stronger than they all, since I stand on God's truth, while they stand on a devil's lie!"

He spoke like one inspired.   His words seemed like the voice of a great general calling his hosts to battle. His voice was low and clear, but it thrilled our hearts. I knew that here was a man whom no threats could affright, neither could any danger turn him aside from the course he had marked out.

"But what will you do, Brother Martin?" asked Philip Melanchthon.

"I will do this first, Philip," said Martin Luther.   "I will answer this Bull of Leo's.   After that we shall see. For a long time I have seen this day coming, and because of it I have prepared many things.   My English friend here shall help me."

He went to his desk as he spoke, and, seizing a pen, he wrote on a piece of parchment these words:

"AGAINST THE BULL OF ANTICHRIST."

"That shall be the title of the next treatise I write," he said quietly.

"The Pope will tear thee to pieces," cried the subprior tremblingly.   "He will break thee as a man is broken on a wheel. He will surely encompass thy death."

"Then rest assured of this," said Luther, and as he spoke joy came back to his voice again, and he laughed with his old buoyancy; "at my death I will be as Samson. I will in dying seize the pillars of this thing called the Papacy, and as they fall the whole superstructure shall fall on the head of the Pope."

The next day he started writing and he used me freely according to his promise, not so much in writing as in searching many an ancient document which I found in the library of the monastery. For many days we labored together, and as I worked and as I saw the rock on which his feet rested, I too learned wherein the truth of God lay.

Meanwhile rumors came to Wittenberg concerning the curses by which Luther was cursed in the churches, also of the great fires that were lit, into which his books were thrown. And not only this, but efforts were made to drive Luther out of the University of Wittenberg. Adrian, who was Helian professor and a friend of Duke George, especially urged that, as he was excommunicated, he must be expelled as a heretic. This he did at the command of Duke George, the Bishop of Merseburg, and the theologians of Leipsic, but in this he failed.

"Is Luther doing God's work, and is he standing on God's word?" asked Philip Melanchthon, and when nearly all cried out "Ay," Adrian quitted Wittenberg and went to Dr. Eck at Leipsic.

But not only did news of the great fires which burned Luther's books, and of the curses which were poured upon him reach us, but news of certain events which made his heart glad.

One thing especially made his heart rejoice when he heard of it. The Count of Nassau, Viceroy of Holland, was solicited by the Dominicans for the right to burn Luther's books, upon which the Count sent back this reply: "Go and preach the Gospel with as much purity as Luther doth, and you will have to complain of nobody."

" There is a man who dares to speak his mind," Luther cried. " Nay, but the truth of God shall conquer."

Another story reached us concerning which he was in great glee. The leading prince of the empire gave a banquet to the princes of Germany, at which Luther and his doctrines were discussed. When the Lord of Ravenstein heard the discussion, and was asked his opinion concerning it, he said aloud: " In the space of four hundred years a single Christian hath ventured to raise his head, and the Pope wishes to put him to death."

But these were only rays of sunshine in the midst of the dark thunderclouds. On every hand we heard the rolling of the thunders, but Luther was calm and composed, until the fourth day of November in the year of our Lord 1520, when he sent forth his answer to the Pope's Bull.

I have seen the excitement of an army when it has marched forward to meet an enemy, but it was nothing to the excitement which prevailed when he sent out the treatise entitled, *"Against the Bull of Antichrist."* It seemed as though men held their breath everywhere, and yet that seemed as nothing compared with the consternation caused by the events which were fast hastening on and which I must now set to work to describe.

CHAPTER XXIV

HOW MARTIN LUTHER BURNED THE POPE'S BULL AT WITTENBERG

"WELL, I have answered the Pope, Master Hamilton," said Dr. Martin Luther, after he had finished his treatise.

"It is a call to battle," I replied.

"Ay, to battle," he made answer. "The greatest battle ever known in these latter days, and yet it is as old as the hills. It is the battle between truth and lies. God's will be done."

"The devil will be busy," I could not help saying.

"Ay, he will, but I have not taken a leaf out of the Pope's books, anyhow," he laughed. "I have answered him. What is his method with me? 'Burn him, but do not answer him.' But I have answered him; afterward — but we shall see."

For some days he took life more easily. He still continued to give his lectures to his students, but he had more hours of relaxation. He gathered his friends around him, and had pleasant conversations with them. Even David Granville was allowed to be present at these gatherings, and here he learned to love Dr. Martin Luther even as I learned to love him, indeed, David stayed with us until the end of November, when he was called away from Wittenberg suddenly by a letter which he received from Count Ulrich von Hutten, which besought him to haste to his side with all speed.

"What is the reason for this, David?" I asked.

"The Count is banished from the Court of the Elector Archbishop of Mentz for teaching Luther's doctrines," he said. "The Count's printer is also imprisoned, while his own life is in danger."

"And he needs your aid?" I asked.

"I know not, Brian," said David, "but I fear greatly," and here he blushed mightily.

"Why do you fear?" I asked. "The Count is a brave fighter, and hath many men-at-arms at his command."

"Ay, but, Brian, I have kept something from you because I thought it was too mad to speak of. But when you were brought to his castle the Count had another sister staying there whom you did not see. She also is a believer in Luther's doctrines, and the Count thought it wise for her to leave. I fear me she is in danger."

I looked into his face, and I saw that he was as red as a peony.

"How old is she, David?" I asked.

"She can be but nineteen," he answered, "and — but I must go quickly, Brian. The Count hath sent for me in all haste."

But for the anxious look in his eyes I should have laughed at his words, for I thought I knew his secret. But it was ill laughing at him; besides, I called to mind one whom I had left at the dwelling of Count von Hutten."

"And what of the Lady Elfrida?" I asked.

"She hath been taken under the protection of the Elector Frederick of Saxony," he said.

"You are sure of this?" I inquired eagerly.

"It is written here in this letter," he answered, and his face had become pale again. "But the Lady Rotha, I know not what hath become of her. If the Count is imprisoned she hath no protector."

"But where is the Lady Elfrida?" I asked. "Know you that?"

"Only that she is gone to one of the Elector's castles," he answered. "She is safe, I tell you. I must go. God be with you."

Ordinarily I should have felt very lonely without David Granville, for we had become as brothers to each other, but events happened so thick and fast that I had no time for loneliness. Nevertheless, I missed him greatly, and wondered often how he fared, and how and when we should meet again.

As I have said, Dr. Martin Luther sent out his treatise early in the month of November, and then took some degree of rest for some days. Indeed, some thought that he would take no further steps, but would wait events. We dreaded daily lest Duke George should send an army of men to take him to Rome in spite of the fact that not he, but the Elector Frederick, was ruler of Saxony.

When some days had elapsed, therefore, and naught happened, I saw that Luther became somewhat gloomy and depressed.

"I have not done enough to show how I regard the whole Papacy business," he said. "I have written my treatise, but that is not sufficient. I must set my conscience at rest in this matter."

"But, Brother Martin," said the sub-prior, "you have defied the Pope, you have appealed to Scripture, you have called him Antichrist."

"That is but the preliminary skirmish," said Luther. "That was but a treatise; I must now appeal for a general council. I must entreat the Emperor and the nobles to free Germany of this thing called the Papacy. Since my eyes have been opened I must make known what I see."

In spite, therefore, of the fears of some in the monastery, he called a notary, together with five witnesses, to come to the monastery, and there, before the public officer, he drew up his formal protest against the Pope's Bull.

After it had been written and signed, Luther read it before all.

Even as I write the picture comes back to me. We had all met in the room where I had first seen him. He was sitting at his desk as he signed his protest, but as he read he rose to his feet. Around him were the public officer, the notary, and the witnesses. The sub-prior was also there, as well as many of the professors. This was what he read, while a solemn silence rested on us all: —

"Considering that a general council of the Christian Church is above the Pope, especially in matters of faith;

"Considering that the Pope is not above, but inferior to Scripture.

"I, Martin Luther, an Augustine friar, Doctor of the Holy Scriptures at Wittenberg, appeal by these presents, in behalf of myself and of those who are or who shall be with me, from the Pope Leo to a future general and Christian Council.

"I appeal from the said Pope: *first*, as an unjust, rash, and tyrannical judge, who condemns me without hearing; *secondly*, as a heretic and an apostate, who commands me to deny that Christian faith is necessary to the use of the sacraments; *thirdly*, as an enemy, an Antichrist, an oppressor of the Holy Scriptures, who dares set his own word in opposition to the Word of God; and, *fourthly*, as a despiser, a blasphemer of the Holy Christian Church.

"For these reasons, with all humility, I appeal to Charles, Emperor of Rome, the electors, princes, barons, and knights, and the whole community of the German nation, to resist with me the antichristian conduct of the Pope for the glory of God, the defense of Christian doctrine, and for the maintenance of the free councils of Christendom."

I say a great silence fell upon us as he read. It was his formal defiance of the greatest power in the world, and our hearts thrilled as he read. We all felt that this was the monk's final breach from the Church of Rome — it was his defiance of the powers of the Pope, whether they were temporal or spiritual.

"And now," said the sub-prior, "I trust, Brother Martin, that you have done enough."

"I shall never have done enough," cried Luther, "until the word of God is triumphant, until this thing called Papacy is destroyed."

The sub-prior shook his head.

"I fear the coming of the soldiers every day," he said. "Remember the Elector Frederick is not Emperor."

17

"I would that he were," cried Luther. "The Emperor Charles gained his position through corruption and bribes, and the Church received the bribes."

"Brother Martin, it makes me tremble to hear you speak," said the old man. "As for you, you fear nothing."

"I fear imprisonment and death as much as any man," cried Luther. "When I wake in the mornings I fear that I shall sleep at night in a dungeon. I have dreams concerning the way the fires will burn my poor body. I remember John Huss, and I know what the Pope hath in his heart to do. But what of that? What is the life of Martin Luther, ay, a hundred Martin Luthers, compared with the truth of God?"

"I fear the end is not yet," said the sub-prior.

"Nay, the end is not yet. The work is only just begun. But what then? God demands truth, truth though churches fall and nations are convulsed with war. Better anything, *anything*, ANYTHING than lies and corruption. The tricksters and cheats must be driven out of the temple of the Living God."

For a week after this naught happened. It is true that Luther's treatise, "Against the Bull of Antichrist," and his formal protest against the Pope were the themes of every tongue; news constantly reached us concerning the burning of his books and the anger of monks and priests. But the work of the University went on quietly. Luther was cursed by the Church, yet he continued to lecture to the students as though the curses of the Pope were but the cries of a puling child, indeed, that was the way in which I think he regarded them.

At the end of a week, however, messengers came from Dr. Eck, who was still at Leipsic, bearing lengthy documents. These they placed in the hands of an old Brother who happened to be at the gates, whereupon the messengers rode away with all speed.

The documents were two in number, one being addressed to "Martin Luther, one time Augustinian monk, and Doctor of the Holy Scriptures at the University of Wittenberg, but now, because of his evil living and heresies, deprived by the Holy Father Pope Leo X of all

rights and privileges as a Christian," and the other bore
the name of the prior of the monastery.

The short December day was fast drawing to a close
as it was brought into the room where Dr. Luther and
his friends were sitting during the hour of recreation.

"Ah, more trouble, more trouble," said the sub-prior
as he saw the seals of the documents.

It might seem, however, as though Martin Luther
was expecting something of importance, for he rose
quickly from his chair.

"Methinks the devil is still at it," he said with a laugh.
"Last night he came to me and awoke me out of my
sleep. 'Martin Luther,' he said, 'your end is nearly
come. Before another week comes to an end you will
have made humble submission to the Pope.'

"'And what if I do, Master Devil?' I asked.

"'I should not be surprised if you are not offered
a cardinal's hat,' was his reply."

"And what said you then, Brother Martin?" said
Philip Melanchthon quietly and with a smile.

"I said, 'What, at thy trade again, Master Devil?
Thou wert always a liar, so be pleased to leave me in
peace.' Upon this I went to sleep again. But what is
this?"

He opened the document as he spoke, and read it
aloud. It was a command that he must, seeing he was
excommunicate, leave the University of Wittenberg at
once, and forthwith repair to Leipsic, where Dr. Eck
would let him know the loving will of the Church concerning him.

"This is but mild thunder after the Pope's Bull,"
cried Martin Luther with a laugh. "It is e'en like the
barking of a lap-dog after the roar of a lion. But what
saith the other, Father?"

The other document was then read. This was also
worded with great formality, and contained the command that the faculty of the University of Wittenberg
was to at once eject the notorious evil liver and heretic
Martin Luther from both monastery and university, that
all were to avoid him as a pestilence, that all students
were to refuse to listen to him, and that if they failed

to obey this loving command they were to be regarded as equally guilty with the said Martin Luther.

"It is but the bray of a wild ass," cried Luther, "but it is well we have heard it. It showeth what we may expect. Let the students hear of this command, and let them judge for themselves."

He seemed in great good humor as he spoke, and immediately issued an order that the students should be congregated in the largest hall, and thither we all repaired.

When that part of the document concerning themselves was read, one of the students gave a great laugh, which was immediately taken up by the others, and then I saw that to the students of the university the Pope's thunders were regarded as of no more weight than the rattling of peas in a pan.

"What will you do, Dr. Luther?" cried someone presently.

"If you will come to the square outside the Elster Gate to-morrow morning at nine o'clock, I will show you what I will do," said the monk; "meanwhile I go to prepare my lecture on the Psalms which I am to deliver the day after to-morrow. As for you, Master Brian Hamilton," he said, turning to me, "will you come with me into my room, for I have work for you to do."

On this there was a great shout among the students, many of whom went into the town and told the people of what had taken place.

We returned to the room from which we had come, Martin Luther leading the way. His head was bare, and his sandaled feet plainly showed beneath his brown frock. The cold December wind swept across the courtyard, but I saw by the look on his face that he heeded it not. The fire of a great resolution was burning in his eyes, and his step was as the step of a great general leading his armies into battle.

"Write," said the monk as soon as we were together, "write in large letters what I shall dictate."

This was what I wrote:—

I, MARTIN LUTHER, DOCTOR OF THE HOLY SCRIP-
TURES *and friar of the Augustinian Monastery at
Wittenberg* (in spite of the Pope's curses) ; HEREBY
INVITE THE FATHERS AND BROTHERS OF THE MON-
ASTERY AND THE PROFESSORS AND STUDENTS OF THE
UNIVERSITY OF WITTENBERG, *together with all the
townspeople who are able, to assemble with me at
the Eastern Gate, near the Holy Cross, at Nine
o'clock to-morrow morning, the tenth day of De-
cember, in the year of our Lord* 1520, THAT THEY
MAY WITNESS WHAT I WILL DO WITH THE POPE'S
BULL, DECRETALS, AND SUCH OTHER DOCUMENTS *as
may have any bearing upon the Church's will concerning me.*

(Signed)   MARTIN LUTHER,
the 9th day of December, 1520.

Martin Luther laughed as he read what had been
written, then he said, " Make copies of this, Master
Hamilton, and have them posted on the walls of the
University. It is well that the people should know
what I think of the gilded pagan of Rome and of all his
doings."

This was done with all speed, and before the night
was over I doubt if there was a man or woman in Wittenberg but who knew of what was to take place.

On the day following, when I looked into the streets,
I saw the people flocking in great numbers toward the
Holy Cross, which was but a three minutes' journey
from the monastery. They were conversing eagerly one
with another, and without exception they cast glances
toward the university and to the posters which still remained. I knew that they were wondering in their
hearts what all Germany was wondering — ay, and for
that matter they were asking what all Europe was asking: " What will Martin Luther do? "

It wanted but ten minutes to nine when the professors
and students started a procession from the monastery.
How many there were I do not know, but certainly there
seemed a great host. At the head of them all was
Martin Luther, still garbed in his monk's frock, and his

head bare. In his hands he carried a bundle of parchments, and I saw that his face was set and stern.

The people made way for the procession, but not a
word was spoken. The day was cloudy but windless.
The gray sky seemed to be close upon our heads.

As I looked among the crowds I saw both young and
old, and in their eyes was a look of wondering anxiety.
But, as I said, no man spoke. The silence was the silence
of night, when sun and wind have gone to rest and the
stars show themselves.

As I drew near to the Holy Cross I saw that a scaffold
had been erected, underneath which were placed several
faggots of dry wood.

The people made a huge circle around the scaffold, still
silent, still watching with anxious, eager eyes.

Luther spoke not a word, but I saw that his eyes
burned red, while on the faces of the professors was a
look partly of fear, partly of wonder; but each man
looked at the monk's face steadfastly and questioningly.

An old professor came forward, bearing a lighted
torch. This he placed to the faggots, and the flames
leaped up. Then Luther spoke.

" Fathers, brothers, and children," he said, " you know
me well; you also know my work and my teaching, especially since that day, more than three years ago, when
I nailed certain theses which you wot of against the door
of the Schloss Church. You know whether my teachings
have been based upon the sayings of men or upon the
word of God. You know, too, whether I have spoken
rightly against the evil lives of many of the clergy,
whether my condemnation of the sales of indulgences
was just, and whether I have led you to the way of life
by proclaiming salvation alone through our Lord Jesus
Christ.

" You know, too, what hath been decided concerning
me, because I have loved truth and hated lies.

" Here in my hand are the Pope's decretals, which
are forgeries and lies. The Pope's popedom rests upon
forgeries and lies. This I have proved to you. Here
is the canon law which hath been made to crush those
who love the truth.

" And here also is the Pope's Bull against me.   In it
I am cursed with a great curse.   In it are commandments
to you to treat me as an outcast and a heretic.   You are
forbidden to give me food and shelter, you are commanded to burn all my writings, and to curse my name
to your children, and to your children's children.   By this
thing also you are commanded to bind me and send me
to Rome bound, where it is undoubtedly the Pope's will
to treat my body as he hath already given commandments concerning my writings.

" This thing," and he lifted the parchment high above
his head, and his voice rang out clear and loud over the
assembled throng, " is the Pope's Bull of Excommunication and Cursing.   What shall I do with it? "

Still no man spoke.   In truth, I think we all ceased
breathing, so great was the excitement which prevailed.
Instead, all eyes were fixed on the brown-frocked friar,
as if in wonder what he would do next.

" This will I do," he cried, " since this vile thing
mocks the Holy One of the Lord, and denies His great
salvation, may these fires consume it.   This I do to
show my scorn for the father of lies."

He flung the Pope's Bull into the fire!

The flames shot up, and in a few moments it was
but ashes.[1]

Then the pent-up feelings of the multitude broke forth.
Such a shout as I have never heard before or since burst
from the people.   To me it seemed like a great shout
of liberty, a great shout of the awakening nations.   I
heard it echoing away in the distance, and as I listened
it seemed to be taken up from the people in the distance
and carried away to lands that I knew not of.   It was a
shout of great joy, a shout which told of the breaking
of chains, of light, and of a new life.

Presently the noise, which was as the noise of many
waters, died down.

" My children," said Luther to the people, " you are
wondering what the Pope will do now.   I know not; I
care not.   You see what I have done.   My enemies have

[1] There is to-day in Wittenberg, on the spot where Luther
burnt the Pope's Bull, a great oak tree growing.   It was planted
many years ago to commemorate the event.

been able by burning my books to injure the cause of truth in the minds of the people and destroy their souls. This is my answer. They have not answered my books; they only burned them. I have answered the Pope, and now I have burned his words, which are full of cursings. The struggle has now really begun. Hitherto I have been playing with the Pope, but now the serious work hath begun. I fight in God's name, and with His weapons. May God's truth prevail. That is my prayer. May it be also yours. And may we all walk in the light of God."

I thought then as I think now, that I saw that day one of the greatest scenes in the history of the life of Europe. But it was not the greatest, as my story will show. Nevertheless, Luther's deed that day roused Germany even as it had never been roused before. It seemed that the very foundations of the nation were being broken up, and every man was asking whether the new reign of God was to commence, whether the man in whom, under God, all their hopes lay would triumph over the man who had governed all Christendom, or whether the monk would be crushed and his name become a byword among the nations.

As for me, I had scarce ceased to wonder at all I had seen and heard, when even the convulsions through which Germany was passing — because of the new thoughts which were burning in the heart and brain of the people — became as naught to me. It seems strange to me even yet that the fate of a woman should be nearer my heart than the fate of nations; yet so it was. Scarcely had the shout, caused by the deed that had more daring in it than that of any other man since Europe had become Christian, died away, than I forgot all about it, for a messenger came in hot haste to Wittenberg bearing a letter for me. This was what I read : —

"Dudley and Mainwaring are at work again. The Lady Elfrida is missing. Come to Eisleben as fast as horse can carry you, and make your way to an inn called the Golden Adler.— DAVID."

CHAPTER XXV

No sooner had I read this letter than I made my way
to Dr. Martin Luther, to whom I handed the letter.

As he read I saw his lips tremble and his eyes fill with
tears.

" The lamb is among wolves," he murmured. " You
must go to rescue her right quickly, my son."

" Ay," I replied quietly, for my heart had grown cold
and hard, and a man doth not shout aloud when a great
purpose fills his life. " I will to horse without delay."

" Stay, my son," he said, " I can help you somewhat.
Know you that Eisleben is my birthplace, and I know
something of the district. Moreover, methinks I see
more than appears. Count von Hartz hath a castle not
far from Eisleben."

" Yes, it cannot be far from the region of the Hartz
Mountains." This I said quietly, but the words had no
import to me.

" You have told me that Dudley and Mainwaring are
men of many inventions," he went on. " Methinks they
are in league with Hans of Hartz. They could not act
without him. It is their will to use him to aid their own
purposes. It will be to his castle that they have taken
the Lady Elfrida. Those wily Englishmen have their
purposes in this."

His words gave me comfort in spite of myself. It
caused a vague danger to take definite and tangible
shape.

" What is more," he went on, " the town of Mansfield and the Castle of Mansfield are not far from Eisleben, and there my father and mother live. I will write
you a letter, my son. It may be that he can be of use

to you. Do you make preparations for your journey while I write the letter, and give the matter due consideration. Have you money?"

" I sent a trusty messenger to Magdeberg, and he brought back to me less than a week ago all I shall need for many days," I answered.

" It is well," he replied.

I left the room as I spoke, leaving him in deep thought. I knew that he had forgotten about his own danger that he might render assistance to the woman whom we both loved; he as a father and spiritual adviser, I as one who would lay down my life to render her a service.

An hour later, all my preparations being made, I returned to him to say " God be with you."

" Brian Hamilton," he said, " it may be that you will have to fight with carnal weapons. Not only will a sharp wit be needed, but a heavy hand. The Count von Hartz can command many swords; and it may be that he is in league with the Count of Rothenburg. Yet is that not likely. I will tell you why. The Count hath fallen under the displeasure of the Emperor, because of certain high-handed deeds which he has performed, and he hath for many months been well-nigh a prisoner. That is the reason why the Lady Elfrida hath not been sought after with more diligence. You told me that your friend informed you that the Lady Elfrida was taken under the protection of the Elector Frederick. I doubted this at the time you made the statement to me, for the Elector Frederick constantly sends messages to me, and, knowing my love for the Lady Elfrida, would, I believe, if what you said was true, have told me. But I said nothing to you, as I did not wish to cause you useless alarm. Now this is how I read it: A messenger, purporting to be from the Elector, hath come to the Lady Elfrida, with the request that she take shelter beneath his roof. This messenger hath in fact come from Count von Hartz, who I know hath become friendly with the Englishmen you wot of."

" Then —"

"I believe she will be in the power of those three men."

"Is this mere surmise?" I asked.

"It is more than surmise," he replied. "I, too, have received messengers this day, and I understood not all that was said. Now it is made plain."

"Then must I lose no time," I said, moving to the door.

"Stay, my son," he cried. "I have thought of many things while you have been preparing for your journey. I have been piecing many scraps of information together. I have written a letter to my father, who will give you shelter and, if needs be, help you with money. The Lord hath prospered him greatly, so that he is now a man of substance. But that is not all. Here is a letter, which you must in case of need take to the Count of Mansfield. There is an ancient feud between the house of Mansfield and that of Hartz. If you find things much as I have told you, take him this letter, and then may the God of battles decide the issue."

"And you," I cried. "It was my purpose to remain by your side as your friend and servant."

"The lady hath greater need of you than I," he made answer. "When you are assured of her safety, then come to me again; meanwhile, remember that the Lord of Hosts liveth and reigneth."

It was two o'clock in the afternoon when I set out, taking with me two rough German troopers, both of whom knew the country well, and on whose fidelity Martin Luther declared to me that I could rest with all assurance. They were, so they informed me, twins, and bore the name of Reuben and Simeon Klein; but their surname belied them, for both of them were of colossal proportions, and, although of somewhat sleepy appearance, were keen and alert. And this I found general among the German people. They have not the quick, decided movements of the Latin races, nor do they give you the impression of being wide awake. Nevertheless, they are, though slow of thinking, a thoughtful and reflective people, and although not easily aroused, they are strong and brave and determined. The heat of a German's anger is not the heat of burning sticks which crackle freely, but the heat of burning logs of oak, which, although not so easily lighted, remain burning far longer.

We rode straight to a town called Halle, which is, I should say, thirty or forty miles distant from Wittenberg. Here we waited three hours, for though I sadly wanted to hasten on, the horses needed rest. At eight o'clock that night we were in the saddle again, and there being a moon, we were able to travel at a good speed. I do not believe either of us thought of robbers, although the country beyond Halle had an ill name. Nor did either of us pay heed to the kind of country through which we were passing, except we noticed that we were leaving the level lands and entering more hilly regions. I know I thought only of the work I had to do, while I believe the two troopers were filled with the stern purpose which burned in my heart.

We stopped at an inn somewhere about eleven o'clock that night, simply because I saw that the horses were completely exhausted. Had I been able to exchange them for others, I would have done so, but that was impossible. We were in a desolate region, where few people lived.

As soon as daylight came the next day we were again riding westward, and before the short December day came to an end we saw the town of Eisleben lying in a valley some few miles away.

At another time I should have paid great attention to this town for Dr. Luther had told me the circumstances of his birth there. He had described to me the situation of the house in Eisleben where his father and mother had come many years before. In truth, when he told me the story, I was even reminded of St. Joseph and St. Mary, who came to Bethlehem more than fifteen hundred years before, and who, because there was no room in the inn, made their way to a stable. Hans Luther and his wife came to Eisleben to a fair held there, and they took up their abode at the house of a friend. It was there, close to one of the two churches in Eisleben, that Martin was born, and the day after his birth his father took him to the little church to be chris-

tened. The name Martin was given to him because it
was St. Martin's day on which he was born. Little did
either Hans Luther or the parish priest think that in less
than forty years after the whole land would ring with his
name, and that almost every church in Germany would
resound with new doctrines!

But I thought not of this then, my mind being too
much filled with the thought of my lady's fate. Nevertheless, I noted in a dazed sort of way that the hills
which stood around Eisleben were drear, and rose to
their heights not suddenly but by almost gentle grada-
tions. It is true that patches of wood were to be seen,
but they were gray and bereft of beauty.

When I entered the town I found it to be a larger
place than I had expected. At the bottom of the valley
was a great square, with substantial houses all around,
and a great church, which, standing out in the clear
moonlight, reminded me of a great sentinel keeping
watch. I had no difficulty in finding the inn called the
Golden Adler, and thither I repaired with all speed.
The first person I saw on entering was Tom Juliff,
whose giant form well-nigh filled the passage. Evidently he had been waiting for me, for his eyes lit up at
the sight of me.

"Maaster David is waitin'," he said simply, and led
the way to a bedchamber.

No sooner did I enter the room than I saw by the
look in David Granville's eyes that I must expect serious
news; yet did my heart rejoice, for while I saw anxiety
I saw also stern resolution.

He wasted no words in unnecessary explanations, nor
of the means by which he obtained his information.
Neither of us was in the mood for many words. I
wanted to know the facts, and that right quickly. These
he gave me.

"This is what hath happened, Brian," he said.
"While you were lying unconscious because of the
wounds you received by the swords of Dudley and
Mainwaring, the Count Ulrich von Hutten received a
letter requesting that my Lady Rotha should go to the
castle of the Count of Mansfield."

" But what of the Lady Elfrida ? " I cried.

" Listen," he said, " you will find that in telling the story of one I am telling the story of the other. The Count, knowing that the Lady Rotha had leaned much to the doctrines of Martin Luther, and knowing of his own danger, deemed it best that my Lady Rotha should go to Mansfield Castle, where she would be safe, and she was sent thither with a fitting escort. I was mightily sad at this, but I dared not speak.

" Scarcely had you and I left the house of the Count von Hutten than he was forbidden the Court of the Archbishop of Mayence, and was told that if he did not give up upholding Martin Luther's doctrines all his lands would be confiscated. This troubled him greatly. He did not fear for his eldest sister, for she hated Luther's doctrines, but he feared for the Lady Elfrida, who also lay under the ban of the Church's displeasure. When, therefore, a letter came bearing the seals of the Elector Frederick, telling Count von Hutten that it was the Elector's will that the Lady Elfrida should be taken to the Castle of Wartburg, which stands just above the town of Eisenach, he rejoiced greatly, knowing that she would there be free from all danger. Once there, the Count Rothenburg could not touch her, neither could the Church harm her. He accordingly informed her of the letter he had received, and she started on her journey to Wartburg Castle.

" Some days passed away, and he sent to Mansfield Castle to see how my Lady Rotha fared, and then he learned that not only had she not arrived there, but the Count of Mansfield had never written desiring her presence there, being on a journey to Augsberg at the time he was supposed to have written. As may be imagined, he was torn with grief; his enemies had become more and more angry with him, and by the Archbishop's commands he was forbidden to leave his own house. He therefore sent me the letter that you wot of, whereupon I rode to him with all speed.

" And now, Brian, comes the terrible news. The whole matter of both letters is but a part of a scheme. I discovered that Dudley and Mainwaring had become

friends with Count von Hartz, and that the clown whom
you well-nigh killed in Rothenburg Castle had agreed
with them that if they would help him to secure in
marriage my Lady Rotha von Hutten, on whom he hath,
since the Lady Elfrida's refusal to wed him, cast his eyes,
he would help them secure the Lady Elfrida. He believes that Count von Hutten's estates will fall to my
Lady Rotha, and because of this he hath been persuaded
by Dudley and Mainwaring to do their will."

" Then where are they now ? " I asked.

" They are in the castle of Count von Hartz," cried
Granville. " So much have I discovered. No sooner
was this clear to me than I sent a messenger to you,
and meanwhile I have been doing all that man can to
learn how we can set them free."

" And what have you done ? " I cried.

" I have been to Hartz's castle and studied its forti-
fications. I know the number of men-at-arms he keeps
there. Fifty there are, Brian, besides Dudley and Mainwaring and the men whose services they have been able
to buy."

" And the Lady El —"

" As yet they are safe. They have their tiring
women to tend on them, and no harm hath befallen
them. But they will not be safe long."

I did not speak, but sat looking into his eyes with
dread terror in my heart.

" To-day," he went on, " I went to the castle, which
is some miles from here, clad in a monk's garb. I had
in my endeavors to find out the truth, made acquaintance with a monk who had been sent for to confess one
of the women of the castle who was supposed to be near
death. Hartz, clown though he may be, hath great faith
in the priests' power, and when the monk told me of the
message I persuaded him to let me take his place."

" And he allowed you ? " I asked.

" Were the matter not so serious I could laugh at the
whole business," cried David. " I had no great difficulty
in bribing Father Andrew to let me go instead of him,
and so well did I play my part that I attracted no suspicion. Moreover, such good use did I make of my

chances that I learned that they, the women we love, Brian, for I will no longer try to hide the truth of my heart, are given a week more to consent to marry John von Hartz and Rufus Dudley."

" And if they will not? " I cried.

" I dare not think. God only knows," he answered.

It was then that I bethought me of th' letter which Dr. Martin Luther had written to the Count of Mansfield, and so, although I had ridden many miles that day, we started for Mansfield Castle without the loss of an hour, for there, as David Granville agreed with me, after I told him what I knew, lay our hope.

Now, it is not my purpose to tell in detail of our experiences with the stern German whom we visited, for I have yet much to relate, and this history hath already become long. Suffice to say that he was in his castle at the time of our visit, and although he at first received us coldly and suspiciously, yet no sooner did he read Martin Luther's letter than his eyes were all ablaze.

" Tell me all you have in your heart, Master Englishmen," he cried, whereupon I told him much that I have set down here.

" He of Hartz is a beer-drinking sot," cried the Count of Mansfield. " Yet is he a strong fighter. Moreover, he hath a low cunning which makes him a dangerous enemy. As for these Englishmen, tell me what you know of them."

As may be imagined, this did not take much time. It was easy to tell what all men thought of Rufus Dudley, a daring, clever, handsome freebooter, who ever played for his own hand, and who broke all laws of honor and chivalry in the playing. As for Mainwaring, he was a clever second of his master's will and purpose.

During my recital of these things the Count of Mansfield rose to his feet and laughed with joy.

" Man," he cried, as he gripped my hand, " I am with you heart and body. I have waited for this day. I have an old score against the man of Hartz, yet have I not had sufficient outward cause to seek open quarrel with him. The fellow, fool though he is, hath always played a wily game. Moreover, he hath always been so backed up by Karl of Rothenburg that attacking him meant a serious business. But now, methinks, most of Rothenburg's teeth are drawn, besides which, if the little monk of Wittenberg is right, he is but a thief, and hath been fattening himself upon —, but of that anon."

Upon that David Granville told the Count of Mansfield all he had learned of the Hartz Castle and of the men-at-arms who guarded it. Whereupon the Count of Mansfield laughed again, and called for a huge tankard of beer, which he quaffed with evident relish.

"You did well to come to me," he cried. "To-night will I send out secret orders for every available man-at-arms to be brought thither, and by to-morrow at this time we will be on the way to our work. *Hoch,* man, but I greet you both, for if your looks do not belie you, you can both fight a good fight."

In truth I saw right soon that not even Count Karl of Rothenburg loved a fight more than he of Mansfield, and because of this he welcomed us as though we were brothers.

We stayed at Mansfield Castle that night, for the Count would not hear of our returning to Eisleben, and although I little thought it was possible, I slept soundly. I was awakened in the morning by the clank of horses and looking into the courtyard I saw well-nigh a hundred men who had been brought thither that night.

"The times of Richard of the Lion Heart have come back again," he laughed; "and by all that is holy the man of Hartz shall feel the weight of Mansfield's arm before the morrow's sun shall rise."

Throughout the day the Count's henchman was busy in arming his troopers. Great strapping fellows they were, and looked right royal when their steel breastplates and caps were fastened upon them. As for David and myself, he saw to it that we were each man armed cap-à-pie, for, as he said, there would be serious fighting before the business was over.

"Glad am I to serve Ulrich von Hutten, too — a brave man, Sir Englishman, and a learned. A little fiery of temper, as a man should be, but honest to the heart's core. I know but little about his doctrines; neverthe-

18

less, my heart goes out to him. Methinks also we shall
strike a blow to-night for the little monk of Wittenberg,
for Hartz, fool that he is, is one of his bitterest enemies."

No sooner did the night begin to fall than we left
the courtyard of the castle, and as silently as we could
made our way toward the Hartz Mountains, near which
Count von Hartz's castle stood.

"There is not a man among my followers but will
fight to the last breath," the Count of Mansfield said as
we rode. "They make a brave show," he continued,
after looking proudly at the men whose armor shone
in the bright moonlight. "I trust Hartz will not turn
coward and give up the ladies without first striking a
blow."

"I trust he may," I answered, for although I feared
not for myself, yet did I know that not one hour's peace
should I have until my lady was safe. "But you need
not fear. Even if Hartz would yield without a blow,
be sure that Dudley is not the man to allow him to
do it."

"Trust he may!" cried the Count of Mansfield.
"Trust that now I have a chance of wiping off old
scores that Hartz will show the white feather! Nay,
man, had not thy friend told me of what happened at
Rothenburg Castle, I should think that thou were only a
man of the gray goose quill, and not a man of the
sword!"

I was silent at this, but looked at Granville's face,
for his visor was up, and saw that he looked set and
stern. In truth, never had I seen such an expression
on my friend's face as I saw that night.

"Ay, but you write as well as any clerk whatsoever,"
he went on in high good humor. "I ne'er thought that
words could be arranged so neatly. Ay, we will do the
thing in right knightly style. Repeat the words to me,
Sir Englishman, the words which you have written, and
which the herald hath committed to memory, and which
he will presently take to the man of Hartz."

I repeated the words I had written down, namely
that it having come to our knowledge that he had by
deceitfulness and false strategy secured the persons of

the Lady Elfrida Rothenburg and the Lady Rotha von
Hutten, and held them in thrall, we, the Count of Mansfield, Brian Hamilton, and David Granville, demanded
without parley their immediate deliverance into our
hands as men of high birth and stainless names. And
that, if he failed to do this, we should forthwith storm
the castle and take them away by force. To this document we had each signed our names with whatever
titles to nobility we possessed.

"Ay, it is great. Not even the Lord Abbot of Stutt-
gart monastery, who is said to be the most learned man
in Germany, could have written better," he cried. "And
Nicholas Bauer shall act as herald and take it to them
with proper ceremony."

In due time we drew near the castle, and then Nicholas
Bauer made his way to the castle gates with all speed,
while we waited, wondering what the night would bring
forth.

"It is a good night for the work, Master Hamilton,"
cried the Count of Mansfield after we had waited some
time. "There is light enough for our work, yet not
enough for him to know our strength. Is it not time
that Nicholas should return?"

"Can the Count von Hartz write?" I asked.

"Nay, not he; but you say that your Master Dudley
can, and even if he cannot, I suspect he will have a
churchman of some sort in the house. But look, here he
comes."

A second later Nicholas Bauer came to us, and I
saw by the look on his face that his message was of
grave portent.

CHAPTER XXVI

THE FIGHT AT HARTZ CASTLE

I WILL not here seek to set down the words in which
Hans von Hartz conveyed his answer to us. It was a
badly written affair, and looked to me as though more
than one hand had taken part in the writing. Enough
to say that it was couched in terms of insolent defiance.
Evidently his castle was strongly guarded, and he was
assured that he was able to repel all attacks from whatever source.

The Count of Mansfield laughed as I repeated the
words to him.

"That is just like Hans of Hartz," he cried, "and is
just the answer I desired. We fight now with good
reason. We have approached him in good knightly
fashion, and he hath defied us. No man, neither Emperor nor Elector, can say that it is not according to
the laws of chivalry to rescue the two ladies they have
imprisoned. Forward then, and may God defend the
right."

We had but little difficulty in reaching the outworks
of the castle, but arrived there our real work commenced. David Granville had made no mistake in saying the castle was well guarded. The clang of crossbows and the groans of wounded men were speedily
heard, and we had to fight our way foot by foot toward
the great castle doors. For this I found — although
there were three entrances to the castle grounds, there
was only one by which we could enter the castle itself.
The place was built on an eminence, and had a great
moat all around it, and the only means by which we
could get in, except by climbing the walls, which, to
say the least of it, was a dangerous business, was to
enter in at the great door, which was strongly defended

276

by a number of picked fighting men. Moreover, a number of men was placed behind the battlements, who shot at us with their crossbows while we fought our way toward the great doors, which were made of iron-studded oak.

But the Count of Mansfield made naught of difficulties.

" This is but child's play," he said to me. " It is all noise and no fighting. I leave you and your friend with fifty men to enter if you can. I, on the other hand, know of a low and undefended place in the walls. I marked it years ago when Han's father was alive, and when I came here as a friend. Fight to the last man, Sir Englishman, no matter how black things may look, for presently you will hear me give a shout of victory at another part of the castle."

There was nothing for it, therefore, but to fight our way toward the great postern doors, the which we did with much bloodshed. Nevertheless, we gained our ground, and then I looked eagerly around for the men, who, now that the passion for fighting was upon me, I longed to see. For this I have ever found: when one is in the midst of a fight all tender thoughts depart. The lust of battle is triumphant, and naught but victory will suffice. At that moment I hated Dudley and Mainwaring and Hartz with a deadly hatred, for did they not hold in their power the woman who hour by hour had grown dearer to me?

As for David Granville, he had utterly changed since he had left me at Wittenberg. His boyishness had seemed to depart, his face had become set and stern, and his eyes shone with that steely glitter which only comes to the man who feels that death is stalking everywhere. Never did I see a man fight as he did. He seemed to bear a charmed life. Arrows and other missiles struck his armor only to glance off harmlessly, while every time he lifted his sword a man fell to the ground with a groan.

I had no opportunity to see what our losses were, but I knew that the battle was with us. The soldiers of Count von Hartz fell back from before us until we had reached the drawbridge which led to the great postern door. And here the fight became a carnage, for here lay the very crux of the battle. While they could keep us out of the castle-yard they had us at advantage, but once there we fought on equal terms.

It was at this time that my heart bounded with a great savage joy, for it was at the drawbridge that I first saw two men clad in armor, one of whom I felt sure was Hans of Hartz. I think too that he recognized us, for I heard the voice of the man like his of the Hartz mountains give a rallying cry. A minute later I was standing on the bridge, exchanging blows with this bull-necked German. At that moment I forgot my duties as leader in the fray; the lust of fighting was on me, and the only thought that filled my heart was to bring this man to earth.

"This day the luck goes not with you, cur of an Englishman," he cried. "As for your dainty beauty —"

But he did not finish what he was going to say, for I managed to bring my sword upon his steel cap with such a clang that I cut his sentence in two. For perhaps a minute we fought with equal fortune, and then I knew that I was bearing him back toward the postern door.

The men from the battlements ceased to shoot with their crossbows, for it was impossible for them to distinguish between friend and enemy. How the matter would have ended, I know not, but at that moment I heard a shout within the castle itself — a shout which was like a shout of victory.

I knew what it meant. The Count of Mansfield had succeeded in his design, and was now within the castle walls. It was then that I turned to see how David Granville fared, but to my dismay he was not to be seen, and although my head was turned but a moment it was like to have ended in my undoing, for I felt a blow on my head which stunned me, and before I was my own man again the great doors had closed as if by magic, and I was left outside.

"Down with the doors. Down with them, I say!"

It was David Granville's voice which rang out clear and strong, and hearing it my strength seemed to come back to me. A minute later the soldiers were raining a storm of blows upon the iron-studded portal, which quickly, although it seemed long to me at the time, yielded to the onslaught. A few minutes later both David Granville and I, together with those of our men who were able to follow us, also stood within the walls of the castle itself.

And now I knew that whatever the result of our quest might be the victory was with us. The Count of Mansfield had succeeded in his design, and now that our forces had joined his, we were masters of the situation. The enemy's soldiers yielded to us without parley, but of Dudley and Hans of Hartz and Mainwaring we could see nothing.

"They have some secret passage by which they can take away their prisoners!" I cried. "We must find them."

But here, although David Granville and I quickly found our way into the castle buildings, we seemed as helpless as children, for the place, like that of Rothenburg, was built without plan or order. We lost our way in dark passages, and presently we became separated, for the building was in black darkness, not a single ray of the moon outside reaching us.

I cursed myself for my folly, for now, although we had gained the victory we hoped for, I seemed to be advantaged not a whit, seeing that the men we had attacked had escaped us, and had doubtless taken away those we had come to liberate. I had no light, nor means of obtaining one. I shouted aloud, but heard no answer save the echo of my own voice, which resounded in the now silent building.

It was at the time when I felt like giving way to despair that I heard a woman's cry. Whose it was I could not tell, but although it was a cry of distress it brought me comfort, for after the clang and shout of battle the silence of the great castle had become unbearable. Without hesitation I made my way in the direction of the sound I had heard, and presently found a stairway. Up this I stumbled, and when I had gone some distance I stopped and listened. I heard voices. They seemed to me far away and muffled, yet the words reached me plainly.

" That is right. My lady can scream no more."

" But we must get away from here."

" All is well. He told us of the passage only this morning, so we can proceed without difficulty."

" Where is the noble Count von Hartz? " This Mainwaring asked with a laugh.

" He may be in heaven or in hell. I care not."

" But we must take her away, else all is lost."

" Ay, I was a fool not to force the marriage yesterday. This comes of being tender toward women. But all is not lost. We must get her outside, then to a holy Father I know of, and when the sacred bonds of marriage bind us both she and her possessions are mine. Doth she still swoon? I will carry her to the passage."

I heard these words while I fumbled with my hands to find the door. Had I not been so distraught I had found it more quickly. At length, however, my fingers happened upon an iron ring, the which I turned and entered a room that was evidently fitted up for a lady of quality. A candle burned dimly on the table, but coming as I did from the dense darkness, the light to me seemed brilliant.

Lying on the floor was a woman evidently in a swoon, while above her stood two armed men.

This I saw the moment I entered, but the face of the woman I could not see. Nevertheless, I did not doubt who she was. The moment Dudley and Mainwaring knew that the battle was against them they had come hither so that they might not be robbed of their prey.

Both of them turned to me the moment I entered.

" Deal with him, Mainwaring, and then follow."

It was Dudley who spoke, and his voice was as cool and quiet as if he were telling a lackey to saddle his horse. He lifted the Lady Elfrida in his arms as he spoke, while Mainwaring turned toward me.

Concerning the issue of the fight between Mainwaring and me I did not trouble one whit, for the spirit of battle was upon me and a great anger filled my heart. What I feared was that Dudley should take my Lady Elfrida away, and that I should not be able to find her. Perhaps it was this thought that gave me strength beyond what was ordinary to me. I did not stop to draw my sword, but gripping the steel-capped mace I held in my hand I rushed forward, and before Mainwaring had time to defend himself I brought it down on his head, and that with such good will that in spite of his steel cap he fell like a log at my feet.

"Ah!" cried Dudley. "Is it you, my young fighting cock?" For so quickly had what I done happened that he had barely taken a step toward leaving the room.

Dropping his burden, he leaped back, and drawing his sword as he did so he rushed toward me, but that not so speedily as not to give me time to meet him with equal weapons.

I found, and that right soon, that Mainwaring had been right when he told me many months before that Dudley was my match as a swordsman; moreover, he fought with confidence, and seemed assured of victory.

"It grieves me much to leave a brother Englishman dead in a German castle," he said with a laugh; "but what can I do when that Englishman meddles with my affairs?"

His vaunting spirit had doubtless angered me into doing something foolish, but when I saw the Lady Elfrida lying in a swoon near by, and perchance wounded, I determined to fight warily, knowing that I could not afford to give him chances. Nevertheless, fortune was with him and not with me, for we had scarcely begun the fight when my sword snapped in my hand, and that close to the hilt.

Dudley gave a laugh as the blade clanged on the floor, but he had not time to take advantage of my misfortune before I flung the hilt from me, and leaping upon him gripped him with all my might. It was now a contest not only of skill but of strength. A moment later we were on the floor in a deadly struggle. More than once I thought I was gaining the mastery, and then again

I felt myself conquered by strength greater than my own. Presently, as it seemed to me, I felt a shock, and then the arms of Rufus Dudley became nerveless, while I rose, panting and bewildered, to see the Lady Elfrida looking toward me.

Her face was as white as the driven snow and her eyes shone wildly.

"Have I killed him?" she whispered hoarsely, and then I saw that she held in her hand the mace with which I had felled Mainwaring.

"I do not know how hard I struck," she went on, "but, but —" and then she trembled violently, as though she were filled with fear.

"Come," I cried, "there are friends in the castle-yard; we will go to them. But what is this?"

For at that moment there was the tramp of many feet, and I saw the Count of Mansfield enter, flushed and triumphant.

"Ah," he cried, "you have been busy, Sir Englishman. You have found one of the caged birds — ay, and by the Mass you have dealt with the keepers of the cage. One against two. But you have not mastered them both single-handed?"

"Nay, not I," I cried. "But where is Granville?"

"He is even now paying loving attention to the other caged bird," laughed the Count. "Ay, but this hath been a night of joy. Never have I known a better fight, and by the Mass I have wiped off old scores against Hans of Hartz."

"Where is he?" I asked.

"Where he will be for many a day," replied the Count. "He hath need of a leech right badly," and again he laughed with glee. "But we must away from here," he continued, "and our fair prisoners must be taken to a safe hiding-place."

The Lady Elfrida came to me when he spoke thus, as though I were her natural protector.

"Yes, take me away with you, and that with all quickness," she said; and I saw how much she was wrought upon. "Rotha and I will never forget to our dying day what we have suffered here. You say she is safe and well?" she continued, turning to the Count of Mansfield.

"Ay, safe and well," laughed the Count; and then he turned to Dudley and Mainwaring, both of whom showed signs of returning consciousness. "But let us away," he cried. "These dogs will be able to bite again soon, and I am not one who can kill in cold blood, and this night's work hath left enough blood on my head without shedding more."

"Yes, let us away," repeated the Lady Elfrida with a shudder. "I ought to be glad I did not kill him, and yet I am not."

Ere long we had left the Castle of Hartz behind us, having done the work we had set out to do. Yet did we not do it without the loss of many lives on both sides, for although none of the leaders was slain, many of the Count of Mansfield's soldiers never returned, while some were maimed for life. As to how many of the Count von Hartz's soldiers fell, never to rise again, that night, I have no knowledge even to this day.

"It will not be safe for these ladies to go to Mansfield," said the Count when we were well away from the castle. "They had better go to Wartburg, for there, as I know, both of them will receive a glad welcome."

"Is it your will that we go to Wartburg?" I said to the Lady Elfrida, for at that moment we rode side by side.

"Since it is not your will to take me to England," she said in a tone which I could not understand.

"Would you go to England?" I asked. "Is it your desire that I shall take you thither?"

"Will you take me if it is?" was her answer.

"Ay," I replied. "If you would go of your own free will and because it is the desire of your heart, then it is my duty to take you thither. But I will not if you consent only because you think you will advantage me thereby."

"But did you not come from England to Germany for that purpose? Was not that the mission on which you were sent?" And I again wondered at the tone in which she asked the question.

"I ought not to have told you of my mission," I replied. "Nevertheless, if it is in your heart to obey the King's will, I will even do as you say. For it hath become the one desire of my heart to serve you."

"And if I will not go to England," she said, "is it your purpose still to remain in Germany?"

"When I have taken you to a place of safety, I shall return to Wittenberg," I made answer.

On this I told her of what had taken place at Wittenberg, and of how I had learned to love the man of whom all Germany was talking.

"It may be that some time I shall desire to go to England," she said, "but not now, not yet," and I heard her voice tremble as she spoke.

"I trust you did not suffer much at the — the place from which you have come."

This I said clumsily, and yet I did not know how to express my thoughts better.

"They offered you no violence, did they?" I went on. "That is, they treated you not unkindly?"

"Count von Hartz gave us the chambers his mother used when she was alive," she replied presently, "and in a way tried to be kind. That is, he allowed our own tiring women to tend us. Yet each day was made terrible, seeing that both he and the Englishman came, and tried first by soft words and then by threats to make us consent to the coming of a priest to be wedded to them. But let us not speak of that now. When I think of it I wish that I had killed the Englishman as you struggled with him this night. I will give God thanks every day of my life that He led you to us. May He ever protect you and give you joy, Master Hamilton."

At this I had great difficulty in keeping myself from speaking words of love, for my heart was all aflame. And surely this was not to be wondered at, for had she not been saved from what to her was worse than death, and did she not ride by my side and speak kind words to me? Perhaps, too, I should have spoken them but for the remembrance of the King's command, which came to me then, for, as I knew, she thought of me with great kindness, and her heart was full of gratitude. I minded not the men-at-arms who were near, I heeded not the Count, who rode close by with David Granville and the Lady Rotha von Hutten, and I was filled with a great longing to tell her of all I felt for her. But the thought of the King's command put a weight on my tongue. Even now I felt that I had betrayed my trust, for had I put the desires of my King first, I had accepted her consent to go with me to England, and should not have returned to Wittenberg a second time.

As it was, I said not a word. Moreover, at that moment the Lady Rotha came up to her friend's side.

And here I feel I have told my story badly, for I have said not a word of what befell David Granville after we became separated in the castle, neither have I told how he found the Lady Rotha. But that is another tale, as the story-tellers say; and in truth so selfish was I in love for the lady who had become all the world to me that I paid little heed as to what happened to him. Enough that they were safe together, and that David's voice became as merry as that of a boy again.

I will say nothing here of our journey to Wartburg, nor of the welcome which we received there, for it does not form an important part of my story. Neither, indeed, do I love to think of it, for no sooner had we arrived than I bade good-bye to the Lady Elfrida, and I saw her not once during the hours I remained in the castle. Of this both David Granville and I were assured, however: No man could harm those whom we loved while they remained there. The castle stands upon a mountain, and in such a position that a few men could defy an army. Moreover, the Lady Elfrida found friends there, and so, at the Count of Mansfield's request, I returned with him to his castle with all speed.

"I dare not stay away from my stronghold," he said, "for Hans of Hartz is not dead, and he will not rest until he seeks to have his revenge."

And so we returned to Mansfield, where the Count would have had me be his guest for many months, but to this I could not consent, for I remembered my promise to Dr. Martin Luther, the monk of Wittenberg, whose dangers, I was informed, increased daily. Moreover, much as I would have liked to have stayed with the Count of Mansfield, my heart went out to the little monk who was fighting such a mighty battle, and I longed to be at his side.

No great space of time elapsed, therefore, from the time I left Wittenberg before I returned thither again. But David Granville did not go with me — he remained at Mansfield; and this, I believe, was because Mansfield was nearer to Wartburg than was Wittenberg, and because he hoped to win the Lady Rotha as his bride. But I had no hope in my heart. I dared not return to England without the woman I loved, and if I took her thither it would only be that she should be wedded to one of the King's favorites.

When I entered Wittenberg the third time, I found that the whole town was in great sorrow, for, as everyone said, Martin Luther's death warrant had just been signed.

"But it must be signed by the Elector, surely?" I cried to the first man who gave me this news.

"Nay," was the reply, "but it hath been signed by the Emperor himself, seeing he hath summoned Dr. Luther to the great Diet at Worms, where he will have to answer him and all the Churchmen who will come together to judge him for what he hath dared to do."

CHAPTER XXVII

THE friends of Dr. Martin Luther were gathered with
him in council when at length I found my way into his
presence. The monk, I thought, looked even more worn
than ever, but the brightness of his eyes had not dimmed
one whit, neither were the lines of stern resolution
around his mouth in any degree lessened. In truth he
looked like a lion at bay, even although his friends were
all around him.

"Is all well, my son?" he said as he saw me.

"All is well," I made answer.

"May God be praised. Truly is the Lord on the side
of righteousness, and although sorrow may endure for
the night, joy surely cometh in the morning."

"I have but just returned to Wittenberg, yet have I
heard sad news since I came. I trust I have been misin-
formed." This I said in the hope that he would be able
to put some brighter color on the dread news I had
heard.

"Alack, no," said the sub-prior; "that is, if you have
been informed that Brother Martin hath been summoned by the Emperor to appear before the Diet at
Worms. Truly it is a death warrant, and we have
nearly all of us joined in trying to persuade him not
to go."

"He will not have a single friend in the Diet save
the Elector Frederick," said the old professor who had
lit the faggots on the day when Dr. Luther burned the
Pope's Bull. "Every man save one will be his enemy.
The Emperor, God save his soul, is but a gluttonous
boy, who dares do naught but what the Church tells
him, yet is he ruler of more than half of Europe. The

Archbishop of Mayence and Cardinal Cajetan, together
with all the churchmen who hate Brother Martin's writings will be there. Ambassadors from nearly all the
Courts of Europe will be present, and there is not one
of them but will seek to crush him. If he goes there
will be but two alternatives before him. Either he will
have to recant every word he hath written which is
contrary to the teachings of the Church, and submit
himself unreservedly to the Pope; or he will be taken
and sent bound to Rome. And the Pope will have no
mercy on him; he will treat him as Huss was treated."

"And if he does not go to the Diet?" I asked.

"Ay, Master Hamilton," cried Martin Luther, starting to his feet and his eyes flashing, "you have put
your finger on the pulse of the whole question. What
if he doth not? Everything lies there. Not a man in
Germany but will say that the little monk is a windbag.
That his doctrines will not stand the fire. That his
words are but the braying of an ass. Then will all I
have done all these years be destroyed. The old lies
and the old corruption will be triumphant. True religion
will die out, and the souls of millions will be destroyed.
The enemies of God's truth will rejoice, the Sword of
the Lord will be buried in mountains of lies, and Europe
will lie in chains as it hath been lying. Ay, it seems like
vain boasting to talk of myself as of so much importance,
yet doth it seem that the Lord hath need of me. Poor
as I am, feeble as I am, it seemeth as though the welfare
of religion under God depends on whether I am strong
enough to trust in God or whether I shall hide myself
like a coward."

"But you could go to France," said the sub-prior;
"freer opinions are welcomed there."

"Nay," cried Luther, "I am a German, and in Germany I must do my work. Have not Germans boasted
that they fear God and naught else? And shall I take
the post where there is least danger. Nay, as God is
in heaven I will go to Worms. The people need me,
and, although I say it with fear and trembling, it is
true, God hath need of me."

My heart grew warm as he spoke. Indeed, I thought

then as I think now, that no braver heart lived in the
world at that time than that of Martin Luther. Rough
of speech he undoubtedly was, and that he hath made
many mistakes I do not deny, but standing there that
day I felt that here was a man who could lead armies
to battle, ay, and to victory.

"The truth is," continued the monk, "up to now I
have not been faithful. I have been a coward."

"Thou a coward!" cried the sub-prior.

"Ay," answered Luther, "to my shame I confess it.
I have addressed the Pope in such language that when
the story of this battle is written men will call me a
time-server and a sycophant. I have used honeyed words
to that Antichrist at Rome. I have admitted Romish
teachings which are as false as hell. I have paid homage
to that which I despise. I have been like a dog who
whined because he was afraid of a whipping. When I
think of one of the letters I wrote to Leo, I grow hot
and cold by turns. I am ashamed of it, for it was not
the letter which my heart dictated, but it was dictated
by a false fear, and a desire to serve both God and
Mammon. But that tune hath ended. I will no longer
fight with a sheathed sword, but a naked one. I will
go to Worms, then, and if God gives me life I will rest
neither day nor night till Antichrist is destroyed in our
land."

"Besides, the Emperor hath sent a safe conduct," said
Philip Melanchthon.

"I trust not in that," cried Luther. "I remember
that John Huss had a safe conduct when he was summoned to Constance, yet did Antichrist command him to
be burned. Ay, and he was burned."

"Then in what do you trust?" asked Melanchthon.

"In the justice of the Lord of Hosts and in His
might," cried Luther. "Nay, Father and Brothers, do
not seek to dissuade me. My mind is made up. I shall
stand alone, but because I stand on God's truth and they
on a devil's lie, I shall be stronger than they all."

After that preparations were made for Luther to proceed without undue delay to the great Diet of Worms,
and although in my heart of hearts I rejoiced, yet did

19

I not entertain a single hope that he would return alive.

As may be imagined, I determined to remain near him while he remained at Wittenberg, and to go to Worms with him when he started on his journey. Even yet I did not understand all his doctrines, neither, for that matter, do I understand them now, but I felt he was fighting God's battle, that he was breaking the fetters of those who were in slavery, and more, I loved him with a great love, greater, indeed, than anyone on earth save the one whom I loved with a love that was hopeless, and yet which filled my whole life.

At length the day came when Luther was to start on his journey to Worms. He had expected to walk thither, even as he had walked to Augsberg to appear before the Cardinal Cajetan, but on this journey he fared better, for the town authorities had built a covered car for him and had made it as comfortable as they could. Here he was able to place some of the books he loved, and thus would he be able to read on his journey.

I think the whole town of Wittenberg turned out to see the monk depart. The Imperial herald, wearing his black robe of office, was there, and he led the procession out of the town. Next came Luther in his cart, by the side of which were some of his chosen friends. After the cart came the professors of the university, and then followed a great multitude, most of whom were weeping bitterly.

"He is going to his death."

"Nay, God will not yet let him die."

"But the Pope hath sworn to crush him."

"God is stronger than ten thousand Popes. The best of the Popes are only the breath of His nostrils."

"Ay, but Dr. Luther hath made religion new to thousands. Our Lord Christ hath been revealed to us as a real Savior to me. And I never knew Him till Dr. Luther preached the gospel to me."

"Thousands can say that, but I fear me we shall never see him again. He is going to his death."

"We must all pray for him."

"Ay, and we will."

Thus the people talked as we slowly marched out

of the town. I rode on horseback close by the cart, and I noted the look in the monk's eyes. Full of longing and wonder it was, but no sign of fear was there.

"If my enemies kill me, Philip," he had said to Melanchthon when they parted, "do you carry on my work. If you survive, my death will not be of consequence. That is, if I die true to the faith I have preached."

As we passed near the place where Luther had thrown the Pope's Bull into the fire he caused the cart to stop.

"Yes," he said, "I did right — I did right. God was with me that day."

The cart rumbled through the Elster gate.

"Luther forever!" shouted a large number of the crowd.

At this Luther stopped the cart again.

"No, my children," he said, "not Luther forever, but Christ forever!"

He looked yearningly at the great multitude, and seemed too overcome to speak. But presently his voice rang out clear and resonant.

"God be with you, my children," he said. "Pray for me, but do not fear for me. Whether I live or whether I die, it doth not matter as long as I am true to God. As for you, do you be faithful to the doctrines I have proclaimed to you. God be with you."

The cart rumbled on.

It is not my purpose to describe that journey to Worms, although it was crowded with incidents of interest. Indeed, to tell of all that took place on the way would be to write as much as I have already written. At Leipsic he was received but coldly; at Naunberg an old priest showed him the portrait of Jerome Savonarola, whose body was burned in Florence by the order of Pope Alexander VI for preaching doctrines of which the Church did not approve.

Luther smiled as the old priest held up the picture. "It was Satan's work," said he, speaking of Savonarola's death.

"Stand firmly by God and God will stand firmly by thee," said the priest.

At Weimar the town was in great excitement because of the proclamation of the Emperor's condemnation of Luther, but Luther only said:

"Let us on in God's name."

When we came to Erfurt, where Dr. Luther had been a student, and where he had taken a monk's vows, one might have thought that he was a conquering king. A troop of horsemen met us, and followed by a shouting multitude we marched into the city. Here we spent some time, and here Luther preached to great multitudes.

But if his entrance into Erfurt was triumphant, it was naught to his departure, so great were the crowds that thronged his cart. And yet many feared for him, for all knew that the Pope's hand was mighty.

"Ah," said one, "there are so many bishops and cardinals in Worms! They will burn you as they did John Huss!"

"Listen," said Luther, his eyes flashing; "though they should kindle a fire all the way from Worms to Wittenberg, the flames of which reached to heaven, I would walk through it in the name of the Lord; I would appear before them; I would enter the jaws of this behemoth and break his teeth, confessing the Lord Jesus Christ."

Day by day we went on until we came to Eisenach, and there our hearts well-nigh failed us, for there Dr. Luther was taken with a terrible illness; but although he could barely sit up in the cart, yet would he have no delay.

"The Lord hath need of me," he said solemnly, "poor and humble though I am."

And so the journey proceeded. Sometimes only a few accompanied us, and then again, as we were a few miles from a town, a great crowd came out to meet us.

"Do not fail us, Dr. Luther," was the cry oft repeated, "all our hopes are in you!"

"Nay, not in me, the Lord Christ liveth! Yet, God helping me, I will not fail," was his reply.

At length we reached the town of Oppenheim, which is but twenty miles from Worms, and here Luther's purpose was tested as it had never been tested before. For, as we learned afterward, a plot was hatched with the purpose of keeping him out of Worms. Near to Oppenheim is a castle owned by one Francis of Sickingen, and the monk's enemies in Worms conveyed to Francis of Sickingen, who somewhat favored Luther's doctrines, the news, seemingly by friends, that only death waited him at Worms, and besought the knight to offer Luther an asylum at his castle.

Now the subtlety of this will appear when it is explained that Luther's safe conduct expired a few days after he had reached Oppenheim; and thus, if Sickingen could persuade him to stay at his castle for that space of time, then the Emperor's safe conduct having expired, he would be completely in the power of his enemies.

But there was also another device put forward to urge Luther to accept Francis of Sickingen's offer of a refuge at his castle, and this was to the effect that the Emperor's own confessor was sent to Sickingen's castle for the purpose of making terms with the monk.

When, therefore, we came to Oppenheim, and as we were proceeding along the street, a troop of horsemen met us, headed by a man whom Luther had known in Heidelberg.

"Death waits for you in Worms," he cried; "do not go there. Besides, there is no need. Francis of Sickingen offers you refuge, and besides the Emperor hath sent his own confessor to the castle that all your troubles may be removed."

"Death at Worms," repeated Luther quietly.

"Ay, death. · There is no hope for you there. Besides, the Emperor's confessor —"

It seemed as though the monk's eyes had penetrated the plausible statements he had heard.

"If the Emperor's confessor hath aught to say to me he will find me at Worms," he interrupted. "I go whither I am summoned."

"You will not enter this refuge then? You will refuse to take advantage of the Emperor's goodness of heart?"

" The Emperor hath sent for me to Worms to answer before my judges for what I have said and done," replied the monk quietly. " I obey orders. Let us go on."

But the cart had scarcely been set in motion again when a messenger came from one whom Luther greatly respected and loved, and to whom he owed much light on the gospel. His name was Spalatin.

" What will you? " said the monk, and I thought I noted a tone of impatience in his voice.

" My master hath sent me to say that he hath it on good authority, that the Emperor's safe conduct will not be respected at Worms, and that you will be cast into prison and to death without trial."

" Your master, Spalatin, saith that, doth he? " said Luther.

" Ay, that he doth, and he besought me, as you long for the spread of the Kingdom of God, to come no farther."

I watched his face as the man gave his message, and then I noted that his eyes burned with that same red light which I had seen when he read the Pope's Bull.

" Go and tell your master that even should there be as many devils in Worms as there are tiles upon the roofs of the houses, still I would go there."

It was like the battle-cry of a great general, and many standing by gave a great shout at his words. His friends were full of fear, but he was not, and his words put life into the hearts even of the most fearful. For strong and great as they are in our own language, they sounded stronger in German, spoken as he spoke them.

He was sitting in the cart, I remember, at the time, and he rose to his feet as he spoke, stretching his right hand toward the city of Worms. Moreover he spoke not as he spoke with the schoolmen, but more as Martin Luther, son of Hans Luther, the miner's son. Something of the roughness of the peasant's manner of speech I heard, and his voice was deep and sonorous.

" *Wenn so viel Teufel zu Worms wären, als Zeegel auf den Dächern noch wollt Ich hinein.*" [1]

[1] There is a stone slab in the main street of Oppenheim which marks the place where Luther uttered these words.

After that no man bade him desist. He had made up his mind to go to Worms, and to Worms he would go. It was about nine o'clock in the morning of an April day, I remember, in the year 1521. The birds were singing in the tree branches, and we could, in the morning sunlight, see the River Rhine coiling its way along the broad, marshy valley. For the neighborhood of the city of Worms is not beautiful. It is flat and uninteresting, even although away in the distance the mountains rise up grandly. Still, had not such momentous issues rested on our journey, I think I could have found pleasure in the journey from Oppenheim to Worms. The air was soft and balmy, the sun shone brightly, the birds were singing gaily, and there seemed something in the bursting of the new life everywhere which made one's heart rejoice.

We had gone scarcely half the way from Oppenheim to Worms, when many of the people from that city came to meet us.

"Look," I heard them cry, "Luther is coming!" And they thronged around the cart to look at the face of the man who, standing alone, dared to defy the ruler of Christendom.

"Great God, give me strength," I heard him pray as, looking over the sea of eager, earnest faces, his lips trembled.

When we entered the gateway of the city there seemed scarce room for a man to move. The people thronged everywhere. Not only in the streets and at every window, but on the roofs of the houses they sat, each and all eager to see the man who was fighting for the liberty of the nations.

For this I found: although many denied his doctrines and declared that he was doing the devil's work in denying what for ages had been obeyed, all admired his courage.

"He may be a heretic, but he is a brave man," I heard men say again and again, as, amidst the thronging multitude, some pouring forth maledictions and more uttering blessings, the monk sat, now giving a smile to

the people, but more often looking straight on like one
trying to read the future.

How many people had gathered in Worms I know
not, but there were many thousands from various parts
of the country.   So many were there that thousands had
to sleep in the streets, while there was not a village for
miles around but gave shelter to those who had come
from afar to see the monk who was shaking the nation
to its very foundation.

No man dared to prophesy what the upshot of the
whole business would be.   Luther had defied all existing
powers.   He had attacked not only the Pope's emissaries,
but the Pope himself.   He had declared that the Church
of Christ had been made filthy, not only in act but in
doctrines, that the lives of thousands of the clergy,
from the highest to the lowest, were a byword and a
shame, and that their doctrines bore not the slightest
resemblance to the doctrines of Christ.   He had resisted
all appeals, and instead of repenting of what the Church
called his heresy, he had grown more and more pronounced in it.   He had hurled his defiance at Rome when
he had sent out his appeal for a general council; he had
thrown down his gauntlet to the world when he had
taken the Bull of His Holiness the Pope and had burned
it before the assembled multitude.   At first he had no
thought of going so far, but the curses of the Church
had led him to look into the claims and credentials of
the Church, and now he declared that it must be reformed from the very foundations.   He had appealed
to all classes.   He had met the schoolmen in debate, he
had sent out his books in the language of the people,
and these books were read by every man who could
read, while those who could not read listened eagerly
to those who could.   Moreover, what angered Luther's
enemies so much was the fact, which even Erasmus
testified aloud, that the intelligent and the best living
people were on Luther's side.

And now he had come to Worms to appear before
the Emperor and the greatest Court in the world to
answer for all he had done.   If Luther was wrong he
was guilty of the greatest sins,   He had disturbed the

mind of the nation. Vast multitudes no longer believed
in the Roman Church or the Pope's claims. During
the last three years a new spirit had come over the
country. Men claimed to be free to read the Bible for
themselves, and to interpret its teaching. They had
come to see that it was deeper than a mere matter of doctrine. It resolved itself into a question as to whether
they should be free or enslaved, whether they should
be dragged at the heels of a Roman hierarchy or whether
they should march erect according to the powers which
God had given them.

What would Charles V and the other judges do?
Would the Emperor treat the safe conduct as Sigis-
mund had treated that of John Huss? Would Luther
recant when he was brought before such an august
tribunal? And, if he did not, what would become of
him? These were the questions which filled the minds
of the people as the monk was dragged along in his
cart through the crowded streets of the city.

It seems wonderful to me now as I reflect. All this
vast multitude came there not to see the Emperor or
the princes, but to see a poor monk, a miner's son, who
had dared to boldly proclaim what at heart he believed
to be true.

Lodgings had been prepared for Luther at an inn,
and thither, after much difficulty, we repaired.

"Brian, my son," said the monk when at length we
had got away from the surging crowds, "you have been
a great joy to me. I little thought that a stranger and
an Englishman would have been such a tried friend. I
have had many friends who have loved me, but none
who has given me more heart to go on than you. When
the others have bidden me play the coward's part you
have urged me to go on. Are all Englishmen like
you?"

"The English love truth — ay, and they love a brave
man," I replied.

"Then will the English embrace the truth of God
and cast off Antichrist," he made answer. "For while
we were passing through the multitude a while since, I
saw a vision. I saw that, whether I lived or whether I

died, the truth would go on. What will happen to me I know not. They may kill Martin Luther, but they cannot kill the truth he hath proclaimed. For in my vision I did see this. I saw men of all nations rising up and breaking the bonds by which they were bound. Then was my heart made glad, and I knew that I should praise God for His mercy whether I live or die. And now, my son, I would be alone, for I need time for prayer that I may even gain strength for my work."

He had scarcely said this when there was great commotion in the inn, and a little later a messenger appeared from the Emperor.

"I would see Martin Luther," said the messenger.

"I am Martin Luther," said the monk, standing erect before him in his friar's frock.

"You are commanded before the Emperor to-morrow afternoon at the Archbishop's palace [1] to answer the charges which have been made against you."

"God's will be done," murmured Luther. Aloud he said, "I will obey the summons," and his voice faltered not one whit.

[1] Some historians maintain that the Diet of Worms was held in the town hall, but it is now generally agreed that it was in the great hall of the Archbishop's palace. This building was destroyed during the wars with France in the time of Louis XIV.

CHAPTER XXVIII

THE MONK AND THE EMPEROR

THAT night, Dr. Luther was kept from his bed until a late hour by the many who came to see him. Not only did his friends come to try and give him a word of comfort, but even those who wished his downfall gained admittance " to see," as they put it, " how he would comport himself."

One of these, a knight of some renown, spoke to me afterward. " I thought to find a different man," he said. " He hath been spoken of to me as one who is partly a snarling cur and partly a bag of wind. But in truth I find him to be a good fellow. He laughs at a good joke, but he makes no boasts. Nevertheless, there is a look in his eye which proclaims him a brave man. Never did I see such courage at such a time."

And to this all agreed, even while some of his enemies declared that his courage was given to him by the devil.

It was past three o'clock of the next day, which was the 17th day of April in the year 1521, when we made our way to the Archbishop's palace, which is situated close to the cathedral; but so great was the populace that we could make no headway whatever. Indeed, I was in doubt at one time whether we should ever reach the Emperor's presence. But those who came to conduct Dr. Luther to his trial led the way through some narrow passages, and from thence through some gardens, till at length we reached the entrance of the hall. As I looked around me I saw that not only was every inch of ground covered with people, but the housetops were black with people who had climbed thither.

So crowded were the doors of the hall that the people had to be driven back by soldiers' pikes. Thousands of people had gathered into the antechambers and embrasures of the windows, but no man spoke a word as Luther walked along the passage which led to the great Council Chamber, where the Emperor and the other judges had gathered. At the door of this chamber stood an old knight in armor, who I afterward learned was George of Freundsberg, one of the greatest of the German generals.

As Luther came to the door the old knight placed his gauntleted hand on the monk's shoulder.

" Poor monk! poor monk! " he said. " Thou art now going to make a nobler stand than I or any other captains have ever made in the bloodiest of our battles! But, if thy cause is just, go forward in God's name! "

" Ay, in God's name," answered the monk.

It was by sheer good fortune that I gained admittance, and indeed had not Luther pleaded for me, I should never have seen and heard what I shall never forget to my dying day.

I have been told since that no man ever appeared before such a tribunal, but concerning that I cannot speak with certainty. This I know: two hundred and four persons were among Luther's judges that day. For not only was the Emperor Charles V there, with his brother, the Archduke Ferdinand, there were also six electors, twenty-four dukes, among whom was the Duke of Alva, and a great number of margraves, archbishops and abbots, together with ambassadors from almost every Court in Europe.

In truth, I was well-nigh stunned with such an array of power and greatness. The Emperor sat in the center of three circles of chairs on a temporary throne, while all around him were judges of high degree. Not that the Emperor himself impressed me greatly. He was but an unhealthy-looking boy in appearance, and there were blotches upon his skin as if by over-eating. His brow was small and his lips thick and sensual, while his eyes, as I thought, had no brightness.

A deathly silence prevailed when at length Luther reached an open space in front of the Emperor's throne.

All eyes were turned upon him. The spectators forgot the brave array of judges, and thought only of the one solitary man who stood before them to be judged. As for the monk, he seemed, first of all, to be dazzled by what he saw, but only for a moment. He stood erect, his eyes burning with that ruddy glare which I had seen more than once before.

Three minutes afterward my heart was like lead, for it seemed to me that Luther's enemies were right and that he had turned coward!

And this was what troubled me. Close by Luther's side was a pile of books, but Luther paid no heed to them! he was looking steadily at the face of the Emperor, who was also studying the monk.

"Martin Luther," said a voice, "his sacred and invincible majesty has commanded your presence here to answer certain questions.

"First," pointing to the pile of books, "do you acknowledge that these books were written by you? Second, are you prepared to retract these books and their contents?"

"Let me hear their titles read," answered the monk.

After the titles were enumerated a dead silence again prevailed, and Luther gave his answer. He admitted that the books were his, and as to the question as to whether he would retract them or not, he required time to consider.

I say my heart sunk like lead at this, especially when I heard his enemies give a laugh of satisfaction. The question was simple, and yet it lay at the crux of the whole situation. What need had he of time to consider what had been before him for months?

"It is a sign of weakness. He will recant."

"He is nothing but a wind-bag, after all."

"He fears the fire."

"The presence of the Emperor hath frighted him!"

Such words I heard on all hands.

"Certainly this fellow will never make a heretic of me," said the Emperor aloud, and I saw the sneering smile that came on his thick, sensual lips.

I saw the Emperor hold converse with certain nobles who were near him, and then the Chancellor of Trèves spoke aloud.

"Martin Luther," he said, "his Imperial Majesty of his natural goodness is willing to grant you another day, but under condition that you make your reply *viva voce*, and not in writing."

The Diet broke up for that day, and there were very few but who believed that the man who had spoken so boldly at Wittenberg had become a coward at Worms.

That night the city of Worms was in an uproar. Fighting and bloodshed were witnessed on every hand. The enemies of Luther fought against those who still believed in him. But for the large number of soldiers in the city the whole of the city would have been in a riot.

As for myself, I mingled with the crowd with a sad heart. It seemed to me that all my hopes had come to naught. The man in whom I had believed and loved showed signs of cowardice. In order to buy his life he was willing to sell the truth. Presently I left the town and found myself near the river, and while standing there I felt a man's hand placed on my shoulder.

"You are an Englishman, and your name is Brian Hamilton?"

"Whoever told you that hath been rightly informed," I answered.

"You are a friend of the little monk?"

"Yes," I answered. "It is not your business, but seeing you have asked the question, I have given you my answer."

"Are you prepared to do aught for him?"

"Before I answer that I must know who you are and your right to ask the question."

"As to that, here is a scrap of paper which may suffice."

I took the piece of parchment he gave me and read the words I saw written.

"Do as this man bids you, as you love the truth and as you believe in David Granville."

"Where is the person whose name is written here?"
I asked.

"That is not for you to know," was the answer.
"The question is, will you obey the behest contained
here?"

I looked into the face of the man who spoke, and
saw a young German no older than myself.

"Yes," I said.

"Then be here to-morrow night at this hour, and
before you come bid good-bye to the monk. Tell no
man what you have heard. Be well armed, and have
your horse in readiness for a journey."

"Bid good-bye to the monk?" I queried.

"Yes, and in bidding him good-bye tell him to fear
naught. You have promised."

He left me without a word, and was quickly lost in
the shadows of the evening, while I found my way back
to the inn where Martin Luther was staying.

To my surprise, I found him calm and cheerful. He
seemed very weary, however, and spoke of going to rest
early.

I longed to ask him what he meant by asking for
delay before answering the question which had been put
to him, but I dared not; there was a look in his eyes
which forbade me. I think he understood what was in
my heart, however, for before he bade me good-night
he placed his hand on my shoulder and looked into my
eyes. "To-morrow will be a great day," he said, "and
only God knows what it will bring forth; but be of good
cheer, my son. Expect anything, expect everything save
that which is worst of all."

After he had gone to his bed-chamber I sat wondering what he meant by this, for the thing was not clear
to me. My heart was very heavy, I remember, especially
as his friends who had gathered in the room had seemed
to have lost faith and hope altogether. In all they said
they spoke of what the Pope and the bishops would do
when Luther was silenced, and seemed to have no hope
that he would stand by the books he had written.

"Perhaps it is too much to expect," said one. "How
can a poor monk defy the world?"

"Ay, but John Huss did, and so did the Monk of Florence," said another.

"Ah, well, perhaps he will be bolder than we fear. He seems to have a merry heart to-night."

So they spoke, while I mused over all I had seen and heard that day. I determined not to leave the room, but to sit awake all night, so that I might, if need be, defend him from harm. This I did bearing in mind all the threats I had heard against him. In spite of my determination, however, I fell asleep, and it was much past midnight when I was awoke with a start by the sound of the great cathedral bell in the near distance. When the sound of the bell died away I heard someone speaking in Dr. Luther's chamber; so, fearing enemies were there, I crept close to the door. But I did not enter. It was not an enemy's voice that I heard, but his own. Luther was at prayer, and as I listened my heart was strangely lifted up. I will not write down all I remember, yet, because a man's real nature is more truly revealed in his private devotions, I will set down something of what I heard, especially the words which appealed to me most.

"Lord! where stayest Thou? Come, come, I am ready! I am ready to lay down my life for Thy truth. For the cause is Thine, not mine! I will never separate myself from Thee! And though the world should be filled with devils, though my body should be cut in pieces, my soul is Thine! Yea, Thy word is my assurance of it! My soul belongs to Thee; it shall abide in Thee forever! Oh, God, help me! Amen!"

I would have given much to have seen his face as he prayed, but I did not, for I dared not enter his presence. Yet was my heart greatly comforted, and from that time I had no fears. I knew now that no coward's fear filled his heart, and that whatever the future would bring forth, he would act as became a brave man.

The next morning, as I took my walks through the city, I saw three men in front of me whose figures struck me as strangely familiar. Although I knew not where, I felt sure I had seen them before, and this happening in an unknown city caused me to follow them watchfully. Presently one of them turned his head, and I saw the face of Mainwaring. I thought he looked somewhat pale, yet did he walk upright and with a jaunty step. I did not doubt who the others were, and I wondered what brought Dudley and Hans von Hartz and Mainwaring to Worms. It might be that they had come out of curiosity, as thousands of others had come, yet did I connect their presence with what befell me the previous evening. I knew David Granville's quick mind, and I knew that he was sure, even as I was, that these men were our enemies. More than once we had outwitted them, but they did not belong to the class which gives up easily.

I turned away quickly from them, so as not to be seen; nevertheless their presence gave me much food for thought.

In the afternoon I again made my way with Dr. Luther to the Archbishop's palace, and again we had great difficulty in getting thither. The multitude seemed to have increased rather than to have diminished. Indeed, we had to go through people's houses in order to get to the judgment hall. At length we gained our entrance, and again I stood amidst the great imposing assembly. The Emperor might not have moved from his seat since the previous day. He still sat in the same posture and the same half-cynical and half-indifferent smile was on his lips.

The trial was again opened by the Chancellor of the Elector of Trèves. He said:

" Martin Luther, yesterday you begged for a delay that hath now expired. Assuredly it ought not to have been conceded, as every man, and especially you, who are so great and learned a doctor in the Holy Scriptures, should always be ready to answer any question touching his faith. Now, therefore, reply to the question put by his Majesty, who has behaved with so much mildness: Will you defend your books as a whole, or are you ready to disavow some of them?"

These words he said first in German and then in Latin.

I watched the monk's face as the Archbishop spoke.

20

I saw him standing in an open space before the Emperor, and took note how calm he was. He looked first at the Emperor's face, and then cast his eyes along the benches filled by the other judges. At first there was much smiling and whispering among them, as though they discussed his recantation; but presently they lapsed into silence, and a look of eager expectancy rested upon their faces. A minute later the silence was so great that none seemed to dare to breathe, for the monk opened his mouth to speak.

His first words, I remember, were slow and deliberate, but presently they became more fervid. Yet he spoke quietly, never raving or shouting. Now and then I thought I detected lapses into his peasant mode of speech, but these lapses were rare. In the main he spoke as one of the most learned doctors of his age.

I would I could set down what he said; and yet, even if I did so, I could not convey to paper the tones of conviction, the power of the mighty personality behind the words he uttered. He admitted that the books were his; many of them, he said, were works of a devotional nature, to which no one could find objection. Concerning the books which bore on doctrine, it was possible, nay probable, that errors had crept in them, he being but an erring human being. If, therefore, it were proved to him by Holy Writ and clear reasoning, he would recant them, but not otherwise.

What I have here set down is simple enough, yet did he back all he said by such a weight of argument, by proofs from Scripture and from history, that every man was carried away, so that it seemed as though there were not a word to say against him. When men told me afterward that he spoke for well-nigh two hours, I scarce believed them, for of a truth it seemed but a few minutes.

Up to this time he had spoken in German, and when he had finished, the Emperor commanded that he should repeat what he had said in Latin. For a moment the monk seemed taken aback, but only for a moment, for he repeated his speech in Latin with as little difficulty as he had given it in German.

Looking around among the judges I saw that the Elector Frederick, perhaps the only friend that Luther had there, smiled as if with gladness when he changed his language in order to meet the Emperor's wishes.

When he had ceased for a second time the Chancellor of Trèves said indignantly: "You have not answered the question put to you. You were not summoned hither to call in question the decisions of councils. You are required to give a clear and precise answer. Will you or will you not retract?"

At this great silence again fell upon the assembly, and all eyes were turned toward the monk, whose life, as all felt, hung upon a thread.

"Since your Majesty demands a clear, simple, and precise answer," saith Luther, "I will give you one, and it is this: I cannot submit my faith either to the Pope or to the Councils, *because it is as clear as the day that they have frequently erred and contradicted each other.* Unless, therefore, I am convinced by the testimony of Scripture or by the clearest reasoning — unless I am persuaded by means of the passages I have quoted, and unless they thus render my conscience bound by the Word of God, *I cannot and I will not retract,* for it is unsafe for a Christian to speak against his conscience."

It was at this time, I believe, that the monk really understood what his words meant. He knew that he had defied the cherished traditions of nearly every one of his judges, that he had denied the teaching of the greatest power on earth.

He was very pale, I remember, in spite of the heat of the great hall and the excitement of the hour; and, indeed, it would have been no wonder if he felt afraid. He stood there alone in his monk's robe, his bare head and sandaled feet before the greatest tribunal ever known. He knew that he was helpless, powerless — he, Martin Luther, the miner's son, against the world.

But as he stood there I saw his face change, and the gleam I had noticed so often flashed from his eyes. He looked quietly around on the hushed assembly, which seemed too excited for words, and then he uttered the words which will remain in my memory even although

I live ten times the years allotted to man. I remember, too, that a thrill seemed to run through the assembly as we heard his voice ringing out clearly, sonorously over the hall:

"HERE I STAND. I CAN DO NO OTHER. MAY GOD HELP ME! AMEN!"[1]

It seemed as though he had flung down his challenge to the Emperor, and that he spoke not only to the Diet, but to the world, and that he spoke to the world the words that it longed to hear. Like the shout which I had heard at Wittenberg when he burned the Pope's Bull, it seemed to me that his words were echoed from land to land, and from continent to continent.

The air was full of excitement, the assembly seemed to be spellbound; indeed, no one spoke for, I should think, a minute. Then the Emperor said aloud to the Chancellor of Trèves: "This monk speaks with an intrepid heart and an unshaken courage."

His words seemed to break the spell of excitement, and the Chancellor of Trèves said:

"If you do not retract, the Emperor and the States of the Empire will consult what course to adopt against such an incorrigible heretic."

"May God be my helper," said Luther, "for I can retract nothing."

Of what happened after that I have no distinct remembrance. The orator of the Diet, I believe, harangued Luther concerning his naughtiness, but no one seemed to listen. The monk had seemed to have borne everything before him, so that, after much confusion, I can remember nothing with distinctness save that the Chancellor said: "The Diet will meet again to-morrow to hear the Emperor's opinion." The Emperor arose, and Luther left the hall.

Two Imperial officers kept guard over Luther as he walked out of the palace.

[1] "Hier stehe ich: Ich kann nich anders. Gott helfe mir. Amen."

"Are they taking you to prison, Doctor?" asked someone as he passed along.

"No, I am going to my inn," said Luther, and thither we walked together.

I wondered much at it then; I wonder at it still. This one man, in the strength of God, had won his battle against all who were arrayed against him. This monk, standing on the Word of God, was stronger than the Pope with all his power, temporal and spiritual. He had defied the powers of the world, and although scarce one of the great ones of the earth stood by his side, he had conquered. It seemed to me then, as it seems to me now, that God said: "I have need of Martin Luther, and Martin Luther shall live!"

When we reached the inn I spoke to him privately, and told him of what I had seen and heard the previous night and that morning.

"I like not the thought of leaving you," I said, when I had told him my story. "Yet methinks David Granville had a good reason for writing me."

"Was the handwriting his?" he asked quietly.

"Of that I am certain," I replied.

He remained for some time in thought.

"I know not what it may mean," he said presently, "yet am I sure that God is in it. He hath preserved me so far, and surely He is using you as a means to still preserve me. My heart is sad at the thought of your leaving me, yet is it His will that you should go."

I bade him good-bye as a son might take leave of his father, although he was not so many years older than myself. He kissed me on the brow and said,

"God go with thee, my son. I will pray for thee continuously."

My heart was sad as I made my way to the river's banks, yet did the faith of Martin Luther bear me up, for I felt no fear. I had barely reached the place where the young German had spoken to me the previous night when I felt my arm grasped.

"Brian, is it you? God be thanked, we meet again."

It was David Granville who spoke to me.

CHAPTER XXIX

THE RESCUE AND THE REFUGE

No one was with him, and in the dying light of that spring night I saw that he looked pale and agitated.

"Come, Brian," he said. "Dudley a l Mainwaring and Hans von Hartz are in Worms. We are not safe here. Let us away."

"Whither?" I asked.

"To a place where I will lead you. You trust me, do you not?"

I walked by his side away both from the city and from the river. He led the way quietly through a wood until at length we came to the gates of a large house, which was completely hidden from view till we were close to it.

A man started up suddenly.

"Password!" was his demand.

"*The Little Monk,*" said David, and we were admitted.

We had gone but a hundred yards when another man sprang into view.

"Password!" he also demanded.

"*Liberty,*" said David, and again we passed on.

When we reached the house two more men demanded a password.

"*The Word of God,*" replied David. The great door opened as if by magic, and we entered.

I saw that something important was in my friend's mind, and that he was acting according to a pre-arranged plan. Three different passwords were given at three stages of our journey, and each of them had obtained the right to go forward. I judged, too, that I was going among the friends of Luther. Each of the passwords, "The Little Monk," "Liberty," and "The

Word of God," seemed to be fraught with good meaning. Still, I was naturally anxious, for I had no knowledge of what was before me.

No sooner had I entered the house than I found myself in the midst of a number of men. Nearly all of them were young, and all of them were evidently men of quality. All turned their eyes toward me. One man, as I judged, was looked upon as a leader, for he sat on a place of prominence where all could see him.

"Is this the man?"

"This is the man," replied David.

"And I may speak freely?"

"He hath stood by the little monk for many days. He loves him with a great love. He loves liberty. He believes in the Word of God. But more, he has some of the best blood of England in his veins, and hath never been guilty of aught that could tarnish his name."

"It is well. Master Brian Hamilton, I am the Count Sickingen. For some time we, all of us German nobles, have watched the battle that hath been going on between the little monk of Wittenberg and the Church, and although we have not all agreed with his doctrines, we believe him to be an honest and a brave man. Is not that so?"

"Yes, yes," came from all over the room.

"For that reason we determined that he should be protected from his enemies, who have conceived a plot to kill him. This we did even after yesterday's meeting of the Diet, when many thought he would turn coward. That was why you were followed and spoken to. To-day many of us listened to his defense, and as we listened we were made converts to his faith. We are more than ever determined to protect him. Every good sword will be needed. May we count upon yours?"

"As upon your own, my lord," I replied.

"We do not know what may happen at to-morrow's Diet; but, whatever happens, we are determined to stand by the brave monk who stands by the Word of God. Will you stand by us?"

" As long as God gives me health," I answered, for there was a ring in his voice which stirred my heart.

After that the plans they had made were unfolded to me. These there is no need that I should set down, neither is it necessary that I should tell how what I told them concerning Dr. Luther's wishes led to their alteration. Enough that every man vowed to stand by the little monk, not only because they believed in his courage and honesty, but because his words that day had opened their eyes to the truth he taught.

Before we separated that night, each to do the work allotted to us, I asked David whether he knew aught of the Lady Elfrida. To this he answered no. She was under the protection of the Elector Frederick of Saxony, but he had been told that she had left the castle where we had left her months before. Of the Lady Rotha he said nothing, and I judged that his heart was sore because of what he had heard.

By the next night we heard of what had taken place at the third meeting of the Diet. The Emperor had issued his edict against the monk. He said that seeing a single monk, misled by his own folly, had risen against the faith of Christendom, he had determined, in order to stay such impiety, to sacrifice, if need be, his treasures, friends, and body, blood and soul. He concluded the edict in this fashion:

" I am about to dismiss the Augustine, Luther, forbidding him to cause the least disorder among the people. I shall then proceed against him and his adherents as contumacious heretics by excommunication, by interdict, and by every means calculated to destroy them."

This edict, I discovered, displeased many. First, because he did not consult the Diet before issuing it, and second, because Luther had by his defense made hosts of converts. Indeed, the whole city was in a ferment. Many there were who would have the Emperor regard his safe conduct as but waste parchment, and it was thought that but for the many nobles who had become Luther's friends he would have acted after this fashion,

Mediators were sent repeatedly to Luther in order to persuade him to obey the Emperor's dictates, and Luther's reply to Charles V. was caught up and printed, and was soon posted over the town.

"God, who is the searcher of all hearts, is my witness," it ran, "that I am ready to obey your Majesty in honor or dishonor, in life or in death, with no exception save the Word of God, whereby man lives. Where eternal interests are concerned God wills not that man should submit to man."

When the Archbishop of Trèves called upon him to retract what he had said concerning the Councils of Constance, he replied:

"I would rather lose my life than forsake the clear and true Word of God."

The result of all the negotiations which took place in Worms after the Diet was that Luther, still standing by what he had declared, received a visit from the Chancellor, who came straight from the Emperor.

"Martin Luther," said the Chancellor, "his Imperial Majesty having at sundry times and in various forms exhorted you to submission, but always in vain, the Emperor, in his capacity of advocate and defender of the Catholic faith, finds himself compelled to resort to other measures. He therefore commands you to return home in the space of twenty-one days, and forbids you to disturb the public peace by either preaching or writing on the road."

On hearing this Luther was silent for some time.

"This is the command of the Emperor?" he said at length.

"They are his own words," said the Chancellor.

"Then tell the Emperor this," said the monk. "I desire, and have ever desired, but one thing — a reformation of the Church according to Holy Scripture. I am ready to do and suffer everything in obedience to the Emperor's will, life or death, evil or good repute, with one reservation — the preaching of the gospel. Woe is me if I preach not the gospel."

"Is that your answer?" asked the Chancellor.

"God's will be done, it is."

"Then I cannot promise that the Emperor's safe conduct will be enforced."

When Count Sickingen heard of this, we who had vowed to defend Luther were called together, and a letter was sent to the Chancellor telling him that four hundred nobles who were in Worms were ready to enforce Luther's safe conduct at the point of the sword. The letter also suggested that it would be a sad day for the empire if Charles V., after his first Diet, was false to his word.

What effect this had I know not. This I know. Luther left Worms the next day in the same cart by which he entered the city, and a band of horsemen guarded it even as far as Oppenheim, above which the Count Sickingen's castle stands.

I heard afterward that in spite of the edict of the Emperor, Luther preached at Hirschfeldt by the invitation of the Prince Abbot of that town. Also, when he came to Eisenach, which is only three miles from Wartburg Castle, and the town where he had gone to school as a boy, he again preached to the assembled multitude; but I was not present on either of these occasions. The reason for this can be quickly told. I had discovered that a number of Luther's enemies had arranged to waylay him and carry him away to Italy with the purpose of sending him to Rome. When I told Count Sickingen of this I was ordered to the place where the attack was to take place with a number of nobles, so as to be ready to defend him.

"This I will gladly do, my lord," I said, "and I doubt not concerning my success. But is Dr. Luther to be then escorted to Wittenberg?"

"And why not?" asked the Count. "He will then be in Saxony, and under the dominion of the Elector Frederick, who is his friend."

"Perhaps you have not seen the latest command of the Emperor?" I said.

"What may it be?" he asked.

"It hath been conveyed to me by a trusty messenger, and is to be made known to the world at a time when the Emperor commands," I replied. "He hath commanded that at the expiration of his safe conduct Luther is to be regarded as the vilest of criminals. He is to be refused food and shelter. He is to be seized and put into prison until the Emperor's will be known."

" You are sure of this? "

For answer I gave him a copy of the Emperor's own words.

" Then his enemies have conquered, after all," said Count Sickingen. " Even if Hans of Hartz and your countrymen fail, the man is doomed."

" Unless some means of safety be devised," I replied.

" Can you think of aught? " he asked.

I told him what was in my mind, with a result which will presently be seen.

When we arrived at the Thuringian forests, we waited according to the orders which had been given me, for it was here that Hans of Hartz, with Dudley and many others, had planned to attack Luther and his escort. I learned, too, that strict commands were given that if they did not succeed in capturing the monk they must see to it that he was killed, for such was the will of those who employed them. For this reason we determined to attack them before they should have time to carry out their designs.

But here our plans were likely to miscarry. Although we reached our halting-place without mishap, we could discover no trace of the enemy. The great forests were silent and desolate, and although I took every precaution and sent out spies in all directions, we heard naught of them.

" Dudley is as cunning as the devil," said David Granville. " He hath found out our plans and hath devised other means of accomplishing his purposes."

" The party hath been promised a great reward for capturing the monk or taking his life, this I knew," I made answer, " and Dudley is not the man to forego so great a reward. Moreover, Dr. Luther is to pass along the road to Walterhausen this very night. I have also good knowledge that he cannot be attacked till he reaches the hollow near the church at Gilsbach."

"Then let us make our way to the hollow," cried David.

This we did with great caution. The night had fallen, and although the end of May had come it was somewhat dark because of the shadow of the pine trees. Beyond the cracking of a twig or a low murmur, we made no noise whatever, for the ground underneath our feet was soft, and I had given orders that our journey must be as silent as death.

We had barely reached the hollow of which I have spoken when we heard singing in the distance.

"That is Dr. Luther's voice," said one of the young German nobles who was with me.

"Ay, and I recognize the voice of Arnsdorff," whispered another.

He had scarcely spoken when we saw emerging from the other side of the valley on to an open space a number of armed men. It was evident that they also had heard the voices of the singers.

Their coming was so sudden and unlooked for that we did not move, even although we had but little doubt who they were; and even as we watched them the voices of the singers came upon us on the evening air. The hymn they sang was in Latin, and the words seemed so full of meaning that I set it down here in English: —

> "The man that's resolute and just,
> Firm to his principles and trust,
> Nor hopes nor fears can bind;
> Nor parties, for revenge engaged,
> Nor threatenings of a Court enraged,
> Can shake his steady mind."

The men on the other side of the valley listened as we were listening, but when the singers came to the words:

> "Non vultus instantis tyranni
> Mente quatit solida . . ."

I heard the voice of Dudley. "Let us stop their cater-wauling," he said. "Methinks the little monk will sing another kind of hymn before we have done with him."

They were a party of at least twenty men, armed as

for battle, and I knew that what was done must be done quickly.

"Block their passage down the valley," I cried, and then, as it seemed to me, before one had time to count fifty, swords were clashing.

The thing was done so suddenly that the fight was conducted with but little method. Each swordsman found his man, and each fought with a determination to conquer.

I had but little difficulty in my first encounter. The man not only slipped his foot on a smooth stone, and thus might complain of ill luck, but he was a weak swordsman in any case, and I take no credit for having despatched him easily. Scarcely had he fallen, however, when I was attacked with great fury from another quarter.

"Ay, my English bantam," said Dudley's voice, "and so we meet again. This time you shall not have a lady's help."

"Neither shall you have mercy from me," I cried.

"I do not need it, thanks to our Blessed Lady," he answered with a laugh. "And I must e'en despatch you quickly, for the sweet Lady Elfrida waits for me at a certain castle we wot of, and together we will laugh at the end of Brian Hamilton's mission."

He fought as coolly as if we played with sticks, and spoke as carelessly as though naught depended on the fight; the clashing of twoscore of swords seemed not to trouble him one whit.

But those were Dudley's last words, for the fight became a mêlée, and the moment I had disarmed him the sword of a young German baron fell upon his head and found its way into his brain. Three minutes more those of our enemies who were unharmed fled to the forests.

So quickly was the fight over that I doubt whether the singers in the cart knew aught of it; indeed, such an easy victory did we win that I began to think that the enemy had some ruse in flying from us.

"The six horses!" I cried. "Waste not a moment."

A few minutes later five of us met the cart wherein

Luther sat. I seized the monk without a word of warning, and before he had time to defend himself.

"Fear nothing," I whispered in his ear; "I am Brian Hamilton."

"God's name be praised," he said. "But what will you, my son?"

"You will know all soon," I replied. "Meanwhile all that we do is necessary."

He mounted the horse we provided for him, and we rode away into the night. Hour after hour we journeyed, until at length we came to a great castle situated on the top of a high hill. Morning was breaking.

"Methinks I know this country-side," said Luther, gazing around. "This is Wartburg Castle."

"You know it well," I replied.

"Ay," he said slowly, "the Lord is a strong fortress."

A few minutes later Dr. Luther was ushered into a room of the castle, while I was welcomed by Count Sickingen, who had made ready for our coming.

An hour later I stood on the walls of the castle, looking over the great range of forest-covered hills, and on the town of Eisenach, which lay in the valley three miles beneath. Whether it was because I was suffering from a reaction after the excitement of the night I know not, but it seemed to me that my work in Germany was done. Martin Luther was taken to a place of safety, and none but myself and a few others knew where he was. Here he was to remain until the Emperor's commands concerning him had been withdrawn, or things had become so changed that he could defy the imperial power. I could do naught more for him.

As for the Lady Elfrida, I had been told that she had been taken away from Wartburg Castle, but I knew not whither she had gone. She had told me that if ever she needed me she would send for me, but since that day I had heard nothing from her. Not a word did I hear at Wittenberg, and no message or token had followed me to Worms telling me that she ever thought of me. I longed to go back to England, but I dared not go. The King had bidden me not to return to England without bringing the Lady Elfrida with me. And I had betrayed the King's trust. Once when she had consented to go to England I had refused to take advantage of her words. She had told me that which forbade me to gain the King's smile at the cost of her happiness. Perchance, too, I had thought too much of my own happiness; for I knew that the favor of Henry VIII would be mockery to me if the King gave her in marriage to the man for whom he had destined her.

There seemed naught for me to do then, and although I had brought the man I had learned to love, and who had opened my eyes to the truth of God, to a place of safety, I no longer desired to offer my sword to the Elector Frederick, and I dared not return to my own land. As for the Lady Elfrida, who was I that she should deign to give me a further thought? Perchance by this time the Elector had arranged for her marriage with some German noble to whom her heart went out in love.

I was there alone. David Granville had gone to Wittenberg in order to guard the friends of Luther until they reached that harbor of refuge. The sun of early summer shone upon hill and dale, mountain and forest, while the birds sang from a thousand tree tops, but all was drear to me. My work was done, and I had no hope for the future.

"Still, I must play the man," I remember saying to myself. "I cannot be idle. I will e'en go to the Elector and offer him my sword as I had first intended. As for the future, it is in God's hands."

Whereupon I left the castle walls, and went down the stone steps until I reached the castle-yard. Then my heart stood still. Standing a few yards from me, and looking straight into my eyes, was the Lady Elfrida Rothenburg. It was the first time I had seen the light of joy in her eyes. Hitherto she had been surrounded by danger, and, save once, I had spoken to her only to offer her help. Even when she was under the roof of Ulrich von Hutten she knew that she was not free from those who sought her harm; but here, in the castle of the most powerful baron in the empire and in the home of the ancient Margraves of Germany, naught could harm her. And this, as may be imagined, added to her beauty. The hue of health was on her cheeks, and care had fled from her eyes. In truth, she came to me like a vision from God. She was a part of the beauteous May day, and her presence struck me dumb.

She came to me with laughter on her lips.

" Master Hamilton," she said, " methinks you do not give me a glad welcome."

" It is because my heart is too full for speech," I replied.

" Had I not known that you had it in your heart to bring Dr. Martin Luther hither I should have sent you a messenger bidding you to come to me," she said, and I noted that her voice trembled.

" You have need of me? " I asked quickly.

" Yes," she answered, " when you first came to Germany you had it in your heart to take me to England. Now I ask you to escort me thither."

For a moment I could not speak; her words well-nigh overwhelmed me.

" Knowing what is in the King's mind, you go with a willing heart? " I asked presently.

" Ay, and more," she made answer. " I ask you to escort me thither, because I desire to go."

CHAPTER XXX

Now, as may be imagined, her words well-nigh un-
manned me. It is true, I had come to Germany that I
might take her to England. If she had accepted my offer when I had seen her first, I would have ridden back
to my native land with a glad heart and delivered her
to the King with pride. Nevertheless, when, months
afterward, I met her near the convent into which she
had gone, and she had refused to go to England, I rejoiced. I knew I was not loyal to the King's command
in accepting her refusal tamely, yet did I not seek to
persuade her. Afterward, when she offered to return
with me, I would none of it, for, as she declared, she
consented to sacrifice her own heart's longings because
of a mistaken sense of gratitude to me. Base as I might
have been in disobeying the King, I was not base enough
to accept the King's smile at the cost of her happiness.
Besides, as I have before stated, I had grown to love
her so that the thought of taking her to Henry Tudor,
that she might become the wife of one of his favorites,
was more than I could bear.

Truly, the heart of a woman is a strange thing!
What she had refused with scorn a few months before
she now accepted with eagerness. Even as she spoke
I called to mind the tones of scorn in which she declared
that she refused to be a pawn on the King's chess-board,
a toy which he could bestow on whom he pleased, while
now she declared that it was her heart's desire to obey
the King's bidding.

" Have you considered fully that which you have consented to do? " I asked.

" I have considered it fully," she replied.

" And you do not go to save me from the King's

anger?" I cried. "That is," I stammered, "it is not because of a mistaken gratitude to me that you consent to make this sacrifice?"

"I do not make a sacrifice," she answered. "It is the dearest desire of my heart to go to England."

"Knowing what is in the King's mind?"

"Ay, knowing what is in the King's mind."

"Then must the Lady Elfrida have heard of some new trouble, some new danger which surrounds her here?" I suggested.

"Nay," she made answer, "there is no new trouble or new danger for me. Rather many of the things I once feared have passed away. My uncle no longer persecutes me. It is out of his power to do so."

I longed to ask other questions, but I dared not. She was evidently bent upon going to England, and she had asked me to escort her thither. I looked again into her face, and my love for her became a great burning fire. The King's commands, the promises he had made, and the promises I had made all seemed to become as nothing, so great is the power of a woman over a man. What was everything to me if I lost her? And I knew that I should lose her if I took her to England. She would be wedded to the man Henry VIII had chosen for her, while I should eat out my heart in agony. Ay, perchance the King would command me to the wedding feast, while I should know that I had been false to the love of my heart that I might gain the King's smile.

Up to now I had spoken no word of love, even while all my life went out to her. That she cared aught for me I had never believed, and if ever such a hope had come into my heart the words she had first spoken dispelled it. How could she think of love for me when she desired to go to England that she might enable the King of England to succeed in his designs? I knew well enough that she had great wealth in England, and that the King intended to use that wealth in order to buy the services of a man of great power. And she had not been blind to this. Long months before her mind had pierced the King's designs. And yet she asked me to escort her thither.

I longed to throw myself at her feet, to plead with her not to go. I longed to tell her of the love that burned in my heart. I opened my lips to speak, but the words would not pass. I was tempted beyond words to betray my King and to treat his commands as the words of a spoiled child, yet all the time, even although I had dallied with my duty to him for so long, I could not speak the words which my heart prompted. If I pleaded my own cause, then indeed I were false to my name and false to my King.

"Your mind is set, then, on going to England?" I said, and I spoke the words unthinkingly, for my mind went not with them.

"I go there that my heart's desires may be realized," she said.

"But are you sure they will be realized?" This I said wondering what was in her mind. "Because if you are not, be sure I will not take you thither."

"I trust — I pray they may be," she answered. "I can think of no other way. Can you suggest one?"

Her voice became husky as she spoke and her eyes had a look of pleading in them. It was only by a strong effort that I restrained myself from telling her of another way, yet I dared not say what all my life was urging me to cry aloud.

"I would give my life to make the Lady Elfrida happy," I said.

"Yet you cannot suggest another way?" And again I thought I heard pleading in her voice.

"God forgive me, but I cannot," I replied.

"Yet you do not like the thought of my going to England?"

At this I was silent, for what could I say?

For a moment she watched me speechless, and then I thought a new mood came upon her.

"Forgive me, Master Hamilton," she said, "but methinks I have never made you feel how full of gratitude my heart is to you. You gave me hope at the time my uncle willed that I should wed Count Hans von Hartz. You saved me from the hands of those two Englishmen when I sought shelter at the house of Count von Hutten.

You saved me from worse than death at the castle of Hans of Hartz, and I have never thanked you according to my heart's promptings. Yet I do thank you, and I shall never cease to offer up prayers for you. I ask you now to do what you came to Germany to do. Will you fail me?"

Her words stunned me, and I scarce knew what I was saying.

"You have discovered something of which you were ignorant when you refused to do that which is now in your heart to do?" I said.

"Yes," she said, "that is true; and you will not refuse me, will you?"

She held out her hand to me as she spoke, and I grasped it eagerly.

"You believe that it will mean your — your happiness?" I stammered.

"I will see to it that it shall," she replied.

"Then will I do that which you ask," I answered. "If you asked me to go to my death to give you happiness I would do it. But can you leave this castle without difficulty?"

"Yes," she replied.

"When will you be ready?"

"To-day — no, not to-day, to-morrow," she replied; and then she left me alone to the knowledge that all my future would be black.

I went to see Martin Luther that evening, and I knew by the first words he spoke that the Lady Elfrida had also visited him.

"You leave for England to-morrow," he said.

"She hath told you?" I made answer.

"Ay, she hath told me. Truly, the heart of a woman is a strange thing!"

"Ay, it is," I replied.

The monk looked at me for some seconds, and there was a strange expression in his eyes.

"Guard her safely," he said at length. "She is beautiful and good, and the Lord hath led her into the light."

"I will protect her with my life," I made answer. "I

would I could have had my friend David Granville to
accompany me, but he is gone to Wittenberg, and the
Lady Elfrida wills that we leave here to-morrow. But
I can secure a number of faithful men-at-arms."

"That is well. Besides her tiring maids, the Lady
Elfrida will be accompanied by a German matron whose
name will be known to your King."

"It is well," I made answer, although I felt that
naught was well.

"I shall pray for you," said Dr. Luther presently,
"and I shall ever think of you with gladness and thankfulness, for truly the knowledge of you hath been a
great joy to me. I have been told to-day of the purpose in bringing me hither."

"Your enemies will think you dead, while you will
be in safety," I said.

The monk laughed merrily. "Ay, they think me
dead," he cried, "they think that poor Martin Luther's
voice is silenced forever. They will be rejoicing that
all I have done will come to naught. But they will wake
up one fine morning and find that the devil hath been
defeated! Here in this place I shall have time to do
what was impossible to me at Wittenberg. The work of
the Lord will be done, Master Hamilton."

"But if you are here in idleness, and your friends
as well as your enemies think you are dead, how can
you do the work of the Lord?"

"Idleness!" he cried. "Nay, but I have already begun my work, the work that shall complete what hath
been already begun. What is the weapon with which
I have ever fought, Master Hamilton? It hath ever been
by the Sword of the Lord that I have vanquished mine
enemies. During the time I am here I shall wield it with
more power than ever, for I shall translate into the
tongue of the people the Gospels written by the Evan-
gelists. Let these be read to and by the people, and I
shall know that I can do more even in prison than I
could do at liberty."

"In prison?" I queried.

"Ay, prison!" he laughed. "For can I leave the
castle gates? What think you, the very servants know

not who I am. I am to be clothed in armor when I go forth, I am to let my beard grow, and I am to be known as young George. Fancy Martin Luther masquerading as a knight!"

And again he laughed so heartily that his voice filled the room and echoed into the courtyard.

Presently, however, he became serious again.

" Truly the Lord hath done great things for me," he said; " so great that it seems wondrous beyond words. See how the work of God hath spread. The reformation of the Church is not where it was a month ago. That Diet of Worms, which mine enemies thought would be my destruction, hath meant thousands of converts. The Lord hath not done these things by the wise and the prudent, but even by a poor monk, whose only weapon is the Word of God. Why, the whole country is flooded with the truth of God. And the light shall spread!"

He went to the window of the room and looked out at the wondrous panorama of hill and dale. " We are up among the birds," he laughed. " Listen to them singing! I am in a strong castle, where none can harm me. The Word of God seems to come to me from every side. Shall we fear the future, then? Master Hamilton, I would e'en give thee something by which thou may'st remember the man to whom thou hast been so much."

He handed me a piece of parchment as he spoke. " I have written it to-day," he said; " this strong castle hath put it in my mind. Let us never doubt God, Master Englishman. Let us never fear that He will forsake us. Therefore, let us rejoice with a great joy, knowing that although some endureth for the night joy cometh in the morning."

The piece of parchment which Luther gave me lies before me as I write, and I copy some of it here for all to see. There are but few things in life that I prize more, for it is not only a poem of singular strength and beauty, set to befitting music, but it tells of the spirit in which the monk of Wittenberg did his work. Even now, although I am far away from Germany, I find myself constantly singing the first lines of the poem:

"Ein feste Burg ist unser Gott,
Ein treue Wehr' und Waffen." [1]

The next day the Lady Elfrida and I stood before him before leaving the castle.

"God bless you, my children," he said, "and never do you doubt His word and His power. May the Lord bless you and keep you; may the Lord be merciful unto you; may the Lord cause His face to shine upon you and grant you His peace."

These were the last words he spoke to us as we left the room in which for many months he lived and worked, while his friends mourned him as dead. My heart, I remember, was very heavy, yet did hope come to me, for his words were a benediction indeed.

The journey to England, although the time was early

[1] A safe stronghold our God is still,
A trusty shield and weapon.

summer, was long and wearisome. The somewhat elderly matron who accompanied the Lady Elfrida scarcely deigned to speak a word to me, while she whom I was taking to England according to her desire and according to the King's will was strangely silent. Indeed, I might have been only a paid servant of low degree so little was the cordiality with which they treated me. We had left the castle without difficulty, and I had a band of men-at-arms at my command. But I was not treated as a friend or as an equal. I rode near them and I did all I could to make their journey pleasant, but no word of kindness did they speak. The journey was slow, because the Baroness von Halle was not capable of long rides. She was quickly wearied, and fretted much. Moreover, I saw that her demeanor toward the Lady Elfrida was anything but pleasing.

More than once indeed I was on the point of asking the Lady Elfrida whether she repented the resolution she had formed, and whether she would not return; but when I tried to prepare the way for such a suggestion she gave me a look which silenced me completely.

But little happened on our journey. One day succeeded another with wearisome monotony. This, however, we found: although men believed that Martin Luther was dead, the work he had begun was continued. On all hands we heard of the spread of the reformed doctrines, in spite of threats and persecution.

At length we arrived in England, and I made my way with all speed to London.

The Earl of Devonshire met me when I arrived at the King's palace.

"You have long delayed the fulfillment of your mission, Brian," he said, querulously I thought.

I was silent at this, for it seemed to me that his reception lacked in warmth, and indeed in all else pleasant.

"I will now relieve you of your charge," he said. "Do you go to a place of lodgment, and acquaint me concerning it with all speed. When the King desires your presence do you be ready."

With this I was dismissed from his presence. I turned

to the Lady Elfrida to bid her good-bye, but beyond a low-spoken word of thanks she said nothing. As for the Baroness von Halle, I might have been a lackey who was dismissed for ill-behavior. I laughed bitterly as I found my way into the streets. No man seemed to know me. In truth, I might have come into a strange land instead of to my own country.

I would have gone to Rochford but for the command of the Earl of Devonshire; but, remembering what he said, I repaired to my old lodgings, which by good chance were at my disposal. Here I waited day after day, expecting to be summoned to the King's presence, but day after day I waited in vain. I scarcely went into the streets, for I feared lest I should miss the King's summons; instead I sat and brooded over all that had taken place. I desired no man's company, for, as it seemed to me, all a man longs for in this life was impossible. Often and long did I ponder over the reasons why the Lady Elfrida desired to come to England, but each explanation that came to me seemed madder than the other.

A week passed, and no message came from the King; and, what struck me as more strange, not even the Earl of Devonshire called me to his side to ask me how I fared. As for the Lady Elfrida, not once did I hear anything concerning her. As may be imagined, I conjured up many thoughts to account for this state of things, but all the time I knew that I had not guessed rightly. Of one thing I felt sure, even although I could give no sufficient reason why, and that was that the King was ill-pleased with me. So I waited day by day without scarce a ray of sunshine to brighten the sky of my life.

At the end of a week a messenger came from the Earl, commanding me to appear before the King. I dressed myself in my bravest attire; nevertheless, I went to the Earl's presence with many misgivings.

There was a strange look in his eyes as he met me. He was no longer the frank and loving master I had known.

"The King desires speech with you, Master Hamilton," he said.

"His desire cannot be strong, seeing he hath left me a week in silence," I replied.

"But his speech will be to some purpose," he replied, and he gave a short, mirthless laugh as he spoke.

"It should be," I made answer, for he angered me. "Have I not done his will?"

"Thou hast," he replied grimly; "but how?"

"What he commanded hath been done."

Again he looked at me curiously.

"What caused you to be so long, Master Hamilton? That is what the King wants to know."

"Doubtless the Lady Elfrida will tell him," was my reply.

As will be seen, I was in a desperate humor. I felt sure that the King was angry with me, even although I did not know the reason; yet did I not fear his wrath. At that time I did not much value my life.

"Well, the time hath come, and the King awaits you," he said at length. "By our Lady, Brian, I would help you if I could, but I fear the worst."

For the first time he had spoken like my old friend and master, but, as will be seen, his words were of evil import.

A minute later I stood in the room where Henry VIII had received me before, and as I entered I saw that he sat almost in the same posture as he sat on the night when he sent me on my mission.

"Brian Hamilton," he said, letting his piercing eyes rest on me, "many a month ago I sent you on a mission."

"I have fulfilled it, sire," I replied.

"Ay, but how?"

"I delivered the lady into the hands of the King's most faithful minister," I replied. "That was a week ago, sire, yet no word of thanks have I received."

"Thanks, thanks!" he cried angrily. "For what should I thank thee? Hast thou been faithful?"

"Have I not delivered the lady safe and sound, your Majesty?" I replied. "Your Majesty demanded that she should be brought to England secretly. It hath been done. Your Majesty commanded that she should be treated with as much reverence as one should treat the image of our Lady. Hath this been disobeyed? Hath the lady in aught complained?"

"Since you recall my commands, I will e'en recall another," cried Henry VIII, starting to his feet. "Did I not warn thee against lifting thine eyes to her in love? Did I not tell thee that she was not for thee, but for one whom I had in my heart? Tell me, sirrah, is this true?"

I wondered much at his knowledge of this, and I saw that it caused him to be angry. Yet could I see no sufficient reason why.

"Even the commands of kings cannot avail in such matters," I made answer. "A man cannot control his love, since God hath not made him capable of it. He can only do his duty."

"Then thou dost not deny that thou hast lifted thine eyes to her in love?"

"Nay, sire, I love her with all my life."

"And her heart, knowest thou aught of that?"

"Nay, sire, save that I am naught to her but a serving-man who brought her from one land to another."

"Thou hast never made her see that thou dost love her?" he cried angrily.

"Nay, as to that I cannot answer," I replied. "A man cannot control his heart, and when the heart loves — Ah, but your Majesty knows what love is. Can a man whose heart is full of love help that love flashing from his eyes? Can he help betraying it in every tone of his voice? Will he not reveal it in a thousand ways unknown to himself? I am not a man of brass, your Majesty, and I cannot swear that I have never shown her that my heart beats for no woman on earth but her."

"And yet thou wert spoken of to me as a misanthrope, a woman-hater, a sort of lay monk."

"I had not seen her then," I made answer, "and I call your Majesty to witness that I did not plead to undertake the work of bringing her hither."

Henry VIII was silent for a minute, keeping his keen, searching eyes on me all the time. I met his gaze boldly, for I determined that, seeing he knew what was in my heart and was determined to punish me, I would show him I was not afraid of his anger.

"The lady offered to come to England as long ago as November of last year," he said presently, and thou did'st refuse to bring her hither. Dost thou call that faithfulness?"

"She offered to come only out of a mistaken sense of gratitude to me," I made answer; "her heart loathed the thought of it all the time."

"What had that to do with thee, since it was my will?" And his voice rang with anger.

"Because I was enough of a man not to be willing to wreck a woman's happiness in order to gain a King's smile, your Majesty," I answered desperately. "Her heart went not with her words."

"That was not thy only reason."

"No, your Majesty, it was not," I replied, although I thought I saw death in his eyes.

"And yet thou did'st complain but a few minutes ago that I did not give thee thanks."

"At least your Majesty's will is accomplished," I replied.

Again he started from his seat and walked around the room with quick steps, his hands behind his back.

"A penniless nobody to lift his eyes to such a lady!" he cried at length.

"There is no better name in England than mine, your Majesty," I replied, "and it hath never been tarnished. But what of that? I have done my work, almost against my will if you like, and I will take no reward."

"What is that, sirrah?"

"I will take no reward," I repeated almost sullenly.

"But, by my father's bones, thou shalt!" he cried, and there was a strange look in his eyes. He moved to a door in the room and opened it.

"Come hither, mistress," he said; and then I thought I was losing my senses, for the Lady Elfrida stood before me.

"Elfrida Rothenburg," said Henry VIII, "my desire in bringing thee to England was that thou mightest be the wife of a man of my choice, one of England's greatest noblemen. Dost thou still refuse to obey my will?"

"I do, your Majesty," she said quietly.

"Why?"

"Because my heart is given elsewhere."

"This fellow declares that he hath given his love to thee. In this he hath disobeyed the commands of his King. He hath but the patrimony of a paltry squire. Dost thou still desire to wed him?"

"If it is according to his will, your Majesty. I had not come to England else." And then, as she lifted her eyes to mine, the gates of heaven seemed open to me, although even yet the wonder of it all hath not left me.

"And dost thou love this fellow?" asked the King, and I thought his anger seemed to grow less.

"I have already confessed that love to you," she made answer, and her cheeks became rosy red.

"Ay, and for this thou hast defied thy friends; thou hast flouted thy aunt, the Baroness von Halle; thou hast come hither to England only to mock England's King."

"I have come out of love for the man who hath more than once offered his life for mine, your Majesty. How could I help coming?" Her eyes grew moist as she spoke, and there was a sob in her voice.

"Then thou shalt wed him!" cried the King. "He said he would take no reward, but he shall take thee as a reward. Ay, and he shall have thy estates in Germany which have been robbed from thee by thine uncle, as well as those here in England."

He seized a sword as he spoke, while I in my great gladness knelt before him.

"Rise, Sir Brian Hamilton," said the King, touching my shoulder with his sword. "Perhaps, after all, thou may'st be a more faithful servant to me than any of the house of Lancaster; and now begone, for I have many affairs to deal with."

He nodded to the door by which my love had entered the room, and we entered the adjoining apartment together.

"Do you understand now, Brian?" she said, looking at me with tear-brimming eyes.

For answer I held her close to my heart. In truth, what other answer could I give her? For I understood nothing save that this peerless woman loved me, that she had come to England that I might fulfill the King's command, and that she had refused to wed any man save me. I knew, too, that the King's anger had melted before her love and her pleadings, and that I, who had thought that the winter of death had come upon my life, entered into a joy that I never dreamed could be possible to the sons of men.

Not long after the day on which we were wedded two letters were brought to me by a man who had traveled all the way from Germany. The first I opened was from David Granville. I need not describe it here, save to say that he wrote in great good spirits.

" I shall not return to England," the epistle concluded, " for I have work to do in Germany even as you had. Some time, perchance, I shall have a story to tell you of events, compared with which those we passed through together seem tame; but the time for the telling is not yet. In God's own good time I trust that I may come to your home, and receive not only a welcome from you, but from the beauteous wife you have won."

The other letter was from Martin Luther, and was written from Wartburg Castle.

" I send my greetings to you, my son, Brian," he concluded. " I knew what would befall you even when you left this abode of the birds, for I was not ignorant of the thoughts in my lady's heart. Cherish her beyond all things, for her price is far above rubies. I pray for you both day by day. May happiness be your portion, seeing you have both been led into the light of God.

" Farewell to you both, my children; fear nothing for me. The Lord is a strong tower, and in Him I am safe.

" From the abode of the birds.

" Your loving friend in Christ,

" MARTIN LUTHER.

" P. S.— The word of the Lord spreadeth mightily."

www.ingramcontent.com/pod-product-compliance
Lightning Source LLC
Chambersburg PA
CBHW022208010726
47493CB00002B/469